Forgotten Horrors 3
Dr. Turner's House of Horrors

Forgotten Horrors 3
Dr. Turner's House of Horrors

by Michael H. Price
and John Wooley
with
George E. Turner

Midnight Marquee Press, Inc.
Baltimore, Maryland

Also by Michael H. Price & John Wooley:
The Big Book of Biker Flicks
Southern-Fried Homicide
Also by Michael H. Price:
The Comics Journal Special Edition, Vol. No. 2
Cartoonists on Music (With Mark Martin *et al.*)
Contributing Author:
Peter Lorre: Midnight Marquee Actors Series
Vincent Price: Midnight Marquee Actors Series
It's Christmastime at the Movies
Lon Chaney, Jr.: Midnight Marquee Actors Series

Lex Eicon and the Numerologist
(With Jerome McDonough)
The A-to-Z Encyclopedia of Serial Killers
(Contributing Illustrator)
Krime Duzzin't Pay!
The Guitar in Jazz (Contributing Author)
R. Crumb: The Musical
(With Robert Crumb & Johnny Simons)
The 50 Greatest Cartoons (Contributing Author)
Michael H. Price's Hollywood Horrors Electrified!
(With Timothy Truman)
Bloody Visions, Vols. I-III

Also by John Wooley:
Awash in the Blood
Dark Within
Death's Door (With Ron Wolfe)
Old Fears (With Ron Wolfe)
How To Make It in the Music Business
(With Jim Halsey)

Café Purgatory
(Original Stage Play & Collaborative Screenplay)
Hot Schlock Horror!

Also by Michael H. Price & George E. Turner:
Spawn of Skull Island
The Ancient Southwest (In Preparation)
The Palo Duro Story (In Preparation)
Forgotten Horrors: The Definitive Edition
Forgotten Horrors 2: Beyond the Horror Ban
Southern-Fried Homicide
(With John Wooley *et al.*)
Aw-Shucks Suspense Stories
Mo' Southern-Fried Homicide
Human Monsters: The Bizarre Psychology of Movie Villains
V.T. Hamlin's Collected Alley Oop, Vols. 2 & 3
The Cinema of Adventure, Romance & Terror
The Spider
Roy Crane's Collected Wash Tubbs & Captain Easy, Vol. No. 10
Al Capp's Collected Li'l Abner, Vol. No. 6
Forgotten Horrors: Early Talkie Chillers from Poverty Row (Two Prior Editions)

Portions of this book have appeared, in markedly different form, in *The Cinema of Adventure, Romance & Terror* (A.S.C. Press; 1989); in *Human Monsters: The Bizarre Psychology of Movie Villains* (Kitchen Sink Press; 1996); in *The American Cinematographer* magazine; and in Michael H. Price's talk-radio broadcasts and dispatches of the New York Times News Service.

Copyright © 2003 by Michael H. Price and John Wooley
Cover Design/Layout Design: Susan Svehla

Without limiting the rights under copyright reserved above, no part of this publication may be reproduced, stored in or introduced into a retrieval system, or transmitted, in any form, or by any means (electronic, mechanical, photocopying, recording or otherwise), without the prior written permission of the copyright owners or the publishers of the book.
First Edition ISBN 1-887664-86-6
Library of Congress Catalog Card Number 2003104376
Manufactured in the United States of America
Printed by Sheridan Books, Fredericksburg, VA
First Printing by Luminary Press, an imprint of Midnight Marquee Press, Inc., April 2003
Revised Printing by Midnight Marquee Press, Inc., July 2007, November 2008
Revised Editon ISBN 978-1887664868
Revised Edition Library of Congress Catalog Card Number 2007930772
Acknowledgments: Linda J. Walter

In Memory of
Nat Levine
Sam Katzman
Boris Karloff
John Carradine
John Wayne
Tex Ritter
Lon Chaney, Jr.
Vincent Price
Gene Autry
Maris Wrixon
Roy Rogers
Bruce Cabot
Francis Lederer
Grady Sutton

...Whose Offhanded Conversations with Us Helped To Launch These Books—before We Even Knew These Books Wanted Launching

Prelude

The term *Poverty Row*, though indelibly associated since the Jazz Age and Depression years with a seamier side of the moviemaking industry, actually dates from earlier times and more mundane places: It seems to have originated as a sentimentalized term for social squalor, as codified in a popular song of 1898 called "Down in Poverty Row" by the composer Arthur Trevelyan and the lyricist Gussie L. Davis. "Within a crowded tenement where the poorest folks abound," reads the lyric, "there lives a pretty working girl, the best that can be found... Down in Poverty Row, you will find this girl..." Which might apply just as well to any one of the working actresses who graced these pictures of a more nearly modern-day Poverty Row—whether on her way up or on her way out.

The term *Forgotten Horrors*™, though popularly applied today as a generic variant upon a film-research trademark of the Price-Turner-Wooley coalition—consider *aspirin* vs. *Aspirin*® or *frisbee* vs. *Frisbee*®—actually occurred subconsciously to Mike Price and George Turner when they were seeking a title for the first book in this series during the 1970s. It was not until the tail-end of the 1990s that we recollected where we had first encountered that expression: "That black figure with its eyes of fire struck down through all my adult thoughts and feelings, and for a moment the forgotten horrors of childhood came back to my mind." Let the record credit H.G. Wells, writing in *The Island of Dr. Moreau*.

Contents

9	Foreword by Terry Pace
12	Author's Preface by J.W.
15	Author's Preface by M.H.P.
22	Acknowledgments
24	Annotations, Marginalia & Addenda to Prior Volumes

1943

37	Dr. Terror's House of Horrors
38	A Japanese Pipe Dream
39	Man of Courage
41	Child Bride
46	London Blackout Murders
48	Silent Witness
49	The Pay Off
50	Crime Smasher
52	Dead Men Walk
55	A Night for Crime
58	Haunted Ranch
59	The Lum & Abner Series
63	Fighting Sea Monsters
63	The Ape Man
66	The Ghost Rider
67	King of the Cowboys
69	The Mantrap
70	The Ghost and the Guest
72	Death Rides the Plains
73	I Escaped the Gestapo
75	False Faces
76	The Black Raven
78	Cowboy Commandos
79	Hitler's Madman
82	Wolves of the Range
83	Spy Train
84	Ghosts on the Loose
86	That Nazty Nuisance
88	Isle of Forgotten Sins
89	Headin' for God's Country
91	Tiger Fangs
92	Revenge of the Zombies
95	A Scream in the Dark
97	Unknown Guest
98	The Mystery of the Thirteenth Guest
99	Mystery Broadcast
101	Whispering Footsteps

1944

103	Pride of the Plains
104	Women in Bondage
106	Charlie Chan
119	Voodoo Man
121	Voice in the Wind
125	Lady in the Death House
127	The Lady and the Monster
130	The Monster Maker
132	Shake Hands with Murder
133	Johnny Doesn't Live Here Any More
135	The "Kitty O'Day" Pictures:
138	Return of the Ape Man
141	Nabonga Gorilla
142	Waterfront
144	Secrets of Scotland Yard
145	The Girl Who Dared
147	Seven Doors to Death
149	The Port of Forty Thieves
150	Call of the Jungle
152	Strangers in the Night
154	Marked Trails
155	Code of the Prairie
157	Storm over Lisbon
159	Wild Horse Phantom
160	When Strangers Marry
163	Bluebeard
166	Rogues Gallery
167	Crazy Knights
169	The Whispering Skull

1945

171	Grissly's Millions
172	His Brother's Ghost
174	Fog Island
176	There Goes Kelly
177	Dillinger
180	Fashion Model
181	The Great Flamarion
184	Strange Illusion
187	Crime, Inc.
189	The Phantom Speaks
191	Anoush
191	The Phantom of 42nd Street
193	The Lady Confesses
196	The Vampire's Ghost
198	China's Little Devils
200	The Missing Corpse
201	Road to Alcatraz
203	The White Gorilla
204	Jealousy
206	The Fatal Witness
208	Apology for Murder
210	Dangerous Intruder
211	Scotland Yard Investigator
213	Marshal of Laredo
214	Rough Riders of Cheyenne
216	White Pongo
217	Shadow of Terror
219	The Tiger Woman
221	An Angel Comes to Brooklyn
222	Detour
225	The Enchanted Forest
228	The Woman Who Came Back
230	The Strange Mr. Gregory
232	How Doooo You Do!!!

1946

236	Dirty Gertie from Harlem, U.S.A.
238	Strangler of the Swamp
241	The Face of Marble
243	The Madonna's Secret
246	The Shadow Returns
247	Behind the Mask
249	The Missing Lady
250	The Flying Serpent
251	The Haunted Mine
253	I Ring Doorbells
254	Crime of the Century
256	Swing, Cowboy, Swing
258	Fight That Ghost
261	Fear
263	The Mask of Diijon
264	Strange Impersonation
266	Devil Bat's Daughter
268	The Catman of Paris
270	The Glass Alibi
273	Passkey to Danger
273	Jungle Terror
274	Valley of the Zombies
276	Ghost of Hidden Valley
277	Suspense
280	Avalanche
281	Go Down, Death!
283	The Specter of the Rose
287	Strange Voyage
288	Larceny in Her Heart
289	Night Train to Memphis
291	Queen of Burlesque
292	The Inner Circle
294	Death Valley
296	The Invisible Informer
297	Spook Busters
299	Accomplice
301	Mysterious Mr. Valentine
302	Decoy
304	Outlaws of the Plains
305	The Brute Man
308	Beauty and the Bandit
311	Home in Oklahoma
313	The Chase
316	Afterword
317	Recommended Video Sources
319	About the Authors

Foreword
by Terry Pace

In late 1984, during my days as a cub reporter, I left my home in Muscle Shoals, Alabama, and journeyed south to Birmingham.

On the surface, my mission was purely professional: The occasion was a newspaper interview with John Carradine, the grand old Hollywood character actor, then starring in a stage version of Erskine Caldwell and Jack Kirkland's *Tobacco Road*.

In truth, my pilgrimage was deeply personal: As a connoisseur of classic horror, I was eager to meet one of the grand old masters of cinematic terror.

Although crippled by arthritis, the 78-year-old Carradine was as electrifying as ever. After the show, I slipped backstage. "Come in! Come in!" Carradine bellowed, ushering me into his dressing-room. Facing his makeup mirror, I watched him remove the last traces of Jeeter Lester, his *Tobacco Road* role, from the hollow caverns of his expressive face.

For the next hour, Carradine placed his life and his career at my disposal. I inquired about everyone from John Ford and John Wayne to Boris Karloff and Bela Lugosi. Carradine shared the secrets of *Stagecoach*, *Prisoner of Shark Island*, *Jesse James* and *The Grapes of Wrath*. He re-lived macabre memories of *Bride of Frankenstein*, *The Hound of the Baskervilles*, the intermingled Houses of Frankenstein and Dracula and *The Howling*.

Throughout our dialogue, Carradine kept coming back to a single title over and over again—the 1944 chiller *Bluebeard*.

"*That*," he insisted, "was some of my finest work—my *finest*!"

I had certainly read about this revered Poverty Row production, but I had never seen it.

"You *must*!" he demanded. "It's one of my *best*!"

I returned home from that interview a little after 2 a.m., way too wired for slumber. Out of pure reflex, I flipped on the television. There, through some heavenly twist of fate, my eyes fixed on that elusive title: "PRC Pictures Presents... *Bluebeard*... Starring John Carradine." That portentous first viewing marked my belated baptism into the fascinating world of *Forgotten Horrors*—a world that would soon become my home away from home.

Up until then, my taste in movies had fallen strictly within the bounds of conventional studio fare. In my pseudo-sophisticated opinion, the B-movies were a lower life form, providing little more than peripheral pleasure. But *Bluebeard*, Edgar G. Ulmer's moody masterwork, introduced me to a breed of creepy classics long hidden in the shadows.

From there, I moved on to Ulmer's daring film noir thriller, *Detour*, then found Carradine in *Hitler's Madman* and *Revenge of the Zombies*—the movie that also introduced me to my new screen hero, Mantan Moreland.

Bela Lugosi in *White Zombie*

Then came Lugosi in *White Zombie*, Gene Autry in *The Phantom Empire* and Lionel Atwill in *The Vampire Bat*.

Late-night TV's weekly *John Wayne Theatre* unearthed an even more startling revelation. The bottom half of that weekly double bill featured the '30s-era Duke in the likes of *The Star Packer* and *Randy Rides Alone*—weird, unconventional Westerns with eerie elements of Gothic horror.

In this alternate universe of shoestring shivers and chills, moviemakers achieved their subversive artistry against all odds. Their flair for fly-by-night filmmaking required plenty of penny-pinching, but it also generated inspiration, ingenuity and a refreshing lack of pretense. Within this underground art form, obscure names like Regis Toomey, Frankie Darro, Bob Steele, Charles Gemora and Tom Tyler were elevated to their own mythic marquee status. From time to time, Hollywood's heavyweights even ventured into these seemingly forbidden environs. Some, like the Duke, lingered briefly on their rise to the top. Others, like Lugosi, grabbed hold during their disheartening descent.

In 1986, in the midst of my B-movie awakening, the Movie & Entertainment Book Club offered the Eclipse Books edition of *Forgotten Horrors*, a landmark work in cinematic archaeology. Once again, I experienced an overdue epiphany. That indispensable volume of scholarship, masterminded by George Turner and Michael H. Price, managed to identify, arrange and seamlessly connect all of the random dots representing my newfound love. Pretty soon, I was seeking out new titles and adding discovery upon discovery to the experience.

Later, I inched up within the newspaper ranks, settling happily into my duties as editor of our community's arts-and-entertainment coverage. It was then that I linked the name of wire-service contributor Michael H. Price to that groundbreaking edition of *Forgotten Horrors*. For years, I ran Mike's intelligent, insightful pieces on movies and music alongside my own humble efforts. Together, we introduced—or reintroduced—readers to Peter Cushing and John Agar, to Robert E. Howard and Robert Bloch, to *Inner Sanctum* and *King Kong*, to comic books, rockabilly, Southern soul music and Western swing. We finally met in person in 1999, at Midnight Marquee's all-star Monster Rally movie convention in Crystal City, Virginia. Mike remains my friend, colleague and brother-in-arms.

Mike and George Turner devoted decades of labor and love to this fertile field of *Forgotten Horrors*, covering the genre's early heyday (from the 1920s to 1942) in two brilliant volumes. Building upon his late associate's research, Mike (now ably assisted by John Wooley) carries on valiantly, sleuthing and tracking qualifying candidates from 1943-46 for the pages of this superbly researched, supremely entertaining new volume.

This third collection honors many of my personal favorites from that strange, sinister *oeuvre*—from *Strangler of the Swamp* and *The Lady and the Monster* to the little-known screen work of radio's Lum & Abner and the Poverty Row Purgatory that closed the case on Charlie Chan. You'll also discover herein the Carradine classic *Bluebeard*, that murderous thriller that first opened my eyes to the unearthly pleasures of *Forgotten Horrors*.

May these resurrected spectres be remembered and celebrated forevermore.

Terry Pace writes about movies and music for the *TimesDaily*, **a** *New York Times* newspaper near Muscle Shoals, Alabama. His work has appeared in the *New York Times*, *USA Today*, *Cult Movies*, *Scarlet Street*, *Starlog*, *Fangoria* and other national publications. Pace also is an actor, director and filmmaker. He collaborated with his friend and favorite author on the East Coast stage premiere of *The World of Ray Bradbury* and the world premiere of *The Bradbury Chronicles*. Pace also co-produced the short film *SadoMannequin*, an award-winning homage to classic horror films.

Why Forgotten Horrors Is like the *National Geographic*, and Other Observations: One Author's Preface

by John Wooley

So what is it, exactly, about these old films that make us love them so much, that make us happily hand over our shekels for each volume of *Forgotten Horrors* and then eagerly pore over every entry? What's so great about these unearthed tales of pictures that—even in their prime—skimmed along well below most moviegoers' radar? What makes us want to read the diamond-bright little sketches of the original *Forgotten Horrors* books and study these seldom-seen stills over and over, extracting that unusual, minor-keyed joy and sense of discovery that only good writing on arcane topics can evoke?

I'd like to know, because I've been engaged in a lifelong effort to do it myself—a lifelong effort leading to participation in this very project. My first real essay on low-budget American movies came out in a 1974 one-shot fanzine called *Dreamtrip*, via an article called (rather pretentiously) "The Aesthetics of Bad Cinema, or How I Learned To Stop Worrying and Enjoy the Bombs." At the time, I thought I was writing about *bad* movies, which was sort of the hip term to use at the time. A quarter of a century down the line, I realize that what I was doing, instead, was dissecting my reactions to the cheap movies, the second-string pictures, the Hollywood obscurities, that I had grown up with not only on television, but at my small-town Oklahoma theater as well. As a child of the late '50s and early '60s, I developed a severe crush on the actress Betsy Jones-Moreland after seeing Roger Corman's slice of post-nuke weirdness, *The Last Woman on Earth,* on a double-feature; during the same time period, I also answered a movie-magazine ad that promised "a photo of your favorite star" for only 15 cents. Apparently, they didn't have Allison Hayes in stock, because I received neither a picture of her nor my 15 cents back.

Meanwhile, television introduced me to the pictures first released before I was born, and made me a huge fan of such diversified B-film stars as Rondo Hatton and Veda Ann Borg. (Both of whom, I might add, are nicely remembered in this volume.) I remember feeling emotions approaching a religious fervor when I finally got to see Hatton's elongated visage in a late-night showing of *Jungle Captive,* an event I had been anticipating for weeks. Keep in mind, this was the time when almost anything that wasn't new was obscure and unheralded, and there was little in our popular culture that wasn't contemporary and Happening Now. A little past the midpoint of the '60s, however, a nostalgia craze took hold among the young and/or hip, and trivia contests began springing up on college campuses, full of teams with archly comical old-movie-oriented names like the Fatty Arbuckle Appreciation Society. As a result of this fad, a lot of kids began following the root system of the American cinema off into some pretty unusual places, and while they came to poke fun, they stayed to study and enjoy what they'd dug up.

But as the old saw goes, nostalgia isn't what it used to be, and someone in search of undiscovered cinema has to be willing to go a lot deeper these days, when the backs of video boxes at your local Blockbuster contain nuggets of information that would have been available only to the most dogged cinemaphiles a generation ago. In the Information Age, when doing research means hitting Enter on your computer and waiting, or choosing which commentary track to listen to on a DVD, the joy of digging up something new about those movies you love has been seriously leached out of the whole experience. Losing yourself in old magazines and newspapers and dusty boxes of microfilm, tracking down 16-millimeter prints or showings on one-lung UHF stations at crazy hours in neighboring cities—these had their own special allure.

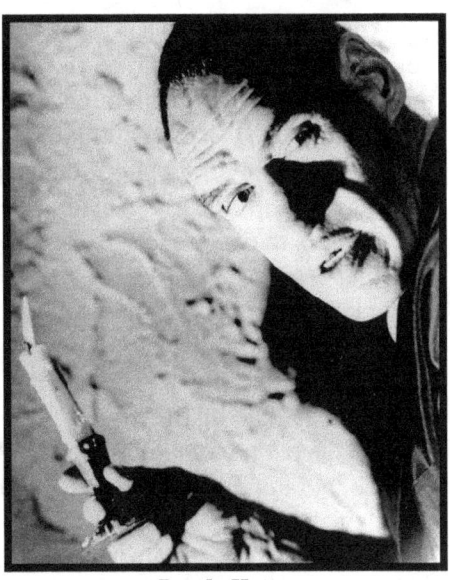

Rondo Hatton

Nowadays, researching something may be a hundred times faster, but it's certainly not a hundred times more fun.

Which brings us, in a roundabout way, to *Forgotten Horrors 3: Dr. Turner's House of Horrors*. Here is a book whose spirit and style reflect the good old way of digging out gems of research and displaying them in a deeply satisfying manner, well adorned with filigrees of opinion. Under the steady (if somewhat skewed) hand of Michael H. Price, with assistance from his late friend and first-class fellow writer, George Turner—and yours truly just now chiming in—this book is calculated to cut both wide and deep. Like its predecessors, *Forgotten Horrors 3* scoots us right past the familiar into the uncharted, and when it does touch down on something only partially obscure, like the *Charlie Chan* or *Shadow* pictures, our *Forgotten Horrors* coalition proposes to offer a fresh take, a new approach, an arcane fact, and we suddenly see the whole thing through a different lens. The approach transforms us—authors and readers alike—into explorers, armchair adventurers; each *Forgotten Horrors* entry is a delightful map to an unexplored world, one whose beauty remains untrampled by the masses. We can read the maps and dream, or we can read the maps and visit the places they show us; either way, they enrich and enliven our lives.

And maybe that's what finally makes the *Forgotten Horrors* approach so doggoned appealing. Maybe those of us who *still* can't quite get around to renting *The Sixth Sense* but might—especially after reading *Forgotten Horrors 3*—walk through hell in a gasoline suit to see *How Doooo You Do!!!* or *Go Down, Death!* are simply the kind of cinematic travelers who choose to vacation in distant places, off the beaten path, where joys await that few have experienced, or even care to experience. We are, in other words, just the right audience for *Forgotten Horrors*. And it's a mark of the genius of Price & Turner that, whether we actually go to any of these specific places or not, their cartography is well worth the price of admission. In fact, this may be a *National Geographic* kind of deal, where reading about something and looking at the pictures is more fun than actually making the trip.

I'm deeply honored that Michael "Aitch" Price has chosen me to become his collaborator on the longer stretch of *Forgotten Horrors*, and I'm fully aware of the awesome legacy left by George Turner, whose shoes I couldn't begin to fill and wouldn't have the temerity to try. The triple byline on this volume acknowledges the fragments of manuscript—backed up by exhaustive research—that George had delivered shortly before his death in 1999; and it remarks the materials that, although I had intended them for an in-progress *Forgotten Horrors 4*, proved better suited to the present chronology.

Michael and I have been friends and fans of each other's stuff for many years, and I welcome this opportunity to work with him again and to continue to add to the *Forgotten Horrors* canon. I hope, with this switcheroo in co-authors, that the subsequent volumes can retain that elusive, indefinable, beautiful spirit of the first ones, the aura that makes you sit back and wonder what it was like to see these pictures in the theaters, and what it would have been like to be a B-movie-obsessed kid back then—with a crush on Louise Currie, maybe, or sending money to a movie magazine ad and watching your mailbox every day, hoping they've finally sent you that picture of Maris Wrixon you asked them for.

—John Wooley
2003, Tulsa, Oklahoma

John Wooley's collaborative novel *Old Fears* [with Ron Wolfe] was first published at about the same time as the original British and American editions of *Forgotten Horrors*, karmically becoming a fictional döppelganger to the Turner & Price book. Wooley has since pursued a sweeping career in radio, newspaper- and-magazine journalism, comic books and playwriting and filmmaking, with such notable outcroppings as the *Dan Turner, Hollywood Detective* telefeature; the indie feature film *Café Purgatory*; and the *Twilight Avenger* and *Miracle Squad* comics. Wooley's more recent novels include *Dark Within* and *Awash in the Blood*.

Dr. Turner's House of Horrors: The Other Author's Preface
by Michael H. Price

You never saw such a house of horrors as George Turner maintained, over a long stretch from the 1950s until well into the 1970s. Compact and more coherently arranged than Forrest J Ackerman's cavernous digs, nowhere near as ornately appointed as the mansion that Charles Addams had built with a fortune in *New Yorker* royalties, the Turner dwelling was superficially quite like its neighboring brick bungalows in suburban West Amarillo, Texas. But the place announced itself as a chamber of Gothic delights the moment one set foot in the entryway.

The living-room doubled as a museum and auditorium, with a Deco-functional 1946-model Revere 16mm motion-picture projector jutting from one end and a reflective glass-beaded movie screen at the opposite, camouflaged by draperies, a cast-iron replica of D.W. Griffith's American Biograph logo and a pulley mechanism. Artifacts from George's innumerable West Texas palæontological digs adorned the bookcases, which housed first editions by the hundreds from the likes of Arthur Machen, H.P. Lovecraft, Edgar Allan Poe, J.B. Priestley, Robert Louis Stevenson and Ambrose Bierce. Gahan Wilson was an occasional visitor; he and George had been art-school chums in Chicago.

Paintings, many of them from George's own studio and the easel of his wife, the soulful portraitist Leona Turner, bedecked the walls, which also were hung with originals by *Weird Tales*' Virgil Finlay, *Prince Valiant*'s Harold R. Foster, the *Tarzan* novels' J. Allen St. John (Foster and St. John had been among George's teachers), *et al.*, *ad infinitum*. These seguéd unobtrusively into a long, narrow den where floor-to-ceiling shelves were given over to an imposing record collection—movie soundtracks, jazz and Euro-classical fare heavy on the great pyrotechnical pianists—and a broadcast-caliber high-fidelity rig that sounded as powerful in 1978 as when George had installed it in 1954. Appliances were built to last in those days, and the generations of technology were so stable that a phonograph disk purchased as long ago as the 1920s could still give up its melodic secrets via newfangled equipment. George preferred his music in monaural; he had upgraded, and grudgingly so, to a stereophonic cartridge-stylus only because the industry would inevitably quit releasing its wares in monophonic editions. ("Stereo makes your ears cross-eyed," he'd grumble, tripping the convert-to-monaural switch.)

George didn't exactly instill in me any revolutionary appreciation of our piebald popular culture—that was already there by the time we began working together—but he taught by example a means of focusing one's interests for greater benefit: Figure out what it is, of all the things you like, that you like best;

George Turner original storyboard from *One from the Heart*

then, once that area has been ordered and indulged, all other appreciations will find their places. George's areas of appreciation were manifold, and he kept the bookcases and filing cabinets to prove this state of being, along with a near-comprehensive elephant's memory to match.

George and Leona had parted ways in 1968, shortly before I joined the newspaper where George served as art director and film critic. Then, after a decade's fulfilling bachelorhood, George hauled off and married a newsroom colleague of ours, a benevolent taskmaster of an editor named Jean Wade, and they moved to Hollywood late in 1978 to begin a career upheaval that wound up with both George and Jean becoming administrative and creative mainstays of the American Society of Cinematographers. The collections and the décor followed suit, bound largely for storage in an L.A. warehouse. Jean indulged George's own personal version of *feng shui* only to a point, and George found it safer to keep the peace than to stand his ground. The Texas ties remained sound, however, and George and I continued building our own series of books about movies, cartooning and whatever else might sound like a kick at any given moment. I was visiting Hollywood almost monthly on newspaper business, at any rate, and it became obvious that the movie capital was where George belonged. He retired, as it were, in 1992—but George defined retirement as a continuation of his labors for *The American Cinematographer* magazine, a beefed-up workload of storyboarding for television and the movies, and a return to his long-dormant keenness on drawing comic-book stories; we published these yarns during 1991-98 via such titles as *Heavy Metal*, *Shriek* and *Southern-Fried Homicide*, while working as commentators and art-restoration consultants for uniform retrospective collections of such celebrated cartoon strips as Al Capp's *Li'l Abner*, Roy Crane's *Wash Tubbs & Captain Easy*, V.T. Hamlin's *Alley Oop* and Stan Lynde's *Rick O'Shay*. George's post-graduate degrees had been, after all, in fine art and commercial illustration.

During 1996-97, while I was assembling a team to launch an annual indie-film expo called the Fort Worth Film Festival, George and I also tackled the 20th-anniversary revision of the original *Forgotten Horrors*. Well in advance of that book's publication, we decided to sustain the momentum into a *Forgotten Horrors 2* and maybe even a *3*. George died unexpectedly in June 1999, just as the revamped *Forgotten Horrors* was shipping, and just as we were writing the first piecemeal chapters for *Forgotten Horrors 2* and *3*. So I enlisted our colleague Scott MacQueen, the ace archivist/restorationist who spent the 1990s bringing order and a prouder sense of history to the Disney studios' vaults, to help convey the working files to my offices in Texas, missing only a few crucial pieces that would turn up sooner or later, and plunged headlong into the sequels. Like I've said: What's to do but carry it on?

When I returned to my offices in Fort Worth, a few days after the memorial ceremony at Cinematographers Clubhouse in H'wood, I found waiting for me a package from George, mailed from Pasadena on the day before his demise. "Here's the file on that picture we'd talked about," he had written. "I think it belongs in the books, but see what *you* think." I wouldn't be so melodramatic as to fancy the note some kind of Voice from Beyond—for that matter, George had believed himself recovering from what he called "a fleeting case of the miseries"—but its arrival at precisely that moment reassured me that the collaboration was far from finished. (The file in question concerns the 1943 exploitationer *Child Bride*, a crepuscular morality fable that of course belongs in the *Forgotten Horrors* canon.)

The simple fact of working alongside such an outspoken and persuasive authority as George Eugene Turner for more than 30 years renders the influence, the very voice, indelible from one's own thoughts and deeds. Not that I'd have things any other way, because this everpresence provides a means of keeping vital George's creative and analytical energies. George as a consequence has posthumously engaged me in innumerable arguments as to what belongs where in which volumes. I'll overrule him as often as not: George, for example, would have omitted that teenage comedy-spooker *Haunted House* from the *FH2* playbill; I included it, if only for the sake of equipping the book with an object of our mutual distaste. His preferences prevail elsewhere, often bordering on a gleeful overkill with the offbeat Westerns.

Although I have written most of the sequels' commentaries and researched the background data from scratch, I still can scarcely resist throwing in George's opinions where they are known and relevant. Compromises figure just as often: *FH2* and *FH3* would have been overrun with Republic Pictures' weirder chapter-a-week serials, had I not limited the selections to a choicer few and then thrown in an appreciative ramble on the cultural importance of those cliffhangers in *FH2*. If I may risk a lightning bolt by adapting a trendy scrap of pop-sanctimony, it boils down to a matter of W.W.G.D.: *What would George do?*

This third volume is in fact the intended balance of *Forgotten Horrors 2: Beyond the Horror Ban* (Midnight Marquee Press; 2001), which originally meant itself to cover the entirety of 1937-46, winding up just at the close of the second cycle of classic-manner Hollywood horror movies, with such last-gasp entries as *The Face of Marble*, *The Flying Serpent* and *The Brute Man* and such infusions of raw vigor into the postwar film noir idiom as *Fear* and *Detour*. Sheer volume of titles forced the split into this third collection, which I have continued on through the end-of-one-era 1946 cutoff. A fourth volume is in progress, tracking the independent chillers on into the escalating Baby Boom years, and additional sequels would seem likely.

The entire point is *context*, which George and I had long ago found to be miserably lacking in most genre studies. For a rigid definition of horror pictures—considered of, by and for themselves—only confines a book to the easier task of preaching to the converted, and such a least-resistance approach fosters no greater appreciation of Film for Film's Sake. By placing conventional monster movies, mad-scientist melodramas and other such easily pigeonholed, genre-fied pieces in a larger context alongside naturalistic and/or stylized crime yarns, propaganda agitators, exotic documentaries, weird Westerns and surreal comedies and patently unclassifiable flights of eccentricity (and all within a real-time chronology) we aim to demonstrate that a wider, and wilder, vista of cultural rediscovery and plain viewing pleasure awaits the enthusiast who is willing to look beyond the obvious. It is to this end that we continue to invoke H.P. Lovecraft's helpful philosophy, which is as true today as it was in Lovecraft's heyday of the 1920s and '30s: Horror is where you find it.

Plans call for *Forgotten Horrors 4*, *5* and so forth to continue until we reach 1985, with the arrival of a picture called *Blood Cult*. This is the ultimate cutting-off point, a made-in-Oklahoma feature that signals an end-of-a-*big*-era turning-point in the independent-studio horror-movie tradition as *Forgotten Horrors* has known, perceived and gone so far as to define it.

Now, *Blood Cult* may seem a tiny effort to bear such a climactic responsibility. But the novelist and cultural historian John Wooley—who weighs in here as co-author of the *Forgotten Horrors* series—has pointed out that *Blood Cult* also holds a historic pride-of-place as the first explicitly made-for-home-video feature in *any* genre, preceding the conventionally acknowledged first direct-to-video picture, the Disney machine's *Love Leads the Way* (1985), by a decent stretch. And whether or not video killed the radio star, as the song would have it, certainly we have seen that the movies-on-video groundswell of the 1980s axed the time-honored practice of looking to low-budget movies on the big picture-show screen as a reliable source of cheap-thrills escapism. The larger studios have since usurped the cheap-thrills function, placing ever-escalating epic-caliber budgets and name-brand ensemble casts at the service of stories better served by chump-change underwriting and adventurous, hungry talents. A defining instance occurred in 1986, when 20th Century-Fox delivered *Predator*, an extravagant and unattributed knockoff of Greydon Clark's perfectly honorable low-budgeter of 1980, *Without Warning*.

The Disney/Touchstone/etc. combine and its embittered-rival spin-off studio, Dreamworks SKG, have become prime offenders, with such noxious and mean-spirited prefabricated-hit fare as *Con Air* (Disney; 1997) and *Road Trip* (Dreamworks; 2000 A.D.)—rancid cheesebags of a strain that even New World Pictures and New Line Cinema outgrew during the 1980s. These very films would be perhaps less offensive if they had issued from trash studios. Had Walt Disney foreseen what manner of big-bucks, star-driven (but otherwise ill-disguised) grindhouse dreck his namesake studio would be delivering by the end of the 20th century, he'd have torched the dump and cashed in on Mickey Mouse's term-life policy. Meanwhile, home video has become the new drive-in, the new grindhouse, bringing the more authentically cheap thrills into the convenient sanctity of the living room—while depriving a massed populace of the forbidden adventure of a trip to watch something scrofulous or provocative in some decrepit backstreet theater on the Wrong Side of Town. My theatreman uncle, Grady L. Wilson (1913-1968), for whom George Turner once worked as an usher-turned-manager, cherished film for the sake of film and enjoyed a good trashola movie as much as a mass-appeal or snob-appeal booking. But Grady also knew better than to book *A Bucket of Blood* or *The Mating Urge* (both of which play out rather quaintly today) into his flagship Interstate Paramount Theatre, or to plunk *The Sound of Music* or *A Man for All Seasons* onto one of his lesser screens. It's called appropriateness, a sensibility that is lost on this age in which such outcroppings of slob-appeal crassness as *There's Something about Mary* and *Me, Myself and Irene* and the *Scary Movie* treadmill will befoul those same classy auditoriums that wait in all-but-vain for higher-minded pictures on the order of *Shakespeare in Love*, *Elizabeth*, *Sling Blade*, *The English Patient* and *Unbreakable*. Even a middlebrow trifle like *Captain Corelli's Mandolin* seems a relief. We gave up a long time ago on a restoration of balance.

I use the collective *we* in a literal sense, by the way. This is neither the Editorial We of lapsed journalistic tradition, nor the Imperious We of 21st century newspaper usage—implying the insulting assumption that trend-gawking, star-sniping, culturally illiterate hack journalists and self-professed critics come prepared to speak for a massed readership. Neither is it the Conspiratorial We, that nudge-and-wink device (so irksome to Australia's savviest film-as-culture columnist, Robin Pen) with which insecure critics seek to rope the unwary reader into the most archly contemptuous of appraisals. It is, rather, a literal *we* in the sense of George Turner, John Wooley and my own self. *We* often agree among ourselves—and when we don't, we allow the disagreement to find its own voice.

What *we* have done in the present volume, is to whip into chronology an array of small pictures that, whether resolutely sleazy or artistically pretentious, knew their places and kept them anchored—and that today add up to a panoramic outlook. This context allows a close examination of Monogram

Pictures and Producers Releasing Corp. as more than tagalongs on the Universal Pictures horror-movie bandwagon; of the rise of both those little studios to greater ambitions, and sometimes even greater accomplishments; of Republic Pictures, in particular, as a force (more commonly ill-acknowledged) in the trial-and-error refinement of the film noir idiom; and, as usual, of the Saturday-matinee Western movies as a vehicle for some bracing crime-and-horror yarns. We find Universal's severely objectified "scream queens," Evelyn Ankers and Anne Gwynne—along with Republic's greatest adventure-serial heroine, Linda Stirling—amply well prepared to demonstrate a greater dramatic range than they usually were allowed.

Producers Releasing Corp., whose prominent initials-only logotype has prompted many a moviegoer to speculate rudely as to what PRC *also* might stand for, comes in for a fairly representative rediscovery, with its shortcomings scarcely in doubt but its strengths coming more clearly into view as the rediscoveries accumulate. Nowhere else does the rift of *attitude* between Old Hollywood's major and minor leagues show through more vividly than in the output of PRC: Overall—and even in its matinee Westerns for the juvenile trade—the scrappy little studio assumed an outlook of no-exit desperation that today seems more intellectually honest, if not necessarily more mature-minded, than the haze of sentimentality that often fogs the work of such big-time masters of rugged cinema as John Ford, Michael Curtiz and Howard Hawks. Such is the stance of a studio with little to lose and everything to prove.

And with the singular guidance of John Wooley (along with Steve Brigati and Jan Alan Henderson as shirtsleeves-cineaste allies), we find the precise moments, in *China's Little Devils* at Monogram and *Shadow of Terror* at PRC, at which low-budget Hollywood beat the big studios to the punch in remarking not only the end of World War II—but also the start of a seemingly endless cycle of atomic-devastation movies, and a decisive infiltration of horror by science fiction.

A conspicuous omission here is a mid-'40s short-feature entry from Toddy Pictures, *Voodoo Devil Drums* (a.k.a. *Virgin Brides of Voodoo*), which has eluded even the American Film Institute's comprehensive cataloguing system but crops up as a tantalizing nugget on various Web sites. No point in parroting the Internet Movie Database, which knows as much or as little as we do about that item. So more later. We hope.

Wooley notes that this present period of concern also finds consummated a relationship between the pulp-magazine trade and the B-movie realm. Writes John: "In addition to John K. Butler, one of that great second tier of hard-boiled pulp writers…, there's Dwight V. Babcock (*Road to Alcatraz*), Frank Gruber (*Accomplice*) and Frederick C. Davis (*Lady in the Death House*). The latter created the unforgettable Moon Man for *Ten Detective Aces* and ghost-wrote that famed slice of '30s paranoia, *Operator Five*.

"John Butler, who's represented in *Forgotten Horrors 3* by *The Vampire's Ghost*, *The Girl Who Dared* and *The Phantom Speaks*, left the pulps in '43 to sign with Republic and never looked back. Also, *Road to Alcatraz* was taken from a *Speed Mystery* story; *Speed Mystery* was a tamed-down version of the notorious *Spicy Mystery Stories*."

John, of course, has been a loyalist in step with *Forgotten Horrors* since back in the day when one volume had seemed quite enough. He has given the deep-reading treatment to all my post-Turner work in rawboned manuscript form, providing not only constructive reality-check suggestions but also nuts-and-bolts proofmarking; both services lend crucial ballast to my entrenched preference for writing hell-bent for Stream of Consciousness, without compromising the spontaneity thus achieved.

I can only find it poignantly appropriate that this third book, the last to boast the direct contributions of George Turner, also reaches back to the very beginnings of George's formal career as a film reviewer: The perfect *lagniappe* is the unearthing of George's W.W. II moviegoing diary—which, as excerpted, lends an on-the-spot immediacy to our 1945 section.

George called this practice the Rediscovery Imperative, a responsibility to consider and re-consider the cultural heritage in search of forward-thinking enlightenment. George preferred plain facts over any interpretation of facts, of course, and he reserved an impatient indignation for anyone (and especially for published theorists) who might try reading subtexts into this film or that. We hold, George's stance notwithstanding, that facts can only invite interpretation. But the basis of interest remains rooted in unembellished information: If one knows not where one's culture has been, then how is one to know where that culture is bound?

Many of these rediscoveries, I must admit, have proved more diverting (and sometimes more annoying) than enlightening, and the search invariably poses the risk of blurring the barrier between legitimate Film Scholarship and mere Movie Nerdism. As though anyone knew where the one leaves off and the other begins. But the digging invariably turns up enough of the Good Stuff to justify the mounds of insignificance, and as usual we leave it up to the reader to decide which is which. There really is No Accounting for Taste—not yours, not mine and decidedly not *ours*.

—Michael H. Price
Cremo Studios, Inc.
2003, Fort Worth, Texas
www.fortworthfilmfestival.com

Acknowledgments

A grateful nod to Kerry Gammill, Terry Pace, Josh Alan Friedman, Jan Alan Henderson, Scott MacQueen, Marty Baumann (www.bmonster.com), Kip Jenkins and Kimball Jenkins (www.missinglink.free-online.co.uk), Michael Weldon, Bill Buckner, John E. Parnum, Christine Bayly (www.lifeisamovie.com), Woody Wise (www.hollywoodsattic.com) and Steve Brigati for their Contributions Beyond the Call; and to these additional sources of information, encouragement and assistance:

Paul Adair; Al Adamson, Ben and Buck Altman; Anthony Ambrogio; Don Ameche; Jim Ameche; Samuel Z. Arkoff; Robert Armstrong; Gene Autry; Vince Barnett; Billy Barty; Spencer Gordon Bennet; Robert Bloch; Ron Borst; Pat Brady; Ryan Brennan; Mel Brooks; T. Sumter Bruton III; Larry Buchanan; Bob Burns; Bruce Cabot; Sam Calvin; Yakima Canutt; Roger Corman; Frank Coughlan, Jr.; Gene Clardy; Mark Clark; Jim and Marian Clatterbaugh; Jim and Susan Colegrove; Cindy Collins; Bob Colman; Mister R. Bob Cooper; Ray "Crash" Corrigan; Buster Crabbe; Robert Crumb; Frankie Darro; Kim Dietch; Guillermo del Toro; Reginald Denny; August W. Derleth; G. Michael Dobbs; Linwood Dunn; Bob Dylan; William K. Everson; David F. Friedman; Kinky Friedman; John Gallaudet; Jimmy Gilmer; Whoopi Goldberg; Richard Gordon; Martin Grams, Jr.; Louis "Buddy" Hale; Isaac Hayes; Robert Heinlein; Charlton Heston; Bob Hope; Richard Horsey; Arthur Housman; Burl Ives; James Janis; Herb Jeffries; I. Stanford Jolley; Dr. G. William Jones; James Earl Jones; Boris Karloff; Sam Katzman; Benjamin Keck; Tom Keene; Cy Kendall; Edgar Kennedy; Fuzzy Knight; Leonard J. Kohl; Steve Kronenberg; David Ladd; Mark Lamberti; Jonathan Lampley; Baxter Lane; Herschell Gordon Lewis; Jerry Lewis; Greg Luce; Bela G. Lugosi [Jr.]; Keye Luke; Arthur Lundquist; Bob Madison; Taj Mahal; Gregory William Mank; Kermit Maynard; Mark Martin; Lee Patrick McCarthy; Jerome McDonough; George "Spanky" McFarland; Don Myers; Rudy Ray Moore; Earl Moseley; Brad Musick; Don Myers; Marian and David Naar; Edwin Neal; John E. Parnum; Bill Paxton; Gregory Peck; Samuel A. Peeples; Robin Pen; Nat Pendleton; Barbara Pepper; Richard Peterson; Norman Petty; Wilson Pickett; John Pierson; Michael R. Pitts; Roland C. Price; Lucien Prival; Luther Joe Pybus; Dr. Bill G. "Buck" Rainey; Fred Olen Ray; Otis Redding; Duncan Renaldo; Gary Don Rhodes; Paul T. Riddell; Tex and Dorothy Fay Ritter; Roy and Dale Evans Rogers; Angelo Rossitto; Reb Russell; Vivian Salazar; John Saxon; Martin Scorsese; Harry Semels; Johnny Sheffield; Sam Sherman; Wayne Shipley; Ryan Simpson; Dennis Spies; Larry D. Springer; Frank Stack; James Stephenson; Brinke Stevens; Patrick Stewart; Billy Gene Stull; Gary and Susan Svehla; Dee Lee Thomas, Jr.; Jeff Thompson; Anthony Timpone; Fred and Mary Kate Tripp; Tom Trusky; Big Joe Turner; Mario Van Peebles; Melvin Van Peebles; Steve Vertlieb; Andrew and Carlela Vogel; Vanessa Vogel; Deborah Voorhees; George Waggner; Loudon Wainwright III; Aaron "T-Bone" Walker; Cindy Walker; Mark Evan Walker; Rich Wannen; Pierre Watkin; John and Pilar Wayne; Tom Weaver; Ian Whitcomb; Chill Wills; Grady L. Wilson; Joanna Wiskowski; Grant Withers; Fay Wray; Carleton Young; Marcella Moreland Young; Tana Young; and Terry Zwigoff.

And on the Corporate/Institutional Front: The Academy of Motion Picture Arts and Sciences; The American Film Institute; The American Society of Cinematographers; The American Society of Composers, Authors and Publishers; Arthouse, Inc. (www.arthouseinc.com); Barnes and Noble Booksellers; the Billy Barty Foundation; the British Film Institute; the Cape Charles (Va.) Historical Society; the Dallas–Fort Worth Film Commission; *Fangoria* Magazine; Gordon Films, Inc., of New York; the Hoblitzelle Theatre Arts Center/University of Texas; Hollywood's Attic (www.hollywoodsattic.com); Independent-International Pictures; the Library of Congress; Life Is a Movie (www.lifeisamovie.com); Little People of America; *Mad about Movies* Magazine; *Midnight Marquee* Magazine; *Monsters from the Vault* Magazine; the National Association of Theatre Owners; the Screen Directors Guild; the Screen Writers Guild; Sinister Cinema (www.sinistercinema.com); and the Southwest Film and Video Archive at Southern Methodist University.

Annotations, Marginalia & Addenda to Prior Volumes

We count the day a loss if we reach its end without having learned something entirely new. Which is as good a reason as any to encourage an interactive relationship between the *Forgotten Horrors* books and their lifeblood readership.

And which is, of course, why we have devoted a section of each sequential volume to the cause of backtracking. Fresh information keeps coming to light: It might serve to amplify or expand the context, to lend a touch of filigree or rectify the occasional inevitable gaffe—we'd rather stand corrected than stand accused—or even to add a dimension beyond the Known.

The following selection of Cine McNuggets will account for the revelations, large and small, and even the occasional challenges, that have declared themselves since *Forgotten Horrors: The Definitive Edition* (1999) and *Forgotten Horrors 2: Beyond the Horror Ban* (2001). There also is the matter of patching in some titles that have impressed our more outspoken Constant Readers as meriting the *Forgotten Horrors* brand. Anybody can play, on the condition of bringing to the table something more than a voracious appetite or a grumpy demeanor.

—M.H.P. and J.W.
mprice@bizpress.net

1930

***Ingagi* (Congo Pictures)**—Though covered in abundant detail in *Forgotten Horrors: The Definitive Edition* and in *Forbidden Fruit* by Felicia Feaster and Bret Wood, this notoriously bogus "African" "documentary" continues to yield the random surprise. The cultural historian Steve Brigati has since determined that *Ingagi* was used, possibly past the midpoint of the 20th century, as a tool of indoctrination by the Ku Klux Klan, which seized upon the film's suggestion of an interbreeding of apes and African tribeswomen. This would seem consistent with the Klan's long-running misappropriation of D.W. Griffith's *The Birth of a Nation* for comparable purposes. So corrupt a use cannot have been part of the strategy of *Ingagi*'s producers, who were more concerned with luring in a thrill-hungry mass audience than with advancing any crackpot socio-political agendas.

1931

***The Galloping Ghost* (Mascot Pictures Corp.)**—What better title for a rip-snorting serial from Mascot than the nickname of a celebrated football player—and who better than Harold "Red" Grange, the Galloping Ghost himself, to tackle the title role? This team-directed serial dodged our radar for the original *Forgotten Horrors* collection—George Turner had remembered it as a sporting adventure with a gambling-racket subplot—but was brought back to our attention by Steve Brigati, who zeroed in on a weirder essence: Theodore Lorch plays a hunchbacked brain surgeon plying his trade for vengeful reasons. The trailblazing black comedians Stepin Fetchit and Fred "Snowflake" Toomes have a bizarre scene in which they ponder the symbolic meaning of Grange's gridiron moniker. Grange, clearly older than his collegiate character, presents an engagingly personality, and his self-stunting is superb.

Mystery Trooper **(Syndicate Pictures)**—Phantom-at-large heroic-adventure serial starring Robert Frazer. Reissued in 1938 by Guaranteed Pictures as *Trail of the Royal Mounted*. The directors are Stuart Paton and Harry S. Webb.

Sign of the Wolf **(Wonder Pictures)**—Team-directed by Forrest Sheldon and Harry S. Webb, this chapter-play deals significantly in alchemy (sand-into-jewels) and features Ed Cobb as a vengeful Mideasterner wielding a blowgun. Rex Lease and Joe Bonomo star.

1932

The Blonde Captive **(North Western Australian Expedition Syndicate/ Harvard University/Imperial Distributing Corp./Columbia Pictures Corp.)**—News commentator Lowell Thomas joins physician Paul Withington and archaeologist Clifton Childs on an expedition to determine whether any remnant of the Neanderthal has survived into the present day. This essentially cruel and exploitative documentary revels in the vivisection of a sea turtle and a seagoing mammal known as a dugong. Concentrating upon Australian Aborigines who have been herded onto a reservation, these meddling eggheads at last pronounce one man to resemble a Neanderthal. (Yes, and *everybody* who lives long enough winds up looking like a monkey, to paraphrase Clarence Williams and/or Milton Brown.) The adventure peaks with the purported shock of finding a white woman living with her Aboriginal husband and their fair-haired offspring; seems the missus had survived the wreck of a pearling schooner and was taken in by the oppressed natives. She nixes the explorers' offer to take her back to civilization. An assortment of versions seems to exist, given the discrepancies between descriptions published in 1932 and our viewings in times more recent.

1933

Jungle Bride **(Monogram Pictures Corp.)**—A castaway melodrama of noteworthy ineptitude, built around a love triangle of predictable unsteadiness among Charles Starrett, as a playboy suspected of murder; Kenneth Thompson,

Charles Starrett in *Jungle Bride*

as a journalist who intends to see Starrett hang; and Anita Page, as Thompson's fiancée—the sister of a cop-killing thug who has implicated Starrett. The jungle setting is more a plot gimmick than a dramatic milieu, although it does allow for a striking set-piece involving a beachfront funeral pyre for the martyred captain (Clarence Geldert) of a doomed ocean liner. Though lacking, the film deserves better than *The New York Times*' cavalier dismissal: "The scene of *Jungle Bride* is that well-traveled veldt somewhere in darkest Hollywood where all bad little melodramas are born and where lions are put out to graze when they become too old and feeble for active service." The directors are Harry O. Hoyt, of 1925's *The Lost World* (attempting a rebound from the absorption of his scuttled *Creation* project into *King Kong* at RKO-Radio Pictures), and Albert Kelley. An inappropriate pop tune, "That's the Call of the Jungle," serves as a bid for ironic resonance.

1934

Blue Steel **(Lone Star Productions/Monogram Pictures Corp.)**—Rejected as fodder for the original *Forgotten Horrors*, then ignored as subsequent volumes took shape, this early starring vehicle for John Wayne still strikes us as a bit too conventional to bear mentioning in the same breath with such out-and-out horseback horrors as *Randy Rides Alone* and *The Star Packer*. The opening reel, however, boasts one of the most unnerving thunderstorm sequences ever captured on film, complete with a stalking. And there *is* a masked-phantom nuisance—after a fashion. His mask, such as it is, is a polka-dot bandanna. The director and screenwriter is the brilliant Robert North Bradbury.

Brides of Sulu **(Exploration Pictures Corp.)**—A culture-clash semi-documentary, in which Islamic fundamentalist zealots (see also *The Black Coin*, under *The Amazing Exploits of the Clutching Hand*, below) pursue a convert to Christianity with murderous intentions. The indignant Sultan of Sulu (played by Armanda Magbitang) finally proves merciful—on condition that the maverick tribesman (Eduardo Castro) revert to Islam. Shot on location along the Philippine Archipelago, with an emphasis upon folkways and scenery.

***Little Men* (Mascot Pictures Corp.)**—Perhaps the classiest production from Nat Levine's rough-and-ready Mascot outfit, this feature-length adaptation of Louisa May Alcott's 1871 novel—companion-piece to the often-filmed *Little Women*—is a sentimental heartwarmer on the face of it. The film draws an appealing core of dread from the threat that Frankie Darro, as a good-natured troublemaker, might be sent away from a nurturing home for orphans to a rightly feared reformatory. One misdeed too many does the trick, and Darro finds himself a prisoner of hawk-nosed Gustav von Seyffertitz, one of Old Hollywood's creepier presences. All ends happily, as all should, but not before Darro has experienced torments better suited to a prison camp.

The film's comparatively classier state, anticipating Levine's move to upscale Republic following Mascot's forced absorption into that studio, reflects Levine's purchase in 1933 of the former Mack Sennett studios on Radford Avenue as a sturdier base of operations. Levine was a crowd-pleasing moneymaker in the low-budget filmmaking racket, and his lapse from productive prominence makes no sense, especially given his producer status at early-day Republic Pictures after that ambitious company had gobbled up Mascot. But then, there is little sense to be made of a frugal businessman's addiction to gambling—which several old-time acquaintances have cited as Levine's downfall.

Little Men was adapted again in 1940, by an independent studio called The Play's the Thing Productions, Inc., but more along the lines of a con-artist scam that threatens the security of a philanthropic school for boys. RKO-Radio Pictures released the 1940 version, whose ensemble cast includes Jack Oakie, Kay Francis and the original Elsie the Cow. Call it *Little Milkmen*.

***The Rawhide Terror* (Security Pictures Corp.)**—Correction, please, and also some amplification: The film historian-turned-producer Sam Sherman thoughtfully cites an error in our description of filmmaker Victor Adamson (a.k.a. Denver Dick and later Denver Dixon) in *Forgotten Horrors: The Definitive Edition*. Adamson was not tall and rangy, but rather compact and wiry, avers Sherman, who should know. Somehow, Adamson's screen presence has always seemed *big* to us. Anyway, it was Adamson who inspired Sherman during the early 1960s to learn moviemaking from the crucial vantage of distribution. With Adamson's son, the ultimately tragic filmmaker Al Adamson, Sherman delivered many of the more memorable Poverty Row jolters of the '60s and '70s, including *Dracula vs. Frankenstein*, *Five Bloody Graves* and *Blood of Dracula's Castle*. We'll require a down-the-line sequel to *Forgotten Horrors* to allow the Adamson-Sherman team a fuller brush with critical justice.

Sherman's larger revelation on *The Rawhide Terror* is that Victor Adamson had intended the film as a serial to be called *The Pueblo Terror*, one of those chapter-a-week rip-snorters, but then reinvented it as a self-contained short feature. Which would help to explain not only the lapses of continuity but also the breakneck pacing of this seminal horror-on-horseback.

The Scarlet Letter **(Larry Darmour Productions/Majestic Producing Corp.)**—Nathaniel Hawthorne's novel of 1850—so often adapted for stage and screen—receives a grisly shock-value reworking in this retelling, which really should have occurred to us back when we cast out the original *Forgotten Horrors* dragnet. (And another grateful nod to Sam Sherman for the heads-up signal.) Colleen Moore is the disgraced Hester Prynne, and Henry B. Walthall plays her vengeful husband. Hardie Albright is the tormented young minister Arthur Dimmesdale, whose secret shame at length drives him to mutilate himself with an *A*-as-in-*adulterer* brand. Robert G. Vignola directs.

The Tell-Tale Heart*, a.k.a. *Bucket of Blood **(Clifton-Hurst Productions/Fox Film Corp.; 1934)**—A British production, with U.S. investment capital. David Plunkett Greene's screenplay takes off strikingly from the famous story by Edgar Allan Poe. Surviving prints vary in running time from 49 minutes to 53 minutes.

Ticket to a Crime **(Beacon Productions)**—Ralph Graves plays a glib private eye who becomes embroiled in a society case involving a jewelry heist, a ransom demand and some pleasingly twisted homicidal treacheries. With Lola Lane as Graves' secretary-turned-sweetheart and Charles Ray, Edward Earle and Hy Hoover as suspects worth suspecting.

1935

Desert Mesa*, a.k.a. *Mormon Conquest **(Art Mix Productions/Security Pictures Corp.)**—Documentation is so lacking on this Victor Adamson film that even a semiformal biography of son Al Adamson—David Konow's *Schlock-o-Rama*, from 1998—cites the film as a 1938 entry under a proxy reissue title, *Mormon Conquest*, and identifies it as a lost work. Certainly the picture eluded the contributions of Price & Turner *et al.* to *The American Film Institute Catalog: Feature Films 1931-1940*, which resorts to cast-list and synopsis files in lieu of any fresh impressions. The story takes place on an embattled ranch, where a menacing character named Lynx Merson holds sway. Lew Meehan plays both Merson and a prowling bandit known either as El Garto or El Gato, depending upon one's source. Enthusiast Steve Brigati has recalled a showcase scene in which Victor Adamson (appearing as Denver Dixon) demonstrates his whip-cracking skills. The Konow book lists Al Adamson, who would have been 6 years old in 1935, among the cast. Likely a more conventional piece than *The Rawhide Terror*—but then, anything bearing the Adamson stamp will exert some bearing here.

Let 'Em Have It! **(Reliance Pictures)**—In the caption in *Forgotten Horrors 2*, Barbara Pepper is mis-identified as Virginia Bruce.

1936

The Amazing Exploits of the Clutching Hand (**Weiss Productions, Inc.**)—See *Forgotten Horrors: The Definitive Edition*. Our original text on this fiend-at-large serial mentions two other chapter-a-week productions from the Weiss agenda for 1936-37—*Custer's Last Stand* and a Mideastern-terrorism thriller called *The Black Coin*—noting that the Weiss & Mintz partnership was dissolved after this batch. Louis Weiss kept up the momentum, however, with three additional serials, which were picked up by Columbia Pictures for its 1937-38 program.

These would be *Jungle Mystery*, starring the explorer Frank Buck; *The Secret of Treasure Island*, from L. Ron Hubbard's novel *Murder at Pirate Castle*; and *Mysterious Pilot*, starring Frank Hawkes. All are generous with the hair-raising weirdness, and all bespeak a decisive infiltration of a major-league studio by one of the hardier Poverty Row outposts. This shadowy corner of the *Forgotten Horrors* canon was brought to our attention by Steve Brigati and *Sinister Serials* author Leonard J. Kohl.

The Black Coin, incidentally, has resurfaced against the odds in a crisp video edition from the Life Is a Movie catalog: www.lifeisamovie.com. This one came to our attention during the summer of 2001. Its tale of deadly intrigues centering upon an outpost of the French Foreign Legion seemed but a quaint echo of bygone days—until the Global Sea Change of September 11, 2001 snapped it squarely back into perspective as something more than a diversionary relic.

For like John Ford's classier *The Lost Patrol* (1934), foremost among any number of other mayhem-in-the-Mideast pictures, *The Black Coin* warns that the clash of social imperatives between disparate cultures can only lead to brutal reciprocal hostilities. Such movies hardly go so far as to indict the vain conceit of the White Man's Burden, which once led the crowned heads of Christiandom to fancy themselves the civilizing landlords of the rest of the world—America included, of course.

But the pictures' grasp of the conflicts thus provoked runs deeper than the misadventures thus portrayed. Their point is not so much to indulge in stereotype (a useful characterizing device, in a form of entertainment that has no space or time for painstaking character development), as it is to demonstrate that civility and zealotry do not mix. This is how missionary evangelists wind up as the Main Course, whether in the Congo or along the South Coast of Texas, and this is how mass murder gets perpetrated as a sacramental offering. In this respect, *The Black Coin* and its ilk prove to have been distant early warnings, probably unwitting and certainly ill heeded, of the consequences of dealing with any society whose rallying cry of "Death to the unbelievers!" is no bluff.

For a tribe that exists along the lines of Live and Let Live has no business mixing with, or even nodding to, any band of nimrods who place greater store in the notion of Kill or Be Killed. The movies told us this much, in terms as explicit as commonplace escapism would allow, a long time ago—using Real

World examples from a day when the cannonade and the sharpshooter rifle were about the heaviest artillery to be had. Now it is too late.

Bridge of Sighs **(Invincible Pictures Corp./Chesterfield Motion Pictures Corp.)**—The sister (Dorothy Tree) of a man wrongfully convicted on a murder rap subjects herself to the terrors of a women's prison in order to get the goods on the truer culprit. Onslow Stevens plays a lovestruck district attorney. Directed by Phil Rosen, of *Devil's Mate* and *The Sphinx*, among other germane titles.

The Lion Man **(Normandy Pictures Corp.)**—Richard Gordon supplies a correction to the caption in *Forgotten Horrors 2*: The actor pictured alongside Kathleen Burke is Ted Adams (a.k.a. Richard Adams), as Sheikh Youssef Ab-Dur. And these additional character names, matched with the players, have come to light since we helped to compile *The American Film Institute Catalog: Feature Films 1931-1940*: Kathleen Burke (Eulilah); Richard Carlyle (Hassan El Dinh); Finis Barton (Sherrifa); Eric Snowden (Sir Ronald Chatham); James "Jimmy" Aubrey (Simmonds); Lal Chand Mehra (Sheikh); Bobby Fairy (Chatham Boy); and Henry Hale.

Murder at Glen Athol, **a.k.a.** ***The Criminal Within*** **(Invincible Pictures Corp./Chesterfield Motion Pictures Corp.)**—George Turner had nixed this one as a candidate for the original *Forgotten Horrors*, back during the 1970s, and he nixed it again when the time came to revamp the book for its 1999 edition from Midnight Marquee Press. Nor did Mike Price see fit to add it to the backtracker section in *Forgotten Horrors 2*, or rather he gave it no fresh consideration. So why the turnabout now? Simply because it might belong, after all, and some enlightened souls have asked that we include the film.

Dapper John Miljan serves *Murder at Glen Athol* as a detective-turned-novelist who stumbles into a tangle of insanity, adultery, blackmail and bludgeonings, stabbings and poisonings. The Legion of Decency and the Production Code Administration must have been snoozing when there came those scenes in which lethal lady Iris Adrian hides incriminating papers in her cleavage and then must fend off attempts to nab them. The papers, that is. The perfectly valid title of this film tends to elicit unwholesome snickering when uttered today—sort of like Warners' *The Amazing Dr. Clitterhouse*.

The President's Mystery **(Republic Pictures Corp.)**—Mentioned in passing in *Forgotten Horrors 2*, this entry bears re-emphasizing in light of one eerie dead-of-night scene in which Henry Wilcoxson, as a wealthy lawyer fleeing an unsavory past life, procures a corpse while en route to staging a false demise. The basis is a vague idea suggested to the novelist/editor Fulton Oursler by Franklin D. Roosevelt, and of course the resulting *Liberty* magazine serial and its movie version exploit that connection to the limit. As a storytelling influence, F.D.R. made a pretty good politician. The director is Phil Rosen, a familiar name among our more diligent readers.

West of Nevada **(Colony Pictures, Inc.)** — This Rex Bell sagebrusher, rediscovered by Sinister Cinema video impresario Greg Luce, is but marginally a *Forgotten Horrors* type of picture, but it does pivot on a curious merger of the gold-mining and taxidermy rackets, with a mob of claim-jumpers attempting to do away with a community of Indian miners.

1937

Blazing Barriers **(Monogram Pictures Corp.)** — Aubrey Scotto's *Blazing Barriers* is a prototypical J.D., or juvenile-delinquency, melodrama with disaster-movie undertones in a forest-fire climax. Frank "Junior" Coghlan and Edward Arnold, Jr., play petty hoodlums given a shot at redemption with the Civilian Conservation Corps. Edwin C. Parsons' original screenplay detours into weirdness with a deranged character known as Crack-Up — who sets out on a murderous rampage of arson and gunplay. Tragedy and redemption result.

The Dead March **(Bud Pollard Productions, Inc./Imperial Distributing Corp.)** — A year before the great French filmmaker Abel Gance remade his war-against-war epic of 1919, *J'Accuse* (*I Accuse*), the not particularly great American filmmaker Bud Pollard made *The Dead March* as an inflammatory pro-war manifesto. This one is by-and-large a documentary piece, utilizing archival footage including the sinking of the *St. Stephan*, an Austrian ship, by an Italian torpedo. A dramatized set-piece portrays the fallen Unknown Soldiers of Germany, France, Italy, England and the United States, rising from their graves to rhapsodize upon their warlike motivations. Pollard timed the release to coincide with the American Legion's national convention in September 1937 in New York. The actors portraying the reanimated dead are, for the record, Solo Daudaux, Al Rigall, Al Ritchie, Don Black and Howard Hagley. Pollard is the artist responsible for *The Horror*, that rickety supporting beam of the *Forgotten Horrors* shelf.

Dybuk*, a.k.a. *Der Dybuk* and *The Dybbuk **(Poland/U.S.)** — Michal Waszynski's supernatural romantic fantasy, filmed in Poland with Jewish American underwriting, concerns a tragic betrothal and the consequences of parental tampering with generations yet unborn. The American release version retained the original Yiddish dialogue track, with English subtitles.

Race Suicide*, a.k.a. *What Price Passion* and *Victims of Passion **(Willis Kent Productions/Real Life Dramas/DeLuxe Distribution Co.)** — Anti-abortion mania hits a fever pitch (way ahead of Roe vs. Wade and its aftershocks) in this alias-ridden mixture of agitprop and legalized voyeurism from the pandering schlockmeister Willis Kent, who dealt in both forbidden kicks and repressive moral conservatism in a single stroke. The back-alley abortion racket is declared tantamount to race suicide—this, in a day when overpopulation and parental default were but distantly grasped concepts among civilized Americans. An upstanding physician moonlights as a clinic-of-horrors operator and murder-for-hire artist; he winds up taking a lethal overdose from a hypo wielded by a disgruntled accomplice. S. Roy Luby directs, with photography by Marcel Le Picard. The film kept playing well into the 1950s, though seldom with the blessing of regional censorship agencies, whose members most likely would have found the politics on parade here right up their alley. The word *abortion* goes un-uttered in the prints we have turned up.

She-Devil Island (**First Division/ Grand National**)—Superficially Americanized release of a 1936 Mexican picture called *Irma la Mala*, starring Pedro Armendariz and directed by Raphael Sevilla. Grand National's advertising campaign promised "Nature in the Raw—Wild Virgins in the Flesh!" Quote/unquote.

1938

Frontier Scout (**Fine Arts Pictures/ Grand National Pictures, Inc.**)— Sam Newfield's history-be-damned Western purports to portray an episode from the career of Wild Bill Hickok (played by the busy adventure-film hero George Houston). A Civil War-era framing story serves as a set-up for a post-bellum scenario, in which Hickok must deal with a phantom sniper and cattle rustler known as One-Shot. The incandescent black comedian Mantan Moreland, still fairly new to the feature-film game, makes much of a conventionally demeaning butler role.

1940

Beyond Tomorrow (**Academy Productions, Inc./RKO-Radio Pictures, Inc.**) — A benevolent haunting, with old-timers Harry Carey, C. Aubrey Smith and Charles Winninger as ghosts returned to help struggling singer Richard Carlson launch his career. Things turn grim after lethal lady Helen Vinson seduces Carlson into a lethal situation. Jean Parker provides the good-girl romantic interest, and Maria Ouspenskaya plays a servant psychically attuned to sense the guardian spirits. Independently produced, with Edward Sutherland directing, and acquired for distribution by RKO.

Midnight Limited (**Sherwill Productions, Inc./Monogram Pictures Corp.**) — An impossible-getaway mystery involving a chain of train robberies between Montreal and Albany. John King stars as diehard sleuth Valentine Lennon, who loses an assistant to a skulking killer before determining that the culprit, in cahoots with baggageman Monte Collins, has been sneaking onto and off the train in caskets. A marginal entry, but even the margins can contain some interesting scribbles.

1941

Borrowed Hero (**Monogram Pictures Corp.**) — Alan Baxter stars as an inept but game lawyer who lands in dutch with a murderous cult-like graft syndicate traveling under the sheep's-clothing name of the Civic League. The money shot comes late, when the killers open fire on their quarry's automobile — slaying two of their own who had stolen the vehicle but neglected to inform the mob.

The Deadly Game (**Monogram Pictures Corp.**) — Marginal science fiction (and wouldn't the language be better off — all due respect — without that fatuous term *sci-fi*?) involving an experimental device to forecast nighttime air raids. Charles Farrell stars as an FBI agent on the trail of spy chief John Miljan.

Emergency Landing (**Producers Releasing Corp.**) — Test pilot Forrest Tucker tackles the development of a remote-controlled aircraft. I. Stanford Jolley plays a hostage-taking German spy. There is some spooky desert-by-night business, along with a leavening of screwball romantic business with Carol Hughes as the headstrong daughter of an aviation-industry big shot.

The Forgotten Village (**Pan-American Films/Mayer-Burstyn, Inc.**) — John Wooley weighs in with amplification upon the chapter in *Forgotten Horrors 2*, citing two biographies: Jackson L. Benson's *The True Adventures of John Steinbeck, Writer* (1984) and Jay Parini's *John Steinbeck* (1995).

Steinbeck, who composed this tale of Third World squalor and superstition directly for the screen, wanted Max Wagner, a lifelong friend who was struggling in Hollywood, to narrate. Producer Herbert Kline wanted a box office name. Spencer Tracy, who admired Steinbeck and later became his friend, was interested, but MGM nixed Tracy's participation—unless the actor would consent to tackle an MGM project he didn't want to do, *Dr. Jekyll and Mr. Hyde*. Tracy agreed, and MGM lined him up to do the narration for *The Forgotten Village*. But just as Tracy had begun preparing for both that job and launched himself into *J&H*, MGM reneged, figuring correctly that the actor would not shut down a big film that was already in production.

Steinbeck was furious, especially now that he had found it necessary to un-invite Wagner. He could scarcely bring himself to ask Wagner again, after so conspicuous a dismissal, and so the author called Burgess Meredith. Before Steinbeck calmed down, he vowed to badmouth MGM's production of *Tortilla Flat* in every way he could. Of course, he didn't follow through on the threat.

Law of the Wolf (**Arthur Ziehm, Inc.**)—More experimental-plane shenanigans, with canine star Rin Tin Tin, Jr., in heroic-ferocious mode against badman George Chesebro. Dennis Moore stars as an escaped jailbird seeking to clear himself of a wrongful murder rap.

Tumbledown Ranch in Arizona (**Range Busters, Inc./George W. Weeks Productions/Monogram Pictures Corp.**)—What was that we were saying about marginal science fiction? Ray "Crash" Corrigan tackles a double role—as himself, more or less, and as the college-boy son of Corrigan's fellow Range Buster John "Dusty" King—in a tale of time travel from the then-present day back to 1900. Nothing particularly fantastical about the adventure, which involves a stock-in-trade land-grabber scheme engineered by a murderous gang and a crooked sheriff (Jack Holmes). But the framing device is remarkable for a Saturday-matinee Western. It all turns out to be a dream, occasioned by a rodeo accident, and ending when Corrigan wakes in a hospital room. An eerie *déjà vu* coda finds Corrigan under the care of a nurse who proves to be the daughter of a ranchwoman who had appeared in his dream.

1942

Jacaré (**Mayfair Productions, Inc./United Artists Corp.**)—The jacaré, or gigantic 'gator-like caiman, menaces an expedition into the Amazon jungles. Explorer Frank Buck entrusts the greater share of adventuring to James M. Dannaldson and Miguel Rojinsky.

Lure of the Islands (**Monogram Pictures Corp.**)—Robert Lowery and Guinn "Big Boy" Williams vs. Japanese infiltrators in Tahiti. Lowery uses a radio-beam gizmo to cause an enemy aircraft to mistake a forested region for a landing strip, with gratifying results.

The Panther's Claw (**Producers Releasing Corp.**)—See *Forgotten Horrors 2*. This one-shot production suggests a false start toward a series featuring Thatcher Colt, an intrepid enforcer created by the novelist Fulton Oursler under the pen name of Anthony Abbot. Our discussion of *The Panther's Claw* should have mentioned two Colt adventures mounted by Columbia Pictures during 1932-33: *The Night Club Lady* and *The Circus Queen Murders*. This oversight was brought thoughtfully to our attention by a California enthusiast, Don Myers; and by Richard Gordon of New York-based Gordon Films, a pivotal figure as executive producer of such favorites as *Grip of the Strangler, Fiend without a Face, First Man into Space* (1958-59) and *Devil Doll* (1964).

Irving Cummings' *The Night Club Lady* finds Colt (Adolphe Menjou) rescuing club owner Mayo Methot from a conventional firearm attack, only to find her slain by inexplicable means at the stroke of a New Year's midnight. The concealed weapon proves to be a scorpion.

Roy William Neill's *The Circus Queen Murder* pits Colt (Menjou) against Dwight Frye as a crazed aerialist who fakes his demise in order to plot a leisurely revenge on his errant wife (Greta Neissen). Frye's climactic mad scene, in which he delivers a magnificent performance before deliberately taking a fatal fall from a high wire, is a jewel.

A third such picture was anticipated, but the series cratered after the two entries. The encyclopedic *American Film Institute Catalog*, a five-foot shelf to which George Turner and Mike Price have contributed research and resources, neglects to acknowledge the *Colt*s as a series. Hence the greater value of the interactive relationship between *Forgotten Horrors* and its readers.

Private Snuffy Smith (**Capital Pictures Corp./Monogram Pictures Corp.**)— The last paragraph of the entry on Page 185 of *Forgotten Horrors 2* makes a great deal better sense if one removes the word *captive*, which represents a glitch that sneaked in while an earlier gaffe was being corrected. Our proofreader's seeing-eye dog was off duty that day.

Scattergood Survives a Murder, a.k.a. *Cat's Claw Murder Mystery* (**Pyramid Pictures Corp./RKO-Radio Pictures, Inc.**)—The independently made *Scattergood Baines* series stars lovable Guy Kibbee as a down-home philosopher-storekeeper in a New England village. The pictures, based upon a phenomenally popular run of stories dating from 1920 in *American Magazine*, spanned 1941-43, serving as a Yankee counterpart to the Deep Southern *Lum & Abner* series. A *Scattergood* radio series, with Jess Pugh and Weldell Holmes, by turns, handling the title role, had originated in 1938 over the CBS network.

Scattergood Survives a Murder, fifth of the movies, boasts a tale of remarkable savagery, involving a killer who does away with two elderly recluses (Margaret McWade and Margaret Seddon) in quest of an inheritance. The weapon of choice is a lynx's severed paw, steeped in poison. (The picture predates Val Lewton's *The Leopard Man* by a year.)

The perpetrator proves to be dependable Wallace Ford, playing both with and against the grain of his familiar lovable smart-aleck type. Ford is rendered helpless by a faceful of dipping snuff, that favorite Controlled Substance of many a folksy 'Way Down Easterner. The work-in-progress title was *Cat's Claw Murder Mystery*, which was restored for a reissue by Favorite Films, after the RKO proprietorship had lapsed. The RKO advertising campaign emphasized the genial dignity of Guy Kibbee; the indie reissue promotion touted a horrific essence.

Another entry in the series, 1941's *Scattergood Pulls the Strings*, pivots on the peculiar tale of a bygone slaying that has severe repercussions in the present day.

And on toward the 1950s

Frankenstein **(George E. Turner; uncompleted)** — The carbon-dating here is approximate, for George Turner kept this home-grown entry in gradual production during a span of several years, postwar. We mentioned in *Forgotten Horrors 2* that the footage, developed but unedited, was destroyed through careless unauthorized handling around 1970. A frame enlargement has since come to light at the bottom of a file of random detritus from George's Pasadena archive. That image, though grainy beyond further refinement, is reproduced herewith as a courtesy to many readers who have wished aloud that they might learn more. So now you know as much about it as we do. Which isn't a great deal, to begin with.

1943

DR. TERROR'S HOUSE OF HORRORS
(National Road Shows)

This notable instance of feature-film vandalism and piracy bobbed briefly back to the surface during the 1960s at a meeting of a Texas film-appreciation society run by George E. Turner and a Southwestern advertising artist-turned-executive named Gene A. Clardy. The reason for the presentation lay in the film's pageant of footage cribbed from mostly rare, mostly foreign films dating from the 1930s, and no one attending the screening was predisposed to appreciate *Dr. Terror's House of Horrors* as a curiosity worth consideration in its own peculiar right. Too bad the picture hasn't seemed inclined to crop up again—bound to be a print slowly falling to rot out there, *somewhere*.

The compilation includes extracts, doubtless unauthorized, of the following:

•Bela Lugosi's starring serial, *The Return of Chandu*, from 1936 (see *Forgotten Horrors: The Definitive Edition*).

•Lugosi's hit starrer of 1932, *White Zombie* (see likewise, as well as A.S.C. Press' *The Cinema of Adventure, Romance & Terror*).

•Carl T. Dreyer's unsettling if marginally coherent *Vampyr* (France-Germany-Denmark; 1931-32), also shown as *Vampire*, *The Strange Adventure of David Gray* and *Castle of Doom*—among other proxy titles.

• The Gabriel Pascal–Richard Oswald production of *Unheimliche Geschicten* (Germany; 1932), also known variously as *Tales of the Uncanny*, *The Living Dead*, *Extraordinary Tales* and *Asylum of Horror*. This most rare of the lot is a gallows comedy based upon Poe and Stevenson, starring Paul Wegener as a murderous lunatic who takes charge of an asylum.

• And Julian Duvivier's *Golem* (Czechoslovakia-France; 1936), also known variously as *Le Golem*, *The Golem*, *The Legend of Prague* and *The Man of Stone*. Ferdinand Hart plays the title role, a uniquely Hebrew instrument of retribution, as a creature described as "half-man and half-spectre."

Gene Clardy recalled seeing the same compilation as part of a midnight spook-show extravaganza during the early 1950s. Yet earlier and more vivid documentation comes from the Pennsylvania-based film historian and stage magician John E. Parnum.

"At the age of 10, I saw *Dr. Terror's House of Horrors* on Saturday, September 22, 1945, at the Studio Theatre in Philadelphia," Parnum told us in 1999. That explicitly remembered date invites Parnum's persuasive conclusion that few prints existed inasmuch as the formal release—such as it was—had occurred in 1943.

"The Studio Theatre showed all kinds of horror and exploitative revivals," added Parnum. "I really don't remember much about the movie, except that there was a long segment about an invincible detective, which may have been the connecting link between the segments from the various films."

The film is not to be confused with the U.S.-British production of *Dr. Terror's House of Horrors* (1963), a portmanteau picture starring Peter Cushing and Christopher Lee.

CREDITS: Released: During 1943 and Thereafter on a State-by-State Basis

A JAPANESE PIPE DREAM
(U.S. Documentary Motion Picture Co.)

As the wife and business partner of the exploitation-film impresario Dwain Esper, Hildegarde Stadie was quite the impresario on her own. She wrote prolifically if not particularly well, and she occasionally lent her artistry—the term is used advisedly—to social concerns larger than that old demon dope (*Marihuana: Weed with Roots in Hell*), the lustful proclivities of mad doctors (*Maniac*), and the recurring problem of ape-rape rampages in the Third World (*Angkor*).

The Japanese menace of World War II was sufficiently entwined with the drug-traffic threat to allow Mrs. Esper to position *A Japanese Pipe Dream* strategically between patriotic propaganda and crass opportunistic sensationalism. Her script, droningly recited throughout an hour's worth of stock footage, declares that Japan had good reason for rejecting an international ban on narcotics several years before: The nation had already decided upon using heroin and morphine to undermine its chosen enemies. The harvesting and processing of the opium poppy is shown in considerable detail. Mme. Chiang Kai-shek complains of "the systematic doping of the populations of Manchuria and Japanese-controlled China," and a 1938 U.S. seizure of Japanese heroin is interpreted as a provocation for the attack upon Pearl Harbor. (Which, in the realm of conspiracy speculation, might pose an intriguing corollary to the prevalent notion of Franklin D. Roosevelt's foreknowledge of Pearl Harbor.) The narrator declares sternly: "The Japanazi shall perish from this earth."

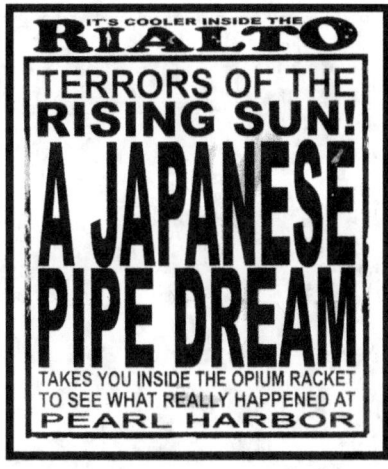

CREDITS: Producer/Writer/Editor: Hildegarde Stadie Esper [Given Elsewhere as Hildagarde]; Running Time: 60 Minutes; Released: During 1943 on a State-by-State Basis

CAST: Earle Ross (Narrator)

MAN OF COURAGE
(Motion Picture Associates, Inc./Producers Releasing Corp.)

Political deception runs neck-and-neck with sadistic murder and kidnapping in this overacted and indifferently directed entry, which Barton MacLane wrote collaboratively as a star vehicle for himself.

MacLane serves *Man of Courage* as "Honest John" Wallace, a reform-minded prosecutor and candidate for governor, whose pal, building contractor Mark Crandall (Forrest Taylor), is secretly his worst enemy, in cahoots with the underworld. A more obvious threat comes from a small-change gambler named George Dickson (Lyle Talbot). Dickson is not only the trigger-man in a high-profile mob slaying; he also is such a rotter as to abandon his family during a fifth-birthday party for his daughter (Patsy Nash) and then take off with a nightclub floozy named Joyce Griffith (Charlotte Wynters).

In the park where the party had been held, a tramp is found murdered—and mutilated beyond recognition. Conveniently planted false evidence convinces the police that the victim must be Dickson, whose wife (Dorothy Burgess) is arrested for murder. Wallace declines to prosecute until he receives forensic conclusions, falsely arranged by Crandall, that identify the corpse as Dickson.

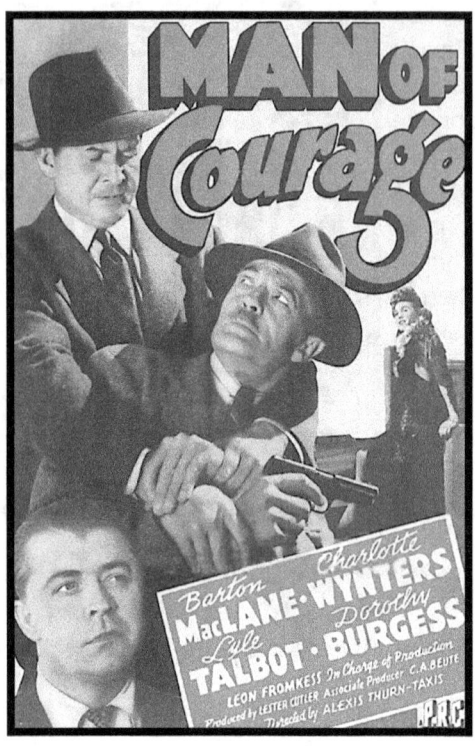

Mrs. Dickson's conviction ensures the election for Wallace, who soon gets wise to Crandall's guise, ultimately to realize that the murder trial was a sham. Wallace resigns, arranges a pardon for Mrs. Dickson and convenes a grand jury to investigate Crandall. He barely escapes a hit squad dispatched by Crandall and finally realizes he has fallen in love with Mrs. Dickson.

Meanwhile, Dickson steals out of hiding, abducting his daughter and demanding a ransom that would settle his gambling debts. Joyce has grown impatient with this pathetic loser, and the kid is the last straw. She returns the child to Mrs. Dickson and implicates Dickson in the mob-contract killing. Dickson is captured while stalking his wife, and Wallace looks forward to changing Mrs. Dickson's name to Mrs. Wallace.

The "true horror of the public enemy"—an expression George Turner coined in 1975 for our coverage of the far superior gangster picture *Let 'Em Have It* (1935)—is here in spades, all right, but it is well hidden underneath all the self-importance and soap-operatics. MacLane makes an insufferably noble title character, so full of himself that he takes 'way too long to spot the chicanery within his most trusted inner circle. Perhaps MacLane's longtime field of specialization, as a tough guy in numerous big-league crime thrillers and Westerns, blurs our perception of his work here. Or perhaps the role is as full of sanctimonious baloney as we're inclined to believe.

Lyle Talbot fares better as the vicious small-time good-for-nothing, but his most treacherous deed, the abduction, is played for so little suspense as to render the climax anticlimactic. Charlotte Wynters makes a pleasingly soft-hearted brassy dame. Veteran stage actress Dorothy Burgess, whose sporadic film career wavered between low-budget leads and big-picture supporting roles, is a study in melancholy beauty as the abandoned-and-accused mother. Patsy Nash is endearing as the menaced child, although she never quite seems convincingly in peril.

Technical contributions make the picture look and sound like a throwback to the early 1930s' primitive state of filmmaking. Marcel Le Picard was a much abler cinematographer than his work here would suggest. The audio is particularly distorted during a gratuitous musical number.

CREDITS: In Charge of Production: Leon Fromkess; Producer: Lester Cutler; Associate Producer: C.A. Beute; Director: Alexis Thurn-Taxis; Dialogue Director: Edith Baldwin Watkins; Original Story: Barton MacLane, Herman Ruby and Lew Pollack; Screenplay: Arthur St. Claire, Barton MacLane and John Vlahos; Photographed by: Marcel Le Picard; Assistant Director: Don Verk; Property Master: George Bahr; Musical Director: Lee Zahler; Song, "Now and Then," by Lew Pollack; Sound: Ben Winkler, RCA Victor; Produced at Talisman Studios; Running Time: 67 Minutes; Released: January 4, 1943

CAST: Barton MacLane ("Honest John" Wallace); Charlotte Wynters (Joyce Griffith); Lyle Talbot (George Dickson); Dorothy Burgess (Sally Dickson); Patsy Nash (Mary Ann Dickson); Forrest Taylor (Mark Crandall); John Ince (Tom Haines); Jane Novak (Mrs. Black); Eddie Cherkose (Stanley Thomas); Claire Grey (Alice); Steve Clark (Judge Roberts); Billy Gray (Mike Wilson); Frank Yaconelli (Pete); Erskine Johnson (Himself)

CHILD BRIDE
a.k.a.: CHILD BRIDE OF THE OZARKS
(Stern Fisher Productions/Astor Pictures)

Hollywood has made room for dwarves and midgets—the more acceptable term nowadays is *Little People*—ever since the age of the silent screen. Such opportunities, unfortunately for that neglected society, have usually amounted to "a spiral, descending into tokenism and exploitation," as the tragic dwarf actor Michael Dunn bitterly informed an interviewer from the Associated Press in 1973.

The most cursory survey bears out Dunn's assertion: Striking examples lie in Stymie Beard's encounter with two troublemaking "fidgets" (played by the carney dwarves Tiny Lawrence and Major Mite) in an *Our Gang* two-reeler called "Free Eats" (1932), and in the Jed Buell–Sam Newfield Western-as-sideshow gimmick film *The Terror of Tiny Town* (1938). Samuel M. Sherman, a latter-day Poverty Row producer, has told us with point-blank frankness, "There's nothing quite as effective as a weird little short guy to let the audience know there's something sick going on." Even MGM's perennially beloved *The Wizard of Oz* (1939), with its helium-voiced chorus of Munchkins, illustrates Dunn's complaint.

The exceptions, however, are likewise striking. A pre-Munchkins Harry Earles (*né* Kurt Schneider) holds forth convincingly as a lovestruck leading man in *Freaks* (1932), and as a calculating menace in two versions of *The*

Unholy Three (1925 and 1930). Michael Dunn landed an Oscar nomination for his portrayal of a philosophical observer of the Human Condition in *Ship of Fools* (1965), and he played an old-fashioned mad doctor of the Karloff/Lugosi school in the teleseries *The Wild Wild West*. Earles, whose truer element was the carnival scene, retired in comfort and lived to the age of 83 in 1985. Dunn died, apparently by his own hand, at age 39 in 1973.

There was a time when Angelo "Little Angie" Rossitto—who with Billy Barty and "Little Billy" Curtis formed the vanguard of Old Hollywood's little-people contingent—would cringe at the mention of his own supporting role in Tod Browning's *Freaks*, although in later years the actor would develop a fonder regard for the film. Rossitto never voiced anything but praise, however, for Harry Revier's *Child Bride*, a cheaply made exploitationer that for all its lurid excesses stands as a proud example of heroic casting for all the Little People who have passed under Hollywood's turnstile.

"I especially liked the part I was lucky enough to get in a little picture called *Child Bride*," Rossitto told us in 1990 while residing in a Los Angeles managed-care apartment, a year before his death at age 83 from complications following surgery. "That was one that could've been just the usual creepy-dwarf business, but they let me *do* some things with it. Unusual, that a picture will let a little guy step in and save the day."

But we're getting ahead of the game: *Child Bride* was made as a roadshow attraction (to use the show-biz parlance of the times), and as such it was released without a Production Code Purity Seal—destined for those lesser theatres that occasionally ran adults-only shows, for burlesque houses and for four-wall situations where the distributor would rent, literally speaking, the four walls of an auditorium for as many weeks as the film could draw a crowd.

Unlike many of its kind, *Child Bride* boasts the competent work of Hollywood professionals. More surprisingly, it presents a fairly realistic story—a sort of poor man's *Swamp Water* and *Tobacco Road* combined—and manages to capture the naturalistic horror that comes with the territory among inbred, isolated communities. The tale is told grimly, with scant conscious humor, although guffaws are the only logical response to Frank Martin's foppish romantic lead and the overplaying of a courageous schoolmarm by Diana Durrell (fiancée of producer Raymond Fridgen).

The cast is peopled largely with unknowns, but Warner Richmond—who does a nice job as the villain—was a veteran of the 1921 *Tol'able David* and a popular heavy in Westerns and serials of the 1930s. The title player, Shirley Mills, fares okay in a difficult role, displaying a defiant mettle to offset her more demeaning moments of conspicuous nudity. Miss Mills had appeared as Ruth Joad in John Ford's 1940 filming of the John Steinbeck novel *The Grapes of Wrath*. She later worked at Columbia, where her assignments included the sorority-house murder mystery *Nine Girls* (1943), and in 1950 she tackled an

anti-sympathetic supporting part alongside the little-guy leading man Paul Dale, in William Castle's *It's a Small World*.

Shirley Mills has recalled the experience in considerable detail in her Web site memoirs: "[For an audition,] they used the scene where I found my father murdered. I was so absorbed with the sadness of the moment, tears flowed down my cheeks and Mr. [Harry] Revier [the director] said, 'That's it! She's perfect for the part.'"

Likewise familiar is Angelo Rossitto, who had received his break in films through the courtesy of John Barrymore in *The Beloved Rogue* (1927) and contributed vigor to the likes of *In Old San Francisco* (1927) and *Seven Footprints to Satan* (1929). Rossitto crops up elsewhere in the 1940s' span of *Forgotten Horrors*, usually as a skulker in league and/or conflict with Bela Lugosi. In addition to his screen work, the two-foot-ten Rossitto operated a well-trafficked newsstand at Hollywood Boulevard and Wilcox; footage showing him at this real-world job, hawking newspapers with the zeal of a carney spieler, turns up in a bizarre all-star revue film from 1946 called *Breakfast in Hollywood*.

Rossitto had begun as early as 1939 to organize the civil-rights group that would become the influential Little People of America. He conducted an aggressive campaign for mayor of Los Angeles in 1941—"finished seventh in a field of eight, yes, I did," as he once told us—and he and Billy Barty and Billy Curtis led successful efforts to have the insurance industry develop actuarial tables for dwarves and to encourage medical schools to develop training programs geared to the treatment of Little People. Many years and quite a few exploitation-thriller assignments later, Rossitto contributed a show-stopping performance to the big-studio production of *Mad Max Beyond Thunderdome* (1985).

Child Bride tells of schoolgirl Jennie Colton (Miss Mills), whose mountaineer father, Ira (George Humphreys), operates a whiskey still in partnership with Jake Bolby (Richmond). Bolby, who trains a lustful eye upon both Jennie and her attractive mother (Dorothy Carrol, Revier's wife), is a thoroughgoing scoundrel, taking especial delight in tormenting the diminutive Angelo (Rossitto, billed here as Don Barrett), and a half-wit boy named Happy (Al Bannon), who help him run the distillery. When Jennie's father bests Bolby in a fistfight, the hillbilly schemes toward revenge.

Meanwhile, Miss Carol (Diana Durrell), the local schoolteacher, campaigns to end the hills' tradition of grown men marrying young girls, with the help of her fiancé, Charles (Martin), a lawyer. Bolby orders the abduction and torture of Miss Carol. Angelo provokes a raid to rescue her.

Bolby murders Jennie's father in the wake of a domestic row. Accusing Ma Colton of the crime, Bolby manipulates her into helping him make the death appear accidental. Now, he can blackmail the mother into giving him her daughter. The brute succeeds in marrying the girl, but before he can consummate the union he is gunned down by Angelo. The dwarf's intervention comes just in time to prevent a schoolboy named Freddie (Bob Bollinger), who loves Jennie, from killing Bolby. Later on, the law against child marriage is passed.

"It all became very real to me," Mills ecalled, "The only hard part was displaying fear of the villain because he was so kind and considerate to me, but the director and my own mother guided me through it all and suddenly he became very ominous because of his own acting ability.

"Everyone on the set really wanted to spoil me—I guess because I was really a nice little girl, and they had fun fussing over me. The prop man, electricians, sound, everyone teased me a lot. Little Angelo found a fresh fig tree and picked some for me every day."

Miss Mills, incidentally, would share the screen with another dwarf player, Paul Dale, in William Castle's 1950 production of *It's a Small World*. The actress has recalled *Child Bride* as a 1938 production, and her Web site goes to far as to cite the film as a provocation to legislation, as early as 1940, outlawing child marriage. Production might conceivably date as far back 1938, but the American Film Institute traces the first showings to 1943. Not to mention that *Child Bride* was hardly in a position to be taken seriously as a socially influential treatise. The distributor was more concerned with selling tickets than with advancing reforms.

The Production Code Administration denied a Purity Seal to *Child Bride*, and for fairly obvious reasons: Nudity and crass misconduct abound, not to mention the overriding degeneracy—and the simple fact that the industry's built-in censorship machine wanted to see the dwarf punished for his murderous act of heroism. There is an effectively nightmarish scene in which the defiant schoolteacher is dragged into a torchlit hollow, there to be stripped and beaten by hooded men. Diana Durrell has a fine enough figure to compensate  for her deficiencies as an actress. The schoolhouse setting is notably true to life, with pigeons roosting nastily in the rafters and a mob of restless students ranging from toddlers to lanky muttonhead grown-ups. Director Harry Revier paces things briskly but dwells rewardingly upon the grotesque details of Southern mountain life.

A queasier element is a skinny-dipping sequence featuring Miss Mills; this apparently served for the benefit of any viewers who might have entertained the same perversity the picture condemns. A similarly glaring dual standard occurs in a foreword stating that the producers have sought to improve the lot of the mountain folk, and that no disparagement is intended. File that one under Yeah, Right. The profuse nudity is, even so, tied to whatever dramatic strength the film possesses—an unusual show of integrity among pictures of this class.

Child Bride's exteriors were photographed at the Iverson Ranch near Chatsworth, site of innumerable movie shoots. The atmosphere rings true for the most part, and the sets, costumes and characters seem authentic enough. The photography by Marcel Le Picard, a busy camera chief at Monogram and PRC, is commendable. The music, by radio composer Felix Mills, evokes the place and the time without lapsing into any cornball blatancy.

CREDITS: Producer: Raymond Friedgen; Director: Harry Revier; Photographed by: Marcel Le Picard [Given Here as Marcel Picard]; Production Manager: Tom Galligan; Editor: Helene Turner; Sound Director: Glen Glenn; Musical Director: Felix Mills; Running Time: 64 Minutes; Released: During January of 1943; Later in Release by: Astor Pictures

CAST: Shirley Mills (Jennie Colton); Diana Durrell (Miss Carol); Warner Richmond (Jake Bolby); Bob Bollinger (Freddie); Dorothy Carrol (Flora [Ma] Colton); George Humphreys (Ira Colton); Frank Martin (Charles)

LONDON BLACKOUT MURDERS
(Republic Pictures Corp.)

Splendid, just splendid. Perhaps the very best of Republic Pictures' double-feature supporters—and fine even by comparison with the bigger-budgeted Republic Specials—is *London Blackout Murders*, an unassuming but innovative and gripping entry from the George Sherman–Curt Siodmak unit.

Scotland Yard had found its workload compounded during the early war years, what with two harrowing cases involving murderers who seemed intent upon making a tradition of the prior century's matter of Jack the Ripper. Wartime conditions tend to bring out the worst in any civilization. Siodmak's script trades strikingly upon these grisly realities but also indulges in editorial commentary—insinuating a willingness on Great Britain's part to allow a negotiated peace with the Hitler mob and suggesting a hysterical vulnerability on the part of the English. Franklin D. Roosevelt's Office of War Information was so appalled by such an attitude that it attempted to suppress *London Blackout Murders* from international distribution, but the President's appointed censor-in-chief of mass media, Byron Price, pronounced the film "ridiculous" but ultimately harmless.

The three-victim rampage of Arthur James Mahoney, alias Bill Layton, had put the Yard's array of newfangled scientific-detection equipment to the test in 1939, and the slaying of four women in 1942 by Royal Air Force Cadet G.F. Cummins had cast official wartime authority in an ugly light that cannot

help but inform Siodmak's script. Republic also had purchased a short story called "London Blackout Murders," written by M.D. Christopher and detailing what the *Los Angeles Times* called "the activities of a killer during the periods of darkness brought about by the war"—a description that suggests the finished film. Christopher receives no screen credit, however.

Innocent Mary Tillett (Mary McLeod) has been orphaned and left homeless in the Nazi bombing raids. Granted a place to stay by Jack Rawlings (John Abbott), a kindly tobacconist, Mary soon begins to sense something dangerous about her host.

Rawlings is actually a fugitive doctor named Vernon, wanted for the slaying of his wife almost 20 years ago. The state of war has moved Rawlings to kill again, using a hypodermic needle hidden in his pipe. Mary has noticed the device, but her fiancé, a soldier from Holland named Peter Dongen (Louis Borell), is unmoved by her suspicions.

Scoland Yard investigators Neil (Lumsden Hare) and Harris (Lloyd Corrigan) keep crossing paths with Rawlings, who kills an associate of a previous victim while traveling by train. A newspaper account of the death of a supposed culprit throws the C.I.D. men off the trail, but Harris obtains fingerprints that identify Rawlings as Dr. Vernon. On trial, Rawlings owns up to his crimes but asserts that the recent victims were Nazi agents. The court seems impressed by the claim—which proves truthful enough—but sentences Rawlings to the gallows, all the same. Rawlings makes a parting gift of his murder pipe to Mary and Peter; the soldier ungratefully destroys the weapon.

London-born John Abbott was a commercial illustrator-turned-actor who resettled in Hollywood in 1941 and quickly became one of the industry's busier and more resilient character men. This rare leading role, as a soft-spoken and philosophical villain with distorted heroic motives, was part of a Republic ploy to use lesser-knowns "to befoozle the public as to who is the hero, the heavy, the ingenue, etc.," as *The Hollywood Reporter* explained things. Although he carries *London Blackout Murders* admirably, Abbott was hardly the type for stardom. Nor was *London Blackout Murders*—like RKO's similarly low-key *Stranger on the Third Floor* (1940)—the type of picture that would make anyone a star. Timid leading lady Mary McLeod and her straight-arrow romantic interest, Louis Borell, likewise kept working thereafter, albeit with modest profiles. Lloyd Corrigan, seen here as a determined inspector, had been a busy backup player since 1926 and would remain so on along into the 1960s. Lesser notable faces include veteran comedian Billy Bevan, the 1931 *Svengali*'s Lumsden Hare and a young Peter Lawford.

London Blackout Murders is more a director's showcase than anything else, and Sherman wrests a generous measure of suspense and mournful longing from every economical moment. His greater accomplishment, however, is to plant in the viewer a forbidden sympathy with Abbott while assuring the audience at every turn that the chap is, indeed, guilty as sin—and proud of it.

CREDITS: Associate Producer and Director: George Sherman; Screenplay: Curt Siodmak; Photographed by: Jack Marta; Art Director: Russell Kimball; Assistant Director: Art Siteman; Editor: Charles Craft; Settings: Otto Siegel; Musical Director: Walter Scharf; Running Time: 59 Minutes; Released: January 15, 1943

CAST: John Abbott (Jack Rawlings); Mary McLeod (Mary Tillett); Lloyd Corrigan (Inspector Harris); Lester Matthews (Oliver Madison); Anita Bolster (Mrs. Pringle); Louis Borell (Peter Dongen); Billy Bevan (Air Raid Warden); Lumsden Hare (Supt. Neil); Frederic Worlock (Eugene Caldwell); Carl Harbord

(George Sandley); Keith Hitchcock (Constable); Tom Stevenson (Doctor); Emory Parnell (Hendrick Peterson); Peter Lawford (Percy); Pax Walker (Girl on Train); Edward Cooper (King's Counsel); Olaf Hytten (Usher); Clifford Brooke (Justice Burford); Carol Curtis-Brown (Betty); Jean Fenwick (Women's Air Force Member); Frank Benson (Driver); Bobby Hale (Worker)

SILENT WITNESS
a.k.a.: ATTORNEY FOR THE DEFENSE
(Monogram Pictures Corp.)

What better name for a family of killers than Manson? These are the brotherly, cowardly marauders played by Milburn Stone and Anthony Ward in *Silent Witness*, a rampaging exercise in sadism and long-deferred justice that unleashes a terrific dog-attack scene for its rousing finale.

Silk importers Joe Manson (Stone) and Lou Manson (Ward) are cleared of a murder rap with the help of conniving lawyer Bruce Strong (Frank Albertson), who in consequence loses his fiancée, Betty Higgins (Maris Wrixon), an investigator with the district attorney's office. Despondent over Betty's new romance with D.A. Bob Holden (Bradley Page), Bruce turns to drink. A Manson flunky, Carlos Jockey (Jimmy Eagles), is slain upon orders from the brothers—but survives long enough to betray his bosses. The Mansons brag to Bruce that they plan to kill Bob; this deed accomplished, Bruce finds himself framed for the slaying. But then, a boy who had rescued the slain prosecutor's pet dog, Major, comes forward with crucial evidence. Later, upon catching sight of one of the Manson hit men, Major lunges forth so violently that the terrified killer spills the beans. The Mansons are hauled in, and a sobered-up Bruce is reunited with Betty.

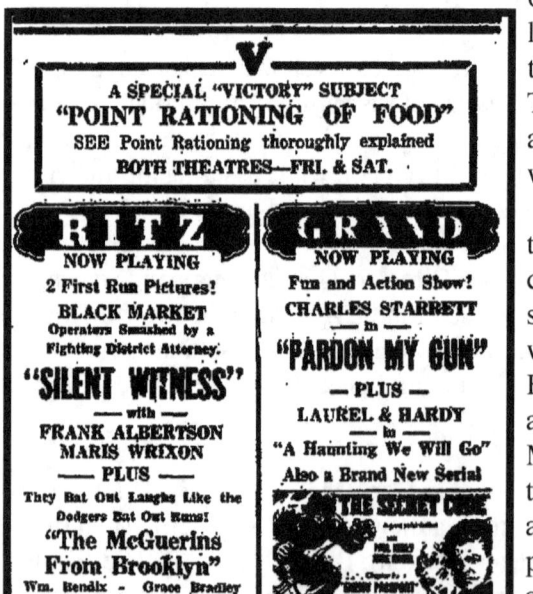

Stone and Ward provide the black heart of the show, contemptuous mock-pillars of society who commission murder with scarcely a second thought. Equally strong, on the side of law and order, is lithe and willowy Maris Wrixon, who had registered so impressively in 1940 as Boris Karloff's experimental patient in *The Ape*. Bradley Page and Frank Albertson make convincing rivals for Miss Wrixon's affections, and Albertson handles nicely his transformation from an arrogant courtroom spellbinder to a down-and-out has-been. Director Jean Yarbrough packs the fleeting running time with suspenseful moments, especially in the sudden puncturing of Page's case against the bad brothers; the deadly attack on Page; and the scene where a friendly Doberman turns vicious upon spotting his master's assassin.

CREDITS: Producer: Max M. King; Director: Jean Yarbrough; Story and Screenplay: Martin Mooney; Photographed by: Mack Stengler; Assistant Director: George Webster; Second Assistant Director: Gerd Oswald; Art Director: David Milton; Editor: Carl Pierson; Musical Score: Edward Kay; Sound: Glen Glenn; Running Time: 62 Minutes; Released: January 15, 1943

CAST: Frank Albertson (Bruce Strong); Maris Wrixon (Betty Higgins); Bradley Page (Bob Holden); Milburn Stone (Joe Manson); Lucien Littlefield (Eastman); Evelyn Brent (Mrs. Roos); Jimmy Eagles (Carlos Jockey); Anthony Ward (Lou Manson); Jack Mulhall (Jed Kelly); John Ince (Mayor); Ace (Major); Joe Eggleston (Rancher); and Paul Bryar, Patsy Nash, John Sheehan, Jean Ames, Kenneth Harlan, Harry Harvey, Charles Jordan, Buzzy Henry, Virginia Carroll, Sam McDaniels, Olaf Hytten, Margaret Armstrong, Herbert Rawlinson, Caroline Burke, Henry Hall

THE PAY OFF
(Producers Releasing Corp.)

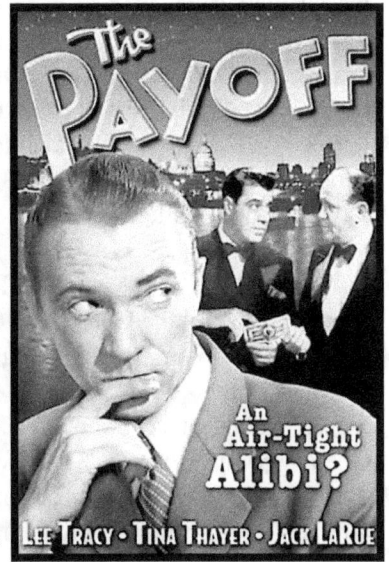

Gruff-voiced Lee Tracy brawls and bellows his way through this slicker-than-average PRC effort as a maverick reporter who butts in on a rackets investigation and uncovers a conspiracy behind the slaying of a special prosecutor. Director Arthur Dreifuss paces the proceedings with a keen sense of terror, bookending Tracy's bravura performance with a genuinely flinch-worthy murder scene at the front end and a desperate capture for the finale. Edward Dein's screenplay is less concerned with the whodunnit element than with Tracy's obsessive vigilante campaign, compensating for the lack of a carefully deployed mystery with sheer force of character.

Tracy is essentially recycling his most famous stage role, that of the fast-talking crackerjack reporter Hildy Johnson in the 1930 Broadway presentation of Ben Hecht and Charles MacArthur's *The Front Page*—a part that Tracy had often echoed and embellished in the movies with scarcely a trace of burnout. *Variety* cited the actor as co-producer of *The Pay Off*, but no such credit graces the screen. Tracy had long since compromised his standing within the industry with a bad-boy public image, alienating MGM as early as 1933, but even in a drawn-out decline he remained a dependable crowd-pleaser. His U.S. government-sponsored radio dramas from the postwar years, ranging from comedy to religious piety to hard-boiled adventure, are particularly delightful.

Tracy receives helpful support in *The Pay Off* from juvenile lead Tom Brown, as a cub reporter whose father runs the paper; leading lady Tina Thayer, as the daughter of a shadowy figure in the investigation; and sympathetic *femme fatale* Evelyn Brent. A romantic subplot involving Miss Thayer and Brown is convincing and unobtrusive.

The German-born Dreifuss had entered show business as a child-prodigy pianist-conductor, then became a choreographer for the stage and settled in Hollywood in 1935 as a dance director. He became a director (and occasional screenwriter) of low-budget films in 1940, specializing in pop musicals and underworld yarns. Dreifuss also helmed PRC's 1943 release *Boss of Big Town*, a crime melodrama with an unusual grocery-racketeer setting, starring John Litel.

CREDITS: Producer: Jack Schwarz; Associate Producer: Harry D. Edwards; Director: Arthur Dreifuss; Original Story: Arthur Hoerl; Scenarist and Dialogue Director: Edward Dein; Photographed by: Ira Morgan; Editor: Charles Henkel, Jr.; Production Manager: Arthur Hammond; Running Time: 74 Minutes; Released: January 21, 1943

CAST: Lee Tracy (Brad McKay); Tom Brown (Guy Norris); Tina Thayer (Phyllis Walker); Evelyn Brent (Alma Dorn); Jack La Rue (John Angus); Ian Keith (Inspector Thomas); Robert Middlemass (Lester Norris); John Maxwell (Vince Moroni); John Sheehan (Sgt. Brennan); Harry Bradley (Dr. Steele); Forrest Taylor (Hugh Walker); Pat Costello (Reporter); and Eddie Borden

CRIME SMASHER
a.k.a.: COSMO JONES IN CRIME SMASHER
(Monogram Pictures Corp.)

In a coda of sorts to the Frankie Darro–Mantan Moreland jive-thrillers (see *Forgotten Horrors 2*), Monogram Pictures paired the ticket-selling comedian Moreland with CBS-Radio personality Frank Graham for this spinoff of Graham's long-running broadcast series, *Cosmo Jones*. The Moreland magic is intact, and Graham accounts nicely for himself as the absentminded would-be detective, Prof. Cosmo Jones, but the picture fizzled as a springboard for anything further on the big screen.

Not to say that it doesn't work. Walter Gering, creator of the *Cosmo* radio adventures, contributes a nifty story: Cosmo is pestering the local police department for a job when he chances to witness a gangland murder—part of a crime wave that has the law baffled. Given the bum's rush despite a display of good citizenship, the nerdy professor accepts a lift from a friendly but trouble-prone cop, Pat Flanagan (Richard Cromwell), and finds himself on the scene of the foiled kidnapping of heiress Phyllis Blake (Gwen Kenyon). Cosmo meets Eustace (Moreland), a janitor who himself harbors the urge to play sleuth, and they plot with Flanagan to lure the crooks out into the open.

Phyllis' treacherous fiancé (Gil Stanley) later accomplishes her abduction. Cosmo and Eustace are taken captive, and a hoodlum named Biff (Charles Jordan) is about to mutilate Eustace with a scalpel when Flanagan and Police Chief Murphy (grumpy Edgar Kennedy) arrive to save the day. Phyllis is rescued by her father (Herbert Rawlinson) and Cosmo, and Eustace gives Flanagan a clear shot at Biff.

The picture is a rowdy delight, with coincidences and situational clichés piled on so thickly as to obscure everything but the spirited portrayals. Charles Jordan plays it sadistic and scary as the meanest of the meanies. Moreland is a fast-talking, quick-reacting marvel, as usual, and his camaraderie with Frank Graham and Richard Cromwell is a particularly forward-thinking touch. Gale Storm offers a hint of her TV-sitcom stardom to come as Richard Cromwell's insistent sweetheart.

CREDITS: Executive Producer: Trem Carr; Producer: Lindsley Parsons; Director: James Tinling; Screenplay: Michael L. Simmons and Walter Gering; Original Story: Walter Gering; Photographed by: Mack Stengler; Technical Director: Dave Milton; Assistant Director/Production Manager: William Strohbach; Editor: Carl Pierson; Musical Director: Edward Kay; Sound: Glen Glenn; Running Time: 62 Minutes; Released: January 29, 1943

CAST: Edgar Kennedy (Police Chief Murphy); Richard Cromwell (Pat Flanagan); Gale Storm (Susan); Mantan Moreland (Eustace Smith); Frank Graham (Cosmo Jones); Gwen Kenyon (Phyllis Blake); Herbert Rawlinson (James J.

Blake); Tristram Coffin (Jake); Charles Jordan (Biff); Gil Stanley (Tommy Hayes); and Vince Barnett, Emmett Vogan, Maxine Leslie, Mauritz Hugo, Sam Bernard

DEAD MEN WALK
(Producers Releasing Corp.)

Le mort troublé, that unquiet death that propels so much of the Gothic literary tradition, has seldom seemed so pernicious as Sam Newfield paints it in *Dead Men Walk*. Universal Pictures is generally credited as the first studio to situate a vampire yarn upon American soil—to wit, the late-1943 release of *Son of Dracula*—but in fact that pride-of-place goes to Producers Releasing Corp., a company with champagne ambitions and a beer-bucket budget. Although the film in question is of an undeniable raggedness, still *Dead Men Walk* has memorable qualities beyond the simple thematic breakthrough. As though anyone had been racing to beat anyone else to the box office with some Stateside takeoff on *Dracula*.

A New England village is so grateful to be rid of Dr. Elwyn Clayton that it allows the known sorcerer and suspected murderer, killed in an (apparently) accidental fall, a polite funeral. Dr. Lloyd Clayton (George Zucco, playing against type), benevolent twin of the deceased, promptly begins destroying Elwyn's library of forbidden magical lore. Elwyn's hunchbacked servant, Zolarr (Dwight Frye), confronts Lloyd and later hides the master's body.

Elwyn Clayton's unholy deeds have earned him a vampiric life-after-death. He pays a taunting visit to his brother, then sets out to prey upon their niece, Gayle (Mary Carlisle). She falls deathly ill and remains so despite a transfusion from Dr. Bentley (Nedrick Young), her fiancé, and Bentley begins to suspect Lloyd in Gayle's decline. Lloyd cannot convince Bentley that a supernatural power is at work until Elwyn (Zucco, on familiar bad-guy turf) materializes to confront them. The villagers, meanwhile, plot a vigilante attack upon Lloyd.

Lloyd locates the body of his brother but is forced into a struggle. A fire engulfs Elwyn's lair, and both Lloyd Clayton and his undead brother are destroyed.

On the most basic level, *Dead Men Walk* is a solid example of Poverty Row craftsmanship, a low-key and inventive reinterpretation of familiar lore. It seems almost a pulp-magazine hair-raiser sprung to life, with all the blesséd randomness of the pulp idiom's prevailing stream-of-consciousness sensibilities. The presence of George Zucco in distinct roles, augmented by a late-in-life portrayal from the formally retired but still-commanding Dwight Frye, takes things to a higher plane. Speaking of planes, that is just where Frye had retrenched of late: An enterprising casting agent found the inimitable character actor working in an aircraft factory.

Dead Men Walk packs nowhere near as much rambunctious fun as PRC's best-remembered picture, the 1940 Bela Lugosi starrer *The Devil Bat*, but it allows a vivid illustration of the audacious storytelling moxie with which the little studio often overcame its chronic limitations of finances and artistry.

PRC, which kept shop in the former studios of the Educational–Fine Arts filmmaking outfit, employed a unit system similar to that established by the somewhat more affluent Monogram Pictures.

George Zucco confronts his evil self in *Dead Men Walk*.

The unit that cranked out most of PRC's meat-and-potatoes Western product, along with exercises in other genres, was headed by the veteran producer-director team of Sigmund Neufeld and Sam Newfield, brothers notwithstanding Sam's Anglicized surname. Sam (*né* Schmuel) also directed on occasion as Samuel Neufeld, in addition to the pseudonyms Peter Stewart and Sherman Scott.

Buster Crabbe, who starred in many Westerns for PRC—and whose horse-opera sidekick, Al "Fuzzy" St. John, appears in *Dead Men Walk*—often recalled with affectionate amusement the pinch-penny tactics of Neufeld and Newfield, and of their production manager, Bert Sternbach.

"I forget which of those epics it was—and really, they were all pretty much alike," Crabbe told us during a marathon interview in 1970, "but in one of our pictures, I was supposed to be leading a posse off into the hills when Mr. Sternbach began complaining that it'd be necessary any second now to go into overtime with the horse-rental agency. The way Mr. Neufeld's company worked, the overtime could just as easily have come out of my pocket. So I improvised a routine that suited Mr. Sternbach just fine. I told Mr. Newfield we were ready to roll, and he cued me, and I yelled out to the posse: 'Dismount! We can get there faster on foot!' The camera panned to follow me and the boys, and the horses were led away off-camera, right ahead of the deadline."

It is rather a leap from horse opera to Gothic horror, but then Newfield was nothing if not versatile, and *Dead Men Walk* bespeaks a deeper immersion in the genre than the director had shown on another starrer for George Zucco,

1942's *The Mad Monster*. Newfield, indeed, handles *Dead Men Walk* with rather more style than he brought to most of his numerous assignments (whatever the genre), using emphatic medium-to-close shots and studying the players' worried faces more so than he dwells upon any overt displays of menace. One bracing moment has the benevolent Zucco reassuring Ned Young that "I don't think we have anything more to worry about"—then glancing up to see his translucent phantom twin grinning at him from a few feet away.

A brief prologue, framing a ghostly view of Forrest Taylor's angular face within a fireplace as he speaks of witchcraft, establishes the foreboding tone. Overall, properties master Fred Preble's barren set dressings, plus the simple effects and stagecraft used to give the illusion of there being two Zuccos, add up to a mixed blessing. This plainness works against camera chief Jack Greenhalgh's strong compositions and lighting but emphasizes the somber mood. Leo Erdody's strident musical score is an asset, if only in its proper context—seeming almost *avant garde* by comparison with the composer's better-known library-stock recordings of familiar classical works for radio stations. (The musical supervisor, David Chudnow, is a recurring presence among these chapters. Chudnow died at age 99 in 2002.)

Newfield avoids shock value altogether and deploys only the most rudimentary double-exposure special effects, generating instead a brooding unease that issues almost entirely from Zucco's air of desperation and impatience as the kindly doctor, a role distinguished further by a handsome toupée. The balding and pallid evil twin is more familiar turf for Zucco, whose show of arrogance and contempt is a cold-blooded delight. But he works harder at the martyred heroic role, leading the viewer to wonder whether this pleasant small-town physician might really have committed murder just to get shed of his wicked brother. One unnerved response, provoked by the bad Zucco's mirage-like appearance, is a small gem of wordless acting. The actor's inexplicable gift for making his eyes seem to glow, no matter what the degree of lighting, is evident throughout.

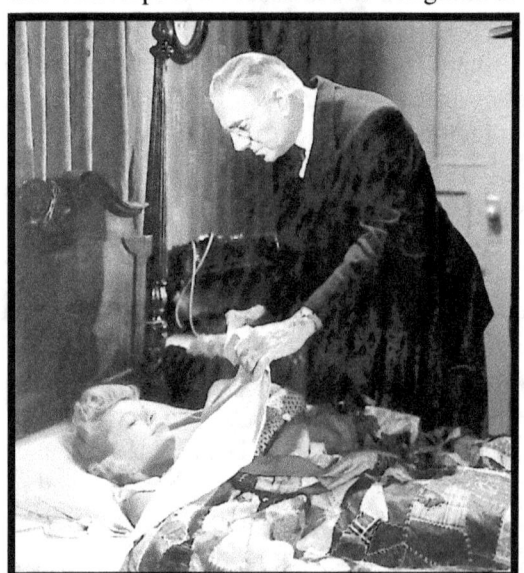

Mary Carlisle is the passive victim in *Dead Men Walk*.

Dwight Frye is almost unrecognizable from his Depression-era heyday at Universal Pictures, where his creeps and sadists had more distinction than the generic hunchback of *Dead Men Walk*. Frye's role here is actually closer to the malicious-idiot type, by turns threatening and absurd, that Mischa Auer had cinched over a decade earlier in *The Monster Walks* and *Murder at Dawn*. Frye enjoys a brief showcase scene, nonetheless, in a snarling encounter with the good Zucco, and he manages to steal some of the bad Zucco's thunder by committing the film's most vile murder.

Mary Carlisle, former leading lady to Bing Crosby at Paramount Pictures, is merely passive here as the victim-in-residence. Nedrick Young—yet to become a busy screenwriter and H.U.A.C. blacklist target—is too surly for anyone's good as Miss Carlisle's short-fused sweetheart. Fern Emmett has some winning tragicomic moments as a local eccentric who, having good reason to despise the vampire-doctor, snoops out his hiding-place. Among the villager ranks, cowboy-movie veteran Hal Price plays a very Western-styled sheriff in this 'Way Down East setting, and Al St. John seems to have wandered in from one of Newfield's own oaters as a townsman who witnesses weird doings. Robert Strange stands out as a snarling rabble-rouser, and old-time comedians Jimmy Aubrey and Frank Rice register in brief appearances as yokels.

Newfield stayed plenty busy in the frontier sector during the same period: His PRC assignments of 1943 also include *Western Cyclone* and *Cattle Stampede*, both of a *Billy the Kid* series starring Buster Crabbe and Al St. John; *Wild Horse Rustlers*, a Nazis-out-West adventure with Bob Livingston and St. John; and *Harvest Melody*, with Rosemary Lane and Johnny Downs.

CREDITS: Producer: Sigmund Neufeld; Director: Sam Newfield; Screenplay: Fred Myton; Photographed by: Jack Greenhalgh; Sound: Hans Weeren; Musical Score: Leo Erdody; Music Supervisor: David Chudnow; Editor: Holbrook N. Todd; Makeup: Harry Ross; Set Designer: Fred Preble; Assistant Director: Melville DeLay; Production Manager: Bert Sternbach; Running Time: 66 Minutes; Released: February 10, 1943

CAST: George Zucco (Dr. Lloyd Clayton and Dr. Selwyn Clayton); Mary Carlisle (Gayle); Nedrick Young (Dr. Bentley); Dwight Frye (Zolarr); Fern Emmett (Kate); Robert Strange (Harper); Forrest Taylor (On-Screen Narrator in Prologue); Hal Price (Sheriff); Sam Flint (Minister); Al St. John, Frank Rice and Jimmy Aubrey (Rubes)

A NIGHT FOR CRIME
(Lester Cutler Productions, Inc./Producers Releasing Corp.)

Just a little *psychopathia sexualis* for the Jung-at-heart: *A Night for Crime* is that rare, psychologically pretentious and artistically ambitious PRC release that justifies a noticeably lengthier running time with a wealth of noir essentials.

Here we have a deadly impersonation, strangulations at every hand, extensive forensics and emotionally manipulative tricks of investigation—and overall, a murder-in-Movieland case as lurid and haunting as anything the *Hollywood Babylon* scum merchants ever dredged out of real life. It comes as little surprise that the original scenarist, Jimmy Starr, was a celebrity-gossip columnist in his own right; Starr and three of his star-gawking colleagues have cameos here.

Tough-talking Glenda Farrell (of 1932's *The Mystery of the Wax Museum*) and adventurous leading man Lyle Talbot (of 1934's *Return of the Terror*) had lapsed decisively from the majors to Poverty Row by now, but they bring to this picture a major-league presence. Which is as it should be, in a little picture pretending to take place among the high rollers of Hollywood.

Movie publicist Joe Powell (Talbot) and his combative girlfriend, newspaperwoman Susan Cooper (Miss Farrell), stumble across the strangulation murder of a neighbor named Ellen Smith (Marjorie Manners) while nosing into the disappearance of movie star Mona Harrison (Lina Basquette). Film producer Hart (Donald Kirke) complains that Mona's latest, unfinished, movie is at stake—a massive investment for the studio. Susan, while snooping about Mona's bedroom, is attacked by a strangler. The assailant flees upon the arrival of the law, and Susan is arrested as a prowler. Once bailed out, Susan meets with Joe at Hart's office, where they are informed that Mona has been found—choked to death. The police aver that Ellen's killer is a man, and Mona's assailant a woman.

Their interest stoked by the delivery of unlabeled movie footage to Hart, Joe and Susan find the film to contain the purportedly unfinished final scenes of Mona's current picture. Joe, remembering that Mona had a twin, comes under attack from a strangler while trying to trace the sister. Reviving, Joe confronts Hart with his knowledge of the film; Hart admits he has found Mona alive. Susan, following a clue to Reno, Nevada, is attacked en route by Mona's chauffeur, Arthur (Ricki Vallin). Arthur is fatally injured when he loses control of his auto. Later, Susan explains that Arthur had confessed to murdering Ellen and Mona's twin, Marie.

Susan contends, however, that it was Mona who was slain and that the woman claiming to be Mona is actually the actress' insane sister, Marie. Susan has used a phony confession to bait Marie into giving herself away. In a fury when faced with this accusation, Marie dies in a fall from a high window. It develops that Marie had agreed to finish the movie for Hart, in exchange for his theft of incriminating papers. Arthur was Marie's husband, and they were blackmailing Mona. Marie had killed Mona, and Arthur had strangled Ellen, a witness.

The convolutions play out better than they read, of course, but even so *A Night for Crime* requires more patience than one is accustomed to giving the more typically straightforward PRC efforts. Director Alexis Thurn-Taxis is not always up to the task of making sense of things, but the players' immersion in character and a tangle of dark secrets make the watching worthwhile. Silent-era star Lina Basquette fares nicely with the roles of the arrogant Mona (in a well-placed flashback) and her deranged sister. Absent from the screen since the late '30s when she tackled this project, Miss Basquette retired permanently following *Night*'s completion. Ralph Sanford is a treat as a lamebrained cop who puts the pinch on Miss Farrell. Real World columnists Starr, Erskine Johnson, Edwin Schallert and Harry Crocker, appearing as themselves, lend the outlandish yarn a helpful credibility.

CREDITS: Producer: Lester Cutler; Associate Producer: C.A. Beute; Director: Alexis Thurn-Taxis; Dialogue Director: Baldwin Watkins; Story: Jimmy Starr; Screenplay: Arthur St. Claire and Sherman Lowe; Additional Dialogue: John Vlahos; Photographed by: Marcel Le Picard; Editor: Fred Bain; Musical Director: Lee Zahler; Sound: Ben Winkler; Running Time: 78 Minutes; Released: February 18, 1943

CAST: Glenda Farrell (Susan Cooper); Lyle Talbot (Joe Powell); Ralph Sanford (Hoffman); Lina Basquette (Mona Harrison and Marie Harrison); Lynn Starr (Carol); Donald Kirke (Hart); Forrest Taylor (Williams); Ricki Vallin (Arthur); Marjorie Manners (Ellen Smith); Edna Harris (Switchboard Operator); Jimmy Starr, Erskine Johnson, Edwin Schallert and Harry Crocker (Themselves); Ruby

Dandridge (Alice); and Joseph M. DeVillard, Niels Baggel, Florence O'Brien, Robert Frazer

HAUNTED RANCH
(Range Busters, Inc./George W. Weeks Productions/ Monogram Pictures Corp.)

Monogram's *Range Busters* series treads onto old-dark-house territory in this slight tale of a fortune in gold, hidden within the forbidding recesses of a ranchhouse whose late owner, a notorious outlaw known as Reno Red, is said to haunt the place. The haunting, of course, is purely human—or subhuman, given the base nature of the owlhoots (a gang led by the intimidating Glenn Strange) who have secretly moved in, hellbent-for-bullion. Seems that Strange and his cronies are fond of lurking in the cellar and scaring off visitors with eerie noises.

The slaying of an heir brings the Range Busters (played here by Dave Sharpe, Dusty King and Max "Alibi" Terhune) into the action. Dusty, impersonating the slain nephew, is delighted to learn that the other inheritor is Helen Weston (Julie Duncan), a beauty from back East. The mystery, apart from the ersatz spooks, involves a will requiring that the kinfolks play Reno Red's favorite song on the ranch's steel-cased pipe organ. Upon the late realization that the tune is "Little Brown Jug," the organ creaks open to reveal the treasure. Helen gets what's coming to her, the outlaws get nabbed, and the U.S. Mint gets its gold back. The Range Busters get to go bust some other ranges. No one in the audience gets particularly scared, but this 20th *Range Busters* series entry is still what *Psychotronic Video* might call "a fun time-waster."

CREDITS: In Charge of Production: William L. Nolte; Producer: George W. Weeks; Director: Robert Tansey; Story: Arthur Hoerl; Screenplay: Harriet Beecher; Photographed by: Robert Cline; Editor: Roy Claire; Music: Frank Sanucci; Songs: "Where the Prairie Meets the Sky," by John "Dusty" King, and "Little Brown Jug," by Joseph E. Winner; Sound: Lyle Willey; Assistant Production Manager: Jim Hawthorne; Running Time: 57 Minutes; Released: February 19, 1943

CAST: John "Dusty" King (Dusty); David Sharpe (Dave); Max "Alibi" Terhune (Alibi and His Dummy, Elmer Sneezeweed); Julie Duncan (Helen Weston); Glenn [Billed Here as Glen] Strange (Rance); Charles King (Chuck); Bud Osborne (Ed); Red Lease (Red); Fred "Snowflake" Toomes (Sam)

THE LUM & ABNER SERIES: TO MARS AND BACK AGAIN
(Jack Wm. Votion Productions, Inc./VoCo, Inc./
RKO-Radio Pictures, Inc.)

The radio program *Lum & Abner* was to rural white-folks America more-or-less what *Amos 'n' Andy* was to citified black America. Each series dealt in affectionate stereotype with a gently satirical subtext—and to generations of viewers, each defined the popular view of its demographic province.

In terms of big-screen potential, *Lum & Abner* managed the more robust spinoff: Where *Amos 'n' Andy* spawned a limited run of animated cartoons and a single feature film during the early years of the Great Depression—and would have to wait until the postwar spread of television for a successful long-term picturization—*Lum & Abner* made a graceful sustained segué to Hollywood, achieving major-studio distribution in the process.

It helped that the industry had developed a taste for caricatured rustic humor during the war years: The stix might have nixed the hix flix (to paraphrase *Variety*'s famous headline) in the day of the conspicuous failure of Phillips H. Lord's *'Way Back Home* (1931), but by now a low-budget homespun comedy could count on a warm reception at the backwoods box office.

Two of the 1940s' *Lum & Abner*s tap decisively enough into the bizarre to want consideration in the present context—not that we feel much need to justify the act of dragging *any* long-neglected movie back into the light. *So This is Washington* hangs upon a crackpot-invention premise, garnishing that indulgence with a spot of delusional derangement. *Two Weeks to Live* touches here on Robert Louis Stevenson's *Dr. Jekyll and Mr. Hyde* and makes a key plot device, elsewhere, of manned rocketry, with detours into ghostly business, a murder-for-profit scam and a Nazi-infiltration conspiracy. All in the name of good-humored hokum, of course. (A final piece, the provincially distributed *Lum & Abner Abroad*, from 1956, will want the fuller treatment a volume or two down the line.)

The War Era entries are below. They issued from an independent studio, Jack Wm. Votion Productions (also known as VoCo), which made no pictures otherwise, and were picked up for first-run distribution by big-time RKO-Radio Pictures. A *Lum & Abner* teleseries took tentative shape during the early 1950s but served chiefly to supply footage for *L&A Abroad*.

•*Dreaming Out Loud* (1940), which combines the essential geezer business with youthful romance and a heart-wrenching tear-jerker element, all at the service of a tale urging improved medical service for the boondocks. The film is marginally a musical, taking its title from an awkward tuneful interlude.

• *The Bashful Bachelor* (1942), which pivots on a late-in-life romantic attraction between grandfatherly Chester Lauck (as Lum Edwards) and spinsterly ZaSu Pitts. Lauck and Norris Goff (as feisty Abner Peabody) had begun impersonating the bickering old-timer chums while still young troupers; they aged more nearly into the roles over the long stretch, but retired the act before they could reach the age range they were portraying.

• *Goin' to Town* (1944), which confronts Lum and Abner's peaceable village of Pine Ridge, Arkansas, with an oil-fraud scam.

• And *Partners in Time* (1946), a fanciful flashback to the origins of the Lum & Abner combo.

And now, the featured attractions:

2 Weeks To Live—The title derives from the bewhiskered old groaner about a doctor's mistaken diagnosis. The party thus pronounced doomed is Abner Peabody (Norris Goff), who has just inherited a railroad line that proves to be a derailed ruin only after friends and neighbors have invested in it. Broke and disgusted by legal fees and estate taxes, Lum Edwards (Chester Lauck) and Abner decide to hire out Abner's services to perform death-defying feats—seeing as how his days seem numbered, anyway—for big bucks.

Their would-be clients include a mad scientist who wants to test a transformation formula on a human guinea pig; a carnival huckster looking to hire a dancing partner for a killer gorilla; one Mrs. Carmen (Kay Linaker), a socialite who *says* she wants to debunk rumors of a house-haunting; and a stunt pilot in search of a stooge willing to walk from the wing of one airplane to another in flight.

Mrs. Carmen's offer proves the most appealing under the circumstances, but in fact the woman intends to discombobulate Abner with a bomb and identify his remains as those of her husband—the better to pull a James M. Cain on an insurance company. She instructs Abner to deliver a violin case to the site. He goes to the wrong address, barging in on a Nazi stronghold and then fleeing in such haste that he forgets to remember the case. Which contains the bomb. Which blows up, obliterating the gang of Fifth Columnists.

Lum (Chester Lauck) and Abner (Norris Goff) in *2 Weeks to Live*

It gets weirder: As the date of his expected demise draws nearer, Abner accepts a cash-money offer to board an experimental spacecraft. Destination: Mars. He reneges at the last moment, returning to his hotel room to await the Reaper. The desk clerk (Jack Rice), noticing that Lum has picked up a case of the sneezing wheezes, summons a doctor. The physician (Edward Earle) examines both men and pronounces Abner hale and hearty. Lum, on the other hand, proves dangerously ill. Lum, expecting the worst, agrees to take Abner's place aboard the rocketship.

Meanwhile, word comes through that the railroad property has turned into a bonanza, counter to all expectations. Just as it looks as though the pals won't need to honor the Mars-shot commitment, after all, Abner accidentally fires the rocket-launching device. Lum, who is bound to recover for another sequel or three, takes off into the void. The craft reaches Mars—Mars, Iowa, that is, thanks to a misfire.

Unspooling with a (fittingly) bucolic plainness of style despite the script's outlandish extravagances, *Two Weeks to Live* bespeaks a mixture of playful innocence and world-weary frankness foreshadowing the much later misadventures of Jim Varney's signature character, Ernest P. Worrell. Lauck and Goff meet the absurdities, as well as the spectre of imminent tragedy, with an indignant directness that keeps things plausible, in context. Each star player has a look in his eyes, a certain set of the jaw, suggesting that if Lum Edwards and Abner Peabody haven't seen it—then it probably hasn't happened. Even so, they're still willing to allow the slickest weasel around the benefit of the doubt.

CREDITS: Producer: Ben Hersh; Director: Malcolm St. Clair; Assistant Director: Charles Kerr; Screenplay: Michael L. Simmons and Rosell Rogers; Photographed by: Jack McKenzie; Art Director: F. Paul Sylos; Editor: Duncan Mansfield; Set Dresser: Ben Berk; Music: Lud Gluskin; Sound: Ferol Redd; Running Time: 73 Minutes; Released: February 26, 1943

CAST: Chester Lauck [Billed Only as Lum] (Lum Edwards); Norris Goff [Billed Only as Abner] (Abner Peabody); Franklin Pangborn (Pinkney); Kay Linaker (Mrs. Carmen); Irving Bacon (Gimpel); Herbert Rawlinson (J.J. Stark, Sr.); Ivan Simpson (Prof. Albert Frisby); Rosemary La Planche (Nurse); Danny Duncan (Mailman); Evalyn Knapp (Secretary); Charles Middleton (Elmer Kelton); Luis Alberni (Van Dyke); Jack Rice (Hotel Clerk); Tim Ryan (Higgens); Oscar O'Shea (Squire Skimp); Edward Earle (Doctor)

So This Is Washington—Inspired by a war-effort appeal to America's common folk to develop practical inventions, Abner jury-rigs a laboratory at his and Lum's general store. The result is a formula for something resembling rubber. The fellows set out to deliver the breakthrough to Washington. By happenstance,

they wind up dispensing folksy wisdom to members of Congress—how to fight a drought, how to keep small-town populations from defecting to the cities and so forth.

Preparations for a demonstration of Abner's formula go awry when he suffers a head injury and develops an obnoxious form of amnesia. The government demands results. A second conk on the noggin clears the inventor's addled mind. The new compound proves to be not rubber, but a valuable new type of sealing compound. Through no asphalt of their own, Lum and Abner are appointed ranking bureaucrats in charge of farm issues.

Norris Goff's Abner finds a generous showcase for his high-pitched voice and his rump-sprung rambunctiousness in the amnesia sequences, which find the spry old boy transformed into a jive-talking hipster in those days of zoot-suited proto-beatniks. Chester Lauck keeps the act anchored in Lum's dry wit, borderline impatience and stabilizing common decency. It probably would be a case of overintellectualizing matters to cite any subversive wit in *So This is Washington*, but then why else would the federal government have pronounced the film a threat to national security? Not that any secrets of synthetic-rubber production are given away here. Rather, the War Department's Office of Censorship socked RKO with a Do Not Export order—complaining that the picture poked fun at rationing, depicted members of Congress as buffoons and razzed a prominent Army physician. All of which sound to us like a few of the very things a wartime comedy is supposed to do.

CREDITS: Producer: Ben Hersh; Director: Raymond McCarey; Assistant Director: Ruby Rosenberg; Dialogue Director: Hal Yates; Screenplay: Leonard Praskins and Roswell Rogers; Story: Roswell Rogers and Edward James; Photographed by: Harry Wild; Art Director: Hans Peters; Editor: Duncan Mansfield; Set Dresser: Ben Berk; Music: Lud Gluskin; Sound: Percy Townsend; Running Time: 64 Minutes; Copyrighted: September 8, 1943, by Jack Wm. Votion Productions, Inc.; Released: On a Region-by-Region Basis during 1943 *et seq.*

CAST: Chester Lauck (Lum Edwards); Norris Goff (Abner Peabody); Alan Mowbray (Chester Marshall); Mildred Coles (Jane Nestor); Roger Clark (Robert Blevine); Sarah Padden (Aunt Charity); Matt McHugh (Stranger); Dan Duncan (Shopkeeper); Barbara Pepper (Cabbie); and Minerva Urecal

FIGHTING SEA MONSTERS
(Times Pictures/Astor Pictures Corp.)

The title alone justifies the inclusion of this one, but some clarification is perhaps in order: No one is fighting sea monsters here; rather, it is the sea monsters that are fighting among themselves. Making no pretense at plot—apart from a fishing-and-diving excursion—and allowing a forcibly droll narration to over-emphasize the action, this undersea documentary captures a pageant of life-and-death struggles among such denizens of the West Indies as the marlin, the manta ray and various types of shark. The photography is occasionally murky, but the brisk editing and adventurous subject matter compensate. *Box Office* magazine's review miscalled the film *Fighting the Monsters*—a thimple typo, perhapth, if not the rethult of hearing the title mith-pronounthed by thome-one with a thlight lithp.

CREDITS: Producer: Capt. John D. Craig; Associate Producer: Herbert T. Edwards; Continuity: Ira Knaster; Musical Score: Edward Craig; Running Time: 59 Minutes; Released: March 9, 1943

CAST: Ted Webbe (Narrator)

THE APE MAN
(Monogram Pictures Corp.)

In a rare attempt at critical insight beyond its basic function of guessing a picture's box office prospects, *Variety* commented in 1943 on *The Ape Man*: "[Bela] Lugosi seems somewhat bewildered and bemused by his role and acts accordingly." The influential tradepaper cannot have been ignorant of the circumstances that had landed Lugosi in the minor leagues, but *Variety*'s on-the-spot critique neglects to recognize Lugosi's struggle to invest his Monogram roles with an intensity that never occurred to his writers or directors. Lugosi bestowed a greater care upon *The Ape Man* than the assignment warranted, and the clash between his artistry and the prevailing shabbiness generates a tension greater than could be expected of any of Poverty Row's man-into-beast fantasies. If

Lugosi may have found himself at the mercy of exploitation and unimaginative casting in *The Ape Man*, but he never let the system grind him down to an indifferent performance.

Boris Karloff had been merely marking time in Monogram's *The Ape* (1940), then Lugosi was hanging on for dear life at the little studio—responding with dignity to the indignities it threw his way. One suspects Monogram didn't know any better, although producer Sam Katzman often voiced regret that "we didn't have the budgets—or the moxie—to give ol' Bela as good as he deserved—I mean, beyond star billing and the freedom to carry his pictures. He seemed grateful enough just to keep working steady."

Lugosi plays Dr. James Brewster, a Jekyll-gone-Hyde who has gorillafied himself. Brewster requires human spinal fluid to regain his natural state for brief intervals, and as a consequence he must resort to murder. Journalists Jeff Carter (Wallace Ford) and Billie Mason (Louise Currie) follow the case so relentlessly that they wind up at the mercy of Brewster and his primate accomplice (Emil Van Horn), but they are saved by the arrival of the police. A gaunt but goofy-looking stranger (played by Ralph Littlefield in baggy-pants burley-cue comic fashion), who has cropped up throughout the adventure to make wisecracks and prod the action along, finally reveals himself to be—within the story's context—the author responsible for this entire load of banana oil.

The *actual* author of the source-story, "They Creep in the Dark," is Karl Brown, who had been a pioneering cinematographer before proving himself a capable enough hand at mad-doctor yarns (including some of the famous Karloff-at-Columbia pictures). The screenwriter is associate producer Barney A. Sarecky, who muddled things considerably. The Littlefield character is a narrative gimmick better left unwritten, an intrusive element that foreshadows the fatuous host-turned-heckler babblings of Cassandra "Elvira" Peterson and the insufferable cheap-shot yammering of the *Mystery Science Theatre 3000* vandals. Sarecky's boneheaded screenplay can only have been composed without any sense of irony beyond its facile self-mockery—more unintentional *sub*-realism than conscious surrealism.

Lugosi seems to have let his work speak for itself throughout this long and all-but-irreversible decline, sending out encrypted signals of his unhappiness via his portrayals rather than making any overt attempt to call popular attention to his plight. As a still-bankable star stranded largely in the low-budget sector, he specialized in embittered, almost pitiable villains—a marked contrast to the flamboyant and authoritative renegades of his Depression-era glory days. A Lugosi hallmark of these declining years is the resentful, regretful soliloquy in which his characters fume over wrongs done them and muse hopefully on vengeance if not vindication. In the PRC production of *The Devil Bat*, Lugosi seems philosophical enough about his typecast entrapment to make a defiantly morbid joke of the proceedings. In *The Ape Man* for Monogram—a slightly more upscale but less adventurous studio than PRC—Lugosi appears less pleased to be on board and crystallizes his predicament with a weary succinctness: "What a mess I made of things!" (Lugosi could not blame himself entirely for his reduced station; studio politics and passive agentry also had figured in the situation.)

But Lugosi propels the simplistic dialogue beyond its laughable context, creating not so much a character as a self-portrait of transcendent nobility under siege. Just as Sam Katzman recalled it, Lugosi was grateful enough to be working steadily, even in reduced circumstances, that he showed the gumption to shade his portrayals with the disappointments he had known as a lapsed major-leaguer. The tone and bearing of this "bewildered and bemused" performance bespeak a personal tragedy vastly more harrowing than the scientist's outlandish predicament.

Lugosi was long since resigned to such conditions, of course—indeed, *The Ape Man* is his sixth of nine prominent turns at Monogram—and today it is fascinating to watch this masterful artist flout the slovenly writing and careless handling that would have overwhelmed a lesser talent. Lugosi may have found himself at the mercy of exploitation and unimaginative casting, but he never let the system grind him down to an indifferent performance.

He is in mixed company in *The Ape Man*, with a likewise transcendent performance from Wallace Ford as a lippy and aggressive newspaperman—not unlike the part Ford had played opposite Lugosi in 1934's *Mysterious Mr. Wong*—and a more genuinely bemused job of acting from Minerva Urecal, who plays the outlaw scientist's worried sister in an inappropriately over-reactive silent-screen style. Louise Curry is a bantering delight as Ford's newsroom colleague. Henry Hall lends a helpful antagonism as Lugosi's treacherous colleague. Emil Van Horn's impersonation of a gorilla is as unwittingly absurd as the same player's hair-suit routine is deliberately preposterous in W.C. Fields' epic of borderline surrealism, *Never Give a Sucker an Even Break* (1941).

Director William Beaudine (1892-1970) was practically a founding father of the movie industry, but apart from some masterful silent pictures (most notably, 1923's *Penrod and Sam* and 1926's *Sparrows*) and the occasional inspired talker he seldom excelled at the craft. *The Ape Man* is a low-water mark even for Beaudine, who seems to have been more concerned with grinding out a salable product than with committing artistry. The film suffers from Beaudine's characteristic inattention to nuances or even plain consistency, but Lugosi provides the usual fascinating subtext.

CREDITS: Producers: Sam Katzman and Jack Dietz for Banner Productions; Associate Producer and Screenwriter: Barney A. Sarecky; Director: William Beaudine; Based upon: Karl Brown's Story, "They Creep in the Dark"; Assistant Director: Arthur Hammond; Photographed by: Mack Stengler; Art Director: David Milton; Editor: Carl Pierson; Sound: Glen Glenn; Musical Director: Edward Kay; Running Time: 64 Minutes; Released: March 19, 1943

CAST: Bela Lugosi (Dr. James Brewster); Wallace Ford (Jeff Carter); Louise Curry [a.k.a. Louise Currie] (Billie Mason); Minerva Urecal (Agatha Brewster); Henry Hall (Dr. Randall); Ralph Littlefield (Zippo); J. Farrell MacDonald (Captain); George Kirby (Randall's Butler); Wheeler Oakman (Brady); Emil Van Horn (Gorilla); Jack Newhall (Reporter); Charles Jordan (O'Toole)

THE GHOST RIDER
(Monogram Pictures Corp.)

That hard-riding Southern gentleman Johnny Mack Brown continues his string of quirky Westerns as a masked vigilante in *The Ghost Rider*. This installment of the loose-knit *Nevada McKenzie* series follows the time-honored—or shopworn, if you prefer—tradition of the hero's search for the gang that had done away with his parents. The yarn hinges just as creakily on a serial-killing mob boss named Lash Edwards (Harry Woods), whose latest victim, Patrick McNally (Jack Daley), lives long enough to inform a wanderer known as Nevada (Brown) about murderous activities around a town known as Dead Creek.

Nevada, who moonlights as the vengeful Ghost Rider, accepts the deed to McNally's slaughterhouse, thwarting a key ploy in Edwards' scam to take over the region's commercial properties. Edwards intends to augment his cattle-rustling racket by sending stolen livestock through the slaughterhouse, eliminating the evidence by rendering it ready-to-roast. Nevada imprisons McNally's son, Joe (Tom Seidel), and an undercover lawman named Sandy Hopkins (Raymond Hatton) lest they interfere with his beyond-the-law campaign. Naturally and also conveniently, the Edwards mob proves to have been responsible for the slaying of Nevada's folks.

Between murder and killings in the name of justice, the body count stacks up alarmingly. Raymond Hatton is too much the hero in his own right to stay hogtied for long, and of course he fancies Brown a crook until the proper debts have been settled. Having finally nabbed Nevada in connection with one hoodlum's death, Sandy then releases the vigilante and invites him to sign up as a federal marshal. Nevada declines, explaining that he prefers to ride the fringes. And more power to him.

CREDITS: Producer: Scott R. Dunlap; Director: Wallace W. Fox; Technical Director: Ernest Hickson; Screenplay: Jess Bowers; Photographed by: Harry Neumann; Assistant Director: William Strobach; Editor: Carl Pierson; Music: Edward Kay; Sound: Glen Glenn; Production Manager: C.J. Bigelow; Running Time: 54 Minutes; Released: April 2, 1943

CAST: Johnny Mack Brown (Jack "Nevada" McKenzie/Ghost Rider); Raymond Hatton (Sandy Hopkins); Harry Woods (Lash Edwards); Beverly Boyd (Julie Wilson); Tom Seidel (Joe McNally); Edmund Cobb (Zack Saddler); Bud Osborne (Lucky Howard); George De Normand (Red); Artie Ortego (Roy Kern); Charles King (Steve Cook); Milburn Moranti (John Wilson)

KING OF THE COWBOYS
(Republic Pictures Corp.)

Roy Rogers, who enjoyed a good cornball joke, told us during the early 1970s about his plan to endorse a new brand of dog food made from bone-meal. "This way," he grinned, "I could call myself the King of the Cow Bones." A nice characterizing touch, it was—a fleeting gag, punctuating a larger conversation about Rogers' perceived regality among Western stars—demonstrating that Republic's once-and-forever King of the Cowboys took himself none too seriously.

The movie that bestowed that rank upon Rogers actually treats him more like a whipping boy for the bad guys. Joseph Kane's *King of the Cowboys* is, for all its tuneful interludes and peppy comic relief, a hard-bitten and rawboned exercise in desperation.

The telling is dominated by Gerald Mohr's portrayal of a killer who specializes in sabotaging American factories on behalf of the Axis powers. Mohr impris-

ons Roy in a doomed warehouse, frames Roy for an act of murder, and generally taunts Roy with impunity—and Rogers doesn't even get the pleasure of capturing the madman. That honor falls to the world-class comical sidekick Lester "Smiley" Burnette. Rogers does, however, get to dispose of the brains behind Mohr's rampage, a crooked government official played by the pudgy-but-vigorous Lloyd Corrigan, and to save a train from a dynamiting. In an upbeat coda to all the mayhem, Rogers is presented with a Big Deal Official Scroll from the Governor of Texas (Russell Hicks) proclaiming him King of the Cowboys. (We cannot help but be reminded here of W.C. Fields' reaction to his "reward" for "heroism," both terms used advisedly, in *The Bank Dick* [1940].)

King of the Cowboys is a classic of its kind: that rare cowboy-crooner entry, with a gaudy rodeo setting and plenty of power-harmony tunesmithery, that never loses sight of the genre's darker origins in the Germanic moviemaking style.

CREDITS: Associate Producer: Harry Grey; Director: Joseph Kane; Screenplay: Olive Cooper and J. Benton Cheney; Story: Hal Long; Photographed by: Reggie Lanning; Art Director: Russell Kimball; Assistant Director: Art Siteman; Editor: Harry Keller; Décor: Charles Thompson; Music: Morton Scott; Songs: "Ride, Ranger, Ride," by Tim Spencer, "Ride 'Em, Cowboy," by Roy Rogers & Tim Spencer, "Roll Along, Prairie Moon," by Ted Fio Rito, Harry MacPherson & Albert von Tilzer, "I'm an Old Cowhand," by Johnny Mercer, "A Gay Ranchero (*Las Alteñitas*)," by Juan José Espinoza, Abe Tuvim & Francia Luban, "Biscuit Blues," by Bob Nolan, and the traditional "Red River Valley"; Locations Manager: Johnny Bourkel; Running Time: 67 Minutes; Released: April 9, 1943

CAST: Roy Rogers (Roy Rogers); Smiley Burnette (Frog Millhouse); Bob Nolan & the Sons of the Pioneers—Hugh Farr, Karl Farr, Tim Spencer, Pat Brady and Lloyd Perryman (Themselves); Peggy Moran (Judy Mason); Gerald Mohr (Maurice); Dorothea Kent (Ruby Smith); Lloyd Corrigan (William Kraly); James

Bush (Dave Mason); Russell Hicks (Governor); Irving Bacon (Alf Cluckus); Norman Willis (Buxton); Trigger (Roy's Horse); Stuart Hamblen (Duke Wilson); Bud Geary, Yakima Canutt, Lynton Brent, Rex Lease (Bad Guys); Eddie Dean (Tex); Forrest Taylor (Cowhand); Harry Burns (Joe); Earle Hodgins (Barker); Dick Rich (Man at Rodeo); Herbert Heyes and William Gould (Sheriffs); Jack Kirk (Bartender); Raphael Bennett (Garageman); John Dilson (Bryson).

THE MANTRAP
(Republic Pictures Corp.)

The old-fashioned concept of the scientific detective, so popular in the early pulps and silent pictures, receives a half-hearted revival in this tedious effort from producer-director George Sherman. As played by the distinguished Henry Stephenson, Sir Humphrey Quilp is a Scotland Yard veteran, long since retired to his writings on criminology but ever progressive in his attitudes—he drives an electric-powered automobile—and eager to show up the younger hotshots. Stephenson's portrayal is winning enough, but Curt Siodmak's screenplay becomes too embroiled in procedural details for the under-an-hour running time.

The joke is, naturally, on the cops, who fool themselves into thinking they have all but solved a murder case before they pretend to consult Sir Humphrey as a condescending courtesy to mark his 70th birthday. The graybeard turns the tables on the authorities, dismissing their ultra-modern methods and announcing a dead-on-the-money conclusion all his own. Suspense is beside the point amid all the mock-forensic gibberish and ill-paced exposition. Sir Humphrey's ingenious means of trapping the suddenly exposed killer, utilizing a barricade of beehives, is a redeeming touch.

The film also retains a helpful sense of humor. Stephenson seems glad enough to be playing the part (though it is hardly in a league with his portrayals of historical figures) that he gets by on his usual air of fine breeding and impeccable manners. Portly Lloyd Corrigan, who tackled *The Mantrap* immediately following *King of the Cowboys*, lends a welcome lighter touch as a Watson to Stephenson's shades-of-Sherlock portrayal. Dorothy Lovett and Joseph Allen, Jr., account for a charming element of romance. Frederic Worlock does well by a dual role as brothers—one the killer, one the victim.

George Sherman had long been known as a director of Westerns when he turned his attention to other genres in the 1940s. He fared better over the long haul of 1943 with *London Blackout Murders* and *Mystery Broadcast*, and then in 1944 delivered *The Lady and the Monster*—still the most impassioned adaptation of Siodmak's renegade-surgeon novel, *Donovan's Brain*. Prolific but seldom a hack, Sherman handled more than 100 big-screen features and some 250 television-series installments from 1937 until his retirement in 1978.

The somewhat belated *Variety* review gave the title as *Man Trap*.

CREDITS: Producer and Director: George Sherman; Screenplay: Curt Siodmak; Editor: Arthur Roberts; Photographed by: William Bradford; Art Director: Russell Kimball; Set Dresser: Otto Siegel; Musical Director: Morton Scott; Running Time: 58 Minutes; Released: April 13, 1943

CAST: Henry Stephenson (Sir Humphrey Quilp); Lloyd Corrigan (Anatol Duprez); Joseph Allen, Jr. (Eddie Regan); Dorothy Lovett (Jean Mason [listed as Jane in Credits]); Edmund MacDonald (Assistant District Attorney Knox); Alice Fleming (Freida Mason); Tom Stevenson (Robert Berwick); Frederic Worlock (Patrick Berwick and Thomas Berwick); Jane Weeks (Frances Woolcott); Joe Cunningham (Joseph); Ralph Peters (Filling Station Attendant)

THE GHOST AND THE GUEST
(Producers Releasing Corp.)

The title is nifty but irrelevant: No ghosts, and no guests to speak of—only unwelcome intruders—figure in this delightfully Thurber-like tale of honeymooners who run afoul of racketeers in a supposedly haunted house. The story comes from the cartoonist and humorist Milt Gross, and its adaptation is the work of Morey Amsterdam, the Borscht Belt wit who nearly a generation later would become a household name as a second-banana scene-stealer via network television's *The Dick Van Dyke Show*.

Star player James Dunn was attempting a rebound from a slump at the majors, where he had registered promisingly as an import from Broadway but soon settled into mild romantic parts in the low-budget ranks. Better some showier leading roles on Poverty Row than second-class citizenship in the big time, so Dunn figured, and the strategy worked—if only briefly. By the middle 1940s, he had landed the choice role of the jovial drunkard Johnny Nolan in *A Tree Grows in Brooklyn* and won the Oscar for Best Supporting Actor. He worked only sporadically, however, after that triumph and spent most of the 1950s out of pictures entirely, returning for *The Bramble Bush* in 1960, *Hemingway's Adventures of a Young Man* in 1962 and *The Oscar* in 1966. Dunn died in 1967.

Dunn is a delight here as the earnest and eager bridegroom, who selects an isolated house in the country as the ideal site for an undisturbed honeymoon—only to find traffic galore, as well as a coffin whose occupant seems to have gone missing; enough hidden doors and ominous passageways for a composite remake of *The Cat and the Canary* and *The Bat*; mobsters in search of a cache of diamonds; a nymphomaniacal gun moll (Mabel Todd); a servant (Sam McDaniel) who could use a stiff shot of nerve tonic; and a professional executioner (Robert Dudley) who takes altogether too much pleasure in his line of work. Dunn's tolerant-to-a-point bride is engagingly played by Florence Rice, who had proved herself a versatile leading lady since 1934 in a sweeping variety of thrillers, musicals, comedies and soapers. This was the last assignment before a premature retirement for the daughter of the popular sports journalist Grantland Rice.

Director William Nigh, a veteran of more earnestly weird films, treats the haunted-house gimmicks as the laughable clichés they had long since become. Nigh never loses sight, however, of the genuine dangers that confront his characters and generates a greater tension than one might expect on the evidence of much of his work. The result is a believable farce that not only looks slicker than the usual PRC production—thanks in great measure to Robert Cline's richly composed photography—but also feels more substantial than its brisk running time might suggest.

CREDITS: Producers: Arthur Alexander and Alfred Stern; In Charge of Production: Leon Fromkess; Director: William Nigh; Original Story: Milt Gross; Screenplay: Morey Amsterdam; Photographed by: Robert Cline; Assistant Director: Lou Perlof; Editor: Charles Henkel, Jr.; Settings: James Altweis; Prop Master: George Bahr; Musical Director: Lee Zahler; Sound: Corson Jowett; Makeup: Bernard Ponedel; Running Time: 61 Minutes; Released: April 19, 1943

CAST: James Dunn (Webster Frye); Florence Rice (Jackie Frye); Robert Dudley (Ben Bowron); Mabel Todd (Mabel); Sam McDaniel (Harmony Jones); Jim Toney (Chief Bagnoc); Eddy Chandler (Herbie); Robert Rice (Smoothie Lewis); Renee Carson (Josie); Tony Ward (Killer Blake); Anthony Caruso (Ted); Eddie Foster (Harold)

DEATH RIDES THE PLAINS
(Sigmund Neufeld Productions, Inc./Producers Releasing Corp.)

Death Rides the Plains is one of the choicer entries in the *Lone Rider* series, a frontier horror picture that pulls no punches.

Those historians who would trace the phenomenon of serial murder only as far back as the civilized last quarter of the 19th century—to the Chicago-based exploits of Herman Mudgett, or to Scotland Yard's unsolvable Jack the Ripper case—would do well to reconsider America's barely settled Western frontier as a font of primordial evil. The popular tendency is to paint this social blight as an urbanized development of almost modern-day origins.

But it was in the John & Kate Bender case of rural Kansas in the early 1870s—a tavernkeeper and his daughter, who lured more than a score of travelers into a robbery-and-murder trap—that the prolific shoot-'em-up scenarists Patricia Harper and Joe O'Donnell found an inspiration for *Death Rides the Plains*.

Its blithe liberties with history notwithstanding, *Death Rides the Plains* captures an essence of the Bender case that poses an ideal challenge for the Lone Rider (played here by Robert Livingston), a welcome throwback to the 1920s' and '30s' grittier breed of Western adventurer.

Ray Bennett and I. Stanford Jolley, as the lurking killers, pose a formidable menace. Bob Livingston is no slouch, either, and his air of determination makes it patent from the outset that the badmen are bound to meet their match. This prevailing severity, in turn, is nicely offset by the comic-relief geezer act of Al "Fuzzy" St. John. Livingston had been as impressive a Lone Ranger (in 1939's *The Lone Ranger Rides Again*) as he had been a founding member of Republic's *Three Mesquiteers* series, and he proved amply prepared to carry on as the hellbent-for-justice Lone Rider.

Ben Gowdey (Bennett) and his accomplice, Rogan (Jolley), advertise a handsome ranch for sale—a steal, at $25,000. One buyer after another receives a hospitable enough welcome, only to be done away with once the money has changed hands. Rocky Cameron (Livingston), who leads a secret life as the masked Lone Rider, pretends to demand a cut of the racket, forcing Gowdey to new depths of treachery. The Rider and Fuzzy spend much of the picture on the run from the law, finally unearthing not only a conclusive paper trail pointing to Gowdey—but also a hideous mass burial ground underneath the ranchhouse. In an inevitable falling-out between crooks, Gowdey saves the law the trouble of dealing with Rogan, only to be captured following a wild chase.

The merciless and intelligently dialogued script is a cut above those of wartime Westerns as a class. Sam Newfield directs with the ruthless intensity of his *Lightnin' Bill Carson* series, and there is a '30s-like near-absence of romance, with pretty Nica Doret occupying but a marginal role. St. John's rustic humor is well deployed, but even his recurring sidekick role assumes an unusually vengeful edge, inasmuch as one of Fuzzy's kinfolks lies buried among the victims.

Other *Lone Rider* entries of 1943 include *Law of the Saddle*, *Raiders of Red Gap* and *Wild Horse Rustlers*.

CREDITS: Producer: Sigmund Neufeld; Director: Sam Newfield; Story: Patricia Harper; Screenplay: Joe O'Donnell; Photographed by: Robert Cline; Assistant Director: Melvlle DeLay; Editor: Holbrook N. Todd; Musical Director: David Chudnow; Sound: Hans Weeren; Running Time: 53 Minutes; Released: April 30, 1943

CAST: Bob Livingston (Rocky "Lone Rider" Cameron); Al "Fuzzy" St. John (Fuzzy Jones); Nica Doret (Virginia); Ray Bennett (Ben Gowdey); I. Stanford Jolley (Rogan); George Cresebro (Trent); John Elliott (James Marshal); Kermit Maynard (Jed); Slim Whitaker (Sheriff); Karl Hackett (James)

I ESCAPED THE GESTAPO
a.k.a.: NO ESCAPE
(K-B Productions/Monogram Pictures Corp.)

I Escaped the Gestapo is not so much Gestapo as it is Fifth Column, but the title is a calculated ticket-seller of the it-happened-to-me variety. John Carradine plays Martin, front man for a Nazi infiltration unit, in an impressive piece of topical sensationalism. Carradine, as usual, can be relied upon to commandeer things despite what is essentially a supporting role—upstaging top-billed Dean Jagger, the *I* of the title, at every opportunity.

Martin engineers a jailbreak for Lane (Jagger), a master counterfeiter, who is then placed in captivity at an amusement park and forced to develop engraving plates that will yield passable fakes of negotiable securities. Lane, whose mother has been abducted to ensure his cooperation, plays along until he can get word to the authorities, who finally close in and discombobulate the gang. Mary Brian has little to do in a vaguely romantic subplot, although the fade-out assures the viewer she will wait for Jagger while he serves out the remainder of his sentence. George "Spanky" McFarland, at age 14, has an incidental

role. McFarland recollected the assignment in 1987 as "a welcome respite, I mean to *tell* you," from his chores in the soon-to-end *Our Gang* comedy series—which by this time, the Texas-native child star had grown to despise. Elsewhere among films of the day, John Carradine can be seen as the Nazi big shot Reinhard Heydrich in *Hitler's Madman*, and as a more supernaturally predisposed servant of the Third Reich in *Revenge of the Zombies*.

Oregon-born director Harold Young is better remembered for Alexander Korda's bombastic production of *The Scarlet Pimpernel* (England; 1935) and one of the Disney machine's bolder combinations of live action with animation, *The Three Caballeros* (1945). Young, a former master film editor in Hollywood and Europe, also excelled in the B-as-in-budget leagues, with such memorable entries as the sentimental comedy *Dreaming Out Loud* (1940; part of RKO's *Lum & Abner* series) and *The Mummy's Tomb* (1942). Young plays *I Escaped the Gestapo* for a wealth of suspense, wisely sublimating Jagger's rather mild antiheroic conflict (criminality vs. patriotism) to Carradine's forceful show of villainy.

Variety's pre-release review, incidentally, gave the title as *I Escaped from the Gestapo*.

CREDITS: A King Bros. Production; Producer: Maurice King; Associate Producer: Franklin King; Director: Harold Young; Story: Henry Blankfort; Based upon an Idea by: George Bricker; Screenplay: Henry Blankfort and Wallace Sullivan; Photographed by: Ira H. Morgan; Musical Score: W. Franke Harling; Musical Supervisor: David Chudnow; Art Director: Dave Milton; Set Dresser: Vin Taylor; Editor: S.K. Winston; Sound: Tom Lambert and Glen Glenn; Assistant Directors: Arthur Gardner and Herman King; Running Time: 75 Minutes; Released: May 14, 1943

CAST: Dean Jagger (Torgut Lane); John Carradine (Martin); Mary Brian (Helen); Bill Henry (Gordan); Sidney Blackmer (Bergen); Ian Keith (Gerard); Anthony Ward (Lokin); Billy Marshall (Lunt); William Vine (Sailor); Norman Willis (Rodt); Charles Waggenheim (Haft); Edward Keane (Domack); Greta Grandstadt (Hilda); George "Spanky" McFarland (Billy)

FALSE FACES
(Republic Pictures Corp.)

The film noir idiom picks up early momentum in this disremembered entry from Republic Pictures. Originating as a forced merger of Poverty Row studios, and better known for its bravura high-adventure serials than for its numerous feature films, Republic hovered between major and minor status—too well heeled to belong to the low-budget indie ranks, and yet not quite on the same aesthetic or social grounds with the bigger, old-line outfits. Despite its mounting ambitions, Republic continued to turn out modest pictures, designed for the lower half of the double-feature booking system, that have more in common with the general output of Monogram and PRC than with that of any major studio. (Where Columbia, Universal and the like had their B-picture units, Republic *was* a B-picture outfit, self-contained, and usually proud of the status.)

The ambitious director-and-screenwriter team of George Sherman and Curt Siodmak brings the crucially noir-ified element of despair to *False Faces*: Craig Harding (played by Rex Williams) is an alienated romantic who finds himself framed for murder. Harding, the son of a hard-nosed district attorney, carries a torch for nightclub singer Joyce Ford (Veda Ann Borg). Her slaying brings suspicion upon Craig and his chum, bandleader Don Westcott (Bill Henry). A menacing stranger hovers over the proceedings, inciting fights and seemingly fixing Craig's guilt in the eyes of the authorities. D.A. Stanley Harding (Stanley Ridges), however, continues to ride herd on the investigation. At length, the true culprit is revealed—none too convincingly—as a pudgy little fuss-budget of a hotel manager. This amply well-camouflaged miscreant is played by one of Hollywood's favorite henpecked husbands, Chester Clute.

Williams seems every bit the tormented noir antihero, a temperamental brooder who courts misery at every turn lest he run out of disappointments to brood over. He is not looking for answers so much as he is hoping somebody will keep repeating the questions. Williams is rather a conventional-looking leading man until he doffs his fedora, revealing a high-rise pompadour that might have served as an inspiration to the present-day musician/actor Lyle Lovett. Bill Henry lends vigor as the nightclub entertainer. Stanley Ridges is the soul of determination as the investigating prosecutor. Chester Clute is as comical here as he had been

a decade earlier in a starring series of short subjects, but he makes a game stab at mustering the right air of possessive madness when found out.

Veda Ann Borg had been a Paramount star on the rise during the 1930s, but her promising career was stalled following a disfiguring accident that required extensive plastic surgery. The successful rebuilding of her face should have been rewarded with bigger opportunities on camera, but she settled instead into a busy regimen of low-budget assignments, alternating many tough-gal character parts with the occasional romantic lead. Her otherworldly beauty and vaguely haunted air make Miss Borg seem precisely the type to attract a lovesick dreamer like Williams' character in *False Faces*.

One of the contributing tunesmiths, Ken Darby, much later developed the distinctive *a cappella* scoring for the popular network-television Western, *The Life and Legend of Wyatt Earp*.

CREDITS: Associate Producer and Director: George Sherman; Screenplay: Curt Siodmak; Photography: William Bradford; Art Director: Russell Kimball; Editor: Arthur Roberts; Assistant Director: Harry Knight; Set Dresser: Charles Thompson; Musical Director: Morton Scott; Songs by: Walter Scharf and Ken Darby; Sound: Tom Carman; Running Time: 58 Minutes; Released: May 26, 1943

CAST: Stanley Ridges (Stanley S. Harding); Bill Henry (Donald Westcott); Rex Williams (Craig Harding); Veda Ann Borg (Joyce Ford); Janet Shaw (Diana Harding); Joseph Crehan (Alan O'Brien); Chester Clute (Apartment Manager); John Maxwell (Stewart); Dick Wessell (Mallory); Billy Nelson (Jimmy); Etta McDaniel (Magnolia); Nicodemus Stewart (Mac); Claire Whitney (Agnes Harding); Mozelle Cravens (Receptionist); Charles McAvoy (Cop)

THE BLACK RAVEN
(Producers Releasing Corp.)

Here we have the very basis of Sam Newfield's unfortunate reputation as a genre-fied hack. With its stock tale of ill-matched souls in collision at a backwoods Northern lodge, *The Black Raven* is not so much a bad movie, or even an inept one, as it is merely a desultory effort, made as if marking time until something more interesting could come along. Newfield was—as we have seen at several points in the *Forgotten Horrors* books—quite capable of inventive, provocative filmmaking, but more often his prolific output reduced him to drudgery.

Recalling *Tangled Destinies* and *The Rogues Tavern* (see *Forgotten Horrors: The Definitive Edition*) more so than any other movies of the old-dark-house type, *The Black Raven* at least deserves props up front for having the most redundant title of its period; its closest rivals in this respect would be 1944's

The Yellow Canary, 1951's *The Flying Missile* and 1958's *The Giant Behemoth*.

No shortage of artistry on screen, though: George Zucco is as usual a champ at glowering condescension in the role of innkeeper Amos Bradford, whose disreputable career as a harborer of criminals is fast approaching a crisis. Championship B-movie villains Noel Madison and I. Stanford Jolley, master of intimidation Charles Middleton (on the side of the law, this time), and milquetoast Byron Foulger help to complicate the complications as the guests, intruders and inmates convene, each bearing various grudges and selfish agendas. The intruders include a convict (Jolley) with a gripe against Zucco; an underage couple fleeing the girl's disapproving father; a crooked politician (Robert Middlemass); a bank clerk (Foulger) who has embezzled $50,000; and a racketeer (Madison) who owes his desperate situation to Middlemass. As though these complications were hardly enough, there also is a series of murders that local sheriff Middleton intends to solve.

The stodgy pace and uninspired writing make the film's scant 62 minutes seem to pass rather slowly, and the resolution feels almost improvised. Middleton, at least, clearly relishes the opportunity to provide a grim variety of comic relief, and Glenn Strange contributes his specialty as a dimwit handyman.

The romantic chores are handled ably by Wanda McKay and the original *Three Mesquiteers* ensemble member Robert "Bob" Livingston, billed uniquely here under his actual name, Bob Randall. Livingston had gone on to solo Western stardom and would remain popular as a character man on through the 1940s and early '50s. He was a brother of Addison "Jack" Randall, a cowboy star who died in a freak accident on horseback while filming *The Royal Mounted Rides Again*, a Universal serial, in 1945.

CREDITS: Producer: Sigmund Neufeld; Director: Sam Newfield; Screenplay: Fred Myton; Photographed by Robert Cline; Editor: Holbrook N. Todd; Musical Supervisor: David Chudnow; Assistant Director: Melville DeLay; Sound: Hans Weeren; Production Manager: Bert Sternbach; Running Time: 62 Minutes; Released: May 31, 1943

CAST: George Zucco (Amos Bradford); Wanda McKay (Lee Winfield); Noel Madison (Mike Bardoni); Bob Randall [Robert Livingston] (Allen Bentley); Byron Foulger (Horace Weatherby); Charles Middleton (Sheriff); Robert Middlemass (Tim Winfield); Glenn Strange (Andy); I. Stanford Jolley (Whitey Cole)

COWBOY COMMANDOS
(Monogram Pictures Corp.)

Nazi predators out West had become a staple by now of the Hollywood oat opera, for Western fans made up one of the more patriotically receptive niche audiences. One of the more outlandish such sagebrushers is S. Roy Luby's *Cowboy Commandos*, which sends Monogram's relentlessly popular *Range Busters* team (Ray "Crash" Corrigan, Denny Moore and Max "Alibi" Terhune) on a War Bonds promotional tour. The excursion just naturally runs afoul of a mining-sabotage campaign engineered by agents of the Third Reich. The inclusion of a forbiddingly peppy Western-swing song called "I'll Get der Fuehrer, Sure as Shootin'" is quite enough to place the film among the few most offbeat of its kind.

More than mere saboteurs, the Nazis here are doubling as masked marauders while two of their more conniving cohorts (John Merton and Frank Ellis) work undercover as miners. This lot is so ruthless as to kill one of their own after he is captured by chief Range Buster Ray "Crash" Corrigan—then to leave Corrigan for dead (which of course, for the sake of the franchise, he cannot be) following an ambush.

Then comes the discovery of a creepy hidden chamber adorned with swastikas, along with the revelation that the local saloonkeepers (played by Edna Bennett and Western-movie dependable Budd Buster) are the ringleaders. The simple capture-and-arrest resolution is rather too mild a comeuppance for these murderous troublemakers. Comical Max Terhune shows slightly more range than most of his pictures allowed him, in a noisy drunk scene where he vows revenge against the mine owners; it's all a sham, calculated to attract the interest of the saboteurs, but Terhune plays the tantrum for full seething measure.

CREDITS: A George W. Weeks Production; in Charge of Production: William L. Nolte; Director: S. Roy Luby; Original Scenarist and Assistant Director: Clark L. Paylow; Screenplay: Elizabeth Beecher; Photographed by: Edward A. Kull; Editor: Roy Claire; Music: Frank Sanucci; Song: "I'll Get der Fuehrer, Sure as Shootin'," by Johnny Lange; Sound: Lyle Willey; Running Time: 53 Minutes; Released: June 4, 1943

CAST: Ray "Crash" Corrigan, Denny Moore and Max "Alibi" Terhune (the Range Busters); Evelyn Finley (Joan Cameron); Johnny Bond (Slim); Budd Buster (Werner); John Merton (Fraser); Frank Ellis (Mario); Steve Clark (Bartlett); Edna Bennett (Katie); Bud Osborne (Hans); and George Chesebro

HITLER'S MADMAN
a.k.a.: HITLER'S HANGMAN
(Angelus Pictures, Inc./Metro-Goldwyn-Mayer Corp.)

Seymour Nebenzal was born in 1899 in New York, but he soon bucked the mounting tide of German Jewish resettlement in America. By the early 1920s, Nebenzal had established himself as a prominent filmmaker in Berlin, where in association with G.W. Pabst and Fritz Lang he produced such enduring works as *Westfront 1918* and *M* (both from 1930). He fled the Nazis to continue his career in Paris later in the '30s, then found himself back in America by 1940. Nebenzal became as seriously artistic a producer as Poverty Row had ever seen, with such fine entries on behalf of the low-budget studios as *Tomorrow We Live* (PRC; 1942) and *Hitler's Madman*.

Anyone who neglects to reckon with the Poverty Row studios as a force bigger than their numerous genre programmers would signify, will do well to reappraise the little guys in light of *Hitler's Madman*. The epic tragedy even merited a prestigious release by an old-line major company, MGM, albeit with MGM's tampering.

The film betrays its humble origins in terms of simple production values and an absence of star power, but still it places tremendous craftsmanship and heavy-duty dramatic resources at the service of an unyielding portrayal of the Nazis' brutality as a matter of Germanic national pride.

The story is that of the burning in June 1942 of the Czechoslovakian village of Lidice, and the methodical slaughter of 1,600 people, in retaliation for the assassination of *Reichprotektor* Reinhard Heydrich, the man most directly responsible for the extermination of European Jews during the early years of World War II. The Lidice massacre had been dramatized in a Paramount short subject of 1942 called "We Refuse To Die," and later that year Fritz Lang and Arnold Pressburger made their version of the tale, which United Artists released in March of 1943 as *Hangmen Also Die!*

In *Hitler's Madman*, Heydrich is invested with an aloof malice by John Carradine, who at the time was

Hitler's Madman, starring John Carradine, concerns the burning of the village of Lidice and the slaughter of 1,600 people.

making rather a career-in-miniature out of Nazi impersonations. Carradine serves not only as a classic-manner Man You Love To Hate in the Stroheim fashion, but also as a mouthpiece for MGM's rather awkward repudiation of Adolf Hitler: At the approach of death, this wishful-thinking version of Heydrich rallies to denounce Hitler and predict the Allies' ultimate triumph while demanding a mass slaughter of the Czechs—a scene ordered among revisions imposed after the big studio stepped in as distributor. Carradine plays the scene beautifully, with just the right air of embittered defiance, but the writing works better as propaganda than as drama. (MGM also insisted upon spicing things up with cameos for a number of its starlets, including Ava Gardner; her appearance as a harassed university student found its way into the official version, but she does not appear in other surviving cuts.)

None of the MGM refinements makes Heydrich any more admirable a character. *Hitler's Madman* is overall an emphatic presentation of Nazi ruthlessness. Carradine makes altogether a more forceful Heydrich than Hans H. von Twardowski's mean-but-prissy impersonation in *Hangmen Also Die!* (Von Twardowski has a lesser role, as a military officer, in *Hitler's Madman*.) The Heydrich impersonation suited Carradine so well that Columbia Pictures hired him to reprise it, after a fashion, with a part modeled after *der Reichprotektor* in 1944's *The Black Parachute*.

Among other pictures of similar concern, *Madman* is a trifle less brutal than the close-in-time Reich-buster pictures *She Defends Her Country* (from Russia) and *Soy Puro Mexicano/I Am a True Mexican* (from Mexico), but notably more harsh than Raoul Walsh's adventurous *Background to Danger*, a Warner Bros. entry starring George Raft, Peter Lorre and Sydney Greenstreet as American, Russian and German spies. All four films reached American screens during the early summer of 1943.

Carradine's Heydrich and Howard Freeman's Heinrich Himmler are the dominant characters in a huge and impressively deployed cast, handily overshadowing Resistance leaders played by Alan Curtis (as a Czech-born British soldier), Ralph Morgan, Edgar Kennedy (yes, the beloved Hal Roach Studios comedian and the impatient police chief of *Crime Smasher*) and Patricia Morison.

The underground fight leads to the patriots' ambush of Heydrich, provoking Himmler to order the Lidice Massacre. Director Douglas Sirk, in his first American assignment, acquits himself particularly well in this sustained show of agony, with the forced gathering of the townspeople, the lining up of the men to face a massed firing squad, the packing off of the women to concentration camps, and the tearing away of children from their parents. Sirk concentrates as severely upon the small human dramas amid the terrorism, as upon the vast wave of destruction.

But for an artist who would leave his most lasting signature on such intimate pieces as *Magnificent Obsession* (1954) and the 1959 remake of *Imitation of Life*, Sirk is surprisingly inept at rendering credible the more tender moments of *Hitler's Madman*. A subplot of romance between Curtis and Miss Morison generates so little interest that her character's unexpected death fails to register the intended impact. Miss Morison fared better over the long haul as a B-movie *femme fatale*. Ralph Morgan's transformation from peacemaker to warrior is somewhat better handled. Edgar Kennedy's meandering presence seems scarcely more than a distraction—a blustery hermit of suspect loyalties—until Kennedy reveals his truer leanings in a bracing instant. Ludwig Stossel is most credible as a small-time politico aligned with the Nazis.

Sirk was born Detlef Sierck in 1900 in Denmark and became a successful stage producer in Germany after assuming the significant middle name of Hans. He stayed in Germany well after the Nazis' rise, despite a reputation as an outspoken leftist, and began concentrating upon filmmaking—an arena that he found less subject to censorship. In 1937, he quit Germany and sojourned in Spain, South Africa and Australia before reaching America, where he rechristened himself Douglas Sirk and became known as one who could get big-looking pictures out of tiny budgets. As adept at action and adventure as at maudlin soapers, Sirk thrived in Hollywood until sidelined by failing health in 1959, when he returned to Germany.

CREDITS: Producer: Seymour Nebenzal; Associate Producer: Rudolph Joseph; Director: Douglas Sirk; Story, "Victims Victorious," by: Emil Ludwig and Albrecht Joseph; Suggested by a Story, "Hangman's Village," by: Bart Lytton; Adaptation: Peretz Hirshbein, Melvin Levy and Doris Malloy; Narrative Poem, "The Murder of Lidice" (Excerpted) by: Edna Saint Vincent Millay; Photographed by: Jack Greenhalgh; Art Directors: Fred Preble and Edward Willens; Musical Score: Karl Hajos; Assistant Director: Melville DeLay; Editor: Dan Milner; Sound Engineers: Percy Townsend and W.M. Dalgleish; Technical Director: Eugen [as Eugene] Schufftan; Production Manager: Ralph Slosser; Technical Advisor, Added Scenes: Felix Bernstein; Unit Publicist: Jack Kelly; Running Time: 85 Minutes; Released: Following Previews as *Hitler's Hangman* in Early June of 1943

CAST: John Carradine (Reinhard Heydrich); Patricia Morison (Jarmila Hanka); Alan Curtis (Karel Vavra); Howard Freeman (Heinrich Himmler); Ralph Morgan (Jan Hanka); Edgar Kennedy (Nepomuk); Ludwig Stossel (Mayor Herman Bauer); Al Shean (Father Semlanik); Elizabeth Russell (Maria Bartonek); Jimmy Conlin (Dvorak); Blanche Yurka (Anna Hanka); Jorja Rollins (Clara Janek); Victor Kilian (Janek); Johanna Hofer (Marta Bauer); Wolfgang Zilzer (Colonel); Tully Marshall (Professor); Richard Bailey (Anton Bartonek); Richard Nichols (Stephen Bartonek); Betty Jean Nichols (Miss Bartonek); Laura Lane (Minna); John Good (Rupert Hanka); Emmett Lynn (German); Peter Van Eyck, Richard Ryen, Otto Reichow and Sigurd Tor (Gestapo Agents); Ben Webster (Masaryk); Arthur Thalasso and Dan Duncan (Policemen); Nellie Anderson (Mrs. Masaryk); John Merton (Guard); Dick Talmadge (Chauffeur); Frank Hagney (Engineer); Hugh Maguire (Boy); Hans von Morhart, Ray Miller and Charles Marsh (Soldiers); James Farley (Town Crier); Solvig Smith (Milkmaid); Budd Buster (Conductor); Chet Brandenburg (Linesman); Ernst Hausman and Sam Waagenaar (Sentries); Dan Fitzpatrick and Frank Todd (Pallbearers); George Lynn, Wilmer Barnes and Carl Neubert (Officers); Dennis Moore (Orderly)

WOLVES OF THE RANGE
(Sigmund Neufeld Productions, Inc./Producers Releasing Corp.)

I. Stanford Jolley comes back to menace the Lone Rider and Fuzzy Jones in this eerie rip-snorter, which pretty well defines the difference between a series entry and a sequel, just in case anybody was wondering. Were *Wolves of the Range* a sequel, then Jolley could not return, on account of he got killed in the previous *Lone Rider* adventure, *Death Rides the Plains*. Here, Jolley is an entirely new character in an entirely new setting—but still as fiendish an *hombre* as ever stalked the frontier. Repetitive casting was a foregone conclusion in the Westerns, whether born of Poverty Row or the bigger studios, and the kids and kids-at-heart who kept these pictures in demand grew to recognize favorites among the bad guys and backup players as certainly as they had their favorite heroes, favorite sidekicks and favorite wonder horses.

Jolley had played more a henchman than a mastermind in *Death Rides the Plains*, but here he handles the venomous leading role of Harry Dorn, a big-shot cattleman whose inexplicable inaction in dealing with a drought hides a secretive campaign to sell an entire Arizona valley to an Eastern syndicate for an irrigation project. This arid zone has become a natural setting for hot tempers, mayhem and murder when Rocky "Lone Rider" Cameron (Bob Livingston) and his pal Fuzzy Jones (Al St. John) butt in on the scam.

Prevailing weird touches include a bout with amnesia for the Lone Rider after he is wounded in an ambush, and a mock-mystical warning that Fuzzy will soon die by violence. Fuzzy is saved by a batch of supposedly charmed medallions, but not in the way he expects: The objects serve as a merely physical kind of bulletproof armor. The Rider's final confrontation with Jolley's Dorn involves one of the most brutal beatings we've ever witnessed in a matinee Western, with superb camera placements and no evidence of stunt doubling.

CREDITS: Producer: Sigmund Neufeld; Director: Sam Newfield; Story and Screenplay: Joe O'Donnell; Photographed by: Robert Cline; Assistant Director: Melville DeLay; Editor: Holbrook N. Todd; Sound: Hans Weeren; Production Manager: Bert Sternbach; Running Time: 60 Minutes; Released: June 21, 1943

CAST: Bob Livingston (Rocky "Lone Rider" Cameron); Al St. John (Fuzzy Q. Jones); Francis Gladwin (Ann Brady); I. Stanford Jolley (Harry Dorn); Karl Hackett (Corrigan); Ed Cassidy (Dan Brady); Jack Ingram (Jack Hammond); Ken Duncan (Adams); Budd Buster (Foster); Bob Hill (Judge Brandon)

SPY TRAIN
(Monogram Pictures Corp.)

The suspense here depends upon the claustrophobic setting of a streamliner where a bomb is set to go blooey at any moment now. A brief running time helps matters, but director Harold Young digresses too often to keep the audience enthralled with the urgency of it all. *Spy Train* holds up in spite of its flagging pace and a topical propaganda plot device, for along the way it trots out a socko show of heroism by Richard Travis; a sharp-tongued return engagement for the under-utilized silent-screen player Thelma White; a winning comic portrayal by Fred "Snowflake" Toomes, subverting Negro stereotype as a philosophical porter; and a choice display of Warren Hymer's famous thickheaded style of acting, as a Nazi agent who seems to have been hanging out with the Damon Runyon crowd.

It's another infestation of those dagnabbed Nazis (with Paul McVey and Evelyn Brent in fine sinister form as the chief culprits) that throws the whole mess into gear, carelessly planting a time bomb in a piece of luggage that is supposed to contain documents crucial to the war effort—a Hitchcock-styled

MacGuffin if ever there were one. The valise and a harmless look-alike bag are kept in constant motion as various interested parties plot to nab the contents. Travis, as a quick-thinking war correspondent, arranges for the Third Reichsters to get themselves blasted to smithereens just as they think they're escaping. Catherine Craig makes a winning love interest for Travis—as if such circumstances would permit romance—and Chick Chandler lends the right touch of martyrdom as a daring photographer who runs afoul of Hitler's goons.

CREDITS: Producer: Max M. King; Director: Harold Young; Dialogue Director: Harold Erickson; Screenplay: Leslie Schwabacker and Bart Lytton; Story: Scott Littlefield; Contributing Writer: Wallace Sullivan; Photographed by: Mack Stengler; Set Construction: David Milton; Assistant Director and Production Manager: Richard L'Estrange; Editor: Martin G. Cohn; Set Dresser: Al Greenwood; Sound: Glen Glenn; Makeup: Harry Ross; Running Time: 61 Minutes; Released: July 9, 1943

CAST: Richard Travis (Bruce Grant); Catherine Craig (Jane Thornwald); Chick Chandler (Stew); Thelma White (Millie); Evelyn Brent (Freida Molte); Warren Hymer (Herman Krantz); Paul McVey (Hugo Molte); Herbert Heyes (Max Thornwald); Steve Roberts (Nazi Commander); Bill Hunter (Detective); Fred "Snowflake" Toomes and Napoleon Whiting (Pullman Porters)

GHOSTS ON THE LOOSE
(Monogram Pictures Corp.)

The Broadway smash *Dead End* moved to Hollywood in 1937, creating a comparable sensation on film and establishing an ensemble act that would stick together on screen well into the 1950s—retaining its members' smart-aleck childlike qualities for an unnaturally long time. From the earnest social-problem histrionics of *Dead End* and its immediate sequel-like follow-throughs, there was scarcely any direction to take beyond the low-comedy route. The Dead End Kids' team devolved gradually along the lines of benevolent near-delin-

quents and forked off into the Little Tough Guys at Universal Pictures and the East Side Kids at Monogram, overlapping to often confusing effect as late as 1943. The ensemble would wind up as the Bowery Boys as Monogram gradually transformed itself into Allied Artists, which at first was a classier outfit; the team changed scarcely at all, save for the process of growing to goofball adulthood.

The transitional year of 1943 saw the act lapse decisively from Universal to Monogram, there to begin a consolidated, long-term agenda of misadventures. One of the better entries, *Ghosts on the Loose*, is an old-fashioned laff-riot in a caricatured mock-horrific setting. It is embellished by what amounts to little more than a walk-through from Bela Lugosi—and it is graced by an early performance of surprisingly mature star power from Ava Gardner, appearing on loan-out from MGM for what amounts to a screen test underwritten by Monogram. The big guys always enjoy letting the little guys pick up the tab, for the deed somehow makes both parties feel important.

The story has to do with a looming old mansion that serves as a hideout for a gang of Nazi spies. East Sider Glimpy (Huntz Hall) has a brother (Richard "Rick" Vallin, whose confusing array of professional names also included Rik and Ricki) who is about to get married (Miss Gardner is the bride). The couple has entertained some notion of spending the honeymoon in a haunted house. By the usual outlandish contrivances, the East Side Kids wind up occupying the place, and after the usual hokum with the usual hidden passages, sliding doors and so forth, the kids almost unwittingly thwart Lugosi and his mob of Nazi infiltrators.

The films of the East Side Kids/Bowery Boys are an acquired taste, all right, but there is no denying their generosity with the lowbrow wit and malaprop-ridden wordplay. *Ghosts on the Loose* is the Kids' show all the way, with ringleader Leo Gorcey mangling the language and mugging the camera as few others would have the gall, guff or gumption to do, and second banana Huntz Hall playing the eager-to-please, sometimes indignant stooge. Sammy Morrison, the former "Sunshine Sammy" of Hal Roach's *Our Gang* comedies, is as personable as when he was a little kid, and he lends a welcome sense of integration based upon friendship—though he cannot help accounting for the occasional demeaning color gag. Billy Benedict and Bobby Jordan are prominent, too, although by this stage Gorcey and Hall have already become the crux of the act.

William Beaudine captures the antics nicely; this is a film that requires little formal direction, accommodating Beaudine's definition of the director as an efficient and helpful traffic cop. Lugosi has scarcely more to do than appear by turns irritable and menacing, but the small role must have been a relief after the insults heaped upon him by *The Ape Man*. Miss Gardner, bound for bigger things, is a knockout in a part that demands far less than the stunning presence she has to offer.

CREDITS: Producers: Sam Katzman and Jack Dietz for Banner Productions; Associate Producer: Barney Sarecky; Director: William Beaudine; Screenplay: Kenneth Higgins; Photographed by: Mack Stengler; Editor: Carl Pierson; Settings: Dave Milton; Musical Director: Edward Kay; Assistant Director: Arthur Hammond; Running Time: 65 Minutes; Released: July 30, 1943

CAST: Leo Gorcey (Mugs); Huntz Hall (Glimpy); Bobby Jordan (Danny); Bela Lugosi (Emil); Ava Gardner (Betty); Rick Vallin (Jack); Sammy Morrison (Scruno); Billy Benedict (Benny); Stanley Clements (Stash); Bobby Stone (Dave); Minerva Urecal (Hilda); Wheeler Oakman (Tony); Peter Seal (Bruno); Frank Moran (Monk); Jack Mulhall (Lieutenant); Bill Bates (Sleepy)

THAT NAZTY NUISANCE
(Hal Roach Studios, Inc./United Artists Corp.)

Hal Roach's on-the-cheap production of *The Devil with Hitler* (see *Forgotten Horrors 2*) succeeded in more ways than its aim to vindicate Roach's patriotism, in a Hollywood that had been slow to forgive him for a naïve prewar business deal with Benito Mussolini. The film proved enough of a hit to justify a prompt sequel, *That Nazty Nuisance*. The jury remains out as to whether the sequel justifies its existence.

It develops here that Adolf Hitler (a recurring portrayal by Bobby Watson) has survived a straight-to-Hades bombing and is up to his usual tricks and then some. In a plot to betray his Axis cohorts Mussolini (Joe Devlin) and Suki Yaki (Johnny Arthur, a favorite within the Roach stock company), Hitler heads for the Island of Norom (*moron*, spelled backwards) and a secretive summit meeting with a dignitary named Paj Mub (played by Ian Keith; and *you* take the bass-ackwards spelling game from here). Mussolini and Suki Yaki horn in on Hitler's excursion, however, and find a gala banquet in store, complete with a magician's act for entertainment. Subbing for the entertainer, however, is an American sailor (Frank Faylen), who causes Suki Yaki

to vanish—and to be replaced with an ape. There follows an American plot to capture the Axis leaders, who wind up as prisoners aboard their own submarine, only to be catapulted like human torpedoes onto a beach.

The humiliating silliness is unrelenting, but *That Nazty Nuisance* lacks the murderous ferocity that actually compounds the humor of *The Devil with Hitler*. Roach told us in 1992: "Well, perhaps I felt I had less to prove, this time 'round. And Bobby Watson had to come back, even though we'd sent him on down to hell in the first picture, because an Axis spoof without Hitler would be like a—well, like, why even bother?" Like *The Devil with Hitler*, the sequel belongs to the producer's low-budget *Streamlined Features* series of four- to five-reel pictures; although this series was a comedown for Roach from his glory days as a satellite of MGM, he philosophically heralded the *Streamlined* entries as a progressive experiment in narrative efficiency. *The Devil with Hitler* and *That Nazty Nuisance* were later cobbled together into a single feature, which retained the title of the source-film. The U.S. copyright record for *That Nazty Nuisance* documents the title only as *Nazty Nuisance*.

CREDITS: Producer: Glenn Tryon; Director: Gordon Douglas; Screenplay: Earle Snell and Clarence Marks; Photographed by: Robert Pittack; Photographic Effects: Roy Seawright; Assistant Director: Holly Morse; Art Director: Charles D. Hall; Editor: Bert Jordan; Décor: W.L. Stevens; Wardrobe: Harry Black; Musical Score: Edward Ward; Running Time: 43 Minutes; Released: August 6, 1943

CAST: Bobby Watson (Adolf Hitler); Joe Devlin (Benito Mussolini); Johnny Arthur (Suki Yaki); Jean Porter (Kela Trams) [Reverse the Spelling]; Ian Keith (Paj Mub); Henry Victor (von Popoff); Emory Parnell (Spense); Frank Faylen (Benson); Ed "Strangler" Lewis and Abe "King Kong" Kashey (Guards); Rex Evans (Hermann Goering); Charles Rogers (Josef Goebbels); Wedgewood Nowell (Heinrich Himmler); and Jiggs (Orangutan)

ISLE OF FORGOTTEN SINS
a.k.a.: MONSOON
(Atlantis Pictures Corp./Producers Releasing Corp.)

Edgar G. Ulmer's downfall while making *The Black Cat* (1934) at Universal Pictures has been amply documented in our survey of Hollywood villainy, *Human Monsters*. The afterlife of Ulmer's nonetheless brilliant career was such that he became an exile on Poverty Row, where he cranked 'em out prolifically and occasionally flirted with greatness. *Detour* (1945) is one such transcendent masterpiece. *Isle of Forgotten Sins* comes close but suffers from tampering by the censors, whose dirty work can be spotted almost frame-for-frame. The title itself represents a bit of patchwork recycling: "Isle of Forgotten Sins" is an Ulmer story, unrelated to the present yarn, that had provided the basis for Arthur Ripley's *Prisoner of Japan* (1942).

Like *The Black Cat*, this tale of destructive greed ran afoul of Hollywood's parasitic Legion of Decency, whose bluenosed Jesuits dictated the removal of a crucial bawdy-house setting, lest a viewing render the audience hellbound *en masse*. The place remains on view but is re-defined as a casino in the forced rewrite; boss-lady Gale Sondergaard still carries herself more like a madam than any operator of any gambling den. The censors also required a happy ending that would have been a great deal happier if the surviving heroes (relatively speaking) had been allowed to keep a salvaged fortune. The booty, like the bad guys, seems to have ended up at the bottom of the sea. Ill-gotten gains couldn't even be gotten by the good guys, not in the cracked understanding of human nature fostered by the Legion of Decency.

Starting out like a conventional equatorial adventure, *Isle of Forgotten Sins* promptly veers into a cutthroat campaign to dredge up $3,000,000 from a sunken steamer. Professional deep-sea explorers John Carradine and Frank Fenton, ostensibly of a heroic bent, have a plan to claim the treasure, but watching their every move are crooked seafaring man Sidney Toler—who had been the captain of the doomed ship—and his accomplice Richard "Rick" Vallin, the purser. No sooner have Carradine and Fenton surfaced with the loot, than Toler's mob ambushes them. A monsoon strikes, and the scoundrels are swept away, along with the gold. Carradine and Fenton are left to take solace in their tropical sweethearts.

Ulmer's original scenario clearly offered no particularly admirable leading characters. This quality remains evident in the truculent, opportunistic attitudes of both Carradine and Fenton. They make a finely matched pair of sea-dogs. Sidney Toler, in a drastic departure from his long-running portrayal of the benevolent detective Charlie Chan, is unremittingly evil as the deceitful captain. Veda Ann Borg is an impossibly glamorous "native" "girl," and we use each term advisedly.

The film looks as polished as something that might have come from, say, Ben Pivar's cheap-but-classy B-picture unit at Universal—so much for the categorical assumption that PRC was capable of only shabby work. Gene Stone's handling of the special-effects storm scene is top-shelf for its time, and Ulmer's pacing is genuinely exciting.

CREDITS: In Charge of Production: Leon Fromkess; Producer: Peter R. Van Duinen; Director: Edgar G. Ulmer; Dialogue Director: Ben Kamsler; Screenplay: Raymond L. Schrock; Story: Edgar G. Ulmer; Photographed by: Ira Morgan; Special Effects: Gene Stone; Art Director: Fred Preble; Assistant Director: Melville DeLay; Associate: Angelo Scibetta; Editor: Charles Henkel, Jr.; Set Dressings: Harry Self; Musical Score: Leo Erdody; Songs: "Sleepy Island Moon," by Leo Erdody & June R. Stillman, and "In Pango," by Leo Erdody and Ann Leavitt; Sound: Percy Townsend; Running Time: 82 Minutes; Released: August 15, 1943

CAST: John Carradine (Mike Clancy); Gale Sondergaard (Marge); Sidney Toler (Krogan); Frank Fenton (Burke); Veda Ann Borg (Luana); Rita Quigley (Diane); Rick Vallin (Johnny Pacific); Tala Birell (Christine); Patti McCarty (Bobbie); Betty Amann (Olga); Marian Colby (Mimi)

HEADIN' FOR GOD'S COUNTRY
(Republic Pictures Corp.)

Director William Morgan applies enough frenzied energy to make the excesses of this awkward propaganda piece exciting, if hardly plausible. The unconventional setting of *Headin' for God's Country* is an isolated settlement in the Alaskan wilderness—actually, savvy location work around Mammoth

Lakes, California—where an outcast stranger named Michael Banyan (William Lundigan) concocts a hair-raising story about an imminent raid by hostile foreigners. Banyan is perpetrating a vengeful hoax, as far as he knows, upon the clannish townsfolk who have persecuted him and his pet German Shepherd, Flash (played by the busy Ace, the Wonder Dog). But meanwhile, the Japanese raid on Pearl Harbor is just about to happen, and an infiltrator has cut off contact with the outside world. Commandeering the local Weather Bureau, Albert Ness (Harry Shannon) guides a Japanese raiding party to the locale. The villagers are surprisingly well prepared for the incursion, having believed a bogus report that Banyan has planted in the town's newspaper. The climactic battle is long on tension if short on spectacle.

Bill Lundigan does top-notch work as the surly hero who rises to the occasion. As his only friends in the forbidding little town, weather-station operator Virginia Dale and local drunk/barber/ newspaperman Harry Davenport contribute colorful support. J. Frank Hamilton and the imposing tough-guy actor Eddie Acuff are memorable as a vile father-and-son combination, and Charlie Lung contributes an ethnically demeaning strain of comic relief as a slow-witted Eskimo. As a Japanese big shot, Chinese actor James B. Leong embodies the concept of stereotype in the service of propaganda—how better to keep the Yellow Peril melodramatic tradition relevant in times of turbulent change? The story is a quick-thinking, however ill thought-out, response to the reality of battles between the Allies and the Japanese in the Aleutian Islands.

Ace, the Wonder Dog would have a showier role in the following year's *The Monster Maker*. The now-lovable, now-fierce Shepherd graced a generous handful of pictures from the late 1930s into 1946.

CREDITS: Associate Producer: Armand Schaefer; Director: William Morgan; Screenplay: Elizabeth Meehan and Houston Branch; Story: Houston Branch; Photographed by: Bud Thackery; Art Director: Russell Kimball; Assistant Director: Phil Ford; Editor: Arthur Roberts; Set Decorator: Otto Siegel; Musical Director: Morton Scott; Song: "Battle Hymn of the Republic," by William Steffe & Julia Ward Howe; Sound: Earl Crain, Sr.; Running Time: 78 Minutes; Released: August 26, 1943

CAST: William Lundigan (Michael Banyan); Virginia Dale (Laurie Lane); Harry Davenport (Clem Adams); Harry Shannon (Albert Ness); Addison Richards (Commissioner); J. Frank Hamilton (Hilary Higgins); Eddie Acuff (Hugo Higgins); Wade Crosby (Jim Talbot); Skelton Knaggs (Jeff); John Bleifer (Nickolai); Eddy Waller (Hank); Charlie Lung (Willie Soha); Ernie Adams (Chuck); Eddie Lee (Gim Lung); James B. Leong (Japanese Officer); Anna Q. Nilsson (Mrs. Nilsson); Ace, the Wonder Dog (Flash); Harrison Greene (Skipper); Frank Lackteen (Minnemook); Charles Miller (John Lane)

TIGER FANGS
(Producers Releasing Corp.)

Playing out more like some self-contained fragment of a serial than a conventional feature film, this rip-snorting jungle adventure is a composite of a rather extreme anti-Axis propaganda piece; a marginal horror yarn based upon Far Eastern superstitions; and a recycling dump for footage from star player Frank Buck's own legitimate documentary pieces.

Buck is out to halt a serious threat to the war effort: Those lousy Nazis have been meddling with nature again, feeding Malay tigers a poison that intensifies the beasts' natural-born appetite for people. The rampages remind the natives of an ancient legend about were-tigers (such superstitions being integral to that region's folkways), and the production of rubber is halted. The story may be presumed to have taken place before Japan gained control of the peninsula, for Buck and his United Nations cohorts manage to scour the territory with little difficulty, barring interference from the Nazis and the tigers.

Frank "Bring 'Em Back Alive" Buck had long since ceased to cut an athletic figure by now, but the beefy explorer still seems authority personified as he confronts the Big Science and Bad Medicine of this culture-clash between the Third Reich and the Third World. Buck finds himself dwarfed, in turn, by a mountainous enemy agent played by Dan Seymour. Often dismissed as a poor man's Sydney Greenstreet, Seymour had in fact trod impressively onto Greenstreet's turf, including *Casablanca* (1942) and the Warners lot at large. Seymour's distinguishing trait was a background in burlesque-theatre comedy, and his customarily intimidating movie and television portrayals benefit from a brisk sense of timing.

Buck's heroic contingent includes J. Farrell MacDonald, Duncan Renaldo and—as an astoundingly gorgeous scientist in the service of the U.N.—June Duprez.

CREDITS: Producer: Jack Schwarz; Associate Producers: Fred McConnell and Harry D. Edwards; Director: Sam Newfield; Dialogue Director: Fred Kane; Screenplay: Arthur St. Claire; Photographed by: Ira Morgan; Art Director: Paul Palmentola; Assistant Director: Lou Perlof; Editor and Production Manager: George M. Merrick; Set Dresser: Glenn T. Thompson; Musical Score: Lee Zahler; Sound: Ben Winkler; Running Time: 58 Minutes; Released: September 10, 1943

CAST: Frank Buck (Frank Buck); June Duprez (Linda MacCardle); Duncan Renaldo (Peter Jeremy); Howard Banks (Tom Clayton); J. Farrell MacDonald (Geoffrey MacCardle); Arno Frey (Dr. Lang); Dan Seymour (Henry Gratz); J. Alex Havier (Ali); Pedro Regas (Takko)

REVENGE OF THE ZOMBIES
(Monogram Pictures Corp.)

The wartime propaganda films of other nations, whether Allied or Axisfied, tend to emphasize the noble bravery of the native-born fighting man and foster solidarity among the populace. The American approach, conversely, is to ridicule and/or exaggerate (the fashionable word today would be *demonize*) the evils of the enemy. The Disney machine gave a literal razzing to the Third Reich in a Donald Duck cartoon, "Der Fuehrer's Face," and the Three Stooges—profoundly *Yiddishe* intellects, masquerading as buffoons—portrayed the leading lights of the Third Reich as the ultimate in stoogery.

Monogram took just as extreme an avenue of attack: The studio's Axis-buster films are distinctively horrific in their slow-burn way, more a simmer than a rolling boil. *Revenge*

James Baskett, Walt Disney's Uncle Remus-in-waiting, summons the title creatures of *Revenge of the Zombies*.

of the Zombies, going somewhat beyond a retread of Monogram's *King of the Zombies* (see *Forgotten Horrors 2*), plants a Nazi scientist (John Carradine) in an isolated Louisiana bayou-country outpost, where he intends to perfect the creation of living-dead servants for the sake of giving Germany "an army that will not need to be fed—that cannot be stopped by bullets."

This elaboration upon *King of the Zombies*, whose tale unfolds in the West Indies, not only suggests the tainting of hallowed American soil by perverse Nazi science but also finds Carradine experimenting upon his own wife (the struggling but still game Veda Ann Borg) in the service of the Reich. Call it *Weiss Zombie*.

John Carradine portrays as cold-hearted a *Seig-Heiler* as ever crossed the screen, a surly menace so dedicated to world domination that he would sacrifice one of the most magnificently beautiful women in Hollywood to the cause. It helps to remember that director Steve Sekely (born Istvan Szekely in Budapest) was a recent fugitive from the Third Reich; his leisurely pacing here suggests a brooding anger that lends metaphorical weight to the supernatural premise. Plain shock value would not serve.

The crucial twist—which has made *Revenge of the Zombies* a surprising favorite in the more culturally well-attuned sectors of the feminist movement—is that Veda Ann Borg resists the hoodoo brainwashing: Though quite dead despite an unnatural mobility, the abused wife retains enough defiance to plot Carradine's downfall. To his further inconvenience, Carradine finds himself playing host to his unwelcome brother-in-law (Mauritz Hugo), a family friend (Robert Lowery), and their chauffeur (Mantan Moreland, Old Hollywood's most energetic comedian). The doctor seems to have an ally in a visiting Nazi agent (played by Bob Steele, the Western star and all-'round character man), who briefly pretends to be a Southern sheriff and finally proves to be an FBI investigator. Steele make a convincing enough show of loyalty to the Axis, but once he changes into frontiersman attire and announces, "I'd better start by givin' this Heinie the once-over," the audience can pretty well conclude that he's no genuine goose-stepper.

Mantan Moreland, that venerable Chitlin' Circuit entertainer, leaves the film's most lasting impression—despite his having less crucial a role than in 1941's *King of the Zombies*. A Moreland performance in *any* movie is an all-but-pure distillation of mid-century black show business, but Monogram allowed him the freest rein: The little studio's production values are a cut above those of the black independent studios where Moreland often worked, and so the cameras and microphones capture more of his exuberance and his nuanced delivery of ad-libbed remarks. At the bigger studios, Moreland received less prominent billing and was too often encouraged to soft-pedal his gift of gab. In *Revenge of the Zombies*, he marks time with an improvised soft-shoe routine, woos one of Carradine's servants (Sybil Lewis) with irrepressible jive talk,

and fires off some inspired patter. Upon hearing a disembodied voice moaning, "Where am I?" Moreland answers, "I don't know where *you*['re] at, but 30 seconds from now, I'm gonna be 'leven miles *away* from here!" Elsewhere, he reports the discovery of a murder victim who has been "shot long, deep, wide and con*sec*utive!"

Moreland has been unfairly dismissed as an Uncle Tom within some fashionable sectors of the black intellectual bourgeoisie. Nowhere do his characters resort to the stereotype of the terrified or cringing servant. And the servant roles he plays, in keeping with the economic and social realities of the period, are hardly deferential. His recurring role of Birmingham Brown, in the Monogram *Charlie Chan* series, is more a fellow sleuth than a hired hand. Nor does Moreland indulge in unreasoning superstition: He exhibits, rather, the pragmatic wisdom to believe what his eyes and ears tell him. Like anyone else with the good gumption to duck out on a threatening situation, Moreland's characters are more indignant than scared in the face of trouble, and resourceful enough to fight or make a run for it as circumstances demand. Moreland is a national treasure, as distinctively fine a comic artist as Bob Hope, Charles Chaplin and W.C. Fields, and it is high time to look past the color bar that has long compromised a popular appreciation of the man.

But we digress. So what else is new? Among the supporting players in *Revenge of the Zombies*, the future TV-sitcom star and pop recording artist Gale Storm appears too lively for the surroundings as Carradine's innocent dim-bulb secretary. Robert Lowery makes a dashing enough hero, although he requires Moreland's help to get out of one hairy scrape. The distinguished black players Mme. Sul-Te-Wan and James Baskett (soon to play Uncle Remus in Disney's *Song of the South*) stand out among the servants who are just biding their time until they can help the movie live up to its title.

CREDITS: Producer: Lindsley Parsons; Director: Steve Sekely; Dialogue Director: Jack Linder; Screenplay: Edmond Kelso and Van Norcross; Photographed by: Mack Stengler; Technical Director: David Milton; Editor: Richard Currier; Musical Director: Edward Kay; Sound: Glen Glenn; Production Manager: Dick L'Estrange; Running Time: 61 Minutes; Released: Sept. 17, 1943

CAST: John Carradine (Dr. von Altermann); Gale Storm (Jennifer Rand); Robert Lowery (Larry Adams); Bob Steele (Agent); Mantan Moreland (Jeff); Veda Ann Borg (Lila von Altermann); Barry McCollum (Dr. Harvey Keating);

Mauritz Hugo (Scott Warrington); Mme. Sul-Te-Wan (Beulah); James Baskett (Lazarus); Sybil Lewis (Rosella); Robert Cherry (Pete)

A SCREAM IN THE DARK
(Republic Pictures Corp.)

Serial murder gets played for macabre wit in this quick-sketch entry from George Sherman. The approach is to present the atrocities with a straight and sinister face, and then let those in the culprits' orbit react to humorous effect. It doesn't always work, and oftentimes the comedy is forced and overobvious. But Sherman keeps the suspense cranked, and there is a pervasive weirdness in Elizabeth Russell's portrayal of an often-bereaved marrying woman who collects on one insurance policy too many.

Sudden death seems to dog Miss Russell's tracks, but it takes an amateur sleuth (Robert Lowery) to spot the obvious and out-perform the police in putting paid to the mayhem. Miss Russell and her accomplices (Frank Fenton and Hobart Cavanaugh) cunningly manage to deflect suspicion onto the one spouse who had escaped her clutches via the simple expedient of divorce. The weapon of choice is an umbrella equipped with a dagger-point, brandished with a formidable accuracy. A subplot involving a headless female corpse establishes abundant reason for the culprits to meet a ghastly end.

Lowery, a former big-band crooner and future chapter-play Batman, is almost boyishly impetuous as the newspaperman-turned-private eye. Edward Brophy contributes dandy support and the film's most engagingly humorous presence as Lowery's no-nonsense assistant. Jack LaRue, as a police captain, is suitably impatient with Lowery's know-it-all sleuthery. Wally Vernon is a hoot as a sardonic attendant at the morgue. Marie McDonald is as lovely and capable as ever as Lowery's sweetheart.

CREDITS: Associate Producer and Director: George Sherman; Screenplay: Gerald Schnitzer and Anthony Coldewey; Based upon: Jerome Odlum's Novel, *The Morgue Is Always Open*; Photographed by: Reggie Lanning; Art Director: Russell Kimball; Assistant Directors: Art Siteman and R.G. Springsteen; Editor: Arthur Roberts; Set Decorator: Otto Siegel; Wardrobe: Adele Palmer; Musical Director: Morton Scott; Sound: Tom Carman; Running Time: 55 Minutes; Released: October 15, 1943

CAST: Robert Lowery (Mike Brooker); Marie MacDonald (Joan Allen); Edward S. Brophy (Eddie Tough); Wally Vernon

(Clousky); Hobart Cavanaugh (Leo Starke); Jack LaRue (Cross); Elizabeth Russell (Muriel); Frank Fenton (Sam Lackey); William Haade (Gerald Messenger); Linda Brent (Stella); Arthur Loft (Norton); Kitty McHugh (Maisie); Charles Wilson (Editor); Jack Rice (Desk Clerk); Mike Jeffries (Cop)

UNKNOWN GUEST
(K-B Productions, Inc./Monogram Pictures Corp.)

A prodigal's return to something less than an enthusiastic welcome provides the edgy set-up for this suspenseful shaggy-dog story from Kurt Neumann. Gaunt Victor Jory carries the piece as a vagabond named Chuck Williams. On the run from the mob after he has witnessed a gangland hit, Chuck reunites with his aunt and uncle (Nora Cecil and Lee "Lasses" White) at their rustic tavern, which they are about to vacate for the off-season. The kinfolks, though estranged from their nephew and well known to be anything but generous, apparently leave Chuck in charge, and he runs the place as though it were his own—finding romance with a waitress (Pamela Blake) in the process.

But a string of coincidences and circumstantial incriminations raises the possibility that Chuck has done away with his relatives—maybe even buried them on the premises. The police are closing in, and even Chuck's new sweetheart seems convinced of his guilt. Two mysterious lodgers are racketeers who intend to kill Chuck, but he proves to be an elusive and dangerous quarry. The presumed victims return home just in time to set the record straight, and Chuck and his new sweetheart can count on a cozy finale.

Here is a story of the sort that would find its truer home in years to come with such popular teleseries as *Alfred Hitchcock Presents* and *Armstrong Circle Theatre*. Such yarns proliferated in the day of dramatized radio and the big-screen double bill, and *Guest*'s rediscovery today by the home-video audience is a godsend for movie buffs who believe that the average running time for a feature film—100 to 120 minutes, at last count—has escalated out of all reasonable control. A similarly slight, macabre yarn, in fact, would stand a good chance today of being overinflated to mock-epic proportions: Witness both *Addams Family* features and the no less morbid *My Girl* comedies. Richard Condon's mob novel *Prizzi's Honor*, as filmed in 1985 by John Huston, is essentially just a tall tale of this very sort, a grisly joke that meanders through two hours in search of a measly lone punchline.

So *Unknown Guest* takes the palm merely for saying what little it has to say and shutting up before boredom can set in. Victor Jory is precisely right for the role of the wrongly accused nephew: He looks and acts guilty as all get-out, to start with, and his every attempt to shed his black-sheep-of-the-family image seems to backfire. Perky Pamela Blake makes for a fine ironic contrast with Jory's saturnine appearance, although Jory should have his head examined for passing over supporting player Veda Ann Borg in favor of Miss Blake; of course, Jory does so because Miss Borg proves too treacherous a big-city girlfriend for his tastes. Dimitri Tiomkin's musical score contributes mightily to the grim whimsy of the telling, serving the now-romantic, now-darkening aspects with a playful authority.

As the miserly aunt and uncle, Nora Cecil and comedian Lee "Lasses" White seem every bit the sort to deserve killing and planting down-cellar. Everything and everybody must turn out for the better, however, including these old crabapples.

Lee White had long been a popular white-guy entertainer feigning Negritude in the blackface minstrel tradition, both as a solo and with Lee David "Honey" Wilds in a comedy act called Honey & Lasses. White had ended a seven-year hitch with Nashville's Grand Ole Opry in 1939, following a stint in Hollywood with Wilds and a singing colleague, Chill Wills. White and Wills remained in the film capital, each to forge a distinctive new career, while Wilds returned to the Opry and formed a new laughmaking partnership. White found a berth at length as one of the more popular comical-geezer sidekicks in the matinee Western tradition, capable of appearing significantly beyond his calendar years—only to run afoul of age discrimination when Monogram Pictures retired him prematurely in favor of more youthful supporting players. White died at 61 in 1949.

Kurt Neumann was already a seasoned hand at directing by the time of *Unknown Guest*, with credentials dating from the silent-screen years. He delivered almost uniformly capable, occasionally brilliant, work in all genres, showing a preference for adventure and mystery. Neumann's signature film, however, lay 15 years into the future: 1958's *The Fly*. The producers of *Unknown Guest* and the slightly earlier *I Escaped the Gestapo*, brothers Maurice and Franklin King, would prove to exert a tremendous influence over the long term upon the gradually escalating quality of Monogram's output.

CREDITS: Producer: Maurice King; Associate Producer: Franklin King; Director: Kurt Neumann; Dialogue Director: Edward E. Kaye; Screenplay: Philip

Yordan; Photographed by: Jackson Rose; Art Directors: Neli McGuire and Dave Milton; Assistant Directors: Clarence Bricker and Herman King; Editor: Martin G. Cohn; Set Dresser: Tommy Thompson; Musical Score: Dimitri Tiomkin; Musical Supervisor: David Chudnow; Sound: Glen Glenn; Production Manager: George Moskov; Running Time: 64 Minutes; Released: October 22, 1943

CAST: Victor Jory (Chuck Williams); Pamela Blake (Julie); Veda Ann Borg (Helen Walker); Harry Hayden (George Nadroy); Paul Fix (Fain); Emory Parnell (Sheriff Dave Larsen); Ray Walker (Swarthy); Lee "Lasses" White (Joe Williams); Nora Cecil (Martha Williams); Edwin Mills (Sidney)

THE MYSTERY OF THE THIRTEENTH GUEST
a.k.a.: THE MYSTERY OF THE 13TH GUEST
(Monogram Pictures Corp.)

Apart from padding out the title with *The Mystery of*, this desultory remake of the first-generation Monogram's *The Thirteenth Guest* (see *Forgotten Horrors: The Definitive Edition*) brings little new to the table. Most crucially, the reconstituted version lacks the rambunctious nihilism of the 1933 original. The source-film had long since been reissued, the better to capitalize upon the mounting popularity of its once-unknown star player, Ginger Rogers, and a fresh reissue on this occasion might have better served all parties concerned.

Helen Parrish assumes Miss Rogers' role as the endangered heiress who must learn the identity of a mysterious guest who never showed up for an accursed, long-ago banquet. This absentee miscreant has now begun systematically

to destroy the surviving members of Miss Parrish's family—and her turn is coming right up. The killings are nowhere near as shocking this time out; in the years between the free-wheelingly violent original film and this pallid remake, a mighty force of institutionalized censorship had sunk its hooks into the film industry.

Picking up the Lyle Talbot role of a maverick private investigator is Dick Purcell, whose heart isn't quite in it. The requisite romantic chemistry never sizzles between Purcell and Miss Parrish, and it falls to Frank Faylen—taking up the moronic cop role that Paul Hurst had done so much with—to supply the remake with what entertainment value he can muster. William Beaudine's directing style is so bland as to neutralize even the traces of horror left over from the original.

CREDITS: Producer: Lindsley Parsons; Associate Producer: Charles J. Bigelow; Director: William Beaudine; Screenplay: Tim Ryan, Charles R. Marion and Arthur Hoerl; Based upon: Armitage Trail's Novel, *The Thirteenth Guest*; Photographed by: Mack Stengler; Technical Director: Dave Milton; Assistant Director: Eddie Davis; Editors: Carl Pierson and Dick Currier; Musical Director: Edward Kay; Sound: Glen Glenn; Production Manager: William Strobach; Running Time: 61 Minutes; Released: November 5, 1943

CAST: Helen Parrish (Marie Morgan); Dick Purcell (Johnny Smith); Tim Ryan (Lt. Burke); Frank Faylen (Speed Dugan); Jacqueline Dalya (Marjorie Morgan); Paul McVey (Adam Morgan); John Duncan (Harold Morgan); John Dawson (Tom Jackson); Cyril Ring (Barksdale); Addison Richards (District Attorney); Lloyd Ingraham (Grandfather Morgan)

MYSTERY BROADCAST
(Republic Pictures Corp.)

George Sherman was on a roll in 1943, and *Mystery Broadcast* holds up as one of his better efforts of an extremely enterprising slate. This one finds the busy producer-director still milking the amateur-sleuth angle, but here he avoids the droll humor that had veered out of his control on *A Scream in the Dark* and concentrates instead upon a mixture of romance, professional rivalries and grisly old secrets better left alone.

Pert Ruth Terry plays Jan Cornell, the author of a radio serial whose gimmick is unsolved crimes. The documentary program is losing its audience fast, and so Jan gets too creative for her own good: She makes up semi-plausible resolutions, and the broadcast catches its second wind. One show, however, comes so near the truth that a new wave of murder commences. The spunky scriptwriter digs in and beats the law to a real case-closer.

There is nothing particularly mysterious about *Mystery Broadcast*, but the sense of danger is palpable, and Miss Terry takes the leading role seriously enough to match the movie's more populous ranks of masculine crimebusters at their game. Frank Albertson is rather a token leading man, playing a rival program writer who is as sweet on Miss Terry as he is keen to compete with her in the ratings. Alice Fleming scores as a radio actress who may know 'way too much about a long-ago murder case. Future Superman Kirk Alyn has a bit as a greenhorn cop. The hustle-and-bustle of radio-studio activity is true to life, with many facets of production covered in the course of deploying the plot.

The real surprise of *Mystery Broadcast* is a return to a brooding romantic presence for the Swedish-born Nils Asther. Asther had been largely inactive since a stay in England, where he made *Abdul the Damned* (1935), and his return to Hollywood had found him taking on a handful of character assignments (including 1942's *Night Monster*) that scarcely echoed his better days as a suave and mysterious leading man in the bigger leagues. His work here, as a studio-orchestra conductor caught up in an affair with the wife (Wynne Gibson) of a patron, echoes the sinister forcefulness Asther had shown in Frank Capra's *The Bitter Tea of General Yen* (1933) and Universal's wonderful *The Love Captive* (1934). Asther followed through impressively with a manipulative lawman role in *Bluebeard* and the commanding lead in *The Man in Half Moon Street*, but eventually returned to Sweden.

CREDITS: Associate Producer and Director: George Sherman; Screenplay: Dane Lussier; Additional Dialogue: Gertrude Walker; Photographed by: William Bradford; Art Director: Russell Kimball; Assistant Director: Kenneth Holmes; Editor: Arthur Roberts; Set Decorator: Otto Siegel; Musical Director: Morton Scott; Sound: Tom Carman; Running Time: 63 Minutes; Released: November 23, 1943

CAST: Frank Albertson (Michael Jerome); Ruth Terry (Jan Cornell); Nils Asther (Ricky Moreno); Wynne Gibson (Eve Stanley); Paul Harvey (A.J. Stanley); Mary Treen (Smitty); Addison Richards (Bill Burton); Joseph Crehan (Chief Daniels); Alice Fleming (Mida Kent); Francis Pierlot (Crunch); Ken Carpenter (Announcer); Emmett Vogan (Don Fletcher); Cecil Weston (Carrie); Maxine Doyle (Operator); Larry Stewart (Associate Producer); George Byron (Actor); Jack Gardner (Technician); Walter Tetley (Studio Page); Ernie Adams (Scriptwriter); Edna Harris (Waitress); Kirk Alyn (Rookie)

WHISPERING FOOTSTEPS
(Republic Pictures Corp.)

The predator at large in *Whispering Footsteps* is known as "the Studious Strangler," on account of a preference for egghead college-coed victims. The point of Gertrude Walker's story is less to follow some thrilling pageant of murders, than it is to consider the dehumanizing effects of gossip and ostracism. Director Howard Bretherton honors that higher-minded intention while still generating a respectable lot of suspense.

In Medallion, Ohio, bank teller Marcus Aurelius Borne (John Hubbard) is known to have been on holiday around Cambridge, Indiana, at the time of the latest such slaying there. Fellow boarders at Mrs. Murphy's (Mary Gordon) rooming-house want to hear the scoop on the crime, but the timid Marcus knows nothing that would satisfy his friends' curiosity. Marcus finds himself followed by an investigator (Cy Kendall), who perceives a resemblance to a police sketch of the supposed killer. The local cops scoff at this presumption, declaring that no one so mousy could be a killer. But the interrogation has thrown the roomers into a tizzy, and to get away from their yammering Marcus goes for a stroll with pretty Helene LaSalle (Joan Blair), a new merchant in town.

Miss LaSalle, like Marcus, is scornful of the town's hypocrites, but even so she hasn't the gumption to resist the lustful attentions of the biggest bigshot hypocrite of them all, banker Harry Hammond (Charles Halton). Marcus agrees to meet with Hammond's daughter, Brooke (Rita Quigley), to discuss the matter, but he dozes off and stands her up. That night, the strangler strikes closer to home, and Marcus becomes a suspect without an alibi. Though worried about his own problems, Marcus consents to ask Helene to stop carrying on with his boss; she defies him. Helene, however, gives Marcus an alibi after yet another slaying takes place. Helene is next to die, and Brooke provides the alibi this time.

Marcus, tormented by scandalous hearsay and self-doubt, begins to wonder whether he might actually be the killer. Finally, however, he understands that his so-called friends have all but convicted him with their mean-spirited nature. He angrily confronts the lot of them and prepares to move away. Just then, Marcus tunes in a news report of the real strangler's capture. Though vindicated, he follows through with his escape from this sorry little hick town.

Serial murder strikes ever closer to home as the tale progresses, but the tightly focused screenplay never veers from the troubled orbit of John Hubbard. His doubts become the viewer's doubts, and his late-dawning determination to speak up for himself is as exhilarating a moment as any murderous encounter could have been. Even so, the tragic case of Joan Blair's Helene LaSalle

FOX STATE

Tuesday - Wednesday
BIG SPANISH SHOW
"TRES HERMANOS"
ALSO
'Whispering Footsteps'

HURRY! IT ENDS
TONIGHT
"NORTHWEST PASSAGE"
ALSO
"Youngest Profession"

comes as a bewildering shock. This complicated backup character emerges as a sympathetic presence with troublesome qualities: She treats Hubbard's unassertive character with kindness and harbors all the right resentments toward the backbiting townsfolk, but she also pursues an illicit romance without heed for its hurtful consequences. Rita Quigley is just as impressive as an entirely good girl—even though she stretches the truth to supply a strategic alibi—who finds herself attracted to Hubbard despite her blowhard daddy's orders.

The denizens of the boardinghouse—from *Sherlock Holmes* series regular Mary Gordon as the mother hen-in-residence to snoopy Matt McHugh and snoopier Marie Blake—are the most loathsome of all, passive voyeurs who derive a palpable thrill from ruining a fellow citizen's reputation for the sake of idle scuttlebutt. An old favorite groaner springs to mind here: "Why did the landlady burn down her boardinghouse?" And the answer? "To get rid of all those ugly roomers."

Howard Bretherton (1896-1969) was a silent-era veteran who also became a favorite editor of directors including William Wellman, for whom he cut the aftermath-of-war drama *Heroes for Sale* in 1933. Bretherton's many assignments include the *Hopalong Cassidy* series classic, *The Eagle's Brood* (1935); the Frankie Darro–Mantan Moreland crime-comedy *Irish Luck*; the rousing serial *The Monster and the Ape* (1945); and a late-in-the-game *Charlie Chan* misfire, *The Trap* (1946).

CREDITS: Producer: George Blair; Director: Howard Bretherton; Screenplay: Gertrude Walker (from Her Story) and Dane Lussier; Photographed by: Jack Marta; Art Director: Russell Kimball; Assistant Director: Joe Dill; Editor: Ralph Dixon; Set Decorator: Otto Siegel; Wardrobe: Adele Palmer; Musical Director: Morton Scott; Running Time: 60 Minutes; Released: December 30, 1943

CAST: John Hubbard (Marcus Aurelius Borne); Rita Quigley (Brooke Hammond); Joan Blair (Helene LaSalle); Charles Halton (Harry Hammond); Cy Kendall (Brad Dolan); Juanita Quigley (Rosie Murphy); Mary Gordon (Mrs. Murphy); Billy Benedict (Jerry Murphy); Matt McHugh (Cy Walsh); Marie Blake (Sally Lukens); Dick Elliott (John Charters); Elizabeth Valentine (Aunt Jennie); Madeline Grey (Daphne Hammond); Horace Carpenter (Farmer); Charles Williams (Townsman); Norman Nesbitt (Newscaster)

1944

PRIDE OF THE PLAINS
(Republic Pictures Corp.)

The *John Paul Revere* series had started out with 1943's *Beyond the Last Frontier*, with Eddie Dew in the leading role. The better-known Bob Livingston took up the starring duties with this third entry, which turns upon the troubling pivot of a man-killing horse. *Pride of the Plains* is a remake of the Depression-era jewel *Hit the Saddle* (see *Forgotten Horrors 2*), another starrer for Livingston as the first-among-equals of Republic's Three Mesquiteers team. Though somewhat less ferocious, the revamp packs its own offbeat charms.

The menacing creature here bears the ominous name of Black Cloud. Although the steed has been trained mainly to provoke wild-horse stampedes—the better to urge the repeal of animal-protection laws—a crooked plainsman named Hurley (Kenneth MacDonald) and a cohort, Bowman (champ stuntman Yakima Canutt), also figure that a good trampling now and again will serve their underhanded schemes quite well. The plan calls for restoring open season on wild horses, so that Hurley can find it easier to slaughter them for the dog-food market.

Conservationist Jasper Darwin (reliable Budd Buster), who has opposed Hurley, is the first to die. Game Commissioner Johnny Revere (Livingston) and his animal-doctor sidekick, Frog Millhouse (Smiley Burnette), arrive just in time to catch two of Hurley's thugs (Kenne Duncan and Bud Geary) up to no good. Hurley's veneer of respectability begins to slip as Johnny deputizes a majority of the citizens. A prominent rancher (Charles Miller) becomes the next victim, and Black Cloud's dirty work is blamed on a wild stallion. Revere's brother, Kenny (Stephen Barclay), is all set to lead a posse against the wild horses, but Johnny proves that the killer is a domesticated animal. When finally the thieves fall out, Black Cloud winds up killing Hurley.

The villains are a fine menacing lot, with a tense alpha-male rivalry between Kenneth MacDonald, as the big-time schemer, and the imposing Yakima Canutt, as the guy who knows the command that will set loose the demon in the horse. There is also a dramatically satisfying tension between

Livingston and Stephen Barclay, as brothers divided on the horse-protection issue, and the pro-conservation argument is quite ahead of its time. Most progressive of all is comedian Smiley Burnette's portrayal of a natural-born horse whisperer—a concept as old as the hills, but unusual in a Hollywood picture. This notion of an almost spiritual communion between man and beast would account for a well-received picture of 1998, starring Robert Redford.

CREDITS: Associate Producer: Louis Gray; Director: Wallace Fox; Adapted Screenplay: John K. Butler and Bob Williams; From Oliver Drake's Screenplay for *Hit the Saddle* and a Story by: Oliver Drake and Maurice Geraghty; Photographed by: John MacBurnie; Assistant Director: Art Siteman; Art Director: Fred Ritter; Editor: Charles Craft; Set Décor: Charles Thompson; Music: Mort Glickman; Sound: Fred Stahl; Running Time: 56 Minutes; Released: January 5, 1944 (Prematurely Shown in Los Angeles on November 25, 1943)

CAST: Robert "Bob" Livingston (John Paul "Johnny" Revere); Smiley Burnette (Frog Millhouse); Nancy Gay (Joan Bradford); Stephen Barclay (Kenny Revere); Kenneth MacDonald (Hurley); Charles Miller (Grant Bradford); Kenne Duncan (Snyder); Jack Kirk (Steve Craig); Bud Geary (Gerard); Yakima Canutt (Bowman); Budd Buster (Jasper Darwin); Bud Osborne (Guard)

WOMEN IN BONDAGE
a.k.a.: HITLER'S WOMEN
(Herman Millakowsky Productions for Monogram Productions, Inc./ Monogram Pictures Corp.)

The clash of imperatives between a high-minded artistic team and a hell-bent-for-box office studio has seldom been so pronounced as in the case of Herman Millakowski's passionately felt production of *Hitler's Women*, an intimate piece of near-epic scope and resonance despite its modest trappings. Millakowski, an accomplished German producer seeking more democratic pastures as a fugitive from the Third Reich, was appalled to find his title changed to *Women in Bondage* on the point of release. More insulting yet was this declaration from *Variety*: "Monogram has a

valuable exploitation picture in *Women in Bondage* and wisely is rushing it into distribution."

And yet—how better to get a sobering indictment of the queasy evils of Hitlerism seen by a thrill-hungry massed audience? It helped the picture's commercial prospects that Frank Bentick Wisbar's original story dwelt upon the voyeuristic perversions of Nazi eugenics, which is a $25 word for good breeding gone bad; and that key players Gail Patrick, Anne Nagel, H.B. Warner, Gertrude Michael and Nancy Kelly all packed a name-brand appeal. The social-issue agenda was helped along, too, by an additional reel's running time beyond the customary length of a Monogram picture (which added not only to the budget but also to the rate of taxation), and by a finer technical gloss than Monogram usually allowed. The customers as a class, of course, could scarcely have cared less that Millakowski, Wisbar and director Steve Sekely had quit Germany before that warlike nation could count them among Hitler's so-called Jewish Problem.

And never mind that the title, *Women in Bondage*, sounds more like something for the adults-only trade. No one drawn by the prospect of a forbidden jolt, however, can have come away disappointed, for Miss Patrick's circumstances are lurid, indeed—and Nancy Kelly's are yet more so. We often speak of that delicate balance between the Cinema of Ideas and the Cinema of Sensationalism, but we seldom find it struck with such authority.

Margot Bracken (Miss Patrick), wife of a German officer stranded with the Reich's fool's-errand Russian Campaign, settles in with her in-laws at the family estate, Brackenfield, and finds herself appointed in charge of a Hitler Youth faction for girls. Among these conscriptées is a servant, Toni Hall (Nancy Kelly), who is in love with S.S. Cpl. Heinz Radtke (Bill Henry). Rejected as marrying material by the Powers That Be because her near-sightedness might mean a genetic deficiency, Toni denounces the Third Reich and finds herself imprisoned. She escapes, only to be gunned down while attempting to reach Radtke.

Gertrude Schneider (Gertrude Michael), the district leader, orders Margot examined for child-bearing fitness. Margot passes muster, but then her husband, Ernst Bracken (Roland Varno), returns home from the front—a paralytic wreck. Gertrude orders Margot's impregnation by Ernst's brother (Alan Baxter). Ernst kills himself. Margot, fed up with the cause, defies a blackout and lights the way for an Allied raid. As the bombs rain down upon Brackenfield, Margot takes solace in the prospect of liberation for the damaged women of Europe.

Producer Millakowsky told *The Hollywood Reporter* that he had drawn factual material for *Hitler's Women*—he would continue to call the film by this title even after its formal rechristening—from observations made at first hand. Houston Branch's shooting script appears to be a faithful representation of Wisbar's original scenario. Director Sekely employs a straightforward approach, achieving a naturalistic you-are-there quality that allows the anger of the material abundant room to seethe. Gail Patrick makes a stalwart heroine-in-a-huff, and H.B. Warner is particularly strong as a priest who takes a lonely stand against the Nazis. Gertrude Michael gives her cold-eyed character just the right shadings of deviance-with-impunity.

CREDITS: Executive Producer: Trem Carr; Producer: Herman Millakowsky; Associate Producer: Jeffrey Bernerd; Director: Steve Sekely; Assistant Director: William Strobach; Second Assistant Director: Eddie Davis; Dialogue Director: Harold Erickson; Original Scenarist and Technical Adviser: Frank Wisbar; Screenplay: Houston Branch; Photographed by: Mack Stengler; Art Director: Dave Milton; Editor: Richard Currier; Décor: Al Greenwood; Music: Edward Kay; Sound: Tom Lambert; Running Time: 72 Minutes; Released as *Women in Bondage*: January 10, 1944, Following Previews as *Hitler's Women*

CAST: Gail Patrick (Margot Bracken); Nancy Kelly (Toni Hall); Bill Henry (Cpl. Heinz Radtke); Tala Birell (Ruth Bracken); Gertrude Michael (Gertrude Schneider); Alan Baxter (Otto Bracken); Maris Wrixon (Grete Zeigler); Rita Quigley (Herta Ruman); Felix Basch (Dr. Mensch); H.B. Warner (Pastor Renz); Anne Nagel (Deputy); Mary Forbes (Gladys Bracken); Frederic Brunn (District Leader); Roland Varno (Ernst Bracken); Ralph Linn (Cpl. Mueller); Francine Bordeaux (Litzi); Aune Franks (Blonde)

CHARLIE CHAN ON POVERTY ROW

Charlie Chan, novelist Earl Derr Biggers' genial and relentless homicide detective, had served long and well as a ticket-selling personality at 20th Century-Fox, but all good things must come to an end. The *Charlie Chan* series lapsed, belatedly, from Fox to Monogram with 1944's *Charlie Chan in the Secret Service*, which—despite the continuing presence of Sidney Toler in the title role—represents a steep drop in quality as well as in continuity. Production values are scarcely everything, but Fox's high-gloss budget-picture unit had so accustomed the customers to a finely wrought, atmospheric treatment that the shift to Monogram's rawboned style can only have come as a disappointment. Where Fox *had* a B outfit, Monogram *was* its own B outfit.

For us unapologetic fans, however, the only bad *Charlie Chan* is no *Charlie Chan*, and *Charlie Chan in the Secret*

> Some of the series turned out to be enormously profitable. Production costs were minimal. Sets were used over and over. No expensive salaries were needed because the actors were [for the most part] contract players. Moreover, a good number of the pictures... were based on already popular fictional characters. And so they were pre-sold. [But] after concentrating their efforts on the opener, many producers allowed their product to deteriorate... [and] audiences dwindled. Television provided the coup de grace.—David Zinman, *Saturday Afternoon at the Bijou*; 1973

Service demonstrates that Monogram and veteran suspense director Phil Rosen came prepared to compensate in other ways. The story is classically weird, even science-fictional, having to do with government agent Chan's investigation of the murder of an inventor, and his search for a stolen cache of documents. Benson Fong makes a suitably overeager son to the great detective, and—in what many followers consider the saving grace of the Monogram *Chans*—Mantan Moreland brings wit and energy to the recurring role of Chan's wisecracking cohort, Birmingham Brown. Toler resumes his stride gracefully from Fox's *Castle in the Desert* (1942).

As the treadmill turns, there comes a significant lapse of time between Toler's death and the arrival of Roland Winters. Although Winters makes a perfectly okay Chan, the series grows to feel ever more desultory until it rallies for the rousing penultimate adventures of *The Golden Eye* and *The Feathered Serpent*—only to stumble again with *The Sky Dragon*.

A Cine McNuggets rundown on the Monogram *Chans* follows herewith, spanning 1944-49:

Charlie Chan in the Secret Service (1944): The *Chan* series was a life sentence—gratefully accepted—for, first, Warner Oland and, then, Sidney Toler. Toler, who had assumed the role upon Oland's death in 1938, at length purchased the movie rights from the Biggers estate, thus seeing to it that he would continue to star as Charlie Chan; the strategy was halted only by Toler's own death in 1947. This creaky but earnest new beginning involves the murder of an inventor and the theft of a device designed to combat U-boats. Phil Rosen directs with more of an ear for dialogue than an eye for action, and the story unfolds for the most part inside the mansion of the victim, lending a claustrophobic quality that places *Secret Service* squarely in the old-dark-house tradition.

CREDITS: Producers: Phillip N. Krasne and James S. Burkett; Director: Phil Rosen; Story: George Callahan; Photographed by: Ira Morgan; Editor: Marty Cohen; Assistant Director: George Moskov; Running Time: 65 Minutes; Released: February 14, 1944

CAST: Sidney Toler (Charlie Chan); Gwen Kenyon (Inez); Mantan Moreland (Birmingham Brown); Marianne Quon (Iris); Arthur Loft (Jones); Lelah Tyler (Mrs. Winters); Benson Fong (Tommy Chan); Gene Stutenroth (Vega); Eddie Chandler (Lewis)

The Chinese Cat **(1944):** An epidemic lust for diamonds provokes an outbreak of murder in this law-baffling locked-room mystery. Extensive on-location shooting in an authentic carnival-midway fun house lends an intriguing subtext and enhances the excitement, which frankly needs all the help it can get. The atmosphere and the spoken word again prevail over any acts of violence or heroism, thanks to an immersion in character by both Sidney Toler and Mantan Moreland. As Chan might phrase it: Owner of monogrammed dagger, carelessly deployed, is murderer.

CREDITS: Producers: Philip N. Krasne and James S. Burkett; Director: Phil Rosen; Screenplay: George Callahan; Photographed by: Ira Morgan; Assistant Director: Bobby Ray; Art Director: Dave Milton; Editors: Fred Allen and Martin Cohn; Décor: Tommy Thompson; Musical Supervisor: David Chudnow: Musical Score: Alexander Laszlo; Sound: Tom Lambert; Production Manager: Dick L'Estrange; Running Time: 65 Minutes; Released: May 20, 1944

CAST: Sidney Toler (Charlie Chan); Mantan Moreland (Birmingham Brown); Joan Woodbury (Leah Manning); Benson Fong (Tommy Chan); Cy Kendall (Webster Deacon); Weldon Heyburn (Harvey Dennis); Anthony Ward (Catlen); John Davidson (Carl Kazdas and Kurt Kazdas); Dewey Robinson (Salos); Betty Blythe (Mrs. Manning); and Ian Keith, Stan Jolley, Jack Norton, Luke Chan, Sam Flint

Black Magic **a.k.a.:** ***Meeting at Midnight*** **(1944):** A more impressively entertaining entry pivots upon a reassuring element of friendship between Moreland's Birmingham Brown and Frances Chan, as Charlie's daughter. Plotwise, it's just a matter of the old-standby fake-seance scam, dusted off for another overworking. The murder weapon is a grisly bullet, fashioned from frozen blood. (One foreign-market alternate title is *La Bala de Sangre*, which translates as *The Bullet of*

Blood.) The reissue title, *Meeting at Midnight*, represented an attempt to avoid confusion with Gregory Ratoff's *Black Magic* (1949), starring Orson Welles.

CREDITS: Producers: Philip N. Krasne and James S. Burkett; Director: Phil Rosen; Screenplay: George Callahan; Photographed by: Arthur Martinelli; Assistant Director: Bobby Ray; Operative Cameraman: Dave Smith; Assistant Camera Operator: Monty Steadman; Gaffer: Joseph Wharton; Stills: Earl Crowley; Special Effects: M.B. Kinne; Art Director: Dave Milton; Editor: John Link; Décor: Al Greenwood; Props: Samuel Gordon and Ralph Martin; Wardrobe: Harry Bourne; Musical Director: David Chudnow; Musical Score: Alexander Laszlo; Sound: Max Hutchinson; Production Manager: Dick L'Estrange; Script Clerk: Marie Messinger; Grips: Lew Dow and George Booker; Running Time: 67 Minutes; Released: September 9, 1944

CAST: Sidney Toler (Charlie Chan); Mantan Moreland (Birmingham Brown); Frances Chan (Frances Chan); Joseph Crehan (Inspector Matthews); Helen Beverly (Norma Duncan); Jacqueline de Wit (Justine Bonner); Geraldine Wall (Harriett Green); Ralph Peters (Rafferty); Frank Jacquet (Paul "Chardo" Hamlin); Claudia Dell (Vera Starkey); Charles Jordan (Tom Starkey); Byron Foulger (Charles Edwards); Joe Whitehead (Dawson); Crane Whitley (Bonner); Darby Jones (Johnson); and Richard Gordon, Harry Depp

The Jade Mask (1945): Edwin Luke, kid brother of Keye "Number One Son" Luke from the earlier Fox *Chan*s, weighs in as Number Four Son, egghead brat Eddie Chan. A gas chamber, poisonous darts and a scam to impersonate murder victims keep the thin plot vigorously stirred. The body count is remarkable, at five. Frank Reicher plays the first casualty as a thoroughly well-despised scientist, automatically padding the suspect roster. Notably weird, however cumbersome, is the ploy of causing a dead man to walk by means of a marionette-strings rigging.

CREDITS: Producer: James S. Burkett; Director: Phil Rosen; Screenplay: George Callahan; Photographed by: Harry Neumann; Assistant Director: Eddie Davis; Second Camera: William Margulies; Technical Director: Dave Milton; Editors: John C. Fuller and Dick Currier; Décor: Vin Taylor; Musical Director: Edward J. Kay; Musical Score: Dave Torbett;

Sound: Tom Lambert; Production Manager: William Strobach; Running Time: 66 Minutes; Released: January 26, 1945

CAST: Sidney Toler (Charlie Chan); Mantan Moreland (Birmingham Brown); Edwin Luke (Eddie Chan); Janet Warren (Jean Kent); Hardie Albright (Walter Meeker); Frank Reicher (Harper); Cyril Delevanti (Roth); Alan Bridge (Sheriff Mack); Ralph Lewis (Jim Kimball); Dorothy Granger (Stella Graham); Edith Evanson (Louise Harper); Joe Whitehead (Dr. Samuel R. Peabody); Henry Hall (Inspector Godfrey); Jack Ingram (Lloyd Archer); Lester Dorr (Michael Strong); and Danny Desmond

The Scarlet Clue (**1945**): Federal agent Chan trails a spy ring bent on stealing radar secrets. The lethal weapon of preference is a deadly gas, activated by tobacco smoke. Mantan Moreland's famous anticipation-and-interruption routine with Ben Carter, a Vaudeville staple in which each finishes the other's sentences with mind-boggling results, receives a generous showcase. Much of the action takes place in the then-exotic setting of a television studio.

CREDITS: Producer: James S. Burkett; Director: Phil Rosen; Screenplay: George Callahan; Photographed by: William Sickner; Assistant Director: Eddie Davis; Second Camera: Vincent Farrar; Technical Director: Dave Milton; Editor: Richard Currier; Music: Edward J. Kay; Sound: Tom Lambert; Re-Recording and Effects Mixer: Joseph I. Kane; Music Mixer: William H. Wilmarth; Production Manager: William Strobach; Running Time: 65 Minutes; Released: May 11, 1945

CAST: Sidney Toler (Charlie Chan); Mantan Moreland (Birmingham Brown); Benson Fong (Tommy Chan); Ben Carter (Himself); Virgina Brissac (Mrs. Marsh); Robert E. Homans (Capt. Flynn); Jack Norton (Willie Rand); Janet Shaw (Gloria Bayne); Helen Devereaux (Diane Hall); Victoria Faust (Hilda Swenson); Milt Kibbee (Herbert Sinclair); I. Stanford Jolley (Ralph Brett); Reid Kilpatrick (Wilbur Chester); Charles Sherlock (Sgt. McGraw); Leonard Mudie (Horace Carlos)

The Shanghai Cobra (**1945**): Deformed villain Addison Richards has a reputation for dispatching victims with cobra venom. The real murderer proves to be a Shanghai police official, disguised as a banker. Benson Fong, who plays Tommy Chan, later developed the popular Ah Fong restaurant chain. This most stark and foreboding of the Monogram *Chan*s boasts a *bona fide* film noir sensibility. Director Phil Karlson later delivered the tough-guy extravaganza *Kansas City Confidential* (1952), with John Payne, Preston Foster, Neville Brand, Lee Van Cleef and Jack Elam.

CREDITS: Producer: James S. Burkett; Director: Phil Karlson; Screenplay: George Callahan, from His Story, and George Wallace Sayre; Photographed by: Vincent Farrar; Assistant Director: Eddie Davis; Second Camera: Al Nicklin; Special Effects: Ray Mercer; Transparency Projection Shots: Mario Castegnaro; Art Directors: Vin Taylor and Dave Milton; Editor: Ace Herman; Music: Edward Kay; Sound: Tom Lambert; Re-Recording and Effects Mixer: Jack Noyes; Music Mixer: William H. Wilmarth; Production Manager: Glen Cook; Technical Director: Ormond McGill; Running Time: 64 Minutes; Released: September 29, 1945

CAST: Sidney Toler (Charlie Chan); Mantan Moreland (Birmingham Brown); Benson Fong (Tommy Chan); James Cardwell (Ned Stewart); Joan Barclay (Paula Webb); Addison Richards (John Adams); Arthur Loft (Bradford Harris); Janet Warren (Lorraine); Gene Stutenroth (Morgan); Joe Devlin (Taylor); James Flavin (H.R. Jarvis); Roy Gordon (Walter Fletcher); Walter Fenner (Inspector Davis); George Chandler (Joe Nelson); Mary Moore (Rita); Cyril Delevanti (Larkin); Stephen Gregory (Samuel Black); Bob Blair (Corning); Bill Ruhl (Gregory); John Goldsworthy (Mainwaring); Tiny Newlan (Guard); Andy Andrews (Cop); Karen Knight (Telephone Supervisor); Diane Quillan (Switchboard Operator); Jack Richardson (Postman)

The Red Dragon **(1946):** A search for secret plans to create a super-bomb finds Chan at large in a festive Mexico City setting, where authentic background shots were filmed during a quick location trip. Willie Best pinch-hits for Mantan Moreland, with agreeable enough results. Bogus nobility, a retired Nazi propagandist and a gun-running and smuggling racket figure in the over-padded plot. Chan is perplexed to learn that a collection of murder bullets betrays no firing marks; it turns out that the ammo was exploded without a gun, by remote control.

CREDITS: Producer: James S. Burkett; Director: Phil Rosen; Screenplay: George Callahan; Photographed by: Vincent Farrar; Assistant Director: Eddie

Davis; Background Photography: William Sickner; Special Effects: Robert Clark; Technical Director: Dave Milton; Editor: Ace Herman; Music: Edward J. Kay; Sound: Tom Lambert; Production Manager: Glenn Cook; Running Time: 64 Minutes; Released: Feb. 2, 1946

CAST: Sidney Toler (Charlie Chan); Fortunio Bonanova (Luis Caverro); Willie Best (Chattanooga Brown); Benson Fong (Tommy Chan); Robert E. Keane (Alfred Wyans); Carol Hughes (Marguerite Fontan); Marjorie Hoschelle (Countess Irena); Barton Yarborough (Joseph Bradish)

Dark Alibi **(1946):** The film is not to be confused with the Cornell Woolrich novel *Black Alibi*, which supplied the basis for a Val Lewton picture, *The Leopard Man*. Here, forged fingerprints implicate innocent persons. Chan places himself in mortal peril by staking out a creepy warehouse where the incriminating equipment has been stashed. *Dark Alibi* is not among Phil Karlson's better work, though the return of the Mantan Moreland–Ben Carter team enlivens things considerably.

CREDITS: Producer: James S. Burkett; Director: Phil Karlson; Screenplay: George Callahan; Photographed by: William Sickner; Assistant Director: Theodore Joos; Second Camera: Al Nicklin; Special Effects: Larry Glickman and Mario Castegnaro; Technical Director: Dave Milton; Supervising Editor: Richard Currier; Editor: Ace Herman; Set Dresser: Max Pittman; Music: Edward J. Kay; Sound: Tom Lambert; Re-Recording and Effects Mixer: Joseph I. Kane; Music Mixer: William H. Wilmarth; Production Manager: Glenn Cook; Running Time: 61 Minutes; Released: May 25, 1946

CAST: Sidney Toler (Charlie Chan); Mantan Moreland (Birmingham Brown); Ben Carter (Himself); Benson Fong (Tommy Chan); Teala Loring (June Harley); George Holmes (Hugh Kensey); Joyce Compton (Emily Evans); John Eldredge (Morgan); Russell Hicks (Warden); Tim Ryan (Foggy); Janet Shaw (Miss Petrie)

Shadows over Chinatown **(1946):** A victim is found bereft of head and limbs. A mass attack of pickpocketing follows, aboard a long-distance bus bearing Charlie Chan to the crime scene. The thief (Jack Norton) proves so grateful to Chan for allowing him a second chance that he winds up using his lightfinger skills to save the detective from a late-in-the-game attack. Mantan Moreland renders the picture better than its script. The routine insurance-scam plot fails to honor the horrific promise of the premise.

CREDITS: Producer: James S. Burkett; Director: Terry Morse; Screenplay: Raymond Schrock; Photographed by: William Sickner; Technical Director: Dave Milton; Assistant Director: William Callahan, Jr.; Supervising Editor: Richard Currier; Editor: Ralph Dixon; Music: Edward J. Kay; Sound: Tom Lambert; Makeup: Harry Ross; Production Manager: Glenn Cook; Running Time: 61 Minutes; Released: July 27, 1946

CAST: Sidney Toler (Charlie Chan); Mantan Moreland (Birmingham Brown); Victor Sen Yung (Jimmy Chan); Tanis Chandler (Mary Conover); John Gallaudet (Jeff Hay); Paul Bryar (Mike Rogan); Bruce Kellogg (Jack Tilford); Alan Bridge (Capt. Allen); Mary Gordon (Mrs. Conover); Dorothy Granger (Joan Mercer); Jack Norton (Cosgrove); George Eldredge (Lannigan); Tyra Vaughn (Miss Chalmers); Lyle Latell (Police Clerk); Myra McKinner (Kate Johnson); Gladys Blake (Myrtle); George Chan and James B. Leong (Chinese-Americans); Jack Mower (Hobart); John Hamilton (Pronnet); Harry Depp (Dr. Denby)

Dangerous Money **(1946):** This one hinges upon Chan's shipboard hunt for a murderer-in-drag whose gun is rigged to fire blades. Allan Douglas plays the purported wife of a bogus missionary (Leslie Dennison), who proves to be the head of a gang trafficking in stolen art objects. Willie Best is back in tow as Chattanooga Brown.

CREDITS: Producer: James S. Burkett; Director: Terry Morse; Screenplay: Miriam Kissinger; Photographed by: William Sickner; Technical Director: Dave Milton; Assistant Director: Wesley Barry; Supervising Editor: Richard Currier; Editor: William Austin; Music: Edward J. Kay; Sound: Tom Lambert; Makeup: Harry Ross and Glenn Cook; Running Time: 64 Minutes; Released: October 12, 1946

CAST: Sidney Toler (Charlie Chan); Victor Sen Yung (Jimmy Chan);

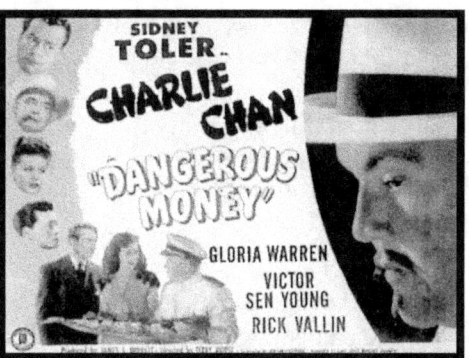

Gloria Warren (Rona Simmonds); Rick Vallin (Tao Erickson); Joseph Crehan (Capt. Black); Willie Best (Chattanooga Brown); John Harmon (Freddie Kirk); Bruce Edwards (Harold Mayfair); Dick Elliott (P.T. Burke)

***The Trap* (1946):** Sidney Toler delivered an unwitting farewell with this picture, which generally is conceded the least of the Monogram *Chan*s. A series of beachfront murders within a show-business community recalls a finer-by-far Fox *Chan*, 1931's *The Black Camel*. There is an unusually great deal of outdoor location shooting. Toler died in February of 1947, at age 72. Production on the series resumed the following August, with *The Chinese Ring*.

CREDITS: Producer: James S. Burkett; Director: Howard Bretherton; Screenplay: Miriam Kissinger; Photographed by: James Brown; Assistant Director: Harold Knox; Technical Director: Dave Milton; Supervising Editor: Richard Currier; Editor: Ace Herman; Décor: Raymond Boltz, Jr.; Music: Edward J. Kay; Sound: Tom Lambert; Makeup: Harry Rose; Production Manager: William Calihan, Jr.; Running Time: 68 Minutes; Released: November 30, 1946

CAST: Sidney Toler (Charlie Chan); Victor Sen Yung (Jimmy Chan); Mantan Moreland (Birmingham Brown); Tanis Chandler (Adelaide); Larry Blake (Rick Daniels); Kirk Alyn (Sgt. Reynolds); Rita Quigley (Clementine); Anne Nagel (Marcia); Helen Gerald (Ruby); Howard Negley (Cole King); Lois Austin (Mrs. Thorn); Barbara Jean Wong (San Toy); Minerva Urecal (Mrs. Weebles); Margaret Brayton (Madge Mudge); Bettie Best (Winifred); Jan Bryant (Lois)

***The Chinese Ring* (1947):** The series regathers self, with Roland Winters as Chan. The historian David Zinman related the transition thusly in a splendid, deep-perspective book called *Saturday Afternoon at the Bijou*: "[Winters'] blond hair and prominent nose made him an unlikely Oriental, but he won the part with a little ingenuity."

"They had never seen me when I was invited... for a screen test," Winters told Zinman. "I'd sent them a picture, of course. But it didn't bear the slightest resemblance to me. I wore a hat and a moustache in it and squinted my eyes because... I assumed this made me look inscrutable."

As to the problem of the honker, Winters added: "I always looked straight into the camera. And when I was talking to someone at the side, I just moved my eyes. I never saw half the people I was supposed to be talking to. But at least my nose didn't give me away."

The forced squint of his tryout portrait proved workable, as well, on screen: "They tried makeup... [and] fiddled around with wax for the eyes, putty and stuff... So I did it myself," said Winters. "Before every shot, the director would say, 'Remember the eyes.'"

The two-weeks-or-less pace of shooting on each late-in-the-game *Chan* has struck some buffs as a marvel of efficiency. Winters held otherwise: "It wasn't amazing," he told Zinman. "It was horrible."

The Chinese Ring is a remake of Monogram's *Mr. Wong in Chinatown* (1939), part of a shorter-lived but overall more satisfying series starring Boris Karloff. *Ring*'s promising first reel finds a doomed Chinese princess (Jean Wong) entrusting the sacred title object to Birmingham Brown (Mantan Moreland). Louise Curry, as an impulsive, interfering news reporter, provokes Winters' Chan to observe that women are incapable of rational conduct—a sentiment guaranteed to drive even most moderate feminists to a dithering rage, as witnessed at screenings in our own homes. These responses invariably proved more entertaining than the movie.

CREDITS: Producer: James S. Burkett; Director: William Beaudine; Screenplay: W. Scott Darling; Photographed by: William Sickner; Assistant Director: William Calihan; Technical Director: Dave Milton; Editor: Richard Heermance; Set Dresser: Ray Boltz, Jr.; Music; Edward J. Kay; Sound: W.C. Smith; Production Supervisor: Glenn Cook; Running Time: 68 Minutes; Released: December 6, 1947

CAST: Roland Winters (Charlie Chan); Warren Young (Sgt. Bill Davidson); Victor Sen Yung (Tommy Chan); Mantan Moreland (Birmingham Brown); Louise Currie (Peggy Cartwright); Philip Ahn (Capt. Kong); Byron Foulger (Armstrong); Thayer Roberts (Capt. Kelso); Jean Wong (Princess Mei Ling); Chabing (Lily Mae); George L. Spaulding (Dr. Hickey); Paul Bryar (Sergeant); Thornton Edwards (Hotel Clerk); Lee Tung Foo (Butler); Richard Wang (Hamishin); Spencer Chan (Officer); Kenneth Chuck (Boy)

Docks of New Orleans (1948): An ill-advised business deal, involving a shipment of a secret chemical formula from Louisiana's Crescent City to South America, finds Chan and his friends theatened by poisonous gas attacks. The

score gets a boost from the use of New Orleans jazz, but there is little in way of suspense, shock value or even local color. The film is a remake of Monogram's *Mr. Wong, Detective* (1938).

CREDITS: Producer: James S. Burkett; Director: Derwin Abrahams; Adapted Screenplay: W. Scott Darling; From a Screenplay by: Houston Branch; Photographed by: William Sickner; Assistant Director: Theodore Joos; Camera Operator: John Martin; Stills: James Fullerton; Technical Director: Dave Milton; Supervising Editor: Otho Lovering; Editor: Ace Herman; Décor: Ken Swarz; Music: Edward J. Kay; Sound: Tom Lambert; Hair Stylist: Lela Chambers; Production Supervisor: Glenn Cook; Script Supervisor: Mary Chaffee; Grip: George Booker; Running Time: 64 Minutes; Released: March 24, 1948

CAST: Roland Winters (Charlie Chan); Virginia Dale (René); Victor Sen Yung (Tommy Chan); Mantan Moreland (Birmingham Brown); John Gallaudet (Capt. Pete McNally); Carol Forman (Nita Aguirre); Douglas Fowley (Grock); Harry Hayden (Oscar Swendstrom); Howard Negley (André Pareaux); Stanley Andrews (Theodore von Scherbe); Emmett Vogan (Henri Castanero); Boyd Erwin (Simon Lafontanne); Rory Mallinson (Thompson); George J. Lewis (Sgt. Dansiger); Diane Fauntelle (Mrs. Swendstrom); Ferris Taylor (Dr. Dooble); Haywood Jones (Mobile); Eric Wilton (Butler); Forrest Matthews (Detective)

The Shanghai Chest (1948): An intruder stabs a judge (Pierre Watkin) to death within hizzonner's private chambers. An executed killer appears to have been brought back to life, if fresh fingerprints can be credited. The chilling notion receives a lukewarm treatment. Mantan Moreland has the distinction of nabbing the fleeing perpetrator, if only by accident.

CREDITS: Producer: James S. Burkett; Director: William Beaudine; Screenplay: W. Scott Darling and Sam Newman, from His Story; Additional Dialogue: Tim Ryan; Photographed by: William Sickner; Assistant Director: Wesley Barry; Operative Cameraman: William Margulies; Stills: James Fullerton; Art Director: David Milton; Supervising Editor: Otho Lovering; Editor: Ace Herman; Décor: Raymond Boltz, Jr.; Music: Edward J. Kay; Sound: Frank McWhorter; Hair Stylist: Lela Chambers; Production Supervisor: Glenn Cook; Script Supervisor: Jules Levy; Grip: Harry Lewis; Running Time: 56 Minutes; Released: July 11, 1948

CAST: Roland Winters (Charlie Chan); Victor Sen Yung (Tommy Chan); Mantan Moreland (Birmingham Brown); Tim Ryan (Lt. Michael Ruark); Deannie Best (Phyllis Powers); Tristram Coffin (Ed Seward); John Alvin (Victor Armstrong); Russell Hicks (Dist. Atty. Frank Bronson); Pierre Watkin (Judge Wesley Armstrong); Milton Parsons (Grail); Olaf Hytten (Bates); Erville Alderson (Walter Somervale); George Eldredge (Pat Finley); Charlie Sullivan (Murphy); Eddie Coke (Thomas Cartwright); William Ruhl (Jailer)

The Golden Eye (**1948**): Chan sojourns out West, investigating murders centering upon a played-out mine that unexpectedly yields a new gold strike. Creepy nun Evelyn Brent proves to be a pistol-packing menace. The picture allows a nice reassertion of eerie ferocity for the flagging series.

CREDITS: Producer: James S. Burkett; Director: William Beaudine; Screenplay: W. Scott Darling; Photographed by: William Sickner; Assistant Director: Wesley Barry; Operative Cameraman: John Martin; Stills: Al St. Hilaire; Art Director: Dave Milton; Supervising Editor: Otho Lovering; Editor: Ace Herman; Décor: Raymond Boltz, Jr.; Music: Edward J. Kay; Sound: Franklin Hansen and John Kean; Makeup: Webb Overlander; Hair Stylist: Lela Chambers; Production Supervisor: Allen K. Wood; Script Supervisor: Jules Levy; Grip: Grant Tucker; Running Time: 69 Minutes; Released: August 29, 1948

CAST: Roland Winters (Charlie Chan); Wanda McKay (Evelyn Manning); Mantan Moreland (Birmingham Brown); Victor Sen Yung (Tommy Chan); Bruce Kellogg (Talbot Bartlett); Tim Ryan (Lt. Mike Ruark); Evelyn Brent (Sister Teresa); Ralph Dunn (Driscoll); Lois Austin (Margaret Driscoll); Forrest Taylor (Manning); Lee "Lasses" White (Pete); Lee Tung Foo (Wong Fai); Michael Gaddis (Pursuer); Sam Flint (Dr. Groves); Geraldine Cobb (Rider); Mary Ann Hawkins and Aileen "Babs" Cox (Bathing Beauties)

The Feathered Serpent (1948): Oliver Drake rewrites his collaborative screenplay for the 1936 Western creepshow, *Riders of the Whistling Skull*. Keye Luke makes an overdue return. The search for a lost Aztec temple turns up a scam to smuggle priceless Mexican Indian artifacts. Bob Livingston, the key hero of *Whistling Skull*, serves this remake in a clever bit of self-referential turnabout casting as a villain.

CREDITS: Producer: James S. Burkett; Director: William Beaudine; Story and Screenplay: Oliver Drake; Additional Dialogue: Hal Collins; Photographed by: William Sickner; Assistant Director: William Calihan; Operative Cameraman: John Martin; Stills: Eddie Jones; Gaffer: Lloyd Garnell; Special Effects: Ray Mercer; Technical Director: David Milton; Supervising Editor: Otho Lovering; Editor: Ace Herman; Décor: Ray Boltz; Music: Edward J. Kay; Sound: Tom Lambert; Makeup: Webb Overlander; Production Manager: Allen K. Wood; Script Supervisor: Ilona Vas; Grip: Harry Lewis; Running Time: 68 Minutes; Released: December 19, 1948

CAST: Roland Winters (Charlie Chan); Keye Luke (Lee Chan); Victor Sen Yung (Tommy Chan); Mantan Moreland (Birmingham Brown); Carol Forman (Sonia Cabot); Robert Livingston (John Stanley); Nils Asther (Prof. Paul Evans); Beverly Jons (Joan Farnsworth); Martin Garralaga (Pedro); George J. Lewis (Capt. Juan); Leslie Dennison (Prof. Farnsworth); Jay Silverheels (Diego); Charles Stevens (Manuel)

The Sky Dragon (1949): A claustrophobic airliner setting helps to suffocate this final entry. Not even a larger-than-usual body count can raise the ante sufficiently to yield the required suspense. There is a helpful climactic struggle between villains Paul Maxey and John Eldredge. Unlike Sidney Toler and Warner Oland, Winters still had plenty of his career ahead of him following the *Chan*s.

CREDITS: Producer: James S. Burkett; Director: Leslie Selander; Screenplay: Oliver Drake and Clint Johnson, from His Story; Photographed by: William Sickner; Assistant Directors: Wesley Barry and Ed Morey, Jr.; Operative Cameraman: John Martin; Gaffer: Robert J. Campbell; Stills: Bud Graybill; Special Effects: Ray Mercer; Technical Director: David Milton; Editors: Roy Livingston and Ace Herman; Décor: Raymond Boltz, Jr.; Music: Edward J. Kay; Sound: Tom Lambert and John Kean; Makeup: Webb Overlander; Hair Stylist: Lela Chambers; Production Manager: Allen K. Wood; Script Supervisor: Ilona Vas; Grip: Harry Lewis; Running Time: 64 Minutes; Released: Following Los Angeles Premiere on April 27, 1949

CAST: Roland Winters (Charlie Chan); Keye Luke (Lee Chan); Mantan Moreland (Birmingham Brown); Noel Neill (Jane Marshall); Tim Ryan (Lt. Mike Ruark); Iris Adrian (Wanda LaFern); Elena Verdugo (Marie Burke); Milburn Stone (Tim Norton); Lyle Talbot (Andy Barrett); Paul Maxey (John Anderson); Joel Marston (Don Blake); John Eldredge (William E. French); Eddie Parks (Jonathan Tibbetts); Louise Franklin (Lena Franklin); Lyle Latell (Ed Davidson); Gaylord Pendleton (Ben Edwards); Emmett Vogan (Doctor); Edna Holland (Old Maid); Joe Whitehead (Doorman)

VOODOO MAN
(Banner Productions/Monogram Pictures Corp.)

Running *The Ape Man* a close second as the silliest of Bela Lugosi's Monogram star vehicles is *Voodoo Man*, which is nonetheless a great deal easier to like. Co-star John Carradine once characterized the picture as "just about the worst thing *I* ever did, even though Lugosi and [George] Zucco were tremendous fun to work with." (The comment dates from the early 1960s, before Carradine's involvement with the likes of *Billy the Kid vs. Dracula* and *Astro-Zombies*.) Marvel Comics honcho Stan Lee once credited the crockheaded self-consciousness of *Voodoo Man* as an inspiration for a recurring gimmick at early-day Marvel: the comic-book story about a comic-book writer whose outlandish yarns somehow spring to life.

Here, the awareness *of* the work, *by* the work, is such that a main character is presented as a screenwriter who is ordered to look into a recent crime wave for the sake of hacking out a scenario. Ralph Dawson (Michael Ames) cares but little for the assignment, being too distracted by the approach of his marriage. It seems that young women have been disappearing near a certain rural spot. Ralph heads for that very region to meet his fiancée, Betty (Wanda McKay). His car conks out, and Ralph hitches a convenient ride with Betty's cousin, Stella (Louise Currie). So then *her* car conks out, and Ralph goes to summon help. Toby (Carradine) and Grego (Pat McKee), servants of one Dr. Marlowe

Ralph (Michael Ames) tries to rescue Betty (Wanda McKay) from Nicholas (George Zucco) in *Voodoo Man*.

(Lugosi), capture Stella. Marlowe places her in a trance, seeing as how he needs to transmigrate her lifeforce into the long-defunct but well-preserved body of his wife (Ellen Hall). His accomplice is Nicholas (Zucco), the title character.

Meanwhile, Ralph hasn't had any better sense than to come knocking at the Marlowe mansion in search of a boost. He receives only the bum's rush; hoofs it back to the roadside; finds Stella and her car gone; arrives the hard way at Betty's house; and learns that Stella has vanished altogether.

The soul-transfer procedure apparently misfires, and Marlowe calls for another abduction. The sheriff (Western-movie stalwart Henry Hall) arrives, with questions. Marlowe is evasive. The dim-witted Toby inadvertently frees Stella, who wanders outside, where she is found and taken to her sister's house. Marlowe pays a neighborly call on the women—then lures Stella back to his place. It should go without saying that Betty is eventually kidnapped. Ralph barges in on a Voodoo ritual. The sheriff shoots Marlowe, whose death breaks the spells all 'round. Ralph records his adventure in a movie script and suggests Bela Lugosi for the starring role.

"We were really scraping the bottom of the barrel with *Voodoo Man*," producer Sam Katzman told us. "Not that we were ever whatcha might call ashamed of scraping bottom, but—now, there's a picture that makes the rest of what we were doing at the time look pretty slick. By comparison, I mean to say." Only Lugosi gets much of a chance to shine, reveling in a tone of sarcastic irony. Carradine and Zucco are stranded in marginal roles that hardly play to their strengths of confident bombast.

Or as Stan Lee might put it: "'Nuff said."

CREDITS: Producers: Sam Katzman and Jack Dietz; Associate Producer: Barney Sarecky; Director: William Beaudine; Story and Screenplay: Robert Charles; Photographed by: Marcel Le Picard; Assistant Director: Art Hammond; Editor: Carl Pierson; Set Designer: Dave Milton; Musical Director: Edward Kay; Running Time: 62 Minutes; Released: February 21, 1944

CAST: Bela Lugosi (Dr. Marlowe); John Carradine (Toby); George Zucco (Nicholas); Wanda McKay (Betty); Louise Currie [a.k.a. Louise Curry] (Stella Saunders [Given as Sally in Screen Credits]); Michael Ames (Ralph Dawson); Ellen Hall (Mrs. Marlowe); Terry Walker (Alice); Mary Currier (Mrs. Benton); Claire James (Zombie); Henry Hall (Sheriff); Dan White (Deputy); Pat McKee (Grego); Mici Goty (Servant)

VOICE IN THE WIND
(Arthur Ripley–Rudolph Monter Productions/United Artists Corp.)

The veteran screenwriter Arthur Ripley had already accredited himself a director, with 1942's *Prisoner of Japan,* by the time he undertook *Voice in the Wind*, a forbidding romance of the war. But it was with *Voice in the Wind* that Ripley meant to announce his arrival as an all-'round filmmaker. Ripley supplied the bleak tale of persecution and morbid obsession. Ripley organized the *ad hoc* company, with Rudolph Monter as an equal-partner producer. And Ripley railroaded the project through such daunting obstacles as a bail-out by its originally contracted distributor and two opportunistic complaints of plagiarism. Ripley cited his practical inspiration in Percy B. Shelley's *Alastor*, that epic confrontation with "sudden darkness and extinction." Shelley, in turn, had acknowledged a debt to these lines from Wordsworth's *Excursion*:

> The good die first
> And those whose hearts
> Are as dry as summer dust
> Burn to the socket.

Misconceptions abound about *Voice in the Wind*, centering upon the notion that the film was developed as a Producers Releasing Corp. venture but proved so impressive that big-time United Artists snatched it up. Granted, PRC had its occasional strivings toward artistry, but the tiny company's idea of artistry was more along the lines of its since-famous Edgar G. Ulmer pictures, *Bluebeard* (1944) and *Detour* (1945). These, of course, are actually ambitious departures from the norms of their idioms more so than they are artistically pretentious films.

With PRC's releasing agreement inked, Ripley and Monter shot the film as a thoroughly maverick effort, brooking no studio interference, during May and June of 1943 at Talisman Studios. A near-final presentation, awaiting music and sound effects, was screened by the end of June for PRC, which according to the *New York Times* rejected *Voice in the Wind* as "too arty." Ripley and Monter sold the picture instead to United Artists, which financed post-production. The musical score, in its context, might have changed PRC's mind, for it is a wondrous job of sound design at the service of storytelling, integrating stirring but ethereal and evocative orchestral works with such homely, mournful sounds as a barroom piano and a solo guitar, a harmonica's wail and the drone of a foghorn. The shooting title had been, for that matter, *Strange Music*.

Just as a modern-day Miramax Pictures or Artisan Entertainment will scour the independent film festivals for the next *Clerks* or *Sling Blade*, the next *Blair Witch Project*, in expectation of another small-budget, anti-formula bonanza, the old-line United Artists distribution group sensed a real coup in *Voice*'s very barrenness of circumstances: "Ripley and Monter... set themselves an audaciously low budget," wrote a UA publicist, "and a shooting schedule that was pushed through in 12 days. Settings were simple and inexpensive; competent actors took the place of box office names; and the luxury of retakes was dispensed with." The cinematographer-of-record is Dick Fryer, but his dense and somber compositions are informed throughout by the counsel of the great German cameraman Eugen Schufftan, who had come to America only to be denied the simple welcome of union credentials. Though barred by regulations from actually laying hands on a camera, Schufftan contributed mightily to the photography of *Voice*.

Maddened by Nazi torture, an outcast known only as *el Hombre* (Francis Lederer) dwells on the desolate island of Guadalupe, a homing ground for refugees. Fragments of a shattered memory occasionally reassemble themselves, and one night *el Hombre* sits at a piano to play a sombre melody. His music catches the ears of three Czechoslovakian fugitives, Dr. Hoffman and his wife, Anna (J. Edward Bromberg and Olga Fabian), and a helpless woman in their care, Marya Volny (Sigrid Gurie). Anna finds the music reminiscent of a great Czech pianist, Jan Volny, and of a happy existence cut short by the German invaders.

El Hombre (in English, "the Man") reads a notice warning refugees to steer clear of those seagoing vessels whose owners will promise to take them to America: These are known as "murder boats," for the crewmen will collect hefty fees and then throw their passengers overboard. In a severe flash of self-recognition, *el Hombre* rushes to destroy one such boat, a fishing ketch owned by his boss, Angelo the Butcher (Alexander Granach). Angelo is a decent enough sort, more or less, despite his reputation for violence and refugee smuggling, but his brothers, Luigi (J. Carrol Naish) and Marco (David Cota) are more the type who'd just as soon kill a man as look at him.

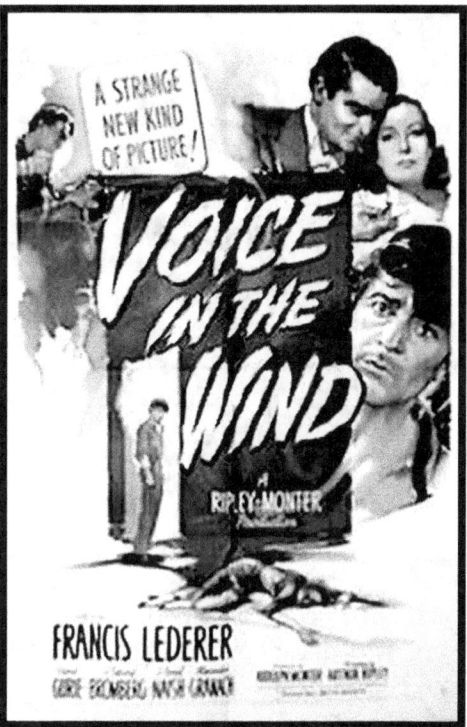

Marya's health is failing fast. Anna reminisces about recent tragedies: Having occupied Prague, the Nazis allowed Jan Volny (Lederer) to present a concert, requiring that he not play a certain patriotic refrain. But when carried away with the rapture of the music, Volny had concluded with a portion of the forbidden composition.

Aware that his impulsive act could only provoke mayhem, Volny had Marya, his wife, smuggled out of the country. His own escape thwarted, Volny was subjected to such cruelties that his mind became unhinged. Overpowering his guards, Volny made his way out of Europe and on to Guadalupe, where, incapable of recalling even his name, he found himself muddling through as *el Hombre*—unwittingly in the service of the murderous racketeers.

In present-day Guadalupe, it becomes plain that Marya is dying of heartbreak. *El Hombre* has finally remembered himself when Luigi suddenly confronts him. Angelo finds Luigi standing over Volny's body, gun in hand. Luigi stabs Angelo. Volny rallies long enough to reach Marya's room—where she has just succumbed. The lovers are reunited in death.

Such a concentration of anguish, laid bare for nearly an hour and a half without resort to such niceties as comic relief or even a shred of hope, pleased a surprising number of critics: "Stirs the emotions," said the *New York Daily News*, and radio gadfly Walter Winchell wished the picture "orchids," which might translate today to a thumbs-up. *Voice in the Wind* fared less agreeably with the theatre operators and their customers, who preferred to take their reminders of Nazi malice in the form of a spy thriller or a slapstick comedy. The Motion Picture Academy anointed *Voice* with Oscar nominations for sound recording and music.

Shortly after the film had opened, a writer named May Davies Martenet sought a restraining order against distribution on grounds of a claim that

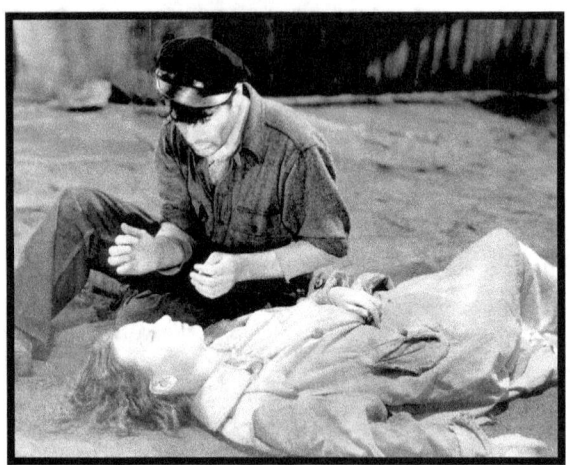
Francis Lederer and Sigrid Gurie—a poignant finale for *Voice in the Wind*

the title and subject matter belonged to a tale she had published two years prior. Her motion was denied. Later, a screenwriter named Jack DeWitt (of 1941's *International Lady*, among others) sued on grounds that *Voice* derived from some of his articles. *The Hollywood Reporter* announced an out-of-court settlement for a percentage of revenues.

Voice transcends its topical limitations most impressively. Francis Lederer is utterly believable as the deranged genius, uncomprehending of his reduced state until the crucial reminders hit him in a shattering instant. Lederer, a Prague-born Hollywood leading man in perceived decline into supporting roles, had grown to cherish his life as a citizen of the film capital, with or without the baggage of celebrity.

"I never really cared, one way or the other," as Lederer told us in 1989, "whether or not anyone in the studio system would let me be a star. Big deal. If the work was there, I would take it. If the work should dry up, why, then, I had my real estate broker's license, and my investments, and my political involvements, and my collection of memorabilia, to occupy my interests." At the formal close of a long career of occasional pictures, Lederer played a formidable visitor from Transylvania in *The Return of Dracula* (1958) and a tormented, Dr. Moreau-like vivisectionist in *Terror Is a Man* (U.S.-Philippines; 1959). A co-founder of the Hollywood Museum and an outspoken proponent of international disarmament, Lederer remained a dapper man-about-town along Sunset Boulevard on into the 1990s. He died in 2000 A.D. at an age disputed as being between 94 and 100.

Voice's ghostly leading lady, Sigrid Gurie, was a product of Samuel Goldwyn's starmaker machine, which billed her as "the Siren of the Fjörds"—the Brooklyn native had been raised in Norway and Belgium—and cast her strikingly but to little popular acclaim in a handful of prewar pictures. *Voice in the Wind* was not formally couched as a comeback, but it did end her three-year absence from the screen. Miss Gurie retired in 1948 and eventually resettled in Mexico, where she died in 1969.

Voice's able supporting ranks are dominated by Alexander Granach (1890-1945), a burly lug who excels at investing a thuggish role with sympathy. As the nearest thing Lederer can find to a pal on the godforsaken island, Granach's Angelo the Butcher is probably every bit as dangerous as his brothers, but Angelo has a soulfully poetic streak and doesn't seem to care who knows it. J. Carrol Naish is more the expected type as the antagonistic schemer behind the refugee-smuggling racket. Luis Alberni is marginally amusing as a curiosity-prone bartender.

Ripley remained in demand as a writer, a script doctor, a film cutter—even as an occasional voice-over actor, a role he serves in *Voice in the Wind*—but rarely directed from this point onward; a chronic drinking problem seems to have compromised his dependability. That quintessential film noir, *The Chase* (1946), is Ripley's—and so is *Thunder Road* (1958), a fondly remembered moonshiners-vs.-revenuers melodrama whose theme song gave star player Robert Mitchum a secondary career as a recording artist.

CREDITS: Produced and Presented by: Arthur Ripley & Rudolph Monter; Director: Arthur Ripley; Screenplay: Frederick Torberg; Story: Arthur Ripley, after Shelley's *Alastor*; Photographed by: Dick Fryer; Second Camera: Arthur "Jockey" Feindel; Miniatures and Special Photographic Effects: Ray Mercer; Editors: Holbrook N. Todd and Arthur Ripley; Settings: Glenn P. Thompson; Musical Score: Michel Michelet, Incorporating Works by Bach, Chopin and Schumann; Musical Director: Yascha Paii; Melody: "The Moldau," by Bedrich Smetana; Sound Recording: P.J. Townsend and W.M. Dalgleish; Mixer: Percy Townsend; Makeup: Ted Larson; Production Manager: Bart Carré; Technical Adviser: Eugen Schufftan; Running Time: 85 Minutes; Released: March 10, 1944

CAST: Francis Lederer (Jan Volny/*el Hombre*); Sigrid Gurie (Marya Volny); J. Edward Bromberg (Dr. Hoffman); J. Carrol Naish (Luigi); Alexander Granach (Angelo the Butcher); David Cota (Marco); Olga Fabian (Anna Hoffman); Howard Johnson (Capt. von Neubach); Hans Schumm (Piesecke); Luis Alberni (Bartender); George Sorel (Detective); Martin Garralaga (Cop); Jacqueline Dalya (Portugese Girl); Rudolph Myzet (Novak); Fred Nurney (Vasek); Bob Stevenson and Otto Reichow (Guards); Martin Berliner (Refugee); Chura Cherassky, Ted Saldenberg and Fred Marvin (Piano Doubles); Arthur Ripley (Narrator)

LADY IN THE DEATH HOUSE
(Producers Releasing Corp.)

Lionel Atwill receives a welcome, though ill-noticed, reprieve from bad-guy typecasting in this tiny double-bill filler from the savvy immigrant director Steve Sekely, courtesy of a newsstand pulp called *Detective Tales*. A stag-party

scandal had compromised Atwill's career early on in the decade, but the artist assumed a chin-up stance and kept working at whatever opportunity. *Lady in the Death House* also tampers with the still-emerging film noir narrative components—desperate situation, bedeviled central character, stale secrets and fresh treacheries, in a layered flashback structure—until it dodges into a more conventionally hopeful ending.

Jean Parker plays Mary Logan, the title character, with an unaccustomed severity; coupled with her close-in-time *Kitty O'Day* pictures, *Lady in the Death House* allows a pleasing showcase for Miss Parker's versatility. Not that many people were paying the actress much attention at this downhill stage of her career.

Miss Logan writes a letter to criminologist Charles Finch (Atwill) while awaiting her date with the executioner. Our reference to the executioner is not merely symbolic: He is Dr. Dwight Bradley (Douglas Fowley), whom Mary had rejected as a suitor some years ago upon learning the nature of his work.

Mary's letter cues the local news-hacks to besiege Finch. He obliges with a flashback, detailing the circumstances that have landed Mary on Death Row—a murder case, sealed by no greater evidence than the crooked victim's having gasped her name before witnesses. Finch had come near saving Mary during the original investigation, and now he renews his campaign. It helps matters that Dr. Bradley stages a sit-down strike at the right moment, and it helps even more that Mary's wayward kid sister (Marcia Mae Jones) finally wises up and implicates her good-for-nothing boyfriend (John Maxwell) in the killing and frame job. Mary is freed, and Bradley quits the executioner's gig.

Atwill is British determination personified as the relentless sleuth who takes one last tilt at a lost cause. Rather like Sir Cedric Hardwicke's heroic character in the more distinguished *A Woman's Vengeance* (1948), Atwill hounds and harasses one headstrong woman to the breaking point, then sets about to pick up the pieces. He clearly relishes the rare opportunity to save the day and carry the show in the process. Marcia Mae Jones is surprisingly capable in the sisterly role, which recalls her better work as a kid player in bigger pictures. John Maxwell works well with Atwill in the urgently deployed flashbacks, which account not only for Maxwell's character's secret shame—a struggling research scientist, reduced to killing for the state—but also for disgraces that Jean Parker's Mary Logan would just as soon keep hidden.

> And apropos of nothing and everything: *Forgotten Horrors* co-creator George E. Turner was stationed with the U.S. Navy at San Diego when Universal Pictures shot its all-star morale-booster revue *Follow the Boys* on location there. George can be seen as a prominent extra in *Follow the Boys*, which was released on March 4, 1944—right about the time of these immediate selections, here.

CREDITS: Producer: Jack Schwarz; Associate Producer: Harry D. Edwards; Director: Steve Sekely; Screenplay: Harry O. Hoyt; Based upon: Frederick C. Davis' 1942 Story, "Meet the Executioner," from *Detective Tales* Magazine; Photographed by: Gus Peterson; Assistant Director: Edward Davis; Art Director: Frank Sylos; Editor: Robert O'Crandall; Décor: Harry Reif; Props: George Bahr; Musical Score: Jan Gray; Orchestra Conducted by: Mort Glickman; Music Supervised by: David Chudnow; Sound: Frank Webster; Running Time: 56 Minutes; Released: March 15, 1944

CAST: Jean Parker (Mary Kirk Logan); Lionel Atwill (Charles Finch); Marcia Mae Jones (Suzy Kirk Logan); Douglas Fowley (Dr. Dwight Bradley); Cy Kendall (Detective); John Maxwell (Robert Snell); Robert Middlemass (State's Attorney); George Irving (Gregory); Forrest Taylor (Warden); Sam Flint (Gov. Harrison); Dick Curtis (Blackmailer)

THE LADY AND THE MONSTER
a.k.a.: THE TIGER MAN
(Republic Pictures Corp.)

This grand adaptation of a bestselling novel by Curt Siodmak promptly inspired a radio miniseries—a two-parter on CBS' *Suspense*, itself starring Orson Welles—and caused a popular sensation wholly at odds with *Variety*'s short-sighted prediction that *The Lady and the Monster* would prove "at best a

Vera Hruba Ralston, Erich von Stroheim and Richard Arlen add up to a tense romantic triangle in *The Lady and the Monster*

dual supporter for the regular runs." The source, of course, is *Donovan's Brain*, published in 1943, which later became the basis for Felix Feist's *Donovan's Brain* (1953); a like-titled CBS telefeature of 1955; and Freddie Francis' *Ein Toter sucht seinen Mörder* (a.k.a. *Vengeance*; England–West Germany; 1962). Numerous other pictures have seized upon Siodmak's notion of telepathic domination by a disembodied intelligence, with or without attribution. Probably the weirdest of the *Donovan* swipes is the Japanese-made *Evil Brain from Outer Space*, a television-derived feature from 1956-59.

The Lady and the Monster benefits not only from pride of place, but also from its mingling of fidelity to the source with an inventive audacity. Producer/director George Sherman and busy screenwriter Siodmak had made a formidable combo earlier in the decade at Republic, and only Siodmak's increasing workload for the larger studios (including *I Walked with a Zombie*, at RKO's Val Lewton unit, and *House of Frankenstein* and *The Climax* at Universal) prevented his direct participation in *The Lady and the Monster*.

The film captures best Siodmak's strategic use of grisly science-fantasy, not as an end in itself, but rather as a disturbing framework accommodating a tangle of murderous old secrets and obsessive jealousy—an area of singular interest to the film's most prestigious player, the great but lapsed director and scenarist Erich von Stroheim.

Stroheim plays Prof. Franz Mueller, a reclusive scientist whose castle lies near the scene of a plane crash in the wastelands of Arizona. The victim is brought to Mueller and pronounced dead, but Mueller finds the brain still vital and removes it with the help of an assistant, Patrick Cory (Richard Arlen). A visit from the widow (Helen Vinson) proves the dead man to have been a hard-hearted plutocrat named William H. Donovan. Donovan's lawyer (Sidney Blackmer) learns that Mueller has preserved the brain but decides not to object, for he and the disinherited Mrs. Donovan are seeking the hiding place of Donovan's fortune.

As Mueller nourishes the brain, it becomes ever more aware of its narrowed orbit and begins exercising a vile control over Cory, driving the scientist to reopen a supposedly solved murder case and at length transferring William Donovan's killing urge to Cory. Donovan's motives prove at length to be benevolent enough—in their diabolical way—but the brain compels Cory to commit such vicious misdeeds that the pawn finally must pay with a stretch in prison. (The penalty was written in as a sop to Hollywood's Production Code, whose pre-production censors also demanded that Donovan be declared officially dead before the doctors could extract his *medulla obnoxiosa*. The *Suspense* radio play perversely allows the removal of the brain from a still-living Donovan, although it ultimately compromises its impact with a curveball finale.)

Forging deeper into the realm of *psychopathia sexualis*, the film not only sets up an inexorably tightening triangle involving Stroheim, Richard Arlen and Vera Hruba Ralston (as Stroheim's ward)—but also expands the tense situation to a quadrangle with Mary Nash, as a housekeeper who once was Prof. Mueller's mistress. Resentful of the boss's affections for the young woman, the servant finally joins forces with her to rescue Cory and do away with both Mueller and the brain. (Stroheim would play a turnabout on the Nash role, as a boss-turned-mate-turned-flunky to Gloria Swanson, in Billy Wilder's *Sunset Boulevard* [1950]. Yet later, Stroheim would speak disparagingly of the *Sunset Boulevard* role as "that stupid butler part," even though the role is wholly consistent with the confrontational themes of lapsed dignity and tarnished brilliance that had dominated the artist's more personally motivated work of the 1920s and beyond.)

A generous nine-reel length marks *The Lady and the Monster* as not only a Republic Special, but also a rather vainly motivated star-debut vehicle for Miss Ralston, a runner-up champion of the 1938 Olympics' ice-skating competition. She had been discovered as a movie star a-borning by Republic's domineering founder and early-day practitioner of the hostile corporate takeover, Herbert J. Yates. Yates nurtured the Czech-born beauty's career from the start, lavishing uncharacteristically vast sums on her pictures, and the two were married in 1952. Miss Ralston never became an A-list star, except within the sheltering confines of Republic, but an ineffable vulnerability distinguishes her performances over the long haul and the camera seems to like her.

Richard Arlen, a burly athlete, aviator and sports journalist who had been a favored silent-era player of the tough-as-a-boot director William Wellman, did abundant distinguished work during the Depression and wartime years (including 1932's *Island of Lost Souls* and that great Paramount B-picture of 1943, *Submarine Alert*) and would continue with a distinguished character-man career on through the 1960s. Arlen is excellent here as a devoted assistant who, despite an attraction to Miss Ralston, takes Stroheim's work-comes-first policy at face value without suspecting the more turbulent romantic intrigues. Arlen's transformation to a lethal puppet is wondrously gradual, and his dawning comprehension of the alien control is accomplished with a greater subtlety than the actor's many tough-guy impersonations might lead one to expect.

Stroheim is a marvel, as usual—a striving artist who professed to despise acting, and who played essentially the same self-absorbed role time and again, but who also brought to each new turn on camera a brooding grandeur and an immersion in character that remain unmatched.

A 1949 reissue of *The Lady and the Monster*, with some dramatically clunky re-edits, would bear the title *The Tiger Man*. Sherman would reunite Stroheim, Arlen and Miss Ralston later in 1944 for the espionage melodrama *Storm over Lisbon*.

CREDITS: Associate Producer and Director: George Sherman; Screenplay: Dane Lussier and Frederick Kohner; Based upon: Curt Siodmak's 1943 Novel, *Donovan's Brain*; Photographed by: John Alton; Special Effects: Theodore Lydecker; Art Director: Russell Kimball; Assistant Director: R.G. Springsteen; Editor: Arthur Roberts; Set Decorator: Otto Siegel; Gowns: Adele Palmer; Music: Walter Scharf; Orchestral Arrangements: Marlin Skiles; Sound: Earl Crain, Sr.; Running Time: 86 Minutes; Released: April 17, 1944

CAST: Vera Hruba Ralston (Janice Farrell); Richard Arlen (Patrick Cory); Erich von Stroheim (Prof. Franz Mueller); Helen Vinson (Chloe Donovan); Mary Nash (Mrs. Fame); Sidney Blackmer (Eugene Fulton); Janet Martin (Singer); Bill Henry (Roger Collins); Charles Cane (Grimes); Juanita Quigley (Mary Lou); Josephine Dillon (Grandmother); Antonio Triana and Lola Montes (Dancers); Jack Kirk (Husky Man); Sam Flint (Phipps); Edward Keane (Manning); Lane Chandler (White); Wallis Clark (Warden); Harry Hayden (Dr. Martin); Maxine Doyle (Receptionist); Billy Benedict (Bellboy); Herbert Clifton (Butler); Harry Depp (Teller); Lee Phelps (Waiter); Frank Graham (Narrator)

THE MONSTER MAKER
(Sigmund Neufeld Productions, Inc./Producers Releasing Corp.)

Of all the show-business arenas that have traded in clinical deformity in fact or in artifice—from carnival sideshows to the movies—Sam Newfield's *The Monster Maker* may be the most generously entertaining. It boasts a fine show

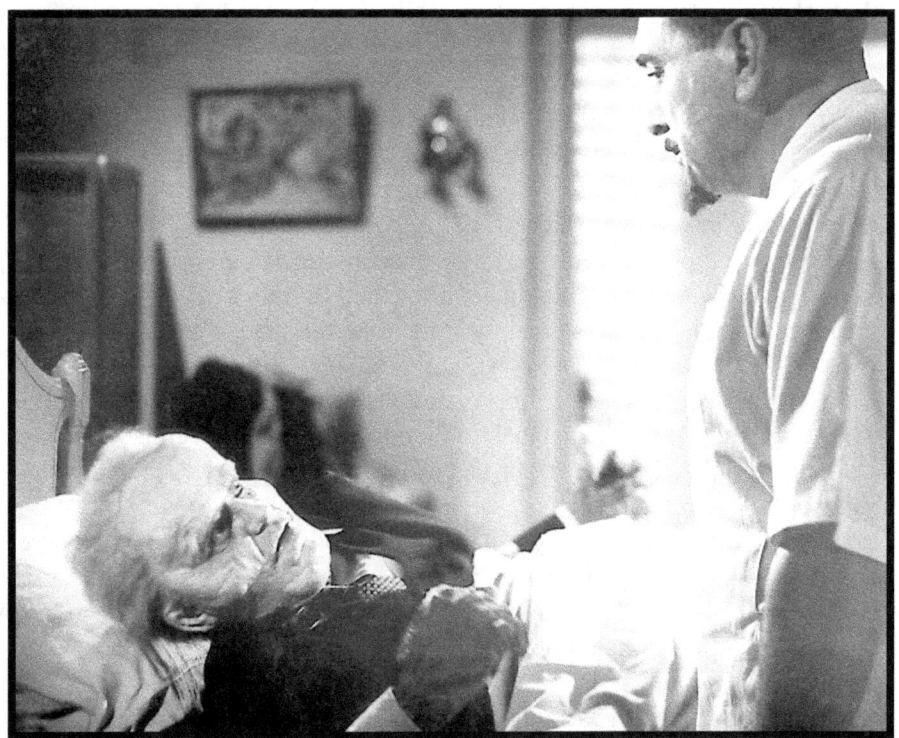

Ralph Morgan and J. Carroll Naish in the entertaining *The Monster Maker*

of controlled malice from J. Carrol Naish in the title role, an equally strong portrayal of resentful near-helplessness from Ralph Morgan as the victimized man-become-monster, and a safe-and-sound resolution that makes reassuringly corny sense. Of course, Rondo Hatton, a Florida-born journalist and publicist who had developed acromegaly following combat duty in World War I, had long since begun exploiting his altered appearance as a screen player. *The Monster Maker* doubtless owes its inspiration to the public profile that Hatton had given his private tragedy.

Morgan plays a celebrated pianist named Anthony Lawrence, whose daughter, Patricia (Wanda McKay), is courted by one Dr. Igor Markoff (Naish). Patricia wants none of the doctor's attentions—indeed, she finds him downright creepy, especially after he reveals that she is the image of his late wife. Markoff escalates from annoyance to threat, and when confronted by Lawrence, Markoff disables the artist and injects him with a disfiguring serum. It develops that Markoff is an assumed identity—the real Markoff had been killed for showing too great an interest in the deranged medico's wife, who had committed suicide after the killer caused her disfigurement. As Markoff, the madman has become a respected expert—in the treatment of acromegaly.

And so where does Lawrence's physician (Sam Flint) send him, as the ailment begins to manifest itself, but to this vile Dr. Markoff? Lawrence's deterioration drives him at length to a killing rage. Markoff's long-suffering assistant and would-be consort, Maxine (Tala Birell), rebels and is ordered slain at the hands of the doctor's pet ape. Maxine's dog, Ace (Ace, the Wonder Dog), rescues her. Markoff tells Patricia he will cure her father—on condition that she become the new Mrs. Markoff. A captive Lawrence breaks free and attacks Markoff, who is killed. Maxine saves the day by declaring her knowledge of the curative formula, which arrests Lawrence's condition. The finale finds Lawrence triumphantly returned to the concert circuit.

Maurice Siederman's nightmarish makeup design, a seeming mixture of malformation and decay, is as much a star of the picture as the thesping of Naish or Morgan. The best-known still from *The Monster Maker*, showing Morgan tearing into Naish, scarcely does the facial alterations justice, freezing a harshly lighted grimace that makes Morgan look almost gleeful. The makeup in motion is altogether more right, and when animated by Morgan's convincing show of savage resentment it can actually cause the absorbed viewer to cringe. (The un-absorbed viewer need not apply.) The busy, emotive musical score is an early work by Albert Glasser, who toiled as a score-transcriber for the major studios until he caught on as a fully fledged composer among the Poverty Row studios. The film belongs almost entirely to the antagonists, but Wanda McKay and Tala Birell make much of their respective reasons to despise Naish. Ace, the Wonder Dog has a pleasingly fierce heroic scene.

CREDITS: Producer: Sigmund Neufeld; Director: Sam Newfield; Screenplay: Pierre Grendon and Martin Mooney; Story: Lawrence Williams; Photographed by: Robert Cline; Assistant Director: Melville DeLay; Editor: Holbrook N. Todd; Sets: Paul Palmentola; Set Dresser: Elias H. Reif; Musical Score: Albert Glasser; Music Supervisor: David Chudnow; Sound Engineer: Ferol Redd; Makeup: Maurice Siederman; Running Time: Minutes; Released: April 15, 1944

CAST: J. Carrol Naish (Dr. Igor Markoff); Ralph Morgan (Anthony Lawrence); Tala Birell (Maxine); Wanda McKay (Patricia Lawrence); Terry Frost (Bob Blake); Glenn Strange (Giant); Alexander Pollard (Butler); Sam Flint (Dr. Adams); Ace, the Wonder Dog (Himself)

SHAKE HANDS WITH MURDER
(American Productions, Inc./Producers Releasing Corp.)

This one is just *too* easy, but the occasional atmospheric moment helps. Frank Jenks plays bail-bondsman Eddie Jones, who believes he has scored a coup with the release of big shot Steve Morgan (Douglas Fowley). Fowley turns out to be a high-risk client, though. Jones attempts to have the bond revoked but learns that Fowley had been the victim of a frame-up.

There follows the murder of Morgan's conniving boss (former serials champ Herbert Rawlinson). Fowley undertakes to convince Jones' business partner (Iris Adrian) that the motive is a hidden stash of negotiable securities that Morgan had been accused of stealing. The reliable booby-trapped bookcase stunt figures in, here, and finally the likeliest suspects are invited to

see which of them will *not* risk triggering the deadly mechanism. Sure enough, sneaky-looking I. Stanford Jolley gives himself away. Jolley has a fine threatening moment at this point, but Miss Adrian—hidden in a suit of armor—saves the day.

Third-billed Fowley is a nifty lesser surprise as the suspect-turned-hero, and he and Miss Adrian make an appealing match. The movie does all the work for the audience in exposing the crook. An ominous hunting-lodge setting and Jolley's snarling show of malice are the larger saving graces.

CREDITS: Producers: Donald C. McKean and Albert Herman; Director: Albert Herman; Story: Martin Mooney; Screenplay: John T. Neville; Photographed by: Robert Cline; Art Director: Paul Palmentola; Assistant Director: Lou Perlof; Editor: Heorge Merrick; Set Decorator: Harry Reif; Property Master: Gene Stone; Musical Director: Lee Zahler; Running Time: 62 Minutes; Released: April 22, 1944

CAST: Iris Adrian (Patsy Brent); Frank Jenks (Eddie Jones); Douglas Fowley (Steve Morgan); Jack Raymond (Joe Blake); Claire Rochelle (Secretary); Herbert Rawlinson (John Clark); Juan de la Cruz (Stanton); I. Stanford Jolley (Haskins); Forrest Taylor (Kennedy); George Kirby (Adams); Gene Stutenroth (Howard); Anita Sparrow (Waitress); Buck Harrington (Sergeant)

JOHNNY DOESN'T LIVE HERE ANYMORE
a.k.a.: AND SO THEY WERE MARRIED
(King Bros. Productions/Monogram Pictures Corp.)

Simone Simon's brief span of American stardom yielded such treasures of supernatural fantasy as *All That Money Can Buy* (1941) and the Val Lewton productions of *Cat People* (1942) and *Curse of the Cat People* (1944). This facile identification with some essential components of a genre tends to obscure the grander sweep of the French-born beauty's career. Miss Simon, who interrupted

her progress in France on two occasions to make a go of Hollywood, was equally well suited to naturalistic drama and romantic comedy; the latter gift is well deployed in Joe May's *Johnny Doesn't Live Here Any More*—a lighthearted bedroom farce that also packs a welcome, though strident, element of other-worldly interference.

One of the King Bros. studio's relentless attempts to lend some class to Monogram Pictures, *Johnny Doesn't Live Here Any More* is a topical spoof involving the wartime homefront and its big-city housing shortages. Kathie Aumont (Miss Simon), a French-Canadian defense worker, arrives on assignment in Washington and finds herself, first, without lodgings and, second, falling in love with a Marine, Johnny Moore (William Terry), who is bound for the battlefront. Taking Johnny's apartment on a sub-lease, Kathie finds the flat overrun with uninvited squatters—pals of Johnny's, and pals of the pals, all in possession of keys to the premises. Romantic complications escalate to a slugfest between rival suitors James Ellison and William Terry, and the matter winds up in night court before an impatient judge (suave Alan Dinehart). The story resolves itself with a flash-forward of several years, revealing that Kathie has settled her domestic quandary by marrying the judge. Not to give away too much, y'know.

Miss Simon's ordeals are symbolized in the person of a gremlin (played by the diminutive Jerry Maren), who seems the annoying embodiment of Murphy's Law. Yet more annoying is the presence of 12-year-old Billy "Froggy" Laughlin, the raspy-voiced child actor who at the time was also helping to diminish the entertainment value of the *Our Gang* comedies. (Laughlin would die at 16 in a motoring accident.) Rondo Hatton turns in a bit as an undertaker named Graves. Robert Mitchum shows up as a Navy officer in possession of one of the errant keys, which are a prized commodity in overpopulous Washington: The serviceman who loses his key won't be getting any new key.

Director Joe May had been a pivotal figure in the development of German cinema and nurtured the filmmaking ambitions of Fritz Lang. May arrived in America during the 1930s, intent more upon putting the Nazis behind him than upon advancing his career. May's Hollywood pictures are as a class less distinguished than his European work spanning 1912-1933, but they include such jewels as *The Invisible Man Returns* and *The House of Seven Gables*, both from 1940. *Johnny Doesn't Live Here Any More* served as the coda for May, who died 10 years later.

Simone Simon quit Hollywood around the end of the war and re-established herself in France, whose film industry welcomed her return. *Johnny Doesn't Live Here Any More* received an energetic reissue in 1948, rechristened *And So They Were Married.*

CREDITS: Producer: Maurice King; Associate Producer: Franklin King; Director: Joe May; Assistant Director: Clark Reynolds; Dialogue Director: Edward E. Kaye; Screenplay: Philip Yordan and John H. Kafka; Story: Alice Means Reeve; Photographed by: Ira Morgan and Robert W. Pittack; Special Effects: Ray Mercer; Art Director: Paul Palmentola; Associate Art Director: George Moskov; Editor: Martin G. Cohn; Décor: Tommy Thompson; Music: W. Franke Harling; RCA Sound: Thomas Lambert; Technical Adviser: Herman King; Running Time: 75 Minutes; Released: May 12, 1944

CAST: Simone Simon (Kathie Aumont); James Ellison (Mike Burke); William Terry (Johnny Moore); Minna Gombel (Mrs. Collins); Chick Chandler (Jack); Alan Dinehart (Judge); Gladys Blake (Sally); Robert Mitchum (Jeff Daniels); Dorothy Granger [as Grainger] (Irene); Grady Sutton (George); Fern Emmett (Grouchy Woman); Chester Clute (Collins); Janet Shaw (Gladys); Jerry Maren (Gremlin); Froggy Laughlin (Jerry Malone); Charles Williams (Court Reporter); George Chandler (Charlie Miller); Harry Depp (David); Mary Field (Subscription Lady); Douglas Fowley (Rudy); Pat Gleason and Emmett Lynn (Passengers); Rondo Hatton (Undertaker Graves); George Humbert (Grocer); Milton Kibbee (Conductor); Sid Melton (Recruit); Dick Rich (Marine Sergeant); Frank J. Scannell (Chauffeur); Michael Vallon (Florist); Duke York (Cabbie); and Lynton Brent, Clarence Straight, George Beatty

THE "KITTY O'DAY" PICTURES: A DEFECTIVE DETECTIVE
(Monogram Pictures Corp.)

This matched pair of airheaded comedy-shockers started out under one nifty working title, *Accusing Corpse*. Retooled as a last-chance star vehicle for the pleasant but often flighty second-string leading lady Jean Parker, the property evolved into *Detective Kitty Kelly* and finally into *Detective Kitty O'Day*. The detective reference is purely tongue-in-cheek, for Miss Parker—whose decline was only hastened by these pictures—plays Kitty O'Day as a secretary and, later, a switchboard operator, whose nosy nature invariably lands her in trouble and complicates the lives of all in her orbit.

Monogram announced that the sequel, *Adventures of Kitty O'Day*, signaled a long-term series, but no additional entries took shape. Another of Monogram's sillier thrillers, *Fashion Model*, has been mistakenly cited in some sources as a third *Kitty O'Day*; the films do boast talents in common. Miss Parker, who had come to Hollywood at age 20 in 1932 as an MGM discovery, retired from the movies before *Adventures* was ready for distribution, retrenching as a stage actress on Broadway and with several touring productions. She returned to the movies as an occasional character player, gracing such memorable pictures as *The Gunfighter* (1950) and *Black Tuesday* (1955). During that patchy resurgence, Miss Parker was married to the actor Robert Lowery; both figure prominently in this volume's concentration of titles.

Detective Kitty O'Day (1944): Accountant Johnny Jones (Peter Cookson) complains to his sweetheart, Kitty O'Day (Miss Parker), that her big-shot boss, Oliver Wentworth (Edward Earle), is requiring too much of her time. Johnny's offhanded, meaningless remark that he'd like to kill Wentworth is overheard by a taxi driver (Pat Gleason). Kitty arrives at the Wentworth mansion to find her employer hanged. The death proves to have been a drowning, with a contrived appearance of suicide.

While the police question Kitty along with Wentworth's attorney, Jeffers (Herbert Heyes), a cop brings in Johnny, who claims that someone knocked him unconscious just outside the house. Mrs. Wentworth (Veda Ann Borg) and her clandestine lover, Harry Downs (Douglas Fowley), arrive. Kitty engages Mrs. Wentworth in a hostile confrontation.

Kitty decides to investigate with or without anybody's help, pestering Johnny until he consents to help her. The police can only resent the intrusion, especially when the two are caught clinging to a hotel's window-ledge in a prowl through Mrs. Wentworth's apartment. Downs is found murdered, and so is Wentworth's butler (Olaf Hytten). It is but a matter of time until Kitty and Johnny find themselves accused of murder, and Kitty hires Jeffers to spring them—only to realize that the lawyer is the killer. Downs and the butler, as Jeffers' accomplices in a securities-theft racket, had outlived their usefulness. Kitty and Johnny are inadvertently rescued when the eavesdropping cabbie sends the police to nab Johnny.

CREDITS: Producer: Lindsley Parsons; Director: William Beaudine; Screenplay: Tim Ryan and Victor Hammond, from His Story; Photographed by: Ira Morgan; Art Director: E.R. Hickson; Technical Director: Dave Milton; Editor: Richard Currier; Music: Edward J. Kay; Sound: Tom Lambert; Production Manager: William Strobach; Running Time: 63 Minutes; Released: Following New York Opening on May 16, 1944

CAST: Jean Parker (Kitty O'Day); Peter Cookson (Johnny Jones); Tim Ryan (Inspector Clancy); Veda Ann Borg (Georgia Wentworth); Ed Gargan (Mike Storm); Douglas Fowley (Harry Downs); Pat Gleason (Cabbie); Olaf Hytten (Charles); Edward Earle (Oliver Wentworth); Herbert Heyes (Robert Jeffers)

Adventures of Kitty O'Day **(1945):**
The prior misadventure would seem to have prompted some career changes for Kitty O'Day (Miss Parker) and Johnny Jones (Peter Cookson), who are now laboring, respectively, as a switchboard-plugger and a travel agent. Hearing gunshots while on duty at the Townley Hotel, Kitty sends Johnny and a porter, Jeff (Shelton Brooks, picking up a role originally meant for Mantan Moreland), to investigate, as it were. An irritable police inspector (co-author Tim Ryan, in a return engagement) responds to Kitty's summons and is as annoyed as ever to find no corpse. Later, however, Kitty finds in her apartment the owner of the hotel—croaked.

The inspector grills the handiest suspects, including the victim's disloyal wife (Lorna Gray), a shady massage therapist (Hugh Prosser) and his girlfriend (Jan Wiley), hotel clerk Roberts (Byron Foulger) and hotel manager Sauter (William Forrest). An undercover private eye (William Ruhl), who has been sent to look into recent jewelry heists at the Townley, turns up slain. Johnny, who has already stumbled into a ladies-only massage room and found himself arrested for lewd behavior, becomes a murder suspect—as does Kitty. Freed on the strength of a timely report from the coroner's office, the meddling sweethearts find only more trouble: Roberts has been electrocuted and crammed into a service elevator. Muddling through as usual, Kitty and Johnny finally expose Sauter as the killer; it all boils down to an intramural theft ring and the old truism about dishonor among thieves.

CREDITS: Producer: Lindsley Parsons; Director: Wiliam Beaudine; Art Directors: Eddie Davis and David Raskov; Screenplay: George Callahan, Tim Ryan and Victor Hammond, from His Story; Photographed by: Mack Stengler; Second Camera: James Knott; Technical Director: Dave Milton; Editor: Richard Pike; Music: Edward J. Kay Sound: John Carter; Production Manager: William Strobach; Running Time: 63 Minutes; Released: January 19, 1945

CAST: Jean Parker (Kitty O'Day); Peter Cookson (Johnny Jones); Tim Ryan (Clancy); Lorna Gray (Gloria Williams); Jan Wiley (Carla Brant); Ralph Sanford (Mac); William Forrest (Sauter); Byron Foulger (Roberts); Hugh Prosser (Nick Joel); Dick Elliott (Bascom); William Ruhl (Michael Tracy); Shelton Brooks (Jeff)

RETURN OF THE APE MAN
(Banner Productions/Monogram Pictures Corp.)

No, this one is no sequel. Its kinship to *The Ape Man* (1943) lies simply in the presence of Bela Lugosi, and in the Banner/Monogram imprimatur. Lugosi's showier Hollywood stardom effectively ends with *Return of the Ape Man*, although there would be close-in-time attempts at resurgence—including a triumphant return to the Count Dracula role in 1948's *Abbott and Costello Meet Frankenstein*—before the artistically disastrous connections that Lugosi would make during the 1950s.

Life eternal is the quest at issue here, and Prof. Dexter (Lugosi) is the obsessive searcher, barely anchored in reality by his level-headed colleague, John Gilmore (John Carradine). The partners are first sighted in their laboratory just as they thaw back to life a vagrant (Ernie Adams), whom they have kept frozen for months. The low-profile success scarcely suits Dexter, who mounts a well-publicized expedition to the Arctic in search of the intact remains of a prehistoric subhuman. The hunt ends in triumph, and so does the defrosting, but the researchers are disappointed to find that the creature (Frank Moran) seems incapable of absorbing civilized ways. Dexter decides he must transplant the reasoning portion of a modern-day human's brain into the ape man.

Rallying from the passive-aggressive, resentful attitude that had characterized even much of his better wartime work along Poverty Row, Lugosi summons a measure of his Depression-era ferocity, becoming more a reflection of his characters in *Murders in the Rue Morgue* and *The Raven*. At a swank party, Prof. Dexter casts a hopeful eye on a young man (Michael Ames) who is engaged to marry Anne (Judith Gibson), the niece of his colleague. Dexter and Gilmore have more in common as truth-seekers than as trusting friends, and Gilmore is outraged when he catches Dexter inviting the unsuspecting fiancé home for a brain extraction. Meanwhile, the ape man glowers menacingly from a cage—at least, as menacingly as an ape man can glower when the makeup department has scarcely bothered to make him look like anything more than a bum in need of a shave and a hangover remedy.

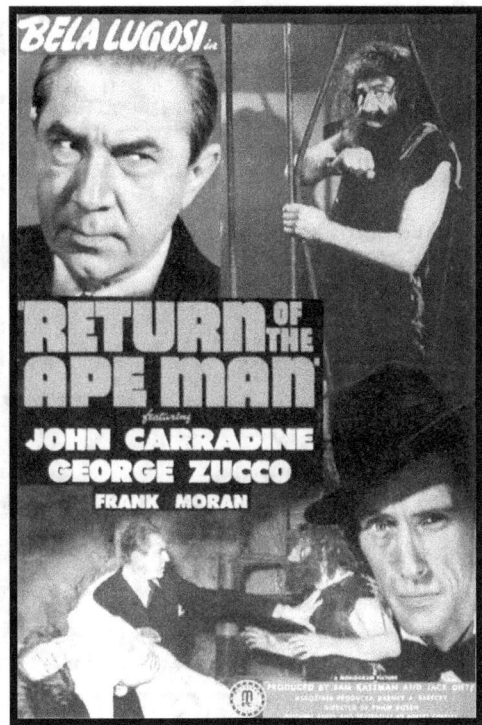

The ape man escapes, killing a policeman before Dexter can drive it back into captivity. A contrite Dexter begs Gilmore's help to destroy the monster, but of course Gilmore is taken captive instead as a brain donor. The film's loss of John Carradine at this point is a crippler—not only because he and Lugosi play so well off one another's Grand Manner intensity, but also because Frank Moran's title creature is such a ridiculous presence.

Hollywood's notion of the sub-hominid as a fear-inducing presence had deteriorated terribly in the years since Bull Montana had played such nightmarishly formidable creatures in *Go and Get It* (1920) and *The Lost World* (1925). By the '40s—*Dr. Renault's Secret* and *Captive Wild Woman* being conspicuously welcome exceptions—even a bigger picture like *One Million B.C.* was content to saddle an actor with pelts and a scruffy hairpiece and call him a caveman. *Return of the Ape Man* takes this line of lesser resistance to its absurd extreme, entrusting the role to sleepy-eyed, slump-shouldered Frank Moran and allowing him to amble through the ostensibly predatory moments while grumbling as if constipated.

The more problematical walk-through here is committed by director Phil Rosen, who seems to have put his characteristically emphatic command of pace and performance on holiday. Carradine and Lugosi hardly require direction, for these fine actors know their proverbial motivations better, probably, than the people who hired them. It is as well that George Zucco, who shares co-billing

with Moran as the ape man, seems not to have suffered the indignity of actually playing the role, except for a production still that was used as a lobby-card image and (possibly) for an early-in-the-game glimpse during a laboratory scene. In any event, only Moran appears on screen as the creature, rampant—and so do his underpants, guaranteeing a chorused horselaugh from the audience at precisely the moment when the suspense should be mounting.

Frank Moran had been a heavyweight prizefighter of some importance, losing a title bout to Jack Johnson in 1914, and battling incumbent Jess Willard to a no-call standstill in 1916. Moran made a more worthwhile mark in Hollywood as a member of Preston Sturges' company, where he registered consistently as a burly lug capable of delivering highfalutin' dialogue with delicacy and droll humor. Moran's finer small moments in such Sturges pictures as *Sullivan's Travels* (1942; as a no-nonsense servant) and *Unfaithfully Yours* (1948; as an indignant fire chief with a fancy vocabulary) go a long way toward lessening the damage of his prolonged exposure in *Return of the Ape Man*.

Another outbreak of guffaws is inevitable when the ape man, now supposedly in possession of a civilized intellect, steals into Carradine's house and begins playing a mournful fragment from Beethoven on a parlor piano. Here is a scene of comparatively sobering depth, intended to show the homing instincts of Carradine's slain character, that benefits from dimmed lighting and a more nuanced reading than any moment that has come before. It occurs too cruelly late, however, to overcome the unintentional hilarity that Rosen has allowed to suffuse the picture, and not even a new fatality can save the sequence.

Phil Rosen was a pioneering camera artist—the first president, during 1918-21, of the American Society of Cinematographers—whose work as a director during the talkie era was usually confined to the smaller studios. Rosen had a sure eye for the proper photographic treatment and usually took a straightforward, practically *anti*-arty approach. This style works well in the more genuinely fine Rosen pictures, most notably 1933's *The Sphinx*, where the grim doings take place in workaday settings. Rosen also knew how to jazz things up a bit when helming the occasional costume melodrama, such as Universal's *The Mystery of Marie Roget* (1942), the ill-acknowledged companion-piece to Robert Florey's *Murders in the Rue Morgue* (1932).

For *Return of the Ape Man*, Rosen takes his customarily unaffected tack, but for once it simply does not work, what with the narrative emphasis upon the yock-inducing title character. Even Lugosi gets done away with prematurely. There follow the abduction of Judith Gibson; a tedious backstage chase at a theatre; a nick-of-time rescue; and a conflagration started by the ape man himself. None too soon.

CREDITS: Producers: Sam Katzman and Jack Dietz; Associate Producer: Barney Sarecky; Director: Phil Rosen; Story and Screenplay: Robert Charles; Photographed by: Marcel Le Picard; Special Effects: Ray Mercer; Assistant Directors: Art Hammond and Dick L'Estrange; Editor: Carl Pierson; Sets: Dave Milton; Music: Edward Kay; Sound: Glen Glenn; Running Time: 61 Minutes; Released: June 24, 1944

CAST: Bela Lugosi (Prof. Dexter); John Carradine (Prof. John Gilmore); Frank Moran (Ape Man; [George Zucco Also Credited]); Judith Gibson (Anne); Michael Ames (Steve Rogers); Mary Currier (Hilda Gilmore); Ed Chandler (Sergeant); Ernie Adams (Bum); Mike Donovan and George Eldridge (Policemen); Horace Carpenter (Watchman)

NABONGA GORILLA
a.k.a.: NABONGA; NABONGA (GORILLA); THE GIRL AND THE GORILLA
(Sigmund Neufeld Productions, Inc./Producers Releasing Corp.)

Nabonga Gorilla, an odd and precarious bridge between *Tarzan* and *Mighty Joe Young*, is a breakthrough semi-starring vehicle for Julie London, who would prove her greater worth to show business as a sultry torch singer. Having graced an expendably small part in 1944's *Jungle Woman* at Universal, Miss London brought an abundance of exotic, vulnerable presence to this premature assignment to help carry a picture.

Miss London's limited range is, really, no debit in a picture that treats her for the most part as scenery. She plays Doreen Stockwell, survivor of a long-ago plane crash that had left her stranded in an African jungle. Doreen's father (the erstwhile cliffhanger champ Herbert Rawlinson) had been a fugitive embezzler, and the fortune he was carrying has become a legendary lost treasure.

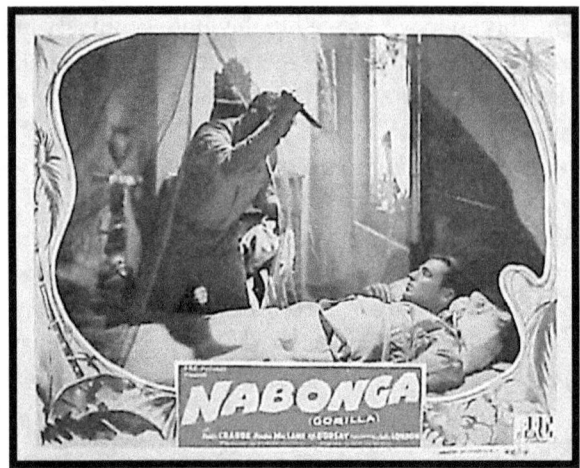

Years have passed, and explorer Ray Gorman (Buster Crabbe) has tied the theft to a persistent legend of a white sorceress. Seems Gorman's late father had been accused in the theft that Doreen's old man committed, and Gorman now intends to clear his dad's reputation. Two crooked hunters (Barton MacLane and Fifi D'Orsay) take an unwholesome interest in Gorman's search. Doreen lives under the protection of Sampson (Ray Corrigan, wearing the ape-suit he called N'Bonga), a mighty gorilla.

It all boils down to romance for Buster Crabbe and Miss London; a fatal thrashing-and-trampling from Sampson for the wicked couple; and a hero's death for the gorilla. Which makes it only too convenient for Miss London to accompany Crabbe back to civilization.

The Neufeld/Newfield family's involvement extends to the portrayal of Miss London as a child by Jackie Newfield, daughter of Sam Newfield.

CREDITS: Producer: Sigmund Neufeld; Director: Sam Newfield; Screenplay: Fred Myton; Photographed by: Robert Cline; Special Effects: Gene Stone; Assistant Director: Melville DeLay; Editor: Holbrook N. Todd; Sets: Paul Palmentola; Music: Willy Stahl; Music Supervisor: David Chudnow; Sound: Corson Jowett; Production Manager: Bert Sternbach; Running Time: 73 Minutes; Released: June 25, 1944

CAST: Buster Crabbe (Ray Gorman); Fifi D'Orsay (Marie); Barton MacLane (Carl Hurst); Julie London (Doreen Stockwell); Bryant Washburn (Hunter); Herbert Rawlinson (T.F. Stockwell); Prince Modupe (Tobo); Jackie Newfield (Young Doreen); N'Bonga [Ray Corrigan] (Sampson)

WATERFRONT
(Alexander-Stern Productions, Inc./Producers Releasing Corp.)

Directed by Steve Sekely and a pinch-hitting Elmer Clifton, this shadowy jewel of a dishonor-among-Nazis thriller also boasts the collaboration of two of Old Hollywood's fiercest experts at villainy, John Carradine and J. Carrol Naish. The treacheries commence with the mugging of a San Francisco optometrist, Carl Decker (Naish)—who nervously informs the police that no such crime has befallen him. Decker is the mastermind behind a spy ring. He promptly consults a fellow agent, Victor Marlow (Carradine), who is dispatched to reclaim a book that has been stolen from Decker. Which Marlow does, killing the thief in the process.

Marlow is a trigger-happy climber within the ranks, and at length his ambitions drive him to murder Decker. *Waterfront* is at its best when both starring antagonists are up and running at full steam, but Carradine carries the final reel relentlessly to a desperate finale. More than just a bloodthirsty menace, Carradine lends the role a sensitive, artistic dimension that figures significantly in his downfall.

Maris Wrixon fares splendidly as a secretary to an outwardly respectable spy (Edwin Maxwell). She also supplies a helpful romantic interest opposite Terry Frost, as a dockworker who is framed for one of Carradine's rub-outs. Olga Fabian is poignantly effective as Carradine's skittish landlady, who has ample reason to fret over the family she has left behind in Germany. Naish's elusive book is a very Hitchcock-styled MacGuffin, motivating mayhem aplenty without bogging down the story in over-explanation.

The co-director situation was not a planned strategy, but rather arose when Sekely was sidelined by illness and Clifton stepped in. Their styles mesh seamlessly.

CREDITS: Producer: Arthur Alexander; Directors: Steve Sekely and Elmer Clifton; Screenplay: Martin Mooney and Irwin R. Franklin; Photographed by: Robert Cline; Art Director: Paul Palmentola; Assistant Director: Lou Perlof; Editor: Charles Henkel, Jr.; Set Decor: Harry Reif; Music: Lee Zahler; Sound: Arthur B. Smith; Running Time: 66 Minutes; Released: July 15, 1944

CAST: John Carradine (Victor Marlow); J. Carrol Naish (Dr. Carl Decker); Maris Wrixon (Freda Hauser); Edwin Maxwell (Max Kramer); Terry Frost (Jerry Donovan); John Bleifer (Oskar Zimmerman); Marten Lamont (Mike Gorman); Olga Fabian (Emma Hauser); Claire Rochelle (Maisie)

SECRETS OF SCOTLAND YARD
(Republic Pictures Corp.)

The secrets on parade here belong as much to the Nazis as to Scotland Yard, and also to a vengeful undercover agent whose brother has been slain in the line of duty. Leading man Edgar Barrier's most urgent secret involves a distinguishing mark that requires him to keep his left hand bandaged lest his undercover assignment be compromised. The bandage also allows him to pack a concealed firearm, which figures in the final showdown. It is hardly giving away too much, too soon, to mention that the picture allows Lionel Atwill a most satisfactory role in keeping with his popular image.

Barrier starts off playing an expert decoder named John Usher, who must contend with a shadowy German cryptographer who has been lurking under a respectably English identity since the end of World War I.

Usher has just cracked a Nazi code when he is murdered, probably by an associate. Sir Christopher Pelt (Sir C. Aubrey Smith), of British Intelligence, summons John's twin, Robert Usher (Barrier), in hopes that an impersonation will jolt the guilty party into self-betrayal. No such luck: All John's co-workers, including his newly hired fiancée (Stephanie Bachelor) and the dignified Waterlow (Atwill), register only their usual genial responses. Robert breaks the sad news to David (Bobby Cooper), John's schoolboy son, and gains the child's promise to keep the imposture a secret. No suspect comes to light. Sir Christopher is murdered, and again suspects are lacking.

Finally, Robert's search for the code-breaking key leads him to a restaurant whose proprietor proves to be a German spymaster known as Josef (Martin Kosleck, in a trademark role). Josef discerns Robert's mission and takes him captive. Robert escapes, returns to headquarters, and translates the code to learn of a campaign to destroy an airplane carrying British military brass to Warsaw. Waterlow reveals himself as the spy who had slain both John and Sir Christopher. Robert, who has kept a gun hidden in the bandage covering his hand, disposes of Waterlow and calls a halt to the endangered flight.

Atwill and C. Aubrey Smith lend a classy substance to the production, which feels suitably English, considering its low-budget Hollywood origins. Edgar Barrier is just right as the patient investigator. The emphasis upon procedural operations is fascinating, with a proper nod to the role of the British Admiralty's decoding unit in trouncing Germany in World Wars past and present. Mary Gordon's housekeeper role seems almost a borrowing from Universal's *Sherlock Holmes* pictures.

The gimmick of the twin drafted into an impersonation of a slain secret-agent brother continues to crop up, most recently in 2002's *Bad Company*, a fish-out-of-water starring vehicle for the satirist and monologue artist Chris Rock, with Sir Anthony Hopkins inheriting Lord Smith's duties.

CREDITS: Executive Producer: Armand Schaefer; Associate Producer and Director: George Blair; Screenplay: Denison Clift, from his 1943 Short Story, "Room 40, O.B.," in *Blue Book* Magazine; Photographed by: William Bradford; Assistant Director: R.G. Springsteen; Art Director: Gano Chittenden; Editor: Fred Allen; Décor: Otto Seigel; Wardrobe: Adele Palmer; Music: Morton Scott; Sound: Earl Crain, Sr.; Running Time: 68 Minutes; Released: July 26, 1944

CAST: Edgar Barrier (John Usher and Robert Usher); Stephanie Bachelor (Sudan Ainger); Sir C. Aubrey Smith (Sir Christopher Pelt); Lionel Atwill (Waterlow); Henry Stephenson (Sir Reginald Meade); John Abbott (Mortimer Cope); Walter Kingsford (Roylott Bevan); Martin Kosleck (Josef); Forrester Harvey (Alfred Morgan); Frederick Worlock (Mason); Matthew Boulton (Col. Hedley); Bobby Cooper (David Usher); William Edmunds (Isaiah Thom); Louis Arco (Col. Eberling)

THE GIRL WHO DARED
(Republic Pictures Corp.)

The popular fascination with radioactive elements combines with a whiff of bogus spiritualism to make a winning garnish for *The Girl Who Dared*, a brisk adaptation of a novel by Medora Field. The retelling benefits further from a dual-role portrayal by the luminous Veda Ann Borg. Coastal Georgia, with its centuried legends of bloodthirsty pirates and buried treasure, is the setting, and John K. Butler's screenplay makes much of the juxtaposition of traditional mystery elements—bickering relatives, gathered for inevitable mayhem at an isolated mansion—with a search for a stolen cache of radium.

An invitation to the island estate of Beau and Chattie Richmond (John Hamilton and Vivien Oakland) promises "a ghost hunt." The arrivals include brother and sister Josh and Ann Carroll (Kirk Alyn and Lorna Gray); mechanic Rufus Blair (Peter Cookson), who has given Josh and Ann a lift; twins Sylvia Scott and Cynthia Harrison (both played by Miss Borg); Sylvia's former husband, David Scott (Roy Barcroft); and a friend, Homer Norton (Grant Withers). Beau and Chattie are flabbergasted at the onslaught of house-guests, for they know nothing of any such invitation. David blames the trickery on Josh, who

had pursued an adulterous affair with Sylvia. Beau seems the ideal host, however ill-prepared. Blair leaves, only to return.

The visitors hear a newscast about a search for one Dr. Paul Dexter, who has disappeared from an Atlanta hospital with a fortune in radium. It develops that Sylvia is acquainted with Dexter. A shadowy intruder attacks Sylvia; among those responding to her screams, David suffers a cut and leaves a bloodstain on one of her shoes. Sylvia denies any attack, claiming she had screamed at sight of a rat.

A ghostly apparition—part of the evening's improvised entertainment—distracts the party, and they return to find Sylvia murdered. The guests' cars have been disabled, and telephone service has been cut off. The body vanishes, but another corpse, identified as the fugitive Dexter, turns up. Cynthia's shoes have gone missing, even though Ann remembers distinctly where she had set them aside while comforting the distressed twin. Blair reveals himself to Ann as an insurance investigator—and the sender of the invitations, in an attempt to nab Sylvia and Dexter. In a cave, Blair and Ann find the two bodies and realize that the slain woman can only be Cynthia, not Sylvia, for neither of her shoes is bloodstained: Sylvia must have used her sister to bait a trap, neglecting to change shoes along with the clothing. A sudden chase leads to the body of Sylvia. Blair informs the assembled survivors that static from a radio will betray traces of radium on the guilty party. Thus unnerved, Homer Norton owns up to the killings. Sylvia and Decker had been expendable accomplices.

Grant Withers' track record as a genial lawman renders his unmasking here a nifty surprise. Lorna Gray makes a gutsy spur-of-the-moment investigator, and Peter Cookson is much more convincing as a genuine sleuth than he is as an amateur snoop in the *Kitty O'Day* pictures. Willie Best contributes his specialty as a nervous servant, whose misfortune it is to discover one of the stiffs. With enough convolutions for an extra 30 minutes' running time, *The Girl Who Dared* covers the bases and still clocks in at under an hour.

CREDITS: Executive Producer: Armand P. Schaefer; Associate Producer: Rudolph E. Abel; Director: Howard Bretherton; Screenplay: John K. Butler; Based upon: Medora Field's 1942 Novel, *Blood on Her Shoe*; Photographed by: Bud Thackery; Assistant Director: Joe Dill; Art Director: Gano Chittenden; Editor: Arthur Roberts; Music: Morton Scott; Running Time: 56 Minutes; Released: August 5, 1944

CAST: Lorna Gray (Ann Carroll); Peter Cookson (Rufus Blair); Grant Withers (Homer Norton); Veda Ann Borg (Sylvia Scott and Cynthia Harrison); John Hamilton (Beau Richmond); Willie Best (Woodrow); Vivien Oakland (Chattie Richmond); Roy Barcroft (David Scott); Kirk Alyn (John Carroll); Tom London (Nielson)

SEVEN DOORS TO DEATH
(Producers Releasing Corp.)

An unusually slick effort from budget-bound PRC, *Seven Doors to Death* also benefits from a captivating title and a layered story to match; a befuddling body-swap murder case; a glib and energetic show of heroism from Chick Chandler; and a rich array of suspects, ranging from a prissy dealer in antiques to an apelike handyman.

The killer's means of diverting suspicion also is a small gem of grisly manipulation—but don't let's get ahead of the game, which begins with the sound of gunfire at Hamilton Court, an upscale shopping center. Jimmy McMillan (Chandler), an architect, hears the noise while parked nearby and sees a young woman running from the courtyard. She hijacks his car at gunpoint, forces it into a crash—then leaps out and disappears. And yes, gallerias and carjackings have been around for longer than one might think.

Jimmy returns to discover the body of a stocky man in a checkered suit. He calls the police, who find instead the corpse of a tall man in evening attire. The victim is identified as Horace Donn, a lawyer who had represented the late Hilda Hamilton, owner of Hamilton Court. Hilda Hamilton's niece, Mary Rawling (June Clyde), is summoned to the police station. Jimmy recognizes Mary as the woman who had commandeered his car. Mary admits she had visited the premises to steal a deed, intending to keep it out of Donn's hands.

Jimmy follows Mary, who operates a shop in the courtyard, to demand that she pay for repairs to his car. The mystery deepens as they realize that a jewelry heist may have triggered the slaying. Other merchants come forth: Donald Adams (Milton Wallace) recalls that an Egyptian chest was stolen from his shop on the night of the murder. Silversmith Claude Burns (Edgar Dearing) seems a likely sort to be harboring stolen jewels. Jimmy and Mary sneak into the courtyard's cellar and find the missing chest—containing the body of the man in the checkered suit. The victim's hands are swathed in bandages. Henry Gregor (Gregory Gay), a photographer, displays to Jimmy and Mary a gallery of portraits of notorious criminals, including swindler Smoky Gordon, who had known Mary's Aunt Hilda. Jimmy learns that furrier Charles Eaton (George Meeker) once was a taxidermist.

Burns is slain while searching for the missing jewels. Mary learns that another merchant, Mabel De Rose (Rebel Randall), was with Eaton at the time of Donn's slaying. Gregor scopes out the scene of another crime—where he finds and photographs a thumbprint that can only belong to Smoky   Gordon.

Timothy Green (Casey MacGregor), the aforementioned apelike handyman, breaks into Mary's shop with apparently no other purpose than to leave a box containing jewelry and a certificate of marriage for Smoky Gordon and Mary's aunt. It finally dawns on Jimmy that the corpse in the cellar must be that of Gordon. No sooner has an anonymous tipster summoned the police to arrest Mary for murder, than Jimmy comes up with a more reasonable reconstruction: Eaton had killed both Donn and Gordon, then cut the flesh from Gordon's thumbs to leave misleading prints. Mabel De Rose had served as Eaton's accomplice, beguiling Green into planting evidence to incriminate Mary. Eaton did away with Burns, as well. Eaton confesses to the works.

Even the victims are a sorry lot in this pleasingly contrived who-and-whydunnit, and the suspects who prove guiltless still seem capable of sneaky intrigues—interesting sorts, if hardly likable. The conniving stereotypes arise from real life, for it is a truism that trendy boutiques, from then to now, tend to harbor misfits and eccentrics. Director Elmer Clifton's screenplay gives June Clyde an air of desperate menace from her first appearance, then softens her character by degrees by establishing in her a childlike impulsiveness, while forcing affable Chick Chandler to play sleuth mainly to keep himself in the clear. Both Chandler and Miss Clyde take a perilously keen interest in the case's twists and turns, finding themselves drawn to one another despite a hostile introduction. Throughout, they upstage Michael Raffetto, as an impatient police captain who'd just as soon nail the most convenient suspect and be done with it.

The *Seven Doors* reference, just in case anyone was wondering, accounts for six retail establishments and an apartment. *Seven Doors to Death* is not to be confused with *Seven Doors of Death*, which is an Americanized proxy title of Lucio Fulci's hellish shocker of 1981, *L'Aldila*, or *The Beyond*.

CREDITS: Producer: Alfred Stern; Director and Screenwriter: Elmer Clifton; Story: Helen Kiely; Photographed by: Robert Cline; Special Effects: Ray Mercer; Assistant Director: Lou Perloff; Art Director: Paul Palmentola; Editor: Charles

Henkel, Jr.; Set Décor: Harry Reif; Music: Lee Zahler; Sound: Arthur B. Smith; Running Time: 64 Minutes; Released: August 5, 1944

CAST: Chick Chandler (Jimmy McMillan); June Clyde (Mary Rawling); George Meeker (Charles Eaton); Michael Raffetto (Capt. William Jaffe); Gregory Gay (Henry Gregor [Given in Screen Credits as Henry Butler]); Edgar Dearing (Claude Burns); Rebel Randall (Mabel De Rose); Milton Wallace (Donald Adams); Casey MacGregor (Timothy Green); and Gene Stutenroth

THE PORT OF FORTY THIEVES
(Republic Pictures Corp.)

Damning secrets and a cruelly vain *femme fatale* worthy of some yarn by Cornell Woolrich or James M. Cain enliven this better-than-routine suspenser from director John English. Character is everything, plot largely incidental. Dane Lussier's original screenplay keeps the emotional tensions and life-or-death (mostly death) urgencies sufficiently cranked that the confining locale, a high-tone penthouse apartment, never becomes tiresome.

Murder has long since been committed by the time the first reel starts unspooling: Muriel Chaney (Stephanie Bachelor) hires a Manhattan lawyer, Scott Barton (Richard Powers), to have her vanished husband, a celebrated author, declared dead. The missing Hartford Chaney III, a financier, had become famous for his book *The Port of Forty Thieves*, an exposé of corruption along Wall Street. In fact, Muriel had murdered Chaney seven years ago. While awaiting the release of the Chaney millions, Muriel kicks back with her money-grubbing sweetheart, Frederick St. Clair (George Meeker).

Barton hits a snag when a bank draft bearing Chaney's signature turns up at a hotel. Muriel is so infuriated that she blurts out the truth of her crime to St. Clair—then threatens him with blackmail if he should blab.

Muriel, growing ever more careless in her fear of discovery, begins a blackmail campaign against captain of industry Charles Farrington (Russell Hicks), whom Chaney had left out of his notorious book on orders from Muriel. She kills St. Clair. The mystery check turns out to be a forgery committed by hotel employee Nancy Hubbard (Lynn Roberts) and her aunt, Caroline (Olive Blakeney), who have a resentful old score to settle with Muriel. Nancy proves to be Chaney's daughter by a prior marriage, which the upper-crust Chaney family had ordered annulled. Nancy has spent years trying to find evidence of Muriel's guilt. Patience finally pays off, but almost at the cost of Nancy's life. Farrington, who has rebelled against the blackmail scam, saves Nancy from a bullet. Muriel is led away to face justice, declaring that she must have a fine wardrobe for her trial.

The miscreant's simple overplaying of a winning hand is the beauty of the script, which is almost a solo vehicle for the under-appreciated Stephanie Bachelor. Only Lynn Roberts, as the grieving but determined daughter, conveys a comparable intensity. Richard Powers is affable and easygoing as the plodding lawyer who becomes more vitally interested in the case as it begins to unravel. Russell Hicks supplies the right bit of impulsive heroism as a defiant victim. Jack Marta's camerawork captures well the pampered confinement that has bred an overconfident killer.

CREDITS: Executive Producer: Armand Schaefer; Associate Producer: Walter H. Goetz; Director: John English; Screenplay: Dane Lussier; Photographed by: Jack Marta; Assistant Director: Allen Wood; Art Director: Russell Kimball; Editor: Richard Van Enger; Décor: George Milo; Costumer: Adele Palmer; Music: Morton Scott; Sound: Tom Carman; Running Time: 58 Minutes; Released: August 13, 1944

CAST: Stephanie Bachelor (Muriel Chaney); Richard Powers (Scott Barton); Lynn Roberts (Nancy Hubbard); Olive Blakeney (Caroline Hubbard); Russell Hicks (Charles Farrington); George Meeker (Frederick St. Clair); Mary Field (Della); Ellen Lowe (Jonsey); Patricia Knox (Gladys Burns)

CALL OF THE JUNGLE
(Krasne-Burkett Productions/Monogram Pictures Corp.)

A murderer described as having "no hands and three legs" hovers ominously over this bushwhacker whodunnit from director Phil Rosen. The promise of a freakish payoff is but ill realized, although *Call of the Jungle* compensates generously otherwise. The mystery is genuinely baffling, and burlesque alumna Ann Corio carries the show nicely as a tropical flirt who winds up spearheading the investigation.

The theft of two black pearls, sacred to the tribe of Tana (Miss Corio), touches off a territorial feud between colonial policeman Jim Forbes (James Bush) and Chief Kahuna (Harry Burns). Tana suspects prospectors Boggs and Carlton (Ed Chandler and I. Stanford Jolley) and warns a trader, Harley (John Davidson), against doing business with them. Tana's suspicions prove correct, but a pearl broker named Dozan (Phil Van Zandt) intimidates Harley into keeping quiet.

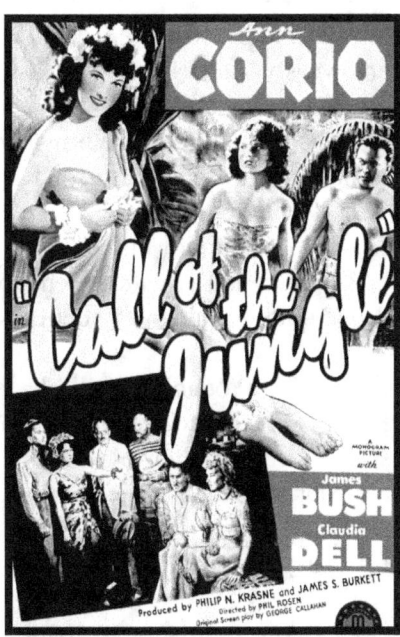

No sooner has Dozan bought the pearls than he is slain and robbed. The killer leaves clues that will implicate Harley. Tana shelters Harley while Forbes, following them into the jungle, is wounded and poisoned by a hidden assailant. Tana saves Forbes' life, and he agrees to bide his time to smoke out the true culprits. Malu (J. Alex Havier), a tribesman who had witnessed the murder, is next to fall. His dying words peg the killer as "a man with no hands and three legs."

Jim exploits the suspects' superstitious fears to keep them on edge while he conspires with the tribe to put the wraps on the case. Carlton and Boggs and a game-legged bartender named Louie (Muni Seroff) and his fiancée, Gracie (Claudia Dell), are seated alongside four burning candles. Tana declares that she will mystically extinguish all the flames except the one shining on the killer. Louie tries to escape but is captured. As Louie stuffs his hands into his pockets, Tana explains that the barkeep's walking-stick is regarded as a third leg by the natives—and his habit of keeping his hands pocketed means "no hands" in the tribal perception. Forbes finds the pearls hidden inside Louie's cane. The snuffing of the candles, the cop explains, was accomplished by a hidden native wielding a blow-gun.

Screenwriter George Callahan's great show of originality here is merely to transplant a generic drawing-room murder mystery into a primitive setting. Miss Corio and James Bush carry out their chores in a manner suggesting some banana-republic *Thin Man* takeoff, with accompanying romantic tensions leading up to a torrid smooch at the fade-out. The use of tribal drumming, slingshots and dart-blowers substitutes ominously for the traffic noise and machine-tooled weaponry of the more conventional setting for such a story. Especially nifty is the trick of making Bush's relentless detective something of an amateur musician—who unnerves his assembled suspects by playing an indigenous death-chant on a barroom piano. Among those suspects, Stan Jolley and Ed Chandler make a fine pair of taboo-busting opportunists. Phil Van Zandt plays the first victim as the sort who would engineer a frame-up just to get his lunch-hooks on a forbidden treasure. Claudia Dell is right at home in a gold-digger role, and weasly Muni Seroff, as a cash-strapped saloon proprietor, makes plenty of his unmasking scene.

The simple jungle settings are expertly rendered in light and shadow by camera chief Arthur Martinelli, whose best-known such hoodoo picture is 1932's *White Zombie*. A derivative but useful musical score bespeaks composer Albert Glasser's admiration of the big-studio maestro Max Steiner; Glasser's brooding brass strains and a rhythmic sense of urgency make the tiny hired-hand orchestra sound quite formidable under the circumstances.

CREDITS: Producers: Philip N. Krasne and James S. Burkett; Director: Phil Rosen; Screenplay: George Callahan; Photographed by: Arthur Martinelli; Assistant Director: Bobby Ray; Art Director: Dave Milton; Editors: Richard Currier and Marty Cohn; Set Décor: Al Greenwood; Musical Director: Dave Chudnow; Musical Score: Albert Glasser; Sound: Tom Lambert; Production Manager: Dick L'Estrange; Running Time: 60 Minutes; Released: August 19, 1944

CAST: Ann Corio (Tana); James Bush (Jim Forbes); Claudia Dell (Gracie); John Davidson (Harley); Muni Seroff (Louie); I. Stanford Jolley (Carlton); Ed Chandler (Boggs); J. Alex Havier (Maui); Harry Burns (Kahuna); Phil Van Zandt (Dozan)

STRANGERS IN THE NIGHT
(Republic Pictures Corp.)

Kindly resist the urge to hum Frank Sinatra's signature song, which came along a generation later and bears no kinship to this compact psychological melodrama. *Strangers in the Night* marks an early directing assignment for Anthony Mann, who would proceed to become one of the sharper handlers of film noir, with 1948's *T-Men* and *Raw Deal* and an uncredited job on *He Walked by Night*; one of the great Western picturemakers, with 1950's *Winchester '73* and 1955's *The Man from Laramie*, among others; and at length a decisive contributor to the big-screen epic style, with 1961's *El Cid* and 1964's *The Fall of the Roman Empire*.

In 1944, however, the director had only recently become Anthony Mann and was searching for a style to underscore the identity. Born Emil Anton Bundmann in San Diego in 1906, he found the family name ill-suited to the prominence he sought in W.W. II Hollywood. In 1942, Mann had moved from an assistant director berth at Paramount to a full-fledged directing career with RKO's low-budget unit and Republic's feature-film factory. *Strangers in the Night* is one of those dues-paying jobs, a potboiler that transcends its bottom-of-the-bill origins with an unnervingly melancholy story; leading portrayals awash in Existential loneliness and a sense of foregone doom; and a shock-value climax that many viewers remember even though they may have long since forgotten the overall narrative thrust.

Strangers in the Night does, of course, require a frank synopsis: A romance has blossomed by correspondence between a wounded Marine, Johnny Meadows (William Terry), and one Rosemary Blake, whose identity Johnny had found inscribed in a book while overseas. Returning to the States, Johnny hastens to Rosemary's hometown of Monteflores, California. En route, he meets Dr. Leslie Ross (Virginia Grey), who is bound for Monteflores to open a clinic. Their train derails, and Johnny helps Leslie care for several injured passengers before the journey can resume.

At the Blake estate, Johnny meets Hilda Blake (Helene Thimig), a crippled eccentric who introduces herself as Rosemary's mother. A massive portrait of Rosemary dominates the main room. Rosemary is traveling, Hilda explains, so Johnny settles in to wait. Meanwhile, Hilda's housekeeper, Ivy Miller (Edith Barrett), nervously visits Leslie's office in a failed attempt to reveal some urgent truth about the situation. Days pass with no sign of Rosemary, and Johnny confides his concerns to Leslie; he realizes that he is falling in love with the doctor—a development that Hilda has perceived. Hilda begins a resentful campaign to ruin Leslie's reputation.

Johnny, his patience exhausted, visits San Francisco to seek information from the artist who had painted Rosemary's likeness. Ivy reveals her misgivings in a letter intended for Leslie, but Hilda intercepts the note and kills Ivy. Johnny learns that Hilda had commissioned a portrait of an imaginary daughter.

Confronted, Hilda admits her deceptions even as she plots to murder Johnny and Leslie before they can find Ivy's corpse. Her trap fails, and Hilda realizes she is as good as nabbed. Just as the madwoman turns to gaze longingly at the portrait, the heavy frame snaps free and falls—crushing her.

Third-billed Helene Thimig (1889-1974), a self-exile from the Third Reich who would eventually return to her native Austria, dominates this intense study in manipulative derangement. She at first radiates a matronly warmth despite her spidery aspect but soon reveals herself as a delusional tyrant who will stop at nothing to sustain the sick fantasies that keep her going. The anticipation of Billy Wilder's famous *Sunset Boulevard* (1950) is unmistakable, as is a longing echo of Charles Dickens' *Great Expectations*, which had come to the screen twice before, in 1917 and 1934, and soon would come again in Sir David Lean's grand adaptation of 1946. William Terry is ideal for *Strangers'* role of a lonesome

searcher whose willingness to believe a romanticized lie almost proves his undoing—until, when helped along by a real woman with plenty of defiant mettle, he saves himself from miseries ahead by taking matters into hand.

The assertive physician is played with plenty of spark by Virginia Grey, a former second-string leading lady at MGM who had turned to free-lancing in 1942 with strategically long-lasting good results. Although she never attained any spectacular stardom, the onetime child actress forged an aggressive and prolific career outside the dominant studio system. She proved memorable in leads and character roles alike and brought as much zest to her smaller assignments (*Unknown Island* and the first *Jungle Jim* feature, later on into the '40s, among them) as to such bigger pictures as *Unconquered* (1947) and *No Name on the Bullet* (1959). Miss Grey retired in 1970 upon completing a featured part in *Airport*. It is trivially noteworthy, in light of Miss Grey's presence in the 1946 *House of Horrors*, that the work-in-progress title of *Strangers in the Night* was *House of Terror*.

CREDITS: Associate Producer: Rudolph Abel; Director: Anthony Mann; Screenplay: Bryant Ford and Paul Gangelin; Story: Philip MacDonald; Photographed by: Reggie Lanning; Assistant Director: Joe Dill; Art Director: Gano Chittenden; Editor: Arthur Roberts; Décor: Perry Murdock; Music: Morton Scott; Sound: Tom Carman; Running Time: 56 Minutes; Released: September 12, 1944

CAST: William Terry (Johnny Meadows); Virginia Grey (Dr. Leslie Ross); Helene Thimig (Hilda Blake); Edith Barrett (Ivy Miller); Anne O'Neal (Nurse Thompson); Audley Anderson (Conductor); Jimmy Lucas (Waiter); Roy Butler (Cabbie); Charles Sullivan (Police Driver); Frances Morris (Nurse)

MARKED TRAILS
(Monogram Pictures Corp.)

Veda Ann Borg takes her *femme fatale* image way out West to enliven *Marked Trails*, a *Trail Blazers* series entry about a Bonnie-and-Clyde rampage that forces Bob Steele to get down to serious business with the family tradition of law enforcement. Veteran lawman Harry Stevens (Steve Clark) is just about to nab a notorious dame named Blanche (Miss Borg) when he is killed in a sneak attack by her accomplice, Slade (Mauritz Hugo). The slaying moves Harry's nephew, Bob Stevens (Steele), and a pal, Hoot (pioneering shoot-'em-up star Hoot Gibson), to take up the killers' trail as U.S. marshals.

Blanche disguises herself as a schoolteacher and then as a flirtatious French settler while en route to a region rumored to be rich in oil. She provokes the murder of a geologist whose maps reveal a potential strike on her newly acquired ranchland, but Bob and Hoot are on the case. The pardners establish an elaborate undercover scheme: Bob will pose as an outlaw, and Hoot will pretend to be an oilfield developer. Bob's mock-courtship of Blanche provokes Slade to betray himself in jealousy.

The outlaws wind up getting less than what should be coming to them, but at least Steele has the pleasure of a snarling confrontation with an unrepentant Miss Borg.

CREDITS: Supervisor: William Strobach; Producer: Lindsley Parsons; Director: J.P. McCarthy; Screenplay: J.P. McCarthy (from His Story) and Victor Hammond; Photographed by: Harry Neumann; Assistant Director: Bobby Ray; Technical Director: E.R. Hickson; Editor: John C. Fuller; Music: Frank Sanucci; Sound: Glen Glenn; Running Time: 59 Minutes; Released: September 30, 1944

CAST: Hoot Gibson (Hoot); Bob Steele (Bob Stevens); Veda Ann Borg (Blanche); Ralph Lewis (Jed); Mauritz Hugh (Slade); Charles Stevens (Denver); Bud Osborne (Sheriff); Lynton Brent (Tex); George Morrell (Liveryman); Allen D. Sewall (Bradley); Steve Clark (Harry Stevens)

CODE OF THE PRAIRIE
(Republic Pictures Corp.)

Bat Matson—a name contrived to sound a whole lot like Bat Masterson—was a stock fictional identity at Republic, where the character might have been developed into a franchise like the long-forgotten *John Paul Revere* series. Which never happened, but by coincidence the Matson character was granted a two-picture showcase during 1943-44. Jack Rockwell played Matson in *Dead Man's Gulch* as a federal marshal who hires Don "Red" Barry to help settle a crime wave.

But woe betide the fan who expects picture-to-picture consistency: When Bat Matson re-surfaces in *Code of the Prairie*, he is now retired—having lost an arm, presumably in the line of duty—and he is played by a different actor, Tom Chatterton. He is also the rabble-rouser and motivating victim whose arrival in lawless Canyon City, Texas, only drives the criminal element to deeds more horrid. Republic's story editors probably never gave a second thought to the cavalier use of the convenient Matson identity. At any rate, *Dead Man's Gulch* is a Red Barry picture, and *Code of the Prairie* is a Sunset Carson–Smiley Burnette adventure.

Matson and his feisty daughter, Helen (Peggy Stewart), en route to establish a newspaper in Canyon City, are rescued from an outlaw attack by Bat's protégé, Sunset Carson (himself), and Sunset's pal, Frog Millhouse (Smiley Burnette). The Matsons' arrival upsets the machinations of Professor Graham (Roy Barcroft), an upstanding barber who enjoys controlling the community from behind the scenes. Matson, upon receiving an arrest-warrant poster for Graham under the villain's real name, confronts the barber—who responds by murdering Matson on the spot. The plot from here hangs on a photograph snapped of Graham as he is disposing of the corpse. Graham retouches the photo to make it appear that his uncomprehending puppet sheriff (Weldon Heyburn) is the culprit. The sheriff receives a royal beating from his impulsive friend Carson before Frog solves the case with a strategic application of down-home common sense.

Roy Barcroft, Republic's most reliable chapter-play villain, gives an expert reading of this demon barber of the Bald Prairie, a model citizen who is a raging sociopath at heart. We've had the displeasure of meeting quite a few of his malicious type in our years on the Texas Plains, where the extraordinary altitudes, endless flatlands and parched climate make an ideal breeding ground for conniving small-time kingmakers.

Sunset Carson hailed from this very region: Born Winifred Maurice (a.k.a. Michael) Harrison in Plainview, Texas, an agricultural hub scarcely an hour's drive south of the setting of *Code of the Prairie*, he assumed the name of his fictional character at Republic and remained a busy outdoors action star until 1950, then became a familiar face in television Westerns. Among the more imposing cowboy-as-hero figures of Old Hollywood, Carson stood six-foot-five—not counting the added height of his riding boots—and seemed tough and friendly in more or less equal measure. Possessed of neither the enduring marquee appeal of John Wayne nor the plutocratic corporate instincts of Gene Autry, Carson nonetheless kept his profile high for the long run, becoming one of the first cult-of-personality figures to lend his engaging presence to provincial movie-fan conventions during the 1960s and '70s.

The slaying of Chatterton's Bat Matson and the near-climactic slugfest are remarkably brutal—especially so, in the context of a picture patently intended for a juvenile clientele. *Code of the Prairie* also features a surreal curtain speech by the singer/comedian Lester "Smiley" Burnette, who makes himself more the star of the show than Carson: Burnette pretends to ask the audience members whether any of them spotted the clue that had given away the retouched photograph, then proceeds to over-explain the resolution. Finally, he says: "You kids go home, now. You've been in here all day." Which was probably true, during the picture's first-run situations.

CREDITS: Executive Producer: William J. O'Sullivan; Associate Producer: Louis Gray; Director: Spencer Gordon Bennet; Screenplay: Albert DeMond and Anthony Coldewey; Story: Albert DeMond; Photographed by: Bud Thackery; Art Director: Fred A. Ritter; Assistant Director: George Webster; Editor: Harry Keller; Set Décor: Otto Siegel; Musical Score: Joseph Dubin; Song: "They Won't Pay Me," by Smiley Burnette; Sound: Ed Borchell; Running Time: 56 Minutes; Released: October 6, 1944

CAST: Smiley Burnette (Frog Millhouse); Sunset Carson (Sunset Carson); Peggy Stewart (Helen Matson); Weldon Heyburn (Jesse Thorpe); Tom Chatterton (Bat Matson); Roy Barcroft (Prof. Graham); Bud Geary (Lem); Tom London (Loomis); Jack Kirk (Boggs); Tom Steele (Burley); Rex Lease (Davis); Howard B. Carpenter (Jackson); Herman Hack (Kent); Hank Bell (Jim); Nolan Leary (Rancher); Frederick Howard (Sam); Charles King, Jr. (Driscoll)

STORM OVER LISBON
(Republic Pictures Corp.)

A stock-company companion-piece to *The Lady and the Monster*, George Sherman's *Storm over Lisbon* affords Erich von Stroheim yet another richly conceived job of villainy, as an overconfident black-marketeer who scarcely could care less whether the Allies or the Axis powers profit from his activities. Stroheim's undoing proves to be the lovely Vera Hruba Ralston, who plays a counterspy feigning subservience to him while undermining his shabby empire from within. Richard Arlen completes the uneasy triangle, as a war correspondent and former prisoner who is anxious to leave Lisbon with documentation of Japanese atrocities in Burma.

Loyalties are a matter of convenience. An enemy spy named Vanderlyn (Otto Kruger) arrives in the Portugese capital believing he is to capture John Craig (Arlen), but in fact Vanderlyn is there to meet death at the hands of casino boss Deresco (von Stroheim). Maritza (Miss Ralston), a famous dancer from Czechoslovakia, has found herself reduced to performing at Deresco's nightclub. Nothing is much as it seems to anyone involved, and Stroheim's Deresco is so oblivious to the affections of his secretary (Mona Barrie) that he cannot notice her exasperated defection to the Allied cause.

The mere betrayal and capture of Stroheim come as a bit of a letdown, but the yarn ends on a note of pleasingly grim determination: Miss Ralston passes

up a shot at safety in the United States to carry on the good fight in Europe. Arlen gets in the last word with a bit of philosophizing about how a heroic life must be pursued alone.

Sherman brings almost a Warners-caliber texture and pacing to *Storm over Lisbon*, in keeping with the tale's *Casablanca*-like attitude. "Mystery-dramas can strangle themselves in too many skeins of intrigue," *Variety* grumped, "and this one ties itself up in knots." The piece is essentially a typical Sherman-at-Republic B-picture, rendered superficially larger by the studio's standing orders to develop pretentious star vehicles for Vera Ralston. (Of course, Warners had harbored no particular pretensions for *Casablanca*, which achieved greatness without any self-conscious artistic strivings.)

Miss Ralston, though never a natural at the acting game, gives the beyond-her-range role a wholehearted try and comes off pretty well. It helps that Stroheim and Arlen—accomplished players whose excellence only seems effortless—refuse to play down to Miss Ralston's rudimentary level, forcing her to reach, with rewarding results. Her dancing sequences are quite good. Followers of the larger perspective of low-budget Hollywood will enjoy spotting future Superman Kirk Alyn and Ed Wood crony-to-be Kenne Duncan in small roles.

CREDITS: Associate Producer/Director: George Sherman; Story: Elizabeth Meehan; Adaptation: Dane Lussier; Screenplay: Doris Gilbert; Photographed by: John Alton; Special Effects: Theodore Lydecker; Assistant Director: R.G. Springsteen; Art Director: Russell Kimball; Editor: Arthur Roberts; Décor: Otto Seigel; Costumer: Adele Palmer; Music: Morton Scott; Sound: Dick Tyler; Running Time: 86 Minutes; Released: October 16, 1944

CAST: Vera Hruba Ralston (Maritza); Richard Arlen (John Craig); Erich von Stroheim (Deresco); Otto Kruger (Alexis Vanderlyn); Eduardo Cianelli (Blanco); Robert Livingston (Bill Flanagan); Mona Barrie (Evelyn); Frank Orth (Murgatroyd); Sarah Edwards (Maude); Alice Fleming (Agatha); Leon Belasco (Nino); Kenne Duncan, Bud Geary and Roy Barcroft (Henchmen); the Aida Broadbent Girls (Dancers); Ruth Roman, Karen Randle and Annyse Sherman (Hat-Check Girls); Marie Day (Maid); Lucien Prival and Muni Seroff (Men in Tuxes); Lester Sharpe (Overfelder); Kirk Alyn (Bandleader); Gino Corrado (Headwaiter); Jack George and George Humbert (Waiters); Will Kaufman (Baron Vallesky);

Alphonse Martell (Maitre d'Hotel); Louis Ludwig Lowy (Croupier); Manuel Paris (Roulette Operator)

WILD HORSE PHANTOM
(Producers Releasing Corp.)

"Waste not, want not" was the watchword on Poverty Row, where a single salvaged prop or a proven crowd-pleasing concept could become the pivot of an entirely new movie. Producer Sigmund Neufeld recycled his *Lightnin' Bill Carson* project of 1936 (which had been appropriated by producer Sam Katzman as the basis of an extensive series) into the *Billy Carson* series at PRC, loosely dovetailing it with a *Billy the Kid* series starring Buster Crabbe and Al "Fuzzy" St. John. Neufeld, who had been a silent-partner supervisor on PRC's *The Devil Bat* (1940), also found it expedient to inform his Western films with traces from his horror thrillers—and vice versa. And what better gimmick to jazz up a *Billy Carson* picture than the Devil Bat itself?

The imposing but hardly realistic bat dummy takes a delightfully surprising encore in *Wild Horse Phantom*, menacing sidekick St. John while he and Crabbe track a gang of robbers through a supposedly haunted mine. Apart from the tunnels—nightmarish in themselves—there is a cackling skulker on hand to pester both the good guys and the bad guys; enough dishonor among thieves to yield a respectable body count; and the creepy-but-comical bat attack, which goes like this:

Fuzzy is standing guard over captive bandit Robert Cason when a hellacious shriek comes out of the darkness. Rushing to investigate, Fuzzy is confronted by the soaring bat. In a mad dash that Lou Costello might have envied, Fuzzy runs smack into Crabbe. Meanwhile, Cason and chief outlaw Kermit Maynard argue over the loot, and Maynard shoots Cason. Re-entering the tunnels, Fuzzy stumbles over Cason's body and reacts by seizing a pickaxe and swinging it blindly. The blow dislodges a cache of stolen money.

Measured by H.P. Lovecraft's scares-are-where-you-find-'em policy, the film's overall tone is not of horrific intent, given the greater concern with reclaiming a fortune and saving a bunch of honest ranchers from economic ruin. But for a rousing moment, there, the classic elements of an *el cheapo* horror movie fall decisively into place, in a

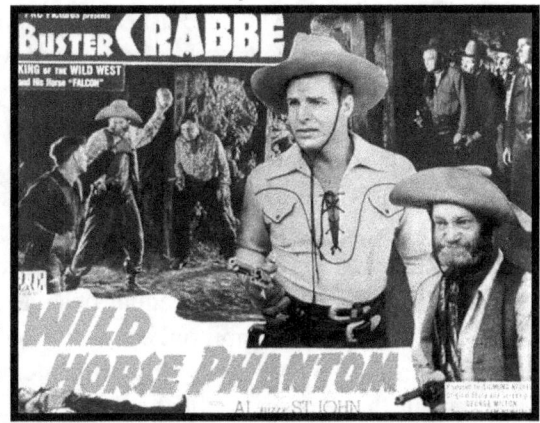

testament to the wisdom of the resourceful frugality that defines independent filmmaking.

CREDITS: Producer: Sigmund Neufeld; Director: Sam Newfield; Story and Screenplay: George Milton; Photographed by: Jack Greenhalgh; Cameraman: Ernest Smith; Special Effects: Ray Mercer; Transparency Projection Effects: Ray Smallwood; Art Director: Paul Palmentola; Assistant Director: Harold E. Knox; Editor: Holbrook N. Todd; Sound Engineer: Arthur Smith; Production Manager: Bert Sternbach; Running Time: 55 Minutes; Released: October 28, 1944

CAST: Buster Crabbe, "King of the Wild West" (Billy Carson); Falcon (Billy's Horse); Al "Fuzzy" St. John (Fuzzy Jones); Elaine Morey (Marian Garnet); Kermit Maynard (Link Daggett); Budd Buster (Ed Garnet); Hal Price (Cliff Walters); Robert Meredith (Tom Hammond); Frank Ellis (Callen)

WHEN STRANGERS MARRY
a.k.a.: BETRAYED
(King Bros. Productions/Monogram Pictures Corp.)

William Castle didn't just materialize one day during the late 1950s as some boisterous pretender to Alfred Hitchcock's "Master of Suspense" title. Castle achieved notoriety by working long and hard for it in comparative obscurity, as a Poverty Row and B-unit director specializing in—what else?—the bizarre and the suspenseful. Precisely such a dues-paying job is *When Strangers Marry*, which paid off for Castle in terms of favorable reviews and brisk box office traffic. *Variety*, which was more often intolerant of the low-budgeter studios' output, liked everything about *When Strangers Marry* but the title, which the trade rag complained "suggests another of the problem plays about newlyweds."

Nope, no domestic soapers here. The film, shot under the title of *I Married a Stranger*, starts out ominously with the strangulation murder of a loudmouthed boozer (Dick Elliott) who had flashed a wad of cash at a bar in Philadelphia. Cut to a train bound for New York, where newlywed Millie Baxter (Kim Hunter), traveling solo, impulsively tells fellow passengers that she is en route to meet her husband, Paul Baxter, a traveling salesman whom she barely knows. Paul has been in Philadelphia.

Paul is nowhere to be found, but Millie meets an old flame, Fred Graham (Robert Mitchum). In the lengthening absence of Paul, Fred offers to help Millie. Rumors of a strangler at large have reached New York. Paul (Dean Jagger) finally turns up, but his peculiar behavior puts Millie on edge. Homicide Detective Blake (Neil Hamilton) connects Paul's luggage to the Philly case and begins questioning Fred and Millie, who attempts to throw the cop off the trail. It turns out that Paul is troubled only by his proximity to the crime, and that

Fred is the culprit, seeking to frame Paul and claim Millie—or, failing that, to kill her. Millie dodges a near-fatal rooftop encounter with Fred, who is finally captured. Millie and Paul embark on an overdue honeymoon.

Not only Castle, but also such heavyweights a-borning as Robert Mitchum and Kim Hunter would owe their careers to such small pictures as *When Strangers Marry*. Mitchum is already in possession of that elusive star quality, using his naturally smoky voice and heavy-lidded eyes to unnerving effect as a predator hiding in plain sight—the right leading man at the right time for the rapidly evolving film noir idiom. Miss Hunter, a David O. Selznick discovery, is likewise fine as the innocent at large and in danger. Dean Jagger, a dependable but bland talent whose larger prospects lay years ahead in the realm of television, completes the triangle as a paranoid schlub who, though guiltless, fancies that he just might be capable of murder. Castle sustains a sense of brooding unease throughout, helped immeasurably by Dimitri Tiomkin's evocative music, but Castle also leavens things with another trademark-in-the-making: welcome bits of nervous humor. The King Bros.' production outfit continues here to raise the standards of Monogram.

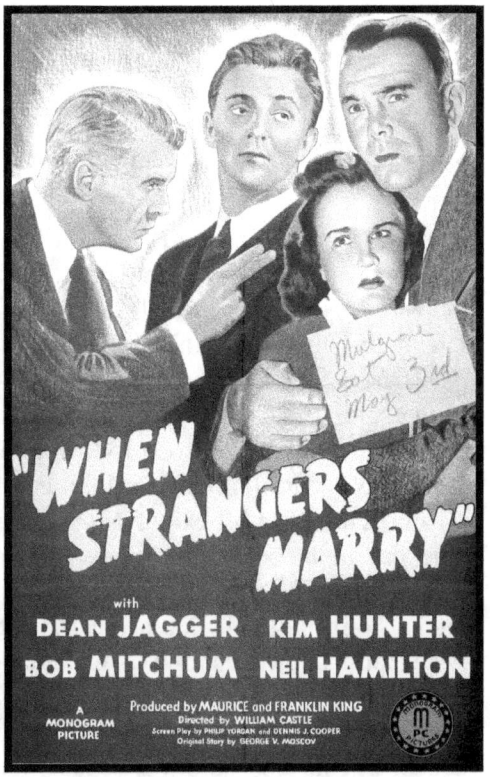

CREDITS: Producers: Maurice King and Franklin King; Director: William Castle; Dialogue Director: Leon Charles; Story: George Moscov; Screenplay: Philip Yordan and Dennis J. Cooper; Photographed by: Ira Morgan; Assistant Directors: Frank Fox and Clarence Bricker; Art Director: F. Paul Sylos; Editor: Martin G. Cohn; Décor: Al Greenwood; Music: Dimitri Tiomkin; Music Editor: Leon Birnbaum; Sound: Thomas Lambert; Technical Adviser: Herman King; Production Manager: Clarence Bricker; Running Time: 67 Minutes; Released: November 24, 1944; Reissued: During 1949 as *Betrayed*

CAST: Dean Jagger (Paul Baxter); Kim Hunter (Millie Baxter); Robert Mitchum (Fred Graham); Neil Hamilton (Blake); Lou Lubin (Jacob Houser); Milt Kibbee (Charlie); Dewey Robinson (News Vendor); Claire Whitney (Middle-Aged Woman); Edward Keane (Middle-Aged Man); Virginia Sale (Maid)

BLUEBEARD
(Producers Releasing Corp.)

The visionary director Edgar G. Ulmer had alienated the nepotistic big shots at Universal Pictures suicidally early in his career: His sin was to woo and win the wife of producer Max Alexander, a nephew of Universal's president, Carl Laemmle. Universal, in thinly veiled retaliation, had subjected Ulmer's perverse masterpiece, *The Black Cat* (1934), to sacrificial scissoring in appeasement of that year's relentless new tide of institutionalized censorship. In a strange karmic turn, Alexander soon followed in Ulmer's wake onto Poverty Row as Laemmle's control of Universal lapsed.

A decade after his exile from the major studios, Ulmer had weathered the blackballing by becoming a respected maker of tightly budgeted independent features and short subjects. In addition to a wide range of general-interest pictures—including the occasional musical—Ulmer was often at the helm of American-made Yiddish and Ukranian-language films, as well as black-ensemble attractions for the separate-and-unequal segregated theatres of the day.

Ulmer was bound sooner or later to develop a film from the legend of Bluebeard, the most notorious seducer-and-slayer in European criminal history and folklore. Ulmer's departure from Universal in 1934 had left unproduced his docketed filming of a version of *Bluebeard*—from a story by Gordon Morris, in which *The Black Cat*'s principal villain, Boris Karloff, was to have starred. Ulmer fared marvelously with the topic at a substantially lesser studio and with an emerging star player whose screen presence at the time suggested a younger, more saturnine Karloff. In John Carradine, Ulmer found an actor with a seldom-explored delicacy of manner that renders this Bluebeard's crueler instincts all the more disturbing. The thunderous Carradine voice is so thoroughly subdued here that when the killer reveals, "I was a very ambitious youth, and extremely sensitive," he seems all the more monstrous for it.

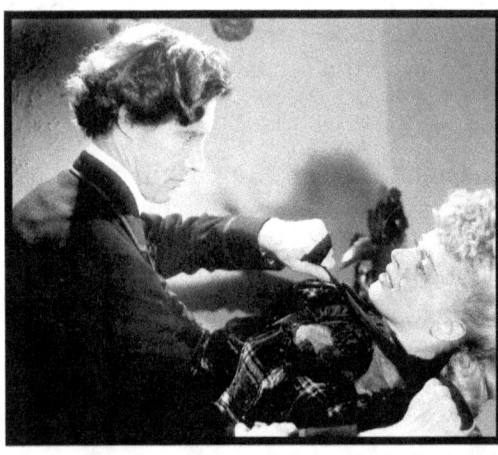

The mad puppeteer Morrell (John Carradine) realizes that his mistress Renée (Sonia Sorel) knows too much to live, in *Bluebeard*.

In 19th-century Paris, the puppeteer Gaston Morell (Carra-

> Aside from Mike Price: My father, the Texas industrialist John A. Price, was one serious film buff, and one of his favorite actors was John Carradine. Dad professed to despise crime-and-horror movies as a class and was wary of my fondness for suchlike, but he'd watch anything with Carradine in it, even *Return of the Ape Man* or *The Face of Marble*. This interest helped us to find a common ground during the generationally divisive 1960s, and when I would occasionally accompany him on his business travels through the Southwest—he ran a company with some remote branch offices—we'd converse a great deal about favorite motion pictures and hit as many movie theatres as time would allow.
>
> We were in Clovis, New Mexico, during the summer of 1961, talking about John Ford over lunch at a town-square café, and Dad started rhapsodizing about *The Grapes of Wrath* (1940). I had seen the film on a reissue, years before, when I was too young to get much out of John Steinbeck's tragic tale of disenfranchisement and defiance, and Dad was allowing as to how we really ought to keep a closer eye on the TV listings on account of one never could tell when *Grapes* might crop up on the Late Show. "Now, for my money, the best character in it is Carradine—you like his monster movies, don't you?—playing this renegade preacher who's kind of the conscience of the story," Dad was saying. "Say, it's like I can hear that voice of his right now, that bombastic Shakespearean voice, just thinking about it."
>
> All of a sudden, that very voice came up over the ambient noise of the short-order eatery. Dad and I looked at one another in a jolt of recognition—neither of us quite managed to utter the name we associated with that unmistakable voice—then shook our heads as if to say, "Naaaww, it can't be." The voice was ordering a chicken-fried steak dinner—"and a bottomless cup of the blackest coffee you can dredge up," as we overheard. I turned around to gaze down the row of booths and saw John Carradine flirting with a waitress. After a moment's hesitation, Dad and I approached his table, figuring the worst he could tell us would be to buzz off.
>
> But no, the Great Man greeted us expansively, inviting us to join him and warming to the opportunity for conversation—even if he didn't seem quite to believe that we'd been talking about him just a moment before. He quoted Shakespeare at some length, to the amused puzzlement of the local regulars, and he inventoried for us a handful of his more fondly remembered assignments from the almost 100 pictures he had graced by that time. His hard-luck Preacher Casy of *The Grapes of Wrath* was mentioned, of course, to my father's delight, and Carradine turned the reference into a joke about an imaginary horror movie he called *The Gripes of Wrath*. He cited his Abraham Lincoln impersonation in *Of Human Hearts* (1938) and his Aaron to Charlton Heston's Moses in *The Ten Commandments* (1956), as well as such fantasies as *The Invisible Man's Revenge* (1944) and the *House of Frankenstein/House of Dracula* combo (1944-1945). It turned out that Carradine was touring Southwestern community playhouses at the time, spreading his passion for Shakespeare to the provinces. Upon returning to Hollywood, he would begin work on *The Man Who Shot Liberty Valance* (1962).
>
> "Another one I have a great deal of affection for," Carradine told us, "is a little period piece called *Bluebeard*. It's a variant on my 'madman' type, and more restrained than I usually come across. Now, I work most commonly just to keep myself working, with the predictable consequence that I have accumulated a sizeable body of work from which comparatively few jobs stand out. I believe *Bluebeard* stands out most admirably."

dine) leads a bizarre secret life. Between engagements of his marionette version of *Faust*, he paints haunting portraits of the beautiful women who fall for him. These are sold under an assumed name through a conniving broker, Lamarte (Ludwig Stossel), who knows a grimmer secret: Morell feels compelled to strangle every woman who poses for him.

Morell drives his mistress, the singer Renée Claremont (Sonia Sorel), beyond her usual jealousy when he courts Lucille (Jean Parker), a modiste. Morell kills Renée when she wonders aloud what has become of his other women. He appears convincingly innocent when questioned by Inspector LeFevre (Nils Asther), but then LeFevre recognizes a victim in one of the canvases, and the police set about to identify the painter.

Lucille's sister, Francine (Teala Loring), visits on undercover business for LeFevre and commissions a portrait through Lamarte. Recognizing the artist

as Lucille's caller, Francine is strangled with a cravat that Lucille had mended for Morell.

Lucille senses a grimness about Morell. He admits his love for her and confesses his killing urge. Rather than risk her turning against him, Morell braces to do away with Lucille. LeFevre and his officers burst in, just in time. Morell, fleeing across the rooftops, plunges to his death in the Seine.

Producers Releasing Corp. and its imposing PRC Pictures logotype are remembered chiefly today with a mock-fondness among a community of bad-cinema devotees whose chief pleasure lies in snarky belittlement. Such PRC releases as *Devil Bat* and *The Black Raven* are familiar entries on the rosters of so-called stinkers, but in fact the studio's output suffers more greatly from constraints of time and money than from ineptitude. Few of the PRCs that we have viewed—and that's a good many, even in just the context of these books—can be accused of inflicting boredom, which is the truer criterion for a bad movie.

During its span of less than a decade, PRC often resolved to part ways with its Poverty Row origins and "strike out for a better trade," as *The Hollywood Reporter* interpreted the studio's ambitions in 1944. *Bluebeard* was begun on the usual 10-day schedule and tiny budget, but after seeing the first two days' rushes, studio chief Leon Fromkess ordered a substantial increase in budget and a few more days' shooting time. Designed to accommodate a maximum of brooding shadowplay by the pioneering European cinematographer Eugen Schufftan—a 1940 immigrant who was barred by union regulations from his usual trade—*Bluebeard* is so polite a study in madness and menace as to render Carradine almost sympathetic.

Carradine had sufficient professional background in common with Schufftan (for both men had worked as portrait artists and sculptors) to make the portrayal of a working artist fit seamlessly into Schufftan's designs of a practical milieu. The dialogue includes a discussion of lighting requirements for a portrait sitting.

Here can be found a remarkable approach to capturing Carradine's face. Resisting the commonplace tactic of exploiting the actor's angular features and overall height in sharply lighted straight-on and low-vantage shots, Schufftan and the official director of photography, Arthur "Jockey" Feindel, concentrated upon Carradine's immense forehead and intense gaze in softly lighted high angles, achieving a soulful aspect. (Feindel and Schufftan had worked together the same year on *Voice in the Wind*.) These values carry over into the gracefully understated dialogue—which helps to mute the broader B-movie coincidences of the screenplay—and into Leo Erdody's delicate musical score. These cues rely largely upon strings and woodwinds, with ominous brass and percussive punctuation. The musical score is based in part upon Mussorsky's *Pictures at an Exhibition*.

The collaborative work of Ulmer and Schufftan compares favorably with the more celebrated teamings of William Wyler and cinematographer Gregg Toland. Schufftan, whose groundbreaking miniature background process system is integral to Fritz Lang's *Metropolis* (Germany; 1927), worked prolifically on an international scale following *Bluebeard*. He eventually won the Oscar for Best Black-and-White Photography for *The Hustler* (1961).

Morell's marionettes play a key part in *Bluebeard*, their portrayal of Gounoud's *Faust* providing an apt complement to the plot enacted by the principals. Many of the puppet scenes are lighted and photographed in such intimate quarters that the mannequins seem almost living performers.

Bluebeard is served with an almost sinister forcefulness by Swedish-born Nils Asther, as the calculating policeman who uses the women as cat's-paws in bringing Carradine to bay. Jean Parker, who was about to retrench to the stage as her H'wood career wound down, appears younger than her 32 years as the resourceful dressmaker.

Austrian stage veteran Ludwig Stossel makes a worthy villain-behind-the-madman. The role is a sharp departure from the genial Germanic type that Stossel had defined in *Pride of the Yankees* (1942) and cinched a generation later in a run of "Little Old Winemaker" commercials for television. Iris Adrian has a hilarious sequence—New York accent and all—as a snippy prostitute. Sonia Sorel (Mrs. Carradine, at the time), does well as Morell's mistress.

CREDITS: Producer: Leon Fromkess; Director: Edgar G. Ulmer; Associate Producer: Martin Mooney; Original Story: Arnold Phillips and Werner H. Furst; Screenplay: Pierre Gendron; Musical Score and Orchestrations: Leo Erdody; Production Design: Eugen Schufftan; Production Manager: C.A. Beute; Assistant Director: Raoul A. Pagel; Art Director: Paul Pamentola; Assistant Art Director: Angelo Scibetta; Set Decorations: Glenn P. Thompson; Sound Engineer: John Carter; Master of Properties: Charles Stevens; Photographed by: Arthur "Jockey" Feindel; Makeup: Milburn Moranti; Marionettes: Barlow & Baker; Running Time: 73 Minutes; Released: November 11, 1944

CAST: John Carradine (Gaston Morell); Jean Parker (Lucille); Nils Asther (Inspector LaFevre); Ludwig Stossel (Lamarte); George Pembroke (Inspector

Renard); Teala Loring (Francine); Sonia Sorel (Renée Claremont); Henry Kolker (Deschamps); Emmett Lynn (Le Soldat); Iris Adrian (Mimi); Patti McCarty (Babette); Carrie Devan (Constance); Anne Sterling (Jeanette)

ROGUES GALLERY
(American Productions, Inc./Producers Releasing Corp.)

Says here that a fantastic new invention can transmit voices over vast distances—and without microphones, yet. Say, listen: The mountain folks have been doing that for centuries; they call it *yodeling*. But about *Rogues Gallery*: News reporter Patsy Clark (Robin Raymond) and photographer Eddie Jones (Frank Jenks) are unwelcome visitors at the laboratory where the device is being tested, but they are right on the spot when the gizmo is strongarmed away from its inventor (H.B. Warner). What starts off as a breezy newspaper caper picture with a sci-fi veneer, turns promptly into a creepy though harebrained murder thriller—never losing sight of its essence of journalistic irresponsibility.

By the time an impatient police lieutenant (Bob Homans) has taken a practical interest in the chase, the yarn has already generated one slaying; a missing corpse that gets found and then goes missing again; a premature headline that gets Robin Raymond's irritating snoop of a journalist fired; and a re-demonstration of the invention that betrays an upstart rival news reporter (Ray Walker) as the culprit. Said culprit gets gunned down for his troubles, and Miss Raymond gets rehired to commit further annoyances-in-print. What business a news-hack would have in taking charge of a radically innovative piece of high technology—now, there's a mystery that should cause absolutely no one to lose any sleep. *Rogues Gallery* is precisely the sort that gives even the better PRCs a tainted reputation.

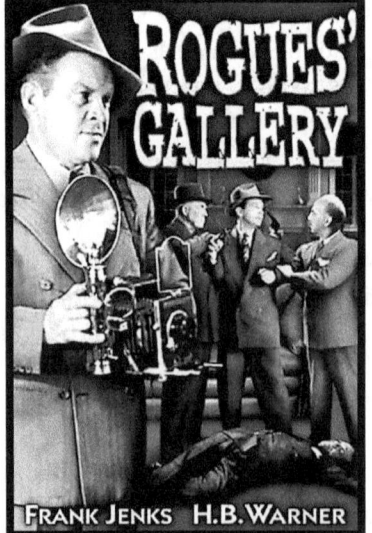

CREDITS: Producers: Donald C. McKean and Albert Herman; Director: Albert Herman; Screenplay: John T. Neville; Photographed by: Ira Morgan; Second Cameraman: Fred Kaifer; Special Effects: Ray Mercer; Assistant Director: Lou Perloff; Art Director: Paul Palmentola; Editors: Fred Bain and Carl Pierson; Décor: Harry Reif; Propmaster: George Bahr; Music: Lee Zahler; Sound: Frank McWhorter; Sound Mixer: John Carter; Re-Recording and Effects Mixer: Jack Noyes; Music Mixer: Eddie Nelson; Makeup: George Gray; Running Time: 60 Minutes; Released: December 6, 1944

CAST: Frank Jenks (Eddie Jones); Robin Raymond (Patsy Clark); H.B. Warner (Reynolds); Ray Walker (Jimmie Foster); Davison Clark (Foster); Bob Homans (Lt. Daniel O'Day); Frank McGlynn (Blake); Pat Gleason (Red); Edward Keane (Gentry); Earl Dewey (Griffith); Milton Kibbee (Wheeler); Gene Stutenroth (Joyce); George Kirby (Duckworth); Norval Mitchell (Joe Seawell)

CRAZY KNIGHTS
a.k.a.: GHOST CRAZY
(Banner Productions/Monogram Pictures Corp.)

Three stooges—not to say *the* Three Stooges—make this scares-laden slapsticker as great a delight as any connoisseur of generically scripted, lowbrow comedy could hope to find. One of the stooges is, in fact, an authentic Stooge: Samuel "Shemp" Howard had long since relinquished his place in the formally acknowledged Vaudeville-to-Hollywood transitional act to kid brother Jerome "Curly" Howard. Shemp's greater strategy was to pursue a solo career, at which he kept busy on into the early 1950s, when he rejoined the Three Stooges, replacing the ailing-and-doomed Curly for the last genuinely inspired stretch of the team's long-running series at Columbia Pictures.

Within or without the family trio, however, Shemp seldom played anything *but* his patented Stooges character. His conspiratorial bartender opposite W.C. Fields in *The Bank Dick* (1940), his dice-throwing routine with Mantan Moreland in *The Strange Case of Dr. Rx* (1942), his teaming with Joe Besser and the Bud Abbott–Lou Costello combo in *Africa Screams* (1949)—all are pure Stoogery, but for the absence of brother Moe Howard and their "adopted cousin," as Moe called him, Larry Fine.

The same goes in volume for William Beaudine's *Crazy Knights* and its companion films, *Three of a Kind* (1944) and *Trouble Chasers* (1945), all produced by Sam Katzman and Jack Dietz in a bid to out-stooge Columbia's *Three Stooges* series. The strategy was to present feature-length misadventures vs. the Columbia short subjects. Katzman and Dietz, of course, enjoyed neither the production resources nor the long-established loyal audience of the Columbias, and this upstart series petered out rapidly.

Where *Three of a Kind* is a backstage show-biz spoof with sentimental overtones and *Trouble Chasers* is a crime-melodrama parody, *Crazy Knights* is an unadulterated horror lampoon—complete with old-dark-house and graveyard shenanigans; a sinister housekeeper played by a reigning expert, Minerva Urecal; and gaping graves, grotesques galore and a gorilla for good measure. Shemp's partners in hilarity are Billy Gilbert, the high-strung and heavy-set *alumnus* of Hal Roach Studios, and Slapsie Maxie Rosenbloom, the prizefighter who earned the nickname via a playfully crowd-pleasing way of slapping his opponents.

Billy Gilbert and Shemp Howard and their circus partner Dave Hammon (Bernard Sell) are traveling to the next engagement with their trained-ape act. They come upon the aftermath of what seems to have been a car-bombing attempt on the life of one Mr. Gardner (John Hamilton). No casualties, but the occupants are shaken and stranded, so Dave offers them a lift home. The destination is a desolate mansion complete with a front-yard burial ground, and niece Joan Gardner (Jayne Hazard) clearly has no business staying in light of the fate that befell her mother—or so the housekeeper, Mrs. Benson (Miss Urecal), cryptically insists. Shemp and Billy want no truck with this joint, but after Joan is frightened by a hideously mutilated prowler and Gardner reports an attack, the buddies agree to stay the night. Dave has become infatuated with Joan.

Shemp and Billy spot what appears to be a ghost. Investigating, they find a movable tombstone over a tunnel; the opening has become hidden by the time they bring help, but Shemp, Billy and Maxie, the Gardners' chauffeur, keep looking until they rediscover it. The gorilla (Art Miles, the title player in 1939's *The Gorilla*) gets loose. Joan is abducted by a cloaked intruder, who is knocked unconscious by Mrs. Benson. The culprit proves to be Gardner, who had hoped to gain control of Joan's inheritance.

Uninspired—though hardly uneventful—plotting would sink the picture if not for the abundant horseplay and lively portrayals. The members of the trio are well-defined personalities, not because the picture renders them so but rather because Howard, Gilbert and Rosenbloom had long since defined themselves: Shemp, the indignant, muttering master of mingled geniality and soreheadedness; Gilbert, the blustering bundle of nerves; and Rosenbloom, the childlike mug. Katzman's independent-among-independents company merely exhibited the good sense to turn these beloved funnymen loose on a yarn that would have defeated lesser artists and repulsed most other name-brand comedians.

CREDITS: Producers: Sam Katzman and Jack Dietz; Associate Producer: Barney Sarecky; Director: William Beaudine; Screenplay: Tim Ryan; Photographed by: Marcel Le Picard; Special Effects: Ray Mercer; Assistant Directors: Art Hammond and Lewis Dow; Editors: John Fuller and Dick Currier; Music: Edward Kay; Sound: Frank Webster; Running Time: 63 Minutes; Released: December 8, 1944

CAST: Billy Gilbert, Shemp Howard and Maxie Rosenbloom (Themselves, More or Less); Tim Ryan (Grogan); Jayne Hazard (Joan Gardner); Tay Dunn (Ralph Williams); Minerva Urecal (Mrs. Benson); John Hamilton (Gardner); Bernard Sell (Dave Hammon); Betty Sinclair (Girl)

THE WHISPERING SKULL
(Alexander-Stern Productions, Inc./Producers Releasing Corp.)

Woodward Maurice "Tex" Ritter (1905-1974) was as unlikely a candidate for Western-movie stardom as his fellow singer Gene Autry had been. Neither artist cut a particularly athletic figure, but each addressed the camera with a glad-to-be-here confidence, and both proved quick studies of the genre's actionful requirements. And like Autry, Ritter proved amenable enough to the Westerns' recurring appetite for weird mystery. *The Whispering Skull* is a middling good example of the Frontier Gothic style—Ritter's lapses into song notwithstanding.

This entry in the *Texas Rangers* series finds lawyer Tex Haines (Ritter) teaming with Rangers Dave Wyatt (stuntman-actor Dave O'Brien) and Panhandle Perkins (Guy Wilkerson) to put down a rampage by a masked marauder known as the Whispering Skull, who prowls by night astride a silent, ghostly horse.

Saloonkeeper Duke Walters (I. Stanford Jolley) announces that he has been warned by the Skull to leave town. Walters rallies a vigilante group that arrests Panhandle on a charge of being the Skull. Tex and Dave arrive in time to save Panhandle from a lynching, and Dave decides to work undercover.

It develops that Walters has been using the Skull's raids as a cover for crimes all his own—no surprise, given the matinee-Western track record of career badman Stan Jolley—and now Walters plots to murder the local sheriff (George Morrell) and frame the Skull. The sheriff survives an attack, however, and Dave conspires to keep the lawman's recovery a secret to smoke out the culprit.

The case boils down to the discovery of an outcropping of rock that Walters has assumed to be a diamond lode. The Skull is at last revealed to be a drifter

known as Arkansas Mike (Wen Wright), who also had discovered the stones and concocted the Skull scam to scare the local ranchers into selling out. The rocks prove worthless, after all. Walters is captured as he attempts to flee, and the Rangers ride on in search of new ranges to rearrange.

The Whispering Skull character is scarier in concept than in execution—gone were the days of such harrowing monsters-out-West fare as *Tombstone Canyon* and *The Crimson Trail*—but the image of a cloaked phantom astride a silently galloping charger is abundantly creepy while it lasts. Leave it to good guy Dave O'Brien to de-mystify the menace, revealing that the Skull's horse is merely an ordinary mount with padded hooves and that the Skull is just a saddle tramp who means no harm other than to rout the locals. Jolley's villainy is made of sterner stuff. The Rangers trio accounts for its star billing more or less equally, with O'Brien handling most of the heroism, Ritter covering the folksy-philosophical and musical bases and Guy Wilkerson serving the all-important sidekick function.

CREDITS: Producer: Arthur Alexander; Director: Elmer Clifton; Screenplay: Harry Fraser; Photographed by: Edward Kull; Assistant Director: Sidney Smith; Second Camera: Ernest Smith; Special Effects: Ray Mercer; Settings: Harry Reif; Editor: Hugh Winn; Music: Lee Zahler; Songs: "In Case You Change Your Mind," by Tex Ritter & Bonnie Dodd, and "It's Never Too Late," by Tex Ritter and Frank Hartford; Sound: Arthur B. Smith; Running Time: 56 Minutes; Released: December 29, 1944

CAST: Tex Ritter (Tex Haines); Dave O'Brien (Dave Wyatt); Guy Wilkerson (Panhandle Perkins); Denny Burke (Ellen Jackson); I. Stanford Jolley (Duke Walters); Henry Hall (Judge Polk); George Morrell (Sheriff Marvin Jackson); Edward Cassidy (Doc Humphrey);

1945

GRISSLY'S MILLIONS
(Republic Pictures Corp.)

Meanness fairly radiates from Muriel Roy Bolton's original screenplay for *Grissly's Millions*, with Virginia Grey accounting for the lone element of kindliness within a household overpopulated with hated and hateful relatives. Even her eventual romantic interest, the lawman played by Paul Kelly, seems to expect the worst of Miss Grey's character, given the company she keeps. He warms to her by degrees—only to realize that she has taken part in a cover-up for homicide. Miss Grey seems unlikely to get out with her life intact, and never mind any inheritance, for the true killer tries to shove Miss Grey over a cliff and later poisons her before making that last defiant stand. Don Douglas is properly shady as an opportunistic lawyer, and Adele Mara contributes an unwitting motivation to the crimes as a would-be actress who'd be just ever so delighted to have the estate underwrite her brilliant career.

CREDITS: Executive Producer: Armand Schaefer; Associate Producer: Walter H. Goetz; Director: John English; Screenplay: Muriel Roy Bolton; Photographed by: William Bradford; Assistant Director: Joe Dill; Second Camera: Joseph Novak; Special Effects: Howard Lydecker and Theodore Lydecker; Transparency Projection Shots: Gordon C. Schaefer; Art Director: Gano Chittenden; Editors: Harry Keller and Richard Van Engler; Décor: George Milo; Costumer: Adele Palmer; Music: Morton Scott; Sound: Earl Crain, Sr; Running Time: 71 Minutes; Released: January 16, 1945

CAST: Paul Kelly (Joe Simmons); Virginia Grey (Katherine Palmor Bentley); Don [Donald] Douglas (Ellison Hayes); Elisabeth Risdon (Leona Palmor);

> From George E. Turner's World War II filmgoing diary (about which, more later):
>
> The entire staff which produced *Grissly's Millions* deserves a pat on the back for making an excellent film out of an inexpensively budgeted mystery story. The film is directed in a very satisfactory manner by former serial director Jack English, [with] good performances from all hands. Musical director Morton Scott adds some superbly disturbing overtones to the suspenseful moments, and the special-effects department of the Lydecker Bros. turns in a job that bests some of the major studios.
>
> Plot concerns old Grissly Palmor's (Robert Barrat) family, all of whom seem to have grisly secrets. Virginia Grey [as a devoted granddaughter] is threatened by her criminal husband (Paul Fix), and Palmor, dying, kills him. To cover up, she and a lawyer (Don Douglas) bury the body with Palmor. The granddaughter receives an inheritance in the millions, but she is found out by a detective (Paul Kelly) on the trail of the vanished husband. The detective falls in love with her. An autopsy shows Grissly was poisoned. The detective proves the granddaughter innocent,... but she is almost killed by the real murderer, [an aunt played by] Elisabeth Risdon—who falls to her death in a ravine.
>
> Best scenes: Special effects shot of the old mansion...; special effects scenes of occurrences at the ravine... Best performances: Kelly, Grey, Risdon.

Robert H. Barrat (Grissly Morgan Palmor); Clem Bevans (Young Tom); Francis Pierlot (Dr. Renny); Addison Richards (Henry Adams); Eily Malyon (Mattie); Adele Mara (Maribelle); Paul Fix (Lewis Bentley); Byron Foulger (Fred Palmor); Joan Blair (June Palmor); Grady Sutton (Robert Palmor, Jr.); Frank Jaquet (Robert Palmor, Sr.); Will Wright (John Frey); Louis Mason (Gatekeeper)

HIS BROTHER'S GHOST
(Producers Releasing Corp.)

The titular ghost is to be taken at face value only by a hysterical majority of the bad guys in this rousing high-water mark of Sig Neufeld's *Billy Carson* series. Those miscreants, however, respond appropriately enough to a bogus haunting to make the film work for *FH's* purposes. More harrowing is the vicious slaying, early on, of that belovedly grizzled career sidekick, Al "Fuzzy" St. John.

Not to worry, though: In a deathbed turning point, Andy Jones (St. John) summons his twin, Jonathan "Fuzzy" Q. Jones (St. John *redux*), who sees to it that the picture lives up to its title. Topliner Buster Crabbe's character, Billy Carson, is all but incidental to this low-rent star vehicle for St. John, who savors every crusty moment of a performance that is by turns comical, distraught and vengeful.

The border town of Wolf Valley is under siege by a gang whose secret leaders include the town doctor, Packard (Karl Hackett), a rancher named Thorne (Charles King) and a deputy sheriff, Bentley (Archie Hall). The Jones estate includes a sprawl of land, and the mob is eager to glom onto the property. So when Thorne's hirelings show up at Andy's villa, Fuzzy crops up to scare them away—then follows them to their hideout for a spot of harassment. The hoodlums become convinced either that they have encountered a ghost or that Andy has survived.

Thorne will abide none of this nonsense, and so he exhumes Andy's corpse to enlighten his thugs. Relieved, the owlhoots return to their lair, only to find Fuzzy resuming the spook act. One of the gang (Roy Brent) becomes so terrified that he submits his resignation to Thorne—who kills him outright. Meanwhile, Billy and Fuzzy rally Andy's tenant farmers against the gang. Billy gives one outlaw (Bob Cason) a sound thrashing, but only the appearance of Fuzzy will move the gangster to name Packard as a conspirator. Billy and Fuzzy then terrify Packard into spilling the plot. Thorne has sensed the truth about Fuzzy, who still has enough mileage left in the ghost routine to scare a near-confession out of Bentley. Bentley is gunned down by Thorne. Just as Thorne is about to force Fuzzy to sign over Andy's property, Billy horns in and disables the ringleader. The sharecroppers attend to the rest of the hoods. Fuzzy declares himself the new law-and-order around these here parts and sentences the surviving racketeers to life in the hoosegow.

One might expect a picture built around Al St. John to be somewhat breezier, but director Sam Newfield keeps things balanced between darkly rambunctious comedy and a greater sense of foreboding. Charles King is just right as the ruthless boss, and St. John never loses sight of his mission to amuse the adolescent-male target audience with the get-up-and-go geezer act while attending to an earnest settling of accounts. Karl Hackett is particularly good as the trusted physician who means but harm to his own townspeople, and King proves the only one of the mob capable of rising above the prevailing irrational fears. Crabbe generously yields control of the yarn to St. John, who is capable of shouldering the burden.

CREDITS: Producer: Sigmund Neufeld; Director: Sam Newfield; Story and Screenplay: George Milton; Photographed by: Jack Greenhalgh; Assistant Director: Harold E. Knox; Special Effects: Ray Mercer; Editor: Holbrook N. Todd; Running Time: 60 Minutes; Released: February 3, 1945

CAST: Buster Crabbe (Billy Carson); Al "Fuzzy" St. John (Andy Jones and Jonathan "Fuzzy" Q. Jones); Charles King (Thorne); Karl Hackett (Doc Packard); Archie Hall (Deputy Bentley); Roy Brent (Yaeger); Bud Osborne (Magill); Bob Cason (Jarrett)

FOG ISLAND
(Producers Releasing Corp.)

A hidden-treasure scam, a disgraced big-shot securities broker and a greedy bunch of disgruntled investors occupy the title patch of sinking real estate, with largely lethal results. If the locale isn't haunted to begin with, then it should be groaning with the spirits of victims by the time the movie has run its course. *Fog Island* is, in one narrow sense, as keen an all-star horror picture as any of Universal's bigger monster-mash teamings, what with George Zucco, Lionel Atwill and Veda Ann Borg on hand to meet the challenges of an audacious, though ill thought-out, script. Bernadine Angus' original stage-play had borne the title *Angel Island* when produced in New York in 1937; PRC's rechristening makes a better fit, if only because the studio's prevailing style is so lovably fogbound in its own right.

Fallen market manipulator Leo Grainger (Zucco), fresh out of stir, has retreated to Fog Island, once a pirates' haven, with his stepdaughter, Gail (Sharon Douglas). The island provides the privacy they require, for the press has awakened to word of the convicted swindler's release—and there remains a mystery involving the slaying of Gail's mother during Grainger's imprisonment. Grainger's former investors, who had let him take the rap for their mis-dealings, are only too ready to believe that he has socked away a fortune.

Although, or perhaps because, he is probably more nearly innocent than anyone will grant, Grainger nonetheless is plotting to kill those who had betrayed him. Promising restitution, he invites the lot of them to spend a jolly weekend on Fog Island. And here they come: Alec Ritchfield (Atwill), John Kavanaugh (Jerome Cowan), Sylvia Jordan (Miss Borg), Emiline Bronson (Jacqueline DeWit) and Jeff Kingsley (John Whitney), Gail's former sweetheart and son of a since-defunct Grainger crony. Joining them is Dr. Lake (Ian Keith), Grainger's creepy bookkeeper and fellow ex-convict.

Treacheries pile up alarmingly from here, starting with a séance during which Ritchfield steals away and murders Grainger, hiding the body down-cellar. A crucial key changes hands by stealth here, force there. Grainger's hidden treasure-box proves to contain only a contemptuous note. The ocean begins to seep in through a leaky foundation. Gail and Kingsley, reassured by a more comforting letter left by her mother, finally decide to leave the assembled crooks to their own cruel devices. Jeff chances to discover a hidden passageway, where he finds not only Grainger's body—but also the corpses of Ritchfield, Kavanaugh, Miss Jordan and Dr. Lake. Jeff decides Gail need not learn of the mass slaughter, and they shove off from Fog Island.

Few enough old-dark-house chillers have the guff to kill off such a hefty percentage of their inmates lest the suspects be depleted, and so *Fog Island* takes the palm for at least that temerity. Lionel Atwill is the most fiendish of a wretched lot of culprits, proving fairly early in the game to have slain host Zucco's wife as a prelude to the present round of horrors. True to George Turner's on-the-spot review, Atwill and Zucco deliver "about the only good performances," although Miss Borg is no slouch if one takes into account her severely under-written role. George Lloyd also has a memorable small turn as Zucco's jailbird butler. Karl Hajos' orchestral score is a jewel of overcranked morbidity.

George Turner, who relished wordplay and especially enjoyed tampering with movie titles, often referred to this picture as *Frog Island*. George Zucco's looks *are* a bit on the batrachian side, at that.

CREDITS: Executive Producer: Leon Fromkess; Associate Producer and Director: Terry Morse; Screenplay: Pierre Gendron; Based upon: Bernadine Angus' 1937 Play, *Angel Island*; Photographed by: Ira Morgan; Assistant Director: William A. Calihan, Jr.; Second Camera: Ralph Ash; Art Director: Paul Palmentola; Editors: George McGuire and Carl Pierson; Décor: Harry Reif; Props: Charles Stevens; Men's Wardrobe: Larry Judge; Women's Wardrobe: Jean Sharpless; Music: Karl Hajos; Sound: William Fox; Running Time: 70 Minutes; Released: February 15, 1945

CAST: George Zucco (Leo Grainger); Lionel Atwill (Alec Ritchfield); Jerome Cowan (John Kavanaugh); Sharon Douglas (Gail); Veda Ann Borg (Sylvia Jordan); John Whitney (Jeff Kingsley); Jacqueline DeWit (Emiline Bronson); Ian Keith (Dr. Lake); George Lloyd (Allerton)

THERE GOES KELLY
(Monogram Productions, Inc./Monogram Pictures Corp.)

Considered here more for the record than on any merits of its own, *There Goes Kelly* is a why-bother? remake of the more significant *Up in the Air*, a 1940 entry in Monogram Pictures' compact series of comedy-thrillers starring Frankie Darro and Mantan Moreland. The annoying Jackie Moran replaces the likable Darro, and Wanda McKay replaces leading lady Marjorie Reynolds. Nobody replaces Moreland, although the Borscht Belt-to-Hollywood comedian Sidney Miller tackles an equivalent role. The plot is all but identical—radio star murdered, case cracked by buttinsky pageboy—right down to the happy ending for all who deserve it.

There is a kinship, as well, to Monogram's 1943 production of *Here Comes Kelly*, which stars Eddie Quillan as bus driver Jimmy Kelly and Sidney Miller as Kelly's pal Sammy Cohn. To complicate matters, Quillan also stars as an overambitious radio page in Universal Pictures' 1944 production of *Hi, Good Lookin'!*, which swipes the essence of *Up in the Air* but omits the murder-mystery angle. It takes a while, but sooner or later such desultory hackwork pictures reach a saturation level.

CREDITS: Associate Producer: William Strohbach; Director: Phil Karlson; Assistant Director: Bobby Ray; Screenplay: Edmond Kelso; Additional Dialogue: Tim Ryan; Photographed by: William A. Sickner; Art Directors: E.R. Hickson and Dave Milton; Décor: Vin Taylor; Western Electric Sound: Tom Lambert; Editor: Richard C. Currier; Running Time: 61 Minutes; Released: February 16, 1945

CAST: Jackie Moran (Jimmy Kelly); Wanda McKay (Anne Mason); Sidney Miller (Sammy); Ralph Sanford (Marty); Dewey Robinson (Delaney); Jan Wiley (Rita Wilson); Anthony Warde (Farrell); Harry Depp (Hastings); George Eldredge (Quigley); Edward Emerson (Martin); Jon [as John] Gilbreath (Tex Watson); Pat Gleason (Pringle); Donald [as Don] Kerr (Bowers); Charles Jordan (Wallis)

DILLINGER
(King Bros. Productions/Monogram Pictures Corp.)

Anyone who cherishes the Monogram spookers—whether earnestly or backhandedly—must of course be drawn to the little company's more naturalistic crime pictures. These movies not only help to define the film noir school of narrative cinema; they also capture the same cinderblock-gray ambiance and the raggedly adventurous milieux in which Bela Lugosi, John Carradine, Veda Ann Borg, Mantan More-land and even Boris Karloff can be found indulging their more outlandish exploits. The King Bros.' *imprimatur* on any Monogram picture is a tip-off that the studio was setting its sights higher than usual. More than one radio comedian of the 1940s would snipe about "dialogue so bad that even Monogram wouldn't use it," and Bob Hope once regaled an Academy Awards gathering with a wisecrack about how Mono-gram's presence at the Oscars banquet would be not a table, but rather a footstool. There but for the grace of Paramount Pictures might have gone Bob Hope.

But when Monogram set out to make a bigger picture, the result could be splendid as often as not. Such an effort is the King Bros. production of *Dillinger*. Although *Variety*, that influential but damnably short-sighted tradepaper, dismissed *Dillinger* as passé in its day—nearly 11 years had passed since the F.B.I.'s ambush slaying of the flamboyant bandit John Dillinger—history has proved the film to hold up as a persuasive retrospective account, nailing a certain truth if not a scrupulous factuality.

Lawrence Tierney, borrowed from RKO-Radio Pictures for this breakthrough star turn, plays Dillinger as a striving hothead of a would-be playboy who carelessly tackles an inaugural holdup, only to net chump-change and a hitch in prison. Incarceration means a networking opportunity for Dillinger, who mounts a break-out for veteran bandit Specs Green (Edmund Lowe), along with two cohorts (Marc Lawrence and Elisha Cook, Jr.). Specs grows ever leerier of John's loose-cannon manner, but Dillinger tries a more calculating strategy for once and fools a bank's sophisticated security system. Demoting Specs as a consequence of this success, Dillinger finds himself promoted to Public Enemy No. 1 by the F.B.I., then lands behind bars once again in what can only have been a betrayal. He escapes via a primitive ruse, kills Specs and finally lands smack in the middle of another betrayal—this one, fatal.

Variety called Tierney "a likely prospect with better roles"—and indeed, the stony-faced heir apparent to Humphrey Bogart's mobster image would go on to a solid handful of essential film noir leads, including *Born To Kill* and *The Devil Thumbs a Ride* (both from 1947). Tierney's career was compromised all along, however, by a turbulent private life, and his arrests for brawling and motoring-while-soused netted him more attention over the long haul than would his uneven involvement with moviemaking. Before *Dillinger*, incidentally, Tierney had appeared in two of Val Lewton's RKO productions of 1943-44: *Ghost Ship* (as the crewman who is crushed beneath a coiled chain) and *Youth Runs Wild*.

Anne Jeffreys, another loan-out from RKO, fares nicely as the romantic interest who turns out to be the feds' lady-in-red decoy, responsible for giving the law a clear shot at Dillinger. The supporting mobsters are a finely varied lot, with Edmund Lowe a standout as the calculating friend-turned-enemy and Elisha Cook, Jr., likewise as the squirmy sort essential to any such picture. Director Max Nosseck, a comparatively new arrival from Europe, gracefully accommodates character development as a function of breakneck pacing, framing the brutal account as a sobering flashback related by Victor Kilian, as the badman's disappointed father.

Variety's review mentions that *Dillinger* "has been banned in Chicago." This reference descends from the Motion Picture Association's attempt to prevent the film's very making, dating as far back as a 1934 edict that "no picture based on the life or exploits of John Dillinger [could be] produced, distributed or exhibited by any member company." (A *non*-member studio, the opportunistic Midland Film Co., cranked out *Dillinger: Public Enemy No. 1* on the quick-and-cheap before 1934 could give way to 1935.)

The mainstream embargo had lapsed before Maurice and Franklin King put *Dillinger* into development on October 10, 1944, but Production Code chief Joseph I. Breen warned Franklin King as early as June of 1944 that a tentative script contained "numerous violations of [the Code's] Special Regulations Re: Crime in Motion Pictures." Breen also advised King to expect protests from "censor boards everywhere." There were no domestic bans other than Chicago's, although Ontario's censorship machine rejected *Dillinger* and the U.S. War Department declined to clear the film for showing at overseas military outposts. Hence the film's conspicuous absence from George Turner's W.W. II moviegoing notes. ("I was especially honked off that the Navy decided that *Dillinger* might inspire us swabs to knock over the commissary," George once said. "This meant I had to wait 'til the re-release.")

The mass-market newspapers, every ready to blame the entertainment industry for Real World social ills, were quick to exaggerate simple robbery cases whose perpetrators supposedly had sat through *Dillinger*. One prominent artist of Hollywood's big-studio establishment, the acclaimed sentimentalist director Frank Borzage, climbed up on his high horse to denounce *Dillinger* in a letter addressed to the Production Code Adminstration—but also leaked to the press *en masse*. Borzage called for "total elimination of the gangster movie," and a retroactive phooey to him from us.

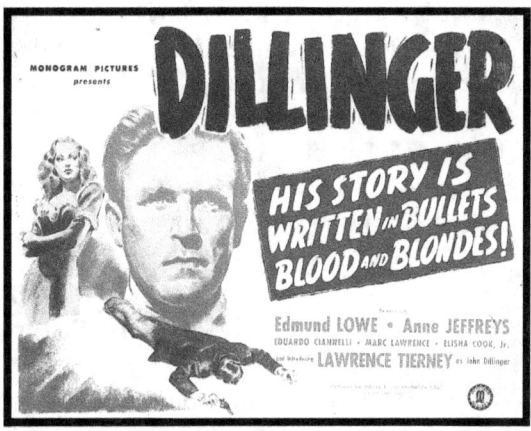

Dillinger's Max Nosseck, to whom an assignment was an assignment, could scarcely have cared less about such grandstanding tactics: Nosseck's other release of 1945 also turned out to be a crime thriller, RKO's *The Brighton Strangler*, which had been produced before *Dillinger*, though issued afterward. Nosseck went on to the diversified likes of *Black Beauty* (1946), *The Return of Rin Tin Tin* (1947) and *Kill or Be Killed* (1950).

Dillinger remains the film on which Tierney's early reputation rests; the actor became briefly resurgent during the 1990s, via Quentin Tarantino's *Reservoir Dogs*. Philip Yordan's *Dillinger* screenplay received an Academy Award nomination—assuring Monogram of a table, and not a footstool, at the Oscars fête. Allied Artists, as successor to Monogram, mounted an ambitious theatrical reissue of *Dillinger* in 1952.

John Dillinger's career receives a shallower but more lurid treatment in Dwain Esper's exploitationer documentary, *The March of Crime*, from 1946. Later such films would include 1973's *Dillinger*, with Warren Oates; 1979's *Lady in Red*, with Pamela Sue Martin and Robert Conrad; 1991's *Dillinger*, with Mark Harmon and Sherilyn Fenn; and 1995's *Dillinger and Capone*, with Martin Sheen and F. Murray Abraham.

CREDITS: Producers: Maurice King and Franklin King; Director: Max Nosseck; Dialogue Director: Leon Charles; Screenplay: Philip Yordan; Photographed by: Jackson Rose; Second Camera: Vincent Farrar; Special Effects: Ray Mercer and Robert Clark; Art Director: F. Paul Sylos; Editor: Edward Mann; Décor: Vince Taylor; Music: Dimitri Tiomkin; Music Editor: Edward Haire; Sound: Thomas Lambert; Production Manager: Clarence Bricker; Technical Adviser: Herman King; Running Time: 74 Minutes; Released: March 2, 1945

CAST: Lawrence Tierney (John Dillinger); Edmund Lowe (Specs Green); Anne Jeffreys (Helen Rogers); Eduardo Cianelli (Marco Minnelli); Marc Lawrence (Doc Madison); Elisha Cook, Jr. (Kirk Otto); Ralph Lewis (Tony); Else Janssen (Mrs. Otto); Ludwig Stossel (Otto); Constance Worth (Nurse); Victor Kilian (Dillinger's Father); Hugh Prosser and Dewey Robinson (Guards); Bob Perry (Proprietor); Kid Chissell and Billy Nelson (Watchmen); Lee "Lasses" White (Salesman); Lou Lubin (Waiter); Judy Brent (Dillinger's Date)

FASHION MODEL
(Monogram Pictures Corp.)

From the sublime of Monogram (*Dillinger*) to the absurd of Monogram: Often mis-recorded as a third entry in the *Kitty O'Day* series (see our 1944 section), this bubbleheaded murder-thriller called *Fashion Model* might as well have been an *O'Day*. For that matter, the *Kitty O'Day*s might as well have been continuations of Monogram's failed attempt to create a *Crime Smasher*, or *Cosmo Jones*, series. *Crime Smasher*, in its turn, looks like nothing so much as a pick-up-where-we-left-off extension of a more important series teaming a brash Frankie Darro with a skittish Mantan Moreland. Somewhere into this mosaic would fit the little studio's single most insipid picture, the Marcia Mae Jones–Jackie Moran starrer *Haunted House*. The constant is the amateur detective whose half-baked sleuthing leads invariably to a hot-water dunking.

For the amateur-sleuth gimmick was an easy perennial with Monogram's story department, and the flakier the would-be detective, the better. *Fashion Model*'s screenwriters, Victor Hammond and actor Tim Ryan, serve the film much as they had served the *O'Day*s, and Ryan's impatient cop character might even be a carry-over but for a significant name-change. Continuity freaks and obsessive-compulsive retentives could lunch out on these trivial pictures for years at a stretch. Take our word for it: Why bother?

For the record: Marjorie Weaver serves *Fashion Model* as Peggy Rooney, the title character, who is first seen cat-fighting with a glamorous colleague, Yvonne (Lorna Gray), over a rivalry for the affections of Jimmy O'Brien (Robert Lowery), a handsome employee of a boutique managed by Mme. Celeste (Dorothy Christie, of *Sons of the Desert* and *The Phantom Empire*, and as haughty as ever). The discovery of Yvonne as a murder victim triggers the revelation of some hateful old secrets, including Yvonne's role in wrecking the marriage of Celeste and proprietor Jacques Duval (Edward Keane). Jimmy is the only employee without an alibi, but Peggy convinces the police that Jimmy would not have had an opportunity to kill Yvonne. Later, Duval's body turns up in Jimmy's delivery van. Peggy muddles through a maverick investigation until she finds the killer to be mousy Harvey Van Alyn (Harry Depp), husband of the salon's most demanding customer (Nell Craig). Van Alyn had given Yvonne a valuable piece from his wife's collection of jewelry, and Yvonne had reciprocated with a blackmail scam. Van Alyn is about to add Peggy to the roster of victims when the police burst in.

Filmed under the more honest work-in-progress title *The Model Murder*, this mercifully brief effort at least packs a respectable body count, and Harry Depp escalates to a scary intensity as the milquetoast philanderer whose secret life has finally caught up with him. Director William Beaudine lets the story run its course practically on auto-pilot, with any nuances of timing or delivery coming strictly from within the ensemble cast. Robert Lowery is playing beneath his level as the hapless almost-patsy, and Marjorie Weaver seems too smart to permit her character such impetuous conduct. Neither seems to have inquired where the motivations might lie—as if Beaudine, to whom nuance and subtext meant only a waste of time, would have known or cared.

CREDITS: Executive Producer: Trem Carr; Associate Producer: William Strobach; Director: William Beaudine; Screenplay: Tim Ryan and Victor Hammond, from His Story; Photographed by: Harry Neumann; Assistant Director: Bobby Ray; Second Camera: Vincent Farrar; Art Director: E.R. Hickson; Technical Director: Dave Milton; Editors: Dan Milner and William Austin; Music: Edward Kay; Running Time: 61 Minutes; Released: March 2, 1945

CAST: Robert Lowery (Jimmy O'Brien); Marjorie Weaver (Peggy Rooney); Tim Ryan (O'Hara); Lorna Gray (Yvonne); Dorothy Christie (Celeste); Dewey Robinson (Grogan); Sally Yarnell (Marie Lewis); Jack Norton (Herbert); Harry Depp (Harvey Van Alyn); Nell Craig (Jessica Van Alyn)

THE GREAT FLAMARION
(Filmdom Productions, Inc./Republic Pictures Corp.)

In shaping a series of sequels to the original *Forgotten Horrors*, we have found ourselves occasionally cannibalizing the 1995-96 edition of *Human Monsters*, a Price & Turner book whose contents we had cherry-picked from a variety of old-line major studios and smaller independent outfits. One such selection is *The Great Flamarion*, whose Republic Pictures pedigree of course plants it more squarely in *Forgotten Horrors'* territory. So yes, you may have caught us weighing in on this one elsewhere.

But more than merely a replay of *Human Monsters'* exploration of *Flamarion*, this revamped chapter contains one of George Turner's earliest stabs at film commentary.

The setting is a music hall in Mexico City, where gunfire backstage presages a wounded man's fall from the rafters. A trouper recognizes the victim as the Great Flamarion (von Stroheim), once renowned as the world's greatest sharpshooter. Dying, Flamarion tells his story:

Flamarion's devotion to his dead-eye artistry had suddenly taken a back seat to his obsession with Connie Wallace (Mary Beth Hughes), wife of Al Wallace (Dan Duryea); both were assistants in Flamarion's stage routine. Connie led Flamarion on when in fact all she saw in him was an end to her unhappy marriage. At length, she persuaded Flamarion to kill the alcoholic Wallace during a performance, making it appear an accident. Connie and Flamarion agreed to meet later in San Francisco, but only Flamarion kept the appointment. At last, he set out to confront his betrayer, eventually finding Connie and her lover, Eddie (Stephen Barclay), here in Mexico. Flamarion berated Connie for her treachery, but she played up to him, pretending she loved him yet, until she could reach his gun and shoot him. With dying strength, Flamarion strangled Connie.

William Lee Wilder left his native Vienna and pursued a career in industry in New York for 20 years before establishing a motion-picture company in Hollywood. His first production, *The Great Flamarion*, was made at the Charlie Chaplin Studio and sold to Republic. This workmanlike job is distinguished by the up-and-coming Anthony Mann's assured hand at directing, and by splendid acting. *Flamarion's* polish and Continental style gained Wilder something of a following, but few of his other productions would live up to the promise shown here.

> Shortly before his death in 1999, George Turner handed down to Mike Price a clothbound U.S. Government Printing Office notebook, which George had filled as a film journal while on Navy duty in the South Pacific during World War II. George's take on *Flamarion* as a newer-than-new release, previewed for the Armed Forces, follows herewith:
>
> This is no doubt the best picture Republic has made in a long time. Most of the credit goes to producer William Wilder [credited as W. Lee Wilder] and director Anthony Mann for keeping an ordinarily just-fair technical staff above their standard, and to [Erich] von Stroheim, [Dan] Duryea and Miss [Mary Beth] Hughes for fine performances. The story is of the daring sex-and-murder type, similar to Wilder's brother Billy's famous *Double Indemnity*. Less pretentious than that film, *Flamarion* is just about as good. By careful dialogue, Wilder's actors manage to put over many lines and actions which would never escape censorship if less skillfully handled. The relationship of Miss Hughes with von Stroheim and another lover is all too obvious to the audience as well as to her pathetic husband, Duryea, who is driven to drink and later becomes the victim of a most cold-blooded murder plot. And his fate is mild as compared with that of von Stroheim, who commits murder only to be jilted by the woman who tricked him into the crime. Not a soul in the audience could feel sorry for the girl when she receives her much-deserved comeuppance. Dialogue is terrific all the way.

The vain and egotistical Flamarion (Erich von Stroheim) is drawn reluctantly to the faithless Connie (Mary Beth Hughes) in *The Great Flamarion*.

Except for the familiar faces and the English dialogue, *Flamarion* could pass for some pre-W.W. II German film. This suggestion dominates the script, the photographic technique, the music and much of the acting. Stroheim's own touches, persisting from his long-sidelined career as a great director, are obvious, particularly in a beautifully played solo sequence where he tidies up a hotel room with a militaristic formality for the never-to-come arrival of his paramour.

Mary Beth Hughes, whom the casting profession thought too pretty for serious dramatic roles, comes through with a satisfyingly shrewish portrayal in this respite from musicals and comedies. Dan Duryea, an alumnus of Samuel Goldwyn's stable of backup actors, is so affecting as a cuckolded drunkard as to rival Stroheim for scene-stealing ability.

The critical and historical consensus has largely ignored *Flamarion* except to cite it as an example of the supposedly worthless fare in which Stroheim took part in the long wake of his big-studio blacklisting as a director during the waning 1920s. (Stroheim had provoked that crippling snub with his characteristic extravagance and stubbornness, and not with any artistic failings.) Stroheim, however, spoke admiringly of the picture in a pre-release statement: "*The Great Flamarion*, in my opinion, has the sort of story which forecasts the motion picture of tomorrow. It is realism at its best, and there are no concessions to hokum."

CREDITS: Executive Producer: Howard Sheehan; Producer: William Lee Wilder; Director: Anthony Mann; Screenplay: Anne Wigton, Heinz Herald and Richard Weil; Based upon: Vicky Baum's 1936 Story, "Big Shot," from *Collier's* Magazine; Photographed by: James S. Brown, Jr.; Assistant Director: Raoul Pagel; Art Director: F. Paul Sylos; Décor: Glenn P. Thompson; Musical Score: Alexander Laszlo; Music Supervisor: David Chudnow; Songs: "Chita," by Faith Watson, and "Lights of Broadway," by Lester Allen; Sound: Percy Townsend; Production Manager: George Moskov; Running Time: 78 Minutes; Released: March 30, 1945

CAST: Erich von Stroheim (Flamarion); Mary Beth Hughes (Connie Wallace); Dan Duryea (Al Wallace); Stephen Barclay (Eddie Wheeler); Lester Allen (Tony); Esther Howard (Cleo); Michael Mark (Watchman); Joseph Granby (Detective); John R. Hamilton (Coroner)

STRANGE ILLUSION
a.k.a.: OUT OF THE NIGHT
(Producers Releasing Corp.)

An unusually lengthy running time by itself announces *Strange Illusion* as one of PRC's statelier efforts, and of course the presence of director Edgar G. Ulmer, like some Continental chef cooking up a storm in a 'burger joint, carries its own pretensions to a higher-minded state. Ulmer told the critic-turned-director Peter Bogdanovich many years after the fact that the greater artistry of *Strange Illusion* belonged to the brilliant cinematographer Eugen Schufftan, operating below the radar of the H'wood union snobs who had sought to nose him out of any career prospects.

Schufftan goes uncredited here in any capacity, with Philip Tannura listed as director of photography. The densely layered and ominous pictorial style of *Strange Illusion* would seem, however, to bear out Ulmer's declaration. As with 1944's *Voice in the Wind* and *Bluebeard*, the immigrant Schufftan found it necessary to toil anonymously if at all as a cinematographer, given a crippling Catch-22 fostered by the American Society of Cinematographers: no work without U.S. credentials, and no credentials without work. Schufftan finally broke through to a respected prominence among America's accredited directors of photography.

The lapsed kid star James "Jimmy" Lydon, late of the *Henry Aldrich* series, asserts a hearty bid for more serious acceptance as Paul Cartwright, a college student whose father, a judge, has died in a car-train collision—ruled an accident, despite a hint of foul play. Paul is beset with a recurring nightmare in which a menacing stranger claims to be his new father. A letter from Paul's genuine father is delivered posthumously: It warns Paul that he must protect his naïve mother, Virginia Cartwright (Sally Eilers), from predatory men.

Too late, Paul learns that his mother has become infatuated with a newly arrived businessman named Brett Curtis (Warren William). Paul is shocked to the point of collapse when his teenaged sister, Dorothy (Jayne Hazard), shows him a bracelet given her by Curtis; such a trinket figures in Paul's nightmare.

Paul sorts through his father's case files and finds a resemblance between Curtis and one Claude Barrington, a postmodern Bluebeard and child molester who has long eluded justice. It develops that Curtis is a disguised Barrington, who had faked his own demise after causing the judge's death. Curtis now plans to marry Virginia as a prelude to further revenge.

Feigning concern for Paul's precarious emotional state, Curtis places him under the psychiatric care of Prof. Muhlbach (Charles Arnt), an accomplice. Suspecting that the men are in cahoots, Paul plays along with the scam while persuading his mother to forestall her marriage to Curtis. Curtis presses Virginia to elope, certain that Muhlbach will kill Paul as soon as the wedding has taken place. A family friend, Dr. Vincent (Regis Toomey), takes Paul from Muhlbach's sanitarium, and Paul and Vincent visit an abandoned farm—similar to the setting of the boy's dream—where they find evidence that can only link Curtis to the train wreck. Mulbach summons Curtis to a meeting, but Curtis has given precedence to his lustful attraction to Dorothy, figuring that even if he must abandon his larger scheme he can still manage a fresh episode of rape and murder before skipping town. Paul trails his sister and Curtis to the Cartwright family's countryside cottage, where Curtis attacks the youth. The police arrive in time to gun down Curtis. Mulbach has meanwhile been captured.

Producer Leon Fromkess paid $10,000, a fortune by PRC's standards, for the rights to Fritz Rotter's original story. This forbidding study of predatory lechery allows sharp-featured Warren William a telling departure from his usual run of suave and witty detectives. William had played such famous sleuths as Philo Vance (in 1934's *The Dragon Murder Case* and 1939's *The Gracie Allen Murder Case*); Perry Mason (in a series including 1934's *The Case of the*

Howling Dog and 1935's *The Case of the Velvet Claws*); a vaguely disguised Sam Spade (in 1936's *Satan Met a Lady*, a takeoff on *The Maltese Falcon*); and the Lone Wolf, but the artist proved strikingly well suited to *Strange Illusion*'s role of oily, calculating evil. The character's depravity is set forth as explicitly as the Production Code Administration would permit, and the climactic attempted seduction of schoolgirl Jayne Hazard remains a dramatically viable cringe-inducer. William died in 1948 at age 52.

James Lydon had been so popular as Paramount Pictures' cheeky teenage proto-nerd, Henry Aldrich, that prominence as a grown-up actor could only elude him. Lydon carried on in secondary roles, all the same, until the late 1950s, when he turned to producing and directing for television. Lydon's portrayal of the nervous hero is a brilliantly controlled job, wavering between terrified indecision and a determination to Do the Right Thing. The youth undermines the scheming simply by allowing himself to be underestimated—while taunting the plotter with unnerving small-talk.

Regis Toomey is likably heroic as a friend in time of need. Soft-spoken Charles Arnt is just right as the murderous quack, who exerts a certain control over the pervert Curtis. Warren William's treacheries notwithstanding, the film's most tense moment comes in a dodgy rooftop interlude involving Lydon and Arnt, interrupted none too soon by Toomey. Jayne Hazard plays the kid-sister role as a vapid if precocious sort, susceptible to William's every smarmy move until quite nearly too late. Mary McLeod leaves a strong impression in a small role as Lydon's girlfriend, who develops good reasons for wanting to help attend to William's comeuppance.

Sally Eilers, considered one of Hollywood's most beautiful stars-in-waiting during the 1920s and '30s, never quite broke through to the prominence promised her despite a busy decade; by the 1940s, she had become an occasional supporting player. Miss Eilers is poignantly clueless as *Strange Illusion*'s preyed-upon widow, conveying well the ill-prepared trusting nature that a life of sheltered pampering can inflict.

CREDITS: Producer: Leon Fromkess; Director: Edgar G. Ulmer; Screenplay: Adele Comandini; Story: Fritz Rotter; Photographed by: Philip Tannura (and Eugen Shufftan, *per* E.G. Ulmer); Assistant Director: Ben Kadish; Dialogue Director: Herman Rotsten; Second Camera: Frank MacDonald; Art Directors: Paul Palmentola and George Van Marter; Editor: Carl Pierson; Décor: E.H. Reif; Properties: Charles Stevens; Wardrobe: Harold Bradow; Music: Leo Erdody; Sound: Frank McWhorter; Running Time: 84 Minutes; Copyrighted and Previewed as *Out of the Night*; Released: March 31, 1945

CAST: James Lydon (Paul Cartwright); Warren William (Brett Curtis); Sally Eilers (Virginia Cartwright); Regis Toomey (Dr. Vincent); Charles Arnt (Prof.

Muhlbach); George H. Reed (Benjamin); Jayne Hazard (Dorothy Cartwright); Jimmy Clark (George); Mary McLeod (Lydia); Pierre Watkin (Armstrong); Sonia Sorel (Charlotte Farber); Vic Potel (Game Warden); George Sherwood (Langdon); Gene Stutenroth (Sparky); John Hamilton (Bill Allen)

CRIME, INC.
(Producers Releasing Corp.)

Lionel Atwill could go slumming with the best of 'em—and he ranks high among Old Hollywood's more distinguished character leads—but what looks like slumming to a player's retrospective admirers might actually be more a case of that old saw about the dignity of honest work at whatever opportunity. There had been here a Downfall-with-a-capital-*D*, stemming from Atwill's guardedly private appetite for pornography and a party on Christmas Eve of 1940 that set the Vice Squad on his case and led to a conviction for perjury following a Grand Jury session. The misadventure prompted a Motion Picture Association blacklisting whose dehumanizing impact is related in respectful, anti-*Hollywood Babylon* detail in Gregory William Mank's splendid book, *Hollywood's Maddest Doctors* (Midnight Marquee Press; 1998). In considering the Mank volume for *Monsters from the Vault* magazine, Steve Kronenberg has remarked it "shocking... that Atwill's relatively innocent 'orgy'... destroyed his career, when actors and actresses today continue to thrive in Hollywood after doing much worse." A chorused "Amen!" would seem in order here, along with a verse or two from the jazz tradition's most righteously defiant manifesto, "'Tain't Nobody's Business What I Do."

But like some virtuoso musician picking up catch-as-can gigs with a hackwork supper-club combo, Atwill seized the near-underground Poverty Row assignments as they came to hand and lent them a calibre of artistry that money could not buy. (Later on in 1945, he would take a prominent turn in Universal's *House of Dracula*, follow-through to the 1944-45 release of *House of Frankenstein*—which features Atwill as another character altogether.)

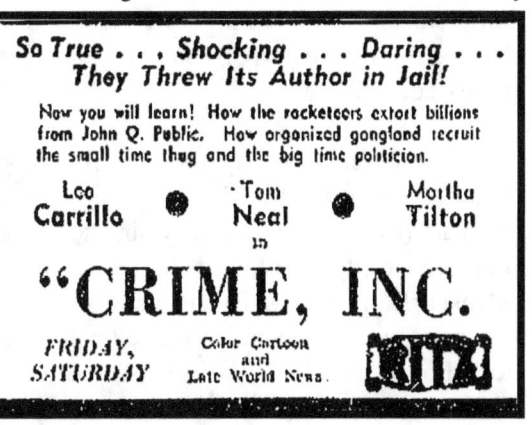

Atwill was nearing the end by now, with scarcely over a year left to him before he would succumb prematurely at 61 to bronchial cancer and pneumonia. Although he appears conspicuously lessened by illness in 1946's *Lost City of the Jungle* and *Genius at*

Work, Atwill is right up to snuff in *Crime, Inc.*, which he serves as a lawyer at the helm of a bloodthirsty mob.

New York mobster Bugs Kelly (Danny Morton) turns fink to the press in retaliation for the gunning-down of two henchmen; abducts a prominent lieutenant (Leo Carrillo) of the offending syndicate and demands a ransom; thwarts one contract on his life; and somehow keeps his racketeering a secret from his nightclub-singer sister (Martha Tilton, a Real World big-band *chanteuse* often billed as "the Liltin' Martha Tilton"). Atwill shows up as syndicate honcho Pat Coyle, who proves less than tolerant of Kelly's strongarm tactics and orders the upstart whacked during a visit to a Coney Island wax museum. Unusually ambitious for a PRC effort, the film is more centrally concerned with a brash newspaper reporter (*Detour*'s Tom Neal), who cranks out a too-hot-to-handle book that hits uncomfortably close to home for both the mob and a corrupt law-enforcement establishment. Think *L.A. Confidential*, Curtis Hanson's Oscar-bait champion of 1997, in rough-hewn prototype.

CREDITS: Producer: Leon Fromkess; Associate Producer: Martin Mooney; Director: Lew Landers (Louis Friedlander); Dialogue Director: Herman Rotstein; Screenplay: Ray Schrock; Photographed by: James Brown; Assistant Director: Lou Perlof; Second Camera: Ralph Ash; Art Director: Paul Palmentola; Editor: Roy Livingston; Décor: Harry Reif; Props: Gene Stone; Men's Wardrobe: Morris Friedman; Women's Wardrobe: Elsie Eppich; Music: Walter Greene; Songs: "Lonely Little Camera Girl" and "I'm Guilty," by Jay Livingston & Ray Evans, and "What a Fool I Was" and "That's It," by Marla Shelton and Nacio Porter Brown, Jr.; Sound: Max Hutchinson; Running Time: 82 Minutes; Released: April 15, 1945

CAST: Leo Carrillo (Tony Marlow); Tom Neal (Jim Riley); Martha Tilton (Betty Van Cleve); Lionel Atwill (Pat Coyle); Grant Mitchell (Wayne Clark); Sheldon Leonard (Capt. Ferrone); Harry Shannon (Commissioner Collins); Danny Morton (Bugs Kelly); Virginia Vale (Trixie Waters); Don Beddoe (Dixon); George Meeker (Barry North); Bud Rogers (Val Lucas); Ed Cronley (Sgt. Hayes); Jack Gordon (Jud Stecker); Monk Friedman (Convict); Harry Hayden (News Editor); Emmett Vogan (Conroy); Gene Stutenroth (Henchman); Earle Hodgins (Waxworks Spieler)

THE PHANTOM SPEAKS
(Republic Pictures Corp.)

In a purely political development at Universal Pictures, the intended Karloff-Lugosi starrer *Black Friday* (1940) had found itself transmogrified into a vehicle-by-default for Stanley Ridges, a distinguished character man from Southampton, England. Ridges inherited a split-personality role intended for Boris Karloff when Karloff assumed the renegade-surgeon part that had been written for Bela Lugosi. Lugosi faced demotion to a backup gangster position, which he nevertheless rendered commanding by sheer force of will and a strategic publicity ploy.

The conflicted scholar-turned-killer portrayal worked well enough for Ridges that he replayed it on a supernatural note for Republic's *The Phantom Speaks*. Either performance is a gem, though of course *Black Friday* is the superior piece in terms of production values and star appeal. *The Phantom Speaks* takes the cake for atmosphere, however. A brooding malevolence underpins the Republic production, which benefits as well from surly Tom Powers' impersonation of a brute whose vengeful ghost takes possession of Ridges at the right moments. Right for the picture, that is.

Harvey Bogardus (Powers) is the truer villain of the piece, a remorseless killer whose capture in connection with a playground slaying attracts the attention of Dr. Paul Renwick (Ridges), a psychic researcher. Renwick, who maintains that the so-called soul is a stream of energy beyond the grasp of death, has staked out Bogardus' Death Row cell in the belief that Bogardus' defiant nature can provide the proof this theory requires.

Following the execution, Renwick concentrates upon summoning the spirit of Bogardus. His experiment seems a success until Bogardus balks at helping with any research and asserts his will over the professor. Renwick becomes Bogardus, in effect, stalking the various objects of the badman's resentment and leaving evidence that suggests a return from the grave. He is about to attack a child (Doreen McCann) who had testified against Bogardus when Renwick's intellect reasserts itself. Bogardus prevents Renwick from committing suicide, then finally overplays his hand by sending Renwick against the district attorney (Jonathan Hale) and a newspaperman (Richard Arlen) who has come too near the truth. Overpowered by these intended victims, Renwick faces up to a death sentence. His final words echo Bogardus' death-march declaration—an oath that he has not finished his rampage.

Ridges' work here and in *Black Friday* would remain unmatched until 1996, when a then-unknown Edward Norton would achieve similarly gripping results as an altar boy accused of murder in *Primal Fear*. Director John English senses vitally that neither top-billed Richard Arlen nor token leading lady Lynne Roberts holds the key to *The Phantom Speaks*, allowing Ridges the dominant presence throughout and closing on a note even grimmer than the manifold tragedies that climax *Black Friday*.

Ridges, too, raises the stakes: Where his character in *Black Friday* is an innocent transformed through the illicitly benevolent intentions of Karloff's character, Ridges makes the professor of *The Phantom Speaks* more of a self-serving manipulator who brings down misfortune upon himself. Tom Powers holds forth admirably as the snarling phantom, and his tense confrontations with Ridges convey a quietly nightmarish quality that render mere shock value quite beside the point.

CREDITS: Executive Producer: Armand Schaefer; Associate Producer: Donald H. Brown; Director: John English; Screenplay: John K. Butler; Photographed by: William Bradford; Second Camera: Joseph Novak; Assistant Director: John Grubbs; Matte Paintings: Howard & Theodore Lydecker; Transparency Projection Photography: Gordon C. Schaefer; Art Directors: Russell Kimball and Frank Arrigo; Editor: Arthur Roberts; Décor: George Milo; Costumer: Adele Palmer; Music: Richard Cherwin; Sound: Earl Crain, Sr.; Music and Effects Mixers: John Stransky, Jr., and Howard Wilson; Running Time: 68 Minutes (Some Television Syndication Prints Run 54 Minutes); Released: April 21, 1945

CAST: Richard Arlen (Matt Fraser); Stanley Ridges (Dr. Paul Renwick); Lynne Roberts (Joan Renwick); Tom Powers (Harvey Bogardus); Charlotte Wynters (Cornelia Willmont); Jonathan Hale (Owen McAllister); Pierre Watkin (Charlie Davis); Marian Martin (Betty Hanzel); Garry Owen (Louis Fabian); Ralf Harolde (Frankie Teel); Doreen McCann (Mary Fabian); Joseph Granby (James J. Kennerley); Frank Fanning, Eddie Parker and Jack Perrin (Policemen); Charles Sullivan (Cabman); Robert Homans (Guard); Tom Chatterton (Chaplain); Ed Cassidy (Doctor); Edmund Cobb (Warden); Nolan Leary (Watchman); Bob Alden (Newsboy); Jack Ingram (Detective); Robert Malcolm (Forensics Officer); Walter Shumway (Deputy)

ANOUSH
(Crown Productions)

Anoush is Armenian in origin but American in execution—with some significant Hollywood talents, including the busy Poverty Row cinematographer Marcel Le Picard, at work behind the scenes. This presumably lost ethnic tragedy seems never to have secured much in the way of general exposure. George Turner recalled seeing it later on during the 1940s while studying at the Art Institute of Chicago, in a 16-millimeter edition bearing English-language subtitles. A folkloric novel and a play, along with a light-opera adaptation by Armen Dickranian, appear to have been followed faithfully here.

Anoush (Zaruhi Elmassian), a young woman of the Caucasus, falls in love with a shepherd named Saro (S.T. Vartian) despite her mother's objections. During a holy celebration, the girls of the village read one another's fortunes. Anoush is dismayed to hear a prediction of violent death for Saro. She believes herself cursed, at any rate, because when she was a baby her mother had refused to help a beggar. Saro bests Anoush's brother, Mosi (Misak Frankian), at wrestling, and Mosi swears to get even. Anoush and Saro attempt to flee the village, but the sheriff (Krish Andikian) kills Saro. Anoush dies of heartbreak, and the lovers' spirits shuffle off this mortal coil.

CREDITS: Producer: Charles Merjanian; Director: Setrag Vartian; Based Upon: Hovannes Toumanian's *Anoush*; Photographed by: Marcel Le Picard; Art Director; Jourken; Editor: John F. Link; Musical Score: Armen Dickranian, from His Operetta, *Anoush*; English Titles: Serene Kassapian; Running Time: Approx. 45-50 Minutes; Released: Following New York Opening on April 27, 1945

CAST: Zaruhi Elmassian (Anoush); S.T. Vartian (Saro); Misak Frankian (Mosi); Satig Logian (Zarnishian); Krish Andrian (Zakar); Haiyastan Baronian (Fortune Teller)

THE PHANTOM OF 42ND STREET
(Producers Releasing Corp.)

A case of serial murder, a show-business legend about an actor-gone-whacko and a treacherous backstage setting provide the right ingredients for this efficient business-as-usual whodunnit from PRC. *The Phantom of 42nd Street* came across in its own day as old-fashioned—a throwback, perhaps, to Paul Leni's show-world shocker *The Last Warning* (Universal; 1929), or even to that film's 1939 *Crime Club* series remake, *The House of Fear*. In any era, however, the pacing is the point, and director Albert Herman keeps *Phantom*'s mayhem zipping along from the opening shockeroo through an underlying tangle of disgraceful

secrets. If *The Phantom of 42nd Street* is consciously a pastiche of the Leni *meisterverk* or its re-*verk*-ing, then at least the upstart embellishes the retracing with a ferocious vigor and a robust sense of humor.

Drama critic Anthony Woolrich (Dave O'Brien) has just glimpsed the Broadway début of Claudia Moore (Kay Aldridge) when he discovers the hanged body of Claudia's wealthy uncle, Jonathan Moore. A note signed "Capt. Kidd" adorns the corpse. Homicide is hardly Tony's beat, but he bows to pressures to cover the case like any other hungry pavement-beating news-hack. During a visit to interview the victim's brother, actor and theatre operator Cecil Moore (Alan Mowbray), Tony meets Claudia, Cecil's daughter, and finds himself romantically attracted to her. Cecil seems shocked to learn of his brother's death. An apparently unrelated second murder-plus-arson, committed by a skulker in a period-piece costume, proves connected upon the discovery of a note signed "Nero." Claudia confides to Tony that her father has been suffering from blackouts. Claudia's behavior is itself somewhat furtive.

As evidence mounts against Cecil, Tony tracks down Claudia's long-missing mother (Edythe Elliott), a former actress who also had been involved with Jonathan Moore. The connection points to another actor, Henry Winters, long presumed to have died in an asylum. There surfaces a third victim with ties to Cecil's repertory company. Tony convinces a homicide cop (Jack Mulhall) to help set a trap, using Cecil as bait—a bogus casting call for Shakespeare's *Julius Caesar*, centering on the assassination scene. Cecil, impersonating Caesar, is attacked, sure enough—and the assailant proves to be the stage manager (Stanley Price), who at length is identified as a surgically altered Henry Winters. Cecil is cleared of suspicion and made certain of a hefty inheritance. Tony begins scheming to win Claudia away from her snooty actor fiancé (John Crawford).

This grim baffler represents PRC in one of its better, not to say even near-brilliant, moments, with prevailing currents of bygone shames better left undisturbed; a whip-smart amateur sleuth who must show the police how to handle their business; and a wealth of incidental wit from Frank Jenks as a nervy cab driver. Dave O'Brien brings a welcome quality of robust, however reluctant, determination to the critic, although most such Real World journalists tend to be ivory-tower types lacking in gumption or even simple newsgathering ability—qualities that O'Brien's Tony develops as the investigation goads him onward. The element of imminent romance never degenerates into mush, and the layered mysteries-within-mysteries keep the absorbed viewer guessing right on up to a well-staged final confrontation.

CREDITS: Executive Producer: Leon Fromkess; Associate Producer: Martin Mooney; Director Albert Herman; Screenplay: Milton Raison, from His and Jack Harvey's 1936 Novel, *Phantom of 42nd Street*; Photographed by: James Brown; Special Effects: Ray Mercer; Assistant Director: William A. Calihan, Jr.; Art Director: Paul Palmentola; Editor: Hugh Winn; Music: Karl Hajos; Sound: Frank Webster; Production Manager: Ray Young; Running Time: 58 Minutes; Released: May 2, 1945

CAST: Dave O'Brien (Anthony "Tony" Woolrich); Kay Aldridge (Claudia Moore); Alan Mowbray (Cecil Moore); Frank Jenks (Romeo); Edythe Elliott (Janet Buchanan); Jack Mulhall (Lt. Matty Walsh); Vera Marshe (Ginger Mason); Stanley Price (Henry Winters); John Crawford (John Carraby); Cyril Delevanti (Roberts); Paul Power (Timothy Wells)

THE LADY CONFESSES
(Alexander-Stern Productions, Inc./Producers Releasing Corp.)

Which lady, and to what she confesses, are mysteries that Sam Newfield's *The Lady Confesses* should be allowed to reveal on its own terms. The renewed availability of this long-buried PRC release, coupled with the tantalizing ambiguity of its title, is enough to prompt us to treat it as something a whole lot like a fresh release and—for a change—call an ixnay on the oilerspays. The horrific quotient here is a strangler-at-large and getting larger, with Hugh Beaumont and Mary Beth Hughes caught up in the midst of an overzealous homicide squad and a compact array of hyperactive red herrings.

We're usually pretty quick to slap a film noir tag on just about anything that packs a suitably dark attitude (lest that idiom be too narrowly regarded), and sure enough, *The Lady Confesses* has been cited as a primitive noir by authorities who got there before we did. But on fresh viewing—we had originally thought this film shouldn't be included in FH3—we find that the thing plays out more like a throwback to the down-and-dirty whodunnit style that had prevailed during the Depression years.

Director Newfield's old-fashioned manner of pacing and blocking; veteran maestro Lee Zahler's melodramatic orchestral cues; the speakeasy-type atmosphere of the main setting; even the Cupid's-bow radiance of babe-in-the-woods Mary Beth Hughes—all signs point to times past, superficially macked out in W.W. II-homefront lapels and hemlines and garnished with a handful of romantically hip floor-show tunes. (One song, Cindy Walker's "It's All Your Fault," about which more later, stands out.) But as to the noir perception: There is no particular sense of alienation or incumbent doom beyond the commonplace mortal perils and police-procedural hassles, and Beaumont's trouble-magnet impersonation of a long-abandoned husband seems breezier than his circumstances warrant.

Innocent Vicki McGuire (Miss Hughes) receives an unwelcome visit from Norma Craig (Barbara Slater), the missing and presumed-dead wife of Vicki's fiancé, Larry Craig (Beaumont). Meanwhile, Craig is making a nuisance of himself at a nitery owned by Lucky Brandon (Edmund MacDonald). Nodding off in the dressing room of entertainer Lucille Compton (Claudia Drake), Craig is awakened by a phone call from Vicki. He hurries to meet her, and together they go to an intended confrontation with Norma—only to find Norma croaked and themselves under suspicion.

Craig's drunken presence at the nightclub is well established by all but Brandon, who lies as if to keep himself in the clear. Vicki conspires to take a job at Brandon's club and turns up information that can only mean danger for herself and death for Lucille. The use of a strangling wire in both murders suggests a serial case.

The investigation is pressed along vigorously by a determined plainclothesman (gruff Emmett Vogan), and the sweetheart relationship between Beaumont and Miss Hughes takes on complications somewhat deeper than the material as she develops an appetite for the amateur-sleuthing game. Unlike many such parts in films of this period (Monogram Pictures' Kitty O'Day mysteries and the Cosmo Jones radio-to-film adaptation come to mind), Miss Hughes' role sidesteps the pitfall of presenting a comical annoyance for the police and takes on a grimmer urgency. The revelation of the killer comes gradually, peaking a bit prematurely but compensating from there with a suspenseful round of events and a plausible, however selfish and simplistic, explanation as to motives. A moody beachfront-by-night scene generates a bracing tension, capped by the sudden intrusion of a stern cop (an unbilled Charles King) just before a new slaying can occur.

A preview-cut running time of 65 minutes suggests that PRC subjected *The Lady Confesses* to some drastic last-minute scissoring. The official general-release length is 58 minutes. Versions of both lengths exist today, the heftier cut indulging in more extensive musical-interlude business.

Featured prominently is the chipper "It's All Your Fault," as warbled by Claudia Drake early in the picture. Although its big-band arrangement obscures its origins, the number is actually the work of Country Music Hall of Fame songwriter Cindy Walker. "It's All Your Fault" was first recorded by Bob Wills & His Texas Playboys in 1941.

"That's one of the first songs I ever had recorded by Bob Wills," the composer told us in 2002. "He did five of my songs at one time...'Cherokee Maiden,' 'Bluebonnet Lane,' 'It's All Your Fault,' 'Dusty Skies' and 'Don't Count Your Chickens.'"

Those other four have become standards of the Western swing idiom, but "It's All Your Fault" remains comparatively obscure; a remake by the countrified star Wade Ray did get some spins during the early 1950s.

Miss Walker was still a teenager, living with her family in Southern California, when she sold "It's All Your Fault" to Wills. She never knew the song had figured as a featured selection in a movie, and hadn't heard the PRC version—which she praised for having "a nice arrangement"—until we brought it to her attention during the final stages of assembling this book.

"I imagine they heard Bob Wills do it, and so they made a pop-band arrangement of it. But I don't guess they ever paid me," Miss Walker added with a chuckle.

CREDITS: Producer: Alfred Stern; Director: Sam Newfield; Assistant Director: Harold E. Knox; Screenplay: Helen Martin; Original Story: Irwin R. Franklyn; Photographed by: Jack Greenhalgh; Camera Operator: Ernest Smith; Film Editor: Holbrook N. Todd; Art Director: Paul Palmentola: Décor: Harry Reif; Costumer: Mona Barry; Music: Lee Zahler; Songs: "Dance Close to Me, Darling," by Robert Unger & Al Seaman, "It's a Fine Old World," by Smith-Kuhstos-Blonder, and "It's All Your Fault," by Cindy Walker; Sound: Arthur B. Smith; Running Time: 65 Minutes (Preview Version) and 58 Minutes (Final Cut); Released: May 16, 1945

CAST: Mary Beth Hughes (Vicki McGuire); Hugh Beaumont (Larry Craig); Edmund MacDonald (Lucky Brandon); Claudia Drake (Lucile Compton); Emmett Vogan (Capt. Brown); Edward Howard (Harmon); Dewey Robinson (Steve);

Carol Andrews (Marge); Ruth Brandt (Gladys); Barbara Slater (Norma Craig); Jack George (Manager); Jerome Root (Bill); Charles King (Beach Patrolman)

THE VAMPIRE'S GHOST
(Republic Pictures Corp.)

Condemned To Live, that radically innovative vampire fable of 1935, had taken pains to couch its traditional Eurocentric terrors in a more radical Third Worldly origin, related via a prologue that anticipates the striking premise of 1972's *Blacula* in its suggestion of a supernatural communion between disparate cultures. *The Vampire's Ghost* takes matters further by concerning itself entirely with a colonial setting—neighboring outposts in Coastal West Africa where Voodoo and vampirism stand at odds with one another, holding roughly equal sway over a helpless populace. John Abbott is the persuasive menace, an underworld mastermind whose campaign of economic corruption appears to be a new undertaking in his unnaturally lengthy existence as one of the undead.

The role is a rare lead for Abbott, who had carried Republic's *London Blackout Murders* abundantly well just two years previous, but whose mannered dependability was usually confined to supporting character parts. Abbott makes a dignified and memorably understated villain here, even though his innovative take on a vampiric presence is hardly anything to challenge the defining portrayal that Bela Lugosi had long since established. Abbott is also the vindication of

John Abbott as the villain in *The Vampire's Ghost*

The Vampire's Ghost, overwhelming the lackluster portrayals surrounding his own and finding in the situation a dire serenity that goes otherwise unheeded in director Lesley Selander's slam-bang approach.

The village of Bakunda is in an uproar over an outbreak of bloodthirsty murder. The local priest, Father Gilchrist (Grant Withers), and a merchant named Tom Vance (Emmett Vogan) discount the natives' superstitious rumblings and seek a plausible explanation. Planter Roy Hendrick (Charles Gordon), who is engaged to marry Vance's daughter, Julie (Peggy Stewart), consults with saloonkeeper Webb Fallon (Abbott), a newcomer who appears conversant with the criminal element. Roy takes Fallon's side in a fight with a seaman named Jim Barrat (Roy Barcroft), who has accused Fallon of running a crooked gambling operation. Invited to dine at the Vance home, Fallon arouses the suspicions of a servant, Simon Peter (Martin Wilkins), who notices that Fallon casts no reflection.

During a visit to a nearby village that seems a hotbed of superstition and insurrection, Fallon rescues Roy from a gunfire booby-trap. Simon Peter learns that Fallon has been hit, but not harmed, by the barrage. Simon Peter impales Fallon upon a silver-pointed spear, but Roy extracts the weapon. Fallon hypnotizes Roy, who carries Fallon to a mountaintop to bathe in the healing rays of a full moon. Fallon reveals his undead nature to Roy and explains that he intends to claim Julie as his bride.

The safari cut short, Roy attempts to learn more about the issues at stake, but Fallon keeps him mesmerized—and places Julie under a spell, while he's about it. A barroom dancer (Adele Mara), jealous of Fallon's attentions to Julie, conspires with Barrat to bilk Fallon; both are killed. The native drums resonate with warnings about a plague of vampirism, accusing Fallon. Vance urges Fallon to leave the district for his safety. Father Gilchrist, convinced that the Voodoo worshippers are hep to the truth, frees Jim from the hypnotic trance through the power of prayer.

Fallon, meanwhile, has taken Julie to an abandoned temple. He is about to transform her when Father Gilchrist intrudes, holding Fallon at bay with a cross. Roy skewers Fallon with the silver spear. Simon Peter sets the temple ablaze, and Julie is taken to safety.

Owing more to John Polidori's dilettante novella *The Vampyre* than to Bram Stoker's *Dracula*, this slight and frenzied film derives from a scenario by Leigh Brackett, who also helped to write the shooting script. John Abbott seems as resistant to the overinsistent pacing of the yarn as his character must be impatient with his pursuers. The richly textured, shadowy camerawork impressively evokes both the underworld and the otherworldly. Les Selander, a prolific director who had worked in Hollywood since the late 1910s, was more comfortably at home with Westerns—although he would show a better-assured grasp of supernatural fantasy on 1946's *The Catman of Paris*.

CREDITS: Executive Producer: Armand Schaefer; Associate Producer: Rudolph E. Abel; Director: Lesley Selander; Screenplay: John K. Butler and Leigh Brackett; Story: Leigh Brackett; Photographed by: Ellis "Bud" Thackery and Robert Pittack; Assistant Cameramen: Al Keller and Enzo Martinelli; Assistant Director: Virgil Hart; Matte Paintings, Miniatures and Special Photographic Effects: Howard Lydecker and Theodore Lydecker; Projection Shots: Gordon C. Schaefer; Art Directors: Russel Kimball and Frank Arrigo; Editor: Tony Martinelli; Décor: Earl Wooden; Musical Director: Richard Cherwin; Choreographer: Jerry Jarrette; Sound: Dick Tyler; Sound Re-Recording and Music-and-Effects Mixers: John Stransky, Jr., and Howard Wilson; Running Time: 59 Minutes; Released: May 21, 1945

CAST: John Abbott (Webb Fallon); Charles Gordon (Roy Hendrick); Peggy Stewart (Julie Vance); Grant Withers (Father Gilchrist); Emmett Vogan (Tom Vance); Adele Mara (Lisa); Roy Barcroft (Jim Barrat); Martin Wilkins (Simon Peter); Frank Jacquet [Given Elsewhere as Jaquet] (Doctor); Jimmy Aubrey (Hobo); and Zack Williams, Floyd Shackelford, George Carlton,

CHINA'S LITTLE DEVILS
(Monogram Pictures Corp.)

The U.S. bombing of Japan lay just over two months into the future when Monogram released this prophetic tribute to China's loyalty to the Allied cause. *China's Little Devils* actually dates from almost a year earlier, having been produced during the summer of 1944. Its climactic bombing predicts no atom-splitting particulars and in fact assumes Tokyo as the target, but the finale captures well the American attitude toward a relentless enemy at this breaking point of World War II. The author is an outspoken playwright of the Old Left, Samuel Ornitz, whose blending here of rambunctious hooligan slapstick, vengeful motivations and unashamed sentimentalism recalls Sidney Kingsley's famous social problem drama, *Dead End*, and its several spinoffs. A supernatural twist at the end is but a gratuitous heartstrings-tugger.

Paul Kelly plays Big Butch Dooley, of the Flying Tigers, who rescues an orphaned boy from the ruins of a Chinese village. The child, adopted by Dooley's squadron, is christened Little Butch and taught commando tactics. At a mission school, Little Butch (played by Ducky L. Louie) trains his fellow refugee orphans in the finer points of guerrilla warfare—the better to prey on Japanese encampments.

Doc Temple (Harry Carey), a kindly missionary, is appalled at these activities, but Little Butch is obsessed with vengeance—preferably, in a spirit of destructive play—that escalates from gasoline-stealing raids to general demolition. Little Butch becomes increasingly reckless, surviving gunshot wounds and losing two of his juvenile warriors as captives. Doc Temple petitions the Japanese for the kids' release, only to find himself taken hostage. Little Butch carries out a reckless scheme to rescue Doc, and the Japanese bomb the mission.

Little Butch's amateur commandos rescue Dooley from the wreckage and return him safely behind Chinese lines. A Japanese unit surrounds the escaping boys, however, and all die in a shoot-out. Suggesting the Allies' only recourse, the picture ends as Dooley drops a payload of explosives onto Tokyo—with the ghost of Little Butch riding along.

The largely Asian ensemble cast serves *China's Little Devils* with conviction, rendering the film more documentarylike in tone than many other Hollywood propaganda pieces. There is a generous use of stock footage, courtesy of the War Department's 1944 documentary *The Battle of China*, in addition to strategic location shooting at Culver City's Army Air Force First Motion Picture Unit. Some surviving prints contain a preface featuring Mme. Chiang Kai-shek.

Grant Withers, the popular B-movie character actor, had already begun moving into the decision-making ranks at Monogram. *China's Little Devils* makes rather an obscure marker for Withers' début as a fully fledged producer. Director Monta Bell's sparse rèsumè also includes 1941's *Aloma of the South Seas* and *Birth of the Blues* and 1942's *Beyond the Blue Horizon*.

CREDITS: Producer: Grant Withers; Associate Producer: William Hanley; Director: Monta Bell; Story and Screenplay: Sam Ornitz; Based upon an Idea by: David Diamond; Photographed by: Harry Neumann; Assistant Director: Bobby Ray; Second Camera: Byron Seawright; Special Effects: Alex Weldon; Art Director: E.R. Hickson; Editors: Dick Currier and Dan Milner; Set Dresser: Vin Taylor; Sound: Tom Lambert; Production Manager: William Strobach; Technical Research: Wei F. Hsueh; Translator: Bruce Wong; Running Time: 75 Minutes; Released: May 27, 1945

CAST: Madame Chiang Kai-shek (Herself, in Prologue); Harry Carey (Doc Temple); Paul Kelly (Big Butch Dooley); Ducky L. Louie (Little Butch); Gloria Ann Chew (Betty Lou); Hayward Soo Hoo (Little Joe Doakes); Jimmy Dodd (Eddie); Ralph Lewis (Harry); Philip Ahn (Farmer); Richard Loo (Col. Huraji); Wing Foo (Capt. Suhi); Jean Wong (Nurse); Fred Mah (Patrick); Nancy Hseuh (Baby); Oie Chan (Farmer's Wife); Aen Ling Chow and Ching Ling Chow (Daughters); Francis Jung, Jr. (Son)

THE MISSING CORPSE
(Producers Releasing Corp.)

Albert Herman's *The Missing Corpse* is more a comedy than anything else—even an inadvertent suggestion of how W.C. Fields might have handled a weird-crime scenario if given the opportunity. The situations are blatantly derivative of Fields, concerning a harassed family man who receives no respect within his household and finds himself subjected to humiliations at every hand. Such put-upon leading men had been popular favorites over the long haul, with Fields preeminent among a pack that also included Lloyd Hamilton, Leon Errol, Edgar Kennedy and Chester Clute. (Two generations later, Rodney Dangerfield would air out that musty mantle as part of his development as an unlikely big-screen leading man.)

Hungarian-born J. Edward Bromberg, a distinguished character man who only occasionally claimed an opportunity to carry a picture, takes the fore here as an irascible publisher who is embroiled in a war of nerves with an unworthy rival. The suggestion of Fields comes in at the home-front level, where neither the wife (Isabel Randolph) nor the children nor even the amply paid servants seem to harbor much appreciation for the breadwinner. Fields, himself a fugitive from a combative marriage, had built a career upon a foundation of such portrayals (particularly in such Depression-era signature pieces as "The Barber Shop" and *It's a Gift* and *The Man on the Flying Trapeze*) and then distilled to a hundred-proof essence the concept of the householder-as-doormat in *The Bank Dick* (1940). Why Fields never wound up nose-deep in a murder case or a haunted house is a mystery that has confounded the Great Man's admirers for generations, for the contradictions that made his characters so fascinating—arrogance and humility, connivance and forthrightness, courage and trepidation, cynicism and sentimentality—would have been a natural match with gallows comedy.

Bromberg is a more realistic player than Fields, but he packs a kindred bluster and put-upon sensitivity. Bromberg is a wonder to behold as *The Missing Corpse*'s Henry Kruger, whose family is irritation enough without the complications posed by enemy publisher Andy McDonald (Paul Guilfoyle). Henry's wayward daughter Phyllis (Lorell Sheldon) is predisposed to landing in compromising situations, and McDonald is constantly at the ready to print another scandalous story. The latest such insult provokes Henry to threaten to kill

MacDonald. The idle threat is overheard by a career hoodlum named Slippery Joe Clary (Ben Welden), who has some old scores to settle against McDonald. So Clary kills McDonald and deposits the body in Henry's car just as Henry is preparing to take an overdue solo vacation.

Much of the hour-plus running time is given over to Henry's flustered attempts to dispose of the corpse; to his chauffeur's (Frank Jenks) similarly flustered attempts to do likewise; and to both men's knockabout misadventures in keeping the corpse from being spotted by a caretaker (Eddy Waller), a dog and a hick constable (Michael Branden). To say nothing of the murderer himself, who can't see fit to stay away. Henry's unwanted family members decide a little togetherness is in order just when Henry needs it the least.

Herman directs with a sense of hair's-breadth urgency, letting any number of intruders get a glimpse of the title stiff but always allowing Bromberg a panicky edge at explaining things away. Isabel Randolph is terrific as the well-meaning but exasperating wife, and Ben Welden is suitably menacing as the opportunistic killer. Frank Jenks' comedy relief is of a high lowbrow order.

CREDITS: Producer: Leon Fromkess; Assosiate Producer: Martin Mooney; Director: Albert Herman; Screenplay: Ray Schrock; Story: Harry O. Hoyt; Photographed by: James Brown; Special Effects: Ray Mercer; Assistant Director: William A. Calihan, Jr.; Art Director: Paul Palmentola; Editor: W. Donn Hayes; Décor: Harry Reif; Propmaster: Gene Stone; Wardrobe: Mona Barry; Music: Karl Hajos; Sound: William R. Fox; Running Time: 62 Minutes; Released: June 1, 1945

CAST: J. Edward Bromberg (Henry Kruger); Isabel Randolph (Alice Kruger;); Frank Jenks (Mike Hogan); Eric Sinclair (James Kruger); Paul Guilfoyle (Andy McDonald); Ben Welden (Slippery Joe Clary); Charles Coleman (Egbert); Eddy Waller (Desmond); John Shay (Jeffry Dodd); Lorell Sheldon (Phyllis Kruger); Michael Branden (Jimmy Trigg); Elayne Adams (Miss Ames); Mary Arden (Madge); Charles Jordan (Draper); Anne O'Neal (Mrs. Swanaker); Jean Ransome (Ken Terrell)

ROAD TO ALCATRAZ
(Republic Pictures Corp.)

Cruelly compact, with nary a distraction from Robert Lowery's self-doubting quest to clear himself of a murder rap, *Road to Alcatraz* is vintage Poverty Row noir, torn raw from genuine pulp-magazine source material. Lowery, Columbia Pictures' Batman-to-be, plays lawyer John Norton, who cannot remember to save his life where he was or what he was doing on the night of his business partner's murder.

A more vivid memory, that he had resented the partner's larger share of the profits in an investment venture, is of no help at all. It develops that John had kept the investment a secret from his wife, Kit (June Storey), and that the broker, Gary Payne (Charles Gordon), is John's college-days fraternity chum—whom Kit has never trusted.

Evidence accumulates against John, but he manages to keep it hidden, blundering only when he searches the home of another investor (Clarence Kolb) and must flee suddenly. While in hiding, John finds a fraternity pin he had believed lost. Eluding the police, he sneaks away to meet Gary—only to realize that the pin belongs to Gary. No sooner has John pegged Gary as the killer, than Gary opens fire on him. The law arrives in time to nab Gary and rescue John. John finally realizes that his blackout had been the result of a drugging administered by Gary.

Lowery is credibly on edge throughout as the unwitting frame-up victim, and Charles Gordon seems the soul of brotherly concern until the whiplash turnabout. Grant Withers delivers a solid portrayal of a determined but open-minded investigator, and Clarence Kolb is as serious as blood poisoning in the role of a colleague who fancies Lowery a threat. June Storey seems less than understanding as Lowery's wife. Lowery's discovery of the murder scene is especially well handled, conveying not only the shock of the occasion but also the onslaught of a crushing imagined guilt.

CREDITS: Executive Producer: Armand Schaefer; Associate Producer: Sidney Picker; Director: Nick Grinde; Screenplay: Dwight V. Babcock and Jerry Sackheim; from Francis K. Allen's 1944 Story, "Murder Stole My Missing Hours," as Published in *Speed Mystery* Magazine; Photographed by: Ernest Miller; Second Cameraman: Herbert Kirkpatrick; Special Effects: Howard Lydecker and Theodore Lydecker; Assistant Director: Don Verk; Transparency Projection Shots: Gordon C. Schaefer; Art Director: Lucious Croxton; Supervising Art Director: Russell Kimball; Editor: Richard L. Van Enger; Décor: George Milo; Music: Richard Cherwin; Sound: Fred Stahl; Re-Recording and Effects Mixer: John Stransky, Jr.; Makeup: Bob Mark; Running Time: 60 Minutes; Released: July 10, 1945

CAST: Robert Lowery (John Norton); June Storey (Kit Norton); Grant Withers (Inspector Craven); Clarence Kolb (Phillip Angreet); Charles Gordon (Gary

Payne); Iris Adrian (Louise Rogers); Lillian Bronson (Dorothy Stone); Harry Depp (Simmons); Kenne Duncan (Servant); Willa Pearl Curtis (Maid); George Sherwood (Hotel Clerk); Si Jenks (Messenger); Frank Meredith, Bill Stevens and Lee Phelps (Cops); Billy Carteledge and Matty Roubert (Newsboys); Jack Daley (Man in Window)

THE WHITE GORILLA
(Louis Weiss/Fraser & Merrick Pictures)

Routinely confused nowadays with Sam Newfield's delightfully dreadful *White Pongo*, *The White Gorilla* is the more fascinating, and even the more straightforwardly entertaining, film on many accounts. This is chiefly because its pinch-penny production company, descended from the pioneering Weiss Bros./Artclass studios, made most of the picture simply by recycling a 1927 Artclass serial called *The Perils of the Jungle*. There was no attempt to correct the projection-rate problems posed by such a self-piracy, and as a consequence much of *The White Gorilla* plays out like a silent movie shown at the faster sound-film speed. Which is precisely what it is.

A veneer of newness was added in footage featuring Ray "Crash" Corrigan as a heroic explorer and directed by H.L. Fraser, screenwriter of *The Perils of the Jungle*. The fresh footage also features Frank Merrill, Eugenia Gilbert, Bobby Nelson and Albert J. Smith, returning with inconsistent results from *Perils*' ensemble cast. The title creature, whose appearance drives Ray Corrigan to a frenzied delirium, appears only in the new scenes, as does Corrigan. Corrigan is added, sort of, to the silent-era bulk of the feature by means of a voice-over narration. Corrigan's presence also ensures that the ape costuming is of a higher grade, for it is his wardrobe of hair-suits—he pursued a lucrative sideline in the movies as a gorilla impersonator—that allows the film to live up to its title.

Unlike *White Pongo*, where the expeditioners want to capture an albino ape for scientific purposes, the point of *The White Gorilla* is to present its title creature for shock value and interspecies intolerance. Neither film has much to say in the way of enlightenment, and animal-rights advocates will find both infuriating.

Legend holds that a white gorilla, banished from its society of otherwise black apes, has grown bitter and murderous. There follows the usual hoo-hah about hostile tribes; a Tarzan-styled boy (Bobby Nelson) who rides an elephant and bosses the natives around; cutthroat intrigues centering on a treasure-laden cave; and the inevitable clashes between the white gorilla and a black gorilla. Lorraine Miller plays the requisite daughter-of-explorer whose beauty attracts the unwanted attentions of the white ape. Corrigan takes the easy way out and shoots the creature. There is an absurdly sobering coda in which the black ape buries its enemy's carcass, deep in the prop-department jungle.

Although *The White Gorilla* was registered for copyright before Producers Releasing Corp.'s *White Pongo*, there is room to doubt there ever was much in the way of direct competition. *Daily Variety* and *The Exhibitor* did not publish reviews of *The White Gorilla* until 1947, when Los Angeles saw a formal opening.

CREDITS: Presented by: Louis Weiss; Supervisor: George M. Merrick; Director: H.L. Fraser; Silent Footage Director: Jack Nelson; Story: Monro Talbot; Recycled Footage from: 1927's Artclass/Weiss Serial, *The Perils of the Jungle*; Photographed by: Robert Cline, William C. Thompson and Bertram Longworth; Settings: Thomas Connoly; Editor: Adrian Weiss; Music: Lee Zahler; Sound: Glen Glenn; Running Time: 62 Minutes; Copyrighted and Announced for Release: July 12, 1945; Los Angeles Opening: December 2, 1947

CAST: Ray Corrigan (Steve Collins); Lorraine Miller (Ruth Stacey); Frank Merrill (Ed Bradford); Bobby Nelson (Wild Boy); Eugenia Gilbert (Wild Boy's Mother); Albert J. Smith (Lou Hanley); Charles King (Morgan)

JEALOUSY
(Republic Pictures Corp.)

Republic Pictures' forté—make that *fortissimo*—was action, and plenty of that. The little company at Studio City (later, the home of CBS Television City) made more robust matinee Westerns and slam-bang serials than any other outfit. Occasional ventures into more prestigious middlebrow fare varied from the excellence of *Man of Conquest* (1938), *The Dark Command* (1940) and *The Quiet Man* (1952) to such misfires as *The Fighting Kentuckian* (1949) and *Belle LeGrand* (1951). Less frequently, Republic emphasized artistic appeal, as in Orson Welles' fascinating but jinxed *Macbeth* (1948) and Gustav Machaty's more fulfilling *Jealousy*. A proper niche for these films eluded the marketing department: Such titles were too highbrow for mainstream theatres and not enough so for the art houses. These forays did, however, bring Republic some unaccustomed critical notice, and they were inexpensive enough to minimize financial risks.

Jealousy chronicles the unraveling of Peter Urban (Nils Asther), once a famous author in Europe but now a refugee wallowing in alcoholic self-pity. His American wife, Janet (Jane Randolph), who works as a cab driver to support Urban, tries to remain loyal despite his suicidal tantrums and manipulative abuses. Janet and a prominent surgeon, Dr. David Brent (John Loder), fall in love—much to the consternation of Brent's colleague, Dr. Monica Anderson (Karen Morley).

Jane Randolph and John Loder in *Jealousy*

Urban, now contemplating murder, becomes ever more vile. Janet leaves their house and returns to find him slain. Suspicion falls upon her. Urban's devoted friend, Hugo (Hugo Haas), a fellow refugee, becomes deranged as as result of the slaying. His testimony is a deciding factor in Janet's conviction. Finally, Brent reveals Dr. Anderson as the killer.

The Czech director Machaty was much admired for the artistry of *Erotikon* (1929) and *Extase* (1932), the latter being the picture that brought fame to Hedy Lamarr. Machaty came Stateside during the late 1930s and made a rather good film for MGM, *Within the Law* (1939). He did not make another until *Jealousy*. His next—and last—was the German-made *Suchkind 312* (1956). Machaty, who made only 11 features in 31 years, died in 1963.

For *Jealousy*, Machaty gathered a company dominated by European talents. (Several participants, including source-author Dalton Trumbo, composer Hanns Eisler and actress Karen Morley, would be blacklisted or worse in the hysterical postwar investigations of the House UnAmerican Activities Committee.) The flavor is strongly European, achieved through the naturalistic filming of familiar Los Angeles street settings, barrooms and cafés. The characters are convincing simply because they lack the conventionality of being entirely good or entirely bad. The decaying writer, set forth splendidly by the sensitive Scandanavian Nils Asther, arouses both pity and dislike.

Hugo Haas, who later would direct several American films in an arch style reminiscent of Machaty, is excellent as a kind-hearted, clumsy man who becomes a paranoid menace. John Loder and Jane Randolph are admirable and long-suffering; their adulterous affair seems a reasonable response to the circumstances. Karen Morley is a dedicated humanitarian who proves willing to sacrifice a colleague and a rival. Machaty kept a Viennese psychiatrist on the set to put the players wise as to how their characters should respond to the script's treacherous emotional tides, and the result of this coaching is exacting and realistic.

The film occasionally wallows overmuch in the miseries at hand, missing the dramatic punch. More often, the impact is just right—as when Miss Randolph suddenly realizes that Asther has poisoned the food he is throwing to a flock of seagulls; here, a subtle use of slow motion lends a mournful gravity. A particularly poignant sequence is a Christmas gathering in the benighted household.

Henry Sharp's photography melds realism and visual poetry into a unified style. Eisler's sophisticated and modernistic score is founded in part upon a bittersweet title song by Rudolf Friml, the popular composer of operettas.

CREDITS: Executive Producer: Howard Sheehan; Associate Producer: George Moskov; Producer and Director: Gustav Machaty; Screenplay: Arnold Phillips and Gustav Machaty; Based upon a Scenario by: Dalton Trumbo; Photographed by: Henry Sharp; Assistant Director: Benjamin Kadish; Art Director: Frank Sylos; Editor: John Link; Décor: Glenn P. Thompson; Costumer: Maria Ray; Music: Hanns Eisler; Song: "Jealousy," by Rudolph Friml; Running Time: 71 Minutes; Released: July 23, 1945

CAST: John Loder (Dr. David Brent); Jane Randolph (Janet Urban); Karen Morley (Dr. Monica Anderson); Nils Asther (Peter Urban); Hugh Haas (Hugo Kral); Herbert Holmes (Melvyn Russell); Michael Mark (Shopkeeper)

THE FATAL WITNESS
(Republic Pictures Corp.)

An extraordinarily popular radio series, CBS' *Suspense*, yielded the source of this twist-ending hair-raiser. *The Fatal Witness* not only generates a lingering chill beyond its ghostly ruse to expose a murderer; the film also provides Evelyn Ankers with a more satisfying star vehicle than even Universal Pictures' horror-movie unit had ever allowed her as a leading lady in the likes of *The Mad Ghoul*, *The Ghost of Frankenstein*, *Captive Wild Woman*, *Son of Dracula* and—but you get the drift.

Miss Ankers is Priscilla Ames, ward of a wealthy and cantankerous Londoner, Lady Ferguson (Barbara Everest). Lady Ferguson accuses her playboy nephew, John Bedford (George Leigh), of theft. John leaves in a huff and makes a point of getting himself jailed for drunken misbehavior.

Lady Ferguson is found slain. John, the likeliest suspect, falls back on his disgraceful alibi. But John proves also to have a paid accomplice in a jailer, Scoggins (Barry Bernard), who had secretly released John for an hour on the night of the murder.

Inspector Trent (Richard Fraser), who is falling in love with Priscilla, becomes ever more determined to nail John. Scoggins turns up strangled after demanding more money from John. Knowing John's superstitious nature, Trent stages a dinner party where an actress will appear as Lady Ferguson; he instructs the other guests to pretend not to see the impostor. John, certain he has encountered a ghost, betrays himself as the killer.

Then comes the belated message so crucial to any such shaggy-dog yarn, explaining that the actress could not appear as planned. Trent and Priscilla realize that the apparition they saw must have been the genuine article. The climax is more a punchline than a resolution—but it works, with all the elemental gooseflesh urgency of a campfire spook-story. Only a grump would resist the urge to cringe.

Miss Ankers (1918-1985), of Chilean birth and British ancestry, had established herself as a screen actress in England several years before she arrived in Hollywood. The contrived English setting of *The Fatal Witness* brings out a more reserved style than Miss Ankers had lavished on her many Hollywood films up to now. For one thing, the little Republic production does not require her to react to any overtly monstrous characters—and, indeed, calls upon her to do more *acting* than *re*acting. Richard Fraser is quite good as the romantically inclined Scotland Yard man, and George Leigh is properly loathsome as a cunning, however impulsive, killer.

The story would reassert itself in 1959—under its original radio-play title, "Banquo's Chair," alluding to a ghostly intrusion in Shakespeare's *Macbeth*—as an episode of Alfred Hitchcock's network teleseries.

CREDITS: Executive Producer: Armand Schaefer; Associate Producer: Rudolph E. Abel; Director: Lesley Selander; Screenplay: Jerry Sackheim; Based upon: Rupert Croft-Cooke's 1943 Radio Script, "Banquo's Chair," as Broadcast on the CBS Network's *Suspense*; Adaptation: Cleve F. Adams; Photographed by: Bud Thackery; Assistant Director: Joe Dill; Special Effects: Howard Lydecker and Theodore Lydecker; Transparency Projection Shots: Gordon C. Schaefer; Art Directors: Russell Kimbell and Gano Chittenden; Editor: Ralph Dixon; Décor: George Milo; Costumer: Adele Palmer; Music: Richard Cherwin; Classical Selection: Beethoven's "Moonlight Sonata" (Piano Sonata No. 2 in C#

Minor); Song: "From Here On In," by Sammy Cahn & Jules Stein; Sound: Vic Appel; Re-Recording and Sound Effects Mixers: Thomas A. Carman and John Stransky, Jr.; Re-Recording, Effects and Music Mixer: Howard Wilson; Makeup: Bob Mark; Running Time: 60 Minutes; Released: September 15, 1945

CAST: Evelyn Ankers (Patricia Ames); Richard Fraser (Inspector William Trent); George Leigh (John Bedford); Barbara Everest (Lady Ferguson); Barry Bernard (Scoggins); Frederic Worlock (Sir Humphrey Mong); Virginia Farmer (Martha); Colin Campbell (Sir Malcolm Hewitt); Crauford Kent (Jepson); Peggy Jackson (Gracie Hallett); Keith Hitchcock (Dowell); Herbert Evans and Cyril Delevanti (Coroners); Eva Novak (Maid); John Meredith (Operator); Hilda Plowright (Lady Mong); Maj. Sam Harris (Elderly Man); Lucy Storm (Daughter); Lillian Talbot (Lady Hewitt); Bruce Carruthers and James Logan (Bobbies); Florence Wix (Elderly Woman); Elaine Lange (Tillie); Boyd Irwin (Tailor); Frank Baker (Police Sergeant); Harry Cording (Gus); Norman Ainsley (Drunkard); Gil Perkins (Detective); Eric Wilson (Clerk);

APOLOGY FOR MURDER
(Sigmund Neufeld Productions, Inc./Producers Releasing Corp.)

Hugh Beaumont (1909-1982), a Methodist minister who financed his church activities with acting roles, became in the process an all-'round capable leading man and backup player in the realm of the Hollywood B-picture. It is an unfortunate cultural hangover that few people can watch Beaumont in *anything* today without feeling compelled to remark on the player's larger identification with the 1950s TV sitcom *Leave It to Beaver*.

If any one piece of Beaumont's rediscovered earlier work could obliterate so overtly wholesome a stigma, it is *Apology for Murder*. Here, the Kansas-born Beaumont plays a passively crooked newspaper reporter, Kenny Blake, who treads onto the turf of *Double Indemnity* and *The Postman Always Rings Twice* via an ill-advised affair with the wife (Ann Savage) of wealthy businessman Harvey Kirkland (Russell Hicks). Blake is unaware at first of Toni Kirkland's marital state, but he hasn't any better sense than to pursue the attraction once he learns the truth. Not only is Blake a lousy reporter, failing to land an assigned interview with the big shot—but he is also susceptible to Toni's suggestion that he help her kill Kirkland.

Blake keeps cool when assigned to write a story about Kirkland's (apparently accidental) death, but then he remembers that he and Toni had neglected to place the victim's car in gear and start its engine before shoving it over a cliff. Which causes the law to smell murder. Kirkland's big-business rival (Pierre Watkin), a likelier suspect, is railroaded into a death sentence. Toni proves disloyal to Blake, who finally barges in on her. The two shoot each other. Mortally wounded, Blake returns to his newsroom, where he bangs out a confession on a literal deadline.

Pure rudimentary noir, *Apology for Murder* keeps the suspense cranked, the tensions between characters varied and unpredictable. It offers persuasive evidence that director Sam Newfield possessed a greater talent than most his work would suggest. Beaumont makes the bad journalist likable enough despite his arrogance and his terminal gumption deficiency, but Blake cannot seem to get along with anyone—not his tough editor (Charles D. Brown), not his illicit lover, not his interview subjects—long enough to develop anything resembling a well-socialized relationship. Blake is an American archetype of the sort most folks will have met,

the brash, affable loser who hardly bears getting to know lest his nature rub off, and Beaumont nails the character. Equally good, though saddled with a role of less challenging depth, is *Detour*'s Ann Savage as the trophy wife who sets out to bag a few trophies on her own.

CREDITS: Producer: Sigmund Neufeld; Director: Sam Newfield; Story and Screenplay: Fred Myton; Photographed by: Jack Greenhalgh; Assistant Director: Kenny Kessler; Second Camera: Ernest Smith; Special Effects: Ray Mercer; Transparency Projection Shots: Ray Smallwood; Art Director: Edward C. Jewell; Editor: Holbrook N. Todd; Set Dresser: Elias H. Reif; Properties: George Bahr; Music: Leo Erdody; Sound: Ben Winkler; Re-Recording & Effects Mixers: Joseph I. Kane, Edward Nelson and Jack Noyes; Running Time: 67 Minutes; Released: September 17, 1945

CAST: Ann Savage (Toni Kirkland); Hugh Beaumont (Kenny Blake); Russell Hicks (Harvey Kirkland); Charles D. Brown (Ward McGee); Pierre Watkin (Craig Jordan); Sarah Padden (Maggie); Norman Willis (Allen Webb); Eva Novak (Maid); Budd Buster (Jed); George Sherwood (Lt. Edwards); Wheaton Chambers (Minister); Archie Hall (Paul); Elizabeth Valentine (Mrs. Harper); Henry Hall (Warden)

DANGEROUS INTRUDER
(Producers Releasing Corp.)

A strategic location shoot in Pasadena opens up the more commonly stage-bound PRC atmosphere, lending Real World scope and texture to the tale of an injured showgirl whose convalescence in a wealthy household is complicated by anguished caterwauling—and worse—in the night.

A speeding car driven by antiques collector Max Ducane (Charles Arnt, the homicidal shrink of *Strange Confession*) strikes Jenny (Veda Ann Borg) while she is attempting to hitch a ride. Insisting that Jenny recuperate at his home, Ducane seems the soul of hospitality until Jenny notices his obsessive devotion to his treasures. Ducane's wife, Millicent (Fay Helm), screams uncontrollably during the night; her daughter, Jackie (Jo Ann Marlowe) explains that Millicent suffers from a chronic ailment, which Ducane has been attempting to treat without medical consultation. Millicent controls the family's wealth, inherited from an aunt who had taken a fatal fall. Jenny overhears Ducane mumbling about shoving someone downstairs.

Jenny falls in love with Curtis (Richard Powers), Ducane's too-trusting brother-in-law. But Curtis rejects her after Millicent dies and Jenny insists that Ducane must be responsible. Jenny has recovered enough to leave and begin prying. Foster (John Rogers), Ducane's helper, confides to Jenny that Ducane is bent upon taking charge of the estate. Learning that Jackie is in line as heir, Jenny concludes that the girl must be the next intended victim; actually, the next victim is Foster, whom Ducane murders outright for blabbing.

Ducane traps Jenny in a blazing automobile with Foster's body. Curtis, who has wised up to Jenny's suspicions, arrives just in time. Ducane, attempting to flee, dies when his car takes a tumble.

Except for a blatantly overacted show of surly menace from top-billed Charles Arnt, the picture plays out nicely until the hurried last reel, which leaves the impression of a hastily concocted wrap-up. Veda Ann Borg, taking a welcome breather from *femme fatale* typecasting, equips the endangered guest with a pleasingly stubborn sense of justice.

CREDITS: Producer: Leon Fromkess; Associate Producer: Martin Mooney; Director: Vernon Keays; Screenplay: Martin M. Goldsmith; Story: Philip MacDonald and F. Ruth Howard; Photographed by: James Brown; Assistant Director: William A. Calihan, Jr.; Art Director: Edward C. Jewell; Editor: Carl Pierson; Décor: Sydney Moore; Wardrobe: Mona Barry; Music: Karl Hajos;

Sound: Max Hutchinson; Makeup: Bud Westmore; Running Time: 62 Minutes; Released: September 21, 1945

CAST: Charles Arnt (Max Ducane); Veda Ann Borg (Jenny); Richard Powers (Curtis); Fay Helm (Millicent Ducane); John Rogers (Foster); Jo Ann Marlowe (Jackie); Helena Phillips Evans (Mrs. Swenson); Roberta Smith (Freckles); George Sorel (Holt); Forrest Taylor (Dr. Bascom)

SCOTLAND YARD INVESTIGATOR
(Republic Pictures Corp.)

Sir C. Aubrey Smith squares off against Erich von Stroheim in *Scotland Yard Investigator*, an art-caper murder thriller that could pass muster as an authentically British production. Lord Smith's presence is the clincher, of course, but the impeccable design by Frank Hotaling and Charles Thompson contributes mightily to the illusion. Even *Variety* liked this one: "[A] mediocre, yet successful, script is made to appear like a well-polished project, simply because it was excellently cast, shrewdly directed and competently produced."

With an imposing height, a jutting browline and protuberant nose and a jowly profile, the London-born Lord Smith (1863-1948) spent the 1930s and '40s as Hollywood's perfect custodian of the Crown's better interests. Here, Smith is the newly knighted Sir James Collison, curator of the National Art Gallery, who has kept the *Mona Lisa* stashed away for safekeeping through the Second World War. Sir James expects the Louvre to reclaim its own any day now, and when two convincingly credentialed Frenchmen, Henri and Jules (George Metaxa and Victor Varconi), arrive, James turns over what he believes to be the da Vinci masterpiece without hesitation.

Sir James has unwittingly assisted the ruthless art collector Carl Hoffmeyer (von Stroheim). When Hoffmeyer realizes the painting is a forgery, he visits Sir James and calmly admits to the theft-by-pretense. Sir James' reaction convinces Hoffmeyer that the curator had been fooled as to the painting's genuineness. Hoffmeyer calls upon a shady dealer in antiques named Sam Todworthy (Forrester Harvey). Todworthy has long since obtained the genuine *Mona Lisa* via a diplomatic leak. Todworthy, who has already committed murder to keep the painting, now demands £100,000 from Hoffmeyer.

Hoffmeyer orders his cohorts to kill Todworthy, and when Jules refuses the command Hoffmeyer stabs him to death. The discovery of Jules' body provokes an investigation by Scotland Yard, which has less to do with the case than the film's title would suggest.

Meanwhile, Sam calls on Sir James and offers to sell the *Mona Lisa*. James' granddaughter and assistant, Toni Collison (Stephanie Bachelor), urges him to contact the Yard, but he fears that a scandal would endanger the precarious health of his wife, Mary (*The Old Dark House*'s Eva Moore). Hoffmeyer's sword-cane rampage continues with the slaying of Todworthy. It all leads to a desperate confrontation between Sir James and Hoffmeyer, who is done in by Todworthy's widow (Doris Lloyd) before he can stab James. Dying, Hoffmeyer attempts to mutilate the genuine *Mona Lisa*, but James rescues the painting. The swap is made secretively, lest the Louvre suspect shenanigans afoot.

Here is one of Stroheim's more rabid villains, a thief whose motive is sheer possession, not profit, and who will kill whoever stands in his way. Aubrey Smith is likewise in his element, the very embodiment of stalwart heroism. As the token title character, an inspector who is conveniently engaged to marry Sir James' granddaughter, Richard Fraser is overshadowed throughout by Lord Smith's droll magnificence. Forrester Harvey, who more often played Cockney comic relief, stands out as a secondary villain, with the bonus of a nicely enacted death scene. Emil Rameau is suitably befuddled as a self-important and clue-deficient official of the Louvre.

CREDITS: Executive Producer: Armand Schaefer; Associate Producer and Director: George Blair; Screenplay: Randall Faye; Photographed by: Ernest Miller and William Bradford; Second Cameraman: Herbert Kirkpatrick; Special Effects: Howard Lydecker and Theodore Lydecker; Transparency Projection Shots: Gordon C. Schaefer; Assistant Director: Joe Dill; Art Director: Frank Hotaling; Editor: Fred Allen; Décor: Charles Thompson; Costumer: Adele Palmer; Music Director: Richard Cherwin; Musical Score: Charles Maxwell; Song: The Traditional "Drink to Me Only with Thine Eyes," Lyrics by Ben Jonson; Sound: Ed Borschell; Re-Recording and Effects Mixers: Thomas A. Carman and Howard Wilson; Makeup: Bob Mark; Running Time: 68 Minutes; Released: September 30, 1945

CAST: Sir C. Aubrey Smith (Sir James Collison); Erich von Stroheim (Carl Hoffmeyer); Stephanie Bachelor (Toni Collison); Forrester Harvey (Sam, Todworthy); Doris Lloyd (Emma Todworthy); Eva Moore (Mary Collison); Richard Fraser (Inspector Bob Cartwright); Victor Varconi (Jules); George Metaxa (Henri); Emil Rameau (Prof. Renault); Colin Campbell (Waters); Frederic Worlock (Col. Brent); George Renavent (Anton Miran); Olaf Hytten (Purvis); Edythe Elliott (Bentley); Simon Oliver (Sir James' Great-Grandson); Eric Wilton

(Inspector); Bob Thom (Cab Driver); Ted Billings (Newsboy); Jean de Briac (Phillipe); Harry Allen (Watchman)

MARSHAL OF LAREDO
(Republic Pictures Corp.)

Roy Barcroft was Republic's most dependably extravagant portrayer of chapter-play villains. But a great many of his 200-odd screen assignments from 1937 until his death in 1969 would find Barcroft holding forth among the supporting badmen in Western features. Such were the economic realities of Poverty Row, where the distinction between stardom and working-actor status was vague at best. Here is a welcome bit of prominence, a *Red Ryder* series entry that allows Barcroft a showy role as a manipulative sadist, paired with a grotesque brute played by Don Costello.

The comic-strip origins of *Red Ryder* usually kept this Saturday-matinee series more on the upbeat side, what with Wild Bill Elliott's dashing title portrayal and kid actor Bobby Blake's annoyingly spirited impersonation of an Indian sidekick called Little Beaver. *Marshal of Laredo* gives the edge to a rabid strain of villainy.

The film opens with a bank-courier robbery in which Marshal Ryder nabs a fleeing bandit (Bud Geary) while a fellow crook, Pretty Boy (Costello), escapes with the loot and reports to mob boss Denver Jack (Barcroft), a superficially respectable saloonkeeper. Pretty Boy, whose nickname is a backhanded reference to a hideously burned face, finds himself continually terrorized by Denver Jack's menacing use of matches. Pretty Boy is more directly sadistic, favoring the bullwhip as a persuasive device. The plot deepens itself with an ambitious lawyer named Larry Randall (Robert Grady), who serves Denver Jack while courting banker's daughter Judy Bowers (Peggy Stewart). Randall promises bank president Mel Bowers (George Carleton) he will part ways with Denver in exchange for Judy's hand in marriage. All of which only sets Randall up to become Red Ryder's chief suspect in the slaying of the banker.

The tale escalates to a near-lynching for Randall and a hostage situation for Red and Little Beaver. Red turns the tables by playing on Pretty Boy's fear of flames.

Barcroft and Costello pretty well steal the show with their brains-heavy/ muscle-heavy combo, seeming to hold an entire town under one threat or another. Bill Elliott is a resourceful and likable hero, and Bobby Blake (formerly Mickey Gubitosi, that world-class pathetic whiner of MGM's post-Hal Roach *Our Gang* comedies) is at best tolerable as the mock-Indian. As Robert Blake in adulthood, the actor would find a greater prominence in television and in the celebrity-gossip news-rags, culminating in a murder case of origins too disgusting to contemplate.

CREDITS: Associate Producer: Sidney Picker; Director: R.G. Springsteen; Screenplay: Bob Williams; Based upon: Fred Harman's Syndicated Comic Strip, *Red Ryder*; Photographed by: Bud Thackery; Second Camera: Enzo Martinelli; Transparency Projection Shots: Gordon C. Schaefer; Assistant Director: Don Verk; Art Director: Hilyard Brown; Editor: Charles Craft; Décor: George Milo; Music: Richard Cherwin; Sound: Earl Crain, Jr.; Re-Recording and Effects Mixer: Thomas A. Carman; Makeup: Bob Mark; Running Time: 58 Minutes; Released: October 7, 1945

CAST: Wild Bill Elliott (Red Ryder); Bobby Blake (Little Beaver); Alice Fleming (Duchess); Peggy Stewart (Judy Bowers); Robert Grady (Larry Randall); Roy Barcroft (Denver Jack); Don Costello (Pretty Boy Murphy); Bud Geary (Ferguson); Sarah Padden (Mrs. Randall); Tom London (Barton); Tom Chatterton (Rev. Parker); Wheaton Chambers (Dr. Allen); George Chesebro (Deputy); George Carleton (Mel Bowers); Dorothy Granger (Suzanne); Dick Scott (Croupier); Mary Arden (Mrs. Paine)

ROUGH RIDERS OF CHEYENNE
(Republic Pictures Corp.)

A hatred-unto-death feud, approaching Hatfields-vs.-McCoys proportions and stoked by covetous outside interests, renders this *Sunset Carson* series shoot-'em-up of interest beyond its built-in nostalgic audience. Texas-born Michael "Sunset Carson" Harrison plays the linchpin in a war of nerves that is further complicated by brother-and-sister twins who might be lurking killers.

The town of Paradise Valley is more valley than paradise, what with an attack on patriarch Andy Carson (Eddy Waller) causing a flare-up of dormant hostilities. Sunset Carson, who has long since put this raggedy little hole-in-the-road behind him, returns to find his father recovering but troubled over the recent slaying of his counterpart, Linc Sterling. Andy stands suspected in the murder, but he is of course innocent.

Sunset learns that Andy and Linc had founded the village—but that Linc married a woman named Harriet (Mira McKinney), whose irrational dislike of the Carsons touched off the feud. In order to save Sunset from Harriet's murderous wrath, Andy had sent his son away. Andy has concluded that his assailant must be one of Harriet and Linc's offspring, Melinda (Peggy Stewart) or Martin (Michael Sloane). Just as the moldy old skeletons have started tumbling out of the closet, a hand snakes in through a window, and Andy is mortally wounded.

Sunset is distracted by an encounter with Pop Jordan (Wade Crosby), the town drunkard. Pursuing a distant rider, Sunset captures Melinda, who insists she is not the culprit. Sunset, too much the gentleman to bully even an antagonistic woman, concludes that Martin must have done the shooting. Melinda, returning home, learns that Martin cannot have committed the deed. Harriet cares not who the slayer might be; she is simply delighted to learn that Andy is dead. The deranged old bat orders her children to finish the Carson line by doing away with Sunset.

A member of a cattle-rustling mob, shot down while attempting to raid the Carson ranch, informs Sunset that both the Carsons and the Sterlings have been "played for suckers." This cryptic death-rattle leads Sunset to conclude that some hidden troublemaker must be trying to provoke him and the Sterlings into killing each other. Each house, after all, owns strategic rangelands.

While attempting to call a truce, Sunset finds himself under fire and blames the Sterlings. He challenges Martin to a duel, and Harriet orders her son to go through with it. Melinda knocks Martin out and dresses in his clothing to keep the appointment. Pop Jordan, who is the secret brains behind a takeover scam, orders his gang to stake out the showdown and kill both shooters. Melinda is wounded. Martin, arriving late, blames Sunset, who establishes his innocence and rallies the twins against their real enemies. Harriet is shot in the resulting bloodbath. Dying, she reveals that she had grown to despise Andy Carson after he jilted her to marry Sunset's mother. So she took up with Linc Sterling, who spent their entire wedded life ridiculing Harriet's thwarted affections. Harriet it was who had killed Linc, hoping to frame Andy.

The fade-out dares suggest that Sunset Carson and Melinda Sterling are bound to fall in love. Peggy Stewart, a recurring leading lady in the *Sunset Carson*s (and once the real-life wife of cowboy star Don "Red" Barry), would return as other characters entirely. So much for picture-to-picture continuity.

CREDITS: Associate Producer: Bennett Cohen; Director: Thomas Carr; Screenplay: Elizabeth Beecher; Photographed by: William Bradford; Assistant Director: Don Verk; Second Camera: Alfred Keller; Miniatures and Special Effects: Howard Lydecker and Theodore Lydecker; Transparency Projection Shots: Gordon C. Schaefer; Art Director: Frank Hotaling; Editor: Fred Allen; Décor: John McCarthy and Robert Hays; Music: Richard Cherwin; Sound: Victor Appel; Re-Recording and Effects Mixer: Howard Wilson; Makeup: Bob Mark; Running Time: 58 Minutes; Released: November 1, 1945

CAST: Sunset Carson (Sunset Carson); Peggy Stewart (Melinda Sterling); Mira McKinney (Harriet Sterling); Monte Hale (Ward Tuttle); Wade Crosby (Pop Jordan); Michael Sloane (Martin Sterling); Kenne Duncan (Lance Davis); Tom London (Sheriff Edwards); Eddy Waller (Andy Carson); Jack O'Shea (Smoke Haley); Bob Wilke (Benjie Cook); Tex Terry (Flapjack); Jack Rockwell (Obediah Jones); Red Lease (Henchman); Hank Bell (Hank); Frank O'Connor (Conductor)

WHITE PONGO
(Producers Releasing Corp.)

For the antithesis of Afrocentric enlightenment, look no further than Sam Newfield's *White Pongo*. Merely a carelessly generous attempt at an exotic entertainment rather than any conscious manifestation of bigotries, the film confronts the viewer with a pageant of mock-tribulations and contrived terrors. It mingles stock expeditionary footage piecemeal with a sound-stage concoction that would have the viewer believe a blond-gorilla-suited player might represent some lost connection between man and ape. The yarn holds that an agent of the Rhodesian police would travel under the name of Mumbo Jumbo and keep a straight face while doing so; that a tribe called the Negritos harbors mostly malice toward white explorers, with strategic exceptions; and that there exists a natural hostility between white gorillas and black gorillas. So much for integration, metaphorically speaking. But such was the state of the color bar during America's strange version of the 1940s that a picture so outlandish could present itself with impunity and even a semblance of seriousness.

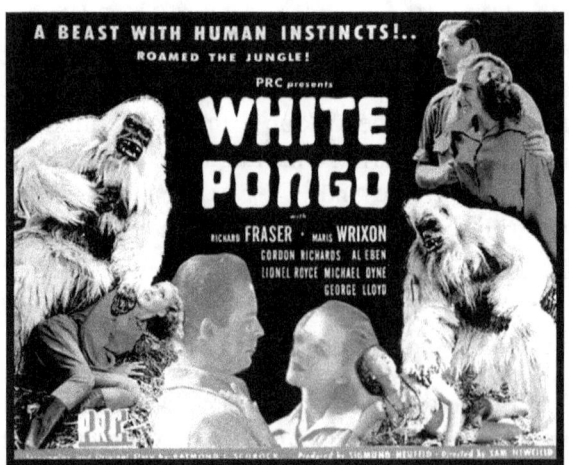

Fleeing tribal captivity in the Belgian Congo, an explorer named Gunderson (Milton Kibbee) sees a mighty white ape kill a native warrior. Gunderson brings his account of the ordeal to civilization, and explorer Sir Harry Bragdon (Gordon Richards) mounts a fresh expedition to look into this missing-link business. Sir Harry's spoiled daughter, Pamela (Maris Wrixon), is among the party, along with guard Jeffrey Bishop (Richard Fraser) and the aforementioned Mumbo Jumbo (Joel Fluellen), purportedly the supervisor of the native bearers. Mutiny follows, along with the abduction of Pamela Bragdon—first by a treacherous guide (Al Eben), and at length by the white gorilla. This beast then is engaged in gratuitous combat by the black gorilla; the albino throws its adversary from atop a cliff. The white ape is captured for shipment to London.

Director Newfield had made finer pictures by far, and he would deliver finer pictures yet to come in a vast body of work whose chief distinction is its very volume. Richard Fraser and Maris Wrixon almost transcend the material, registering a romantic attraction that allows the film to end on something more substantial than just the capture. The balance of the acting is uniformly overwrought, but the ape-suit routines have their entertainingly scary moments. Three generations of American schoolchildren grew up with such cockamamie misperceptions of Africa, thanks to the neighborhood movie theatres and, eventually, the ghostly cinematic afterlife of syndicated television.

CREDITS: Producer: Sigmund Neufeld; Director: Sam Newfield; Story and Screenplay: Raymond L. Schrock; Photographed by: Jack Greenhalgh; Second Camera: Ernest Smith; Special Effects: Ray Mercer; Assistant Director: William O'Connor; Art Director: Edward C. Jewell; Editor: Holbrook N. Todd; Set Dresser: Elias H. Reif; Propmaster: Eugene C. Stone; Costumer: James H. Wade; Music: Leo Erdody; Sound: John Carter; Re-Recording and Effects Mixers: Joseph I. Kane, Edward Nelson and Jack Noyes; Music Mixer: William H. Wilmarth; Production Manager: Bert Sternbach; Running Time: 77 Minutes; Released: November 2, 1945

CAST: Richard Fraser: (Jeffrey Bishop); Maris Wrixon (Pamela Bragdon); Lionel Royce (Dr. Peter Van Doorn); Al Eben (Hans Krogert); Gordon Richards (Sir Harry Bragdon); Michael Dyne (Clive Carswell); George Lloyd (Baxter); Larry Steers (Dr. Kent); Milton Kibbee (Gunderson); Egon Brecher (Dr. Gerig); Joel Fluellen (Mumbo Jumbo)

SHADOW OF TERROR
(Producers Releasing Corp.)

"Further proof," raved *Variety*, "that this company is gradually rising out of the minor leagues." The shadow of the title is the August 6, 1945, bombing of Hiroshima—although this fact was unknown to source-author Sheldon Leon-

ard, or to anyone involved in the preproduction and principal photography of *Shadow of Terror*. The film had wrapped, as a matter of fact, and was ready for cutting when the United States deployed the atomic bomb, and in a quick-thinking response PRC obtained government documentary footage of nuclear-fission tests in New Mexico and spliced it onto the finished feature as a tag-ending, with a savvy added narration that hardly seems an afterthought. What had been merely a cryptic science-fictional melodrama about a struggle for the control of a powerful explosive, suddenly became Hollywood's first explicit flashback to the war's end—and an emphatic opening volley in a vast genre-to-come of atomic-devastation movies. (*China's Little Devils*, of course, had wishfully predicted a bombing raid on Tokyo, just months before.)

A train bound for Washington, D.C., carries research scientist Howard Norton (Richard Fraser), inventor of an explosive of staggering potential. Rival scientist Victor Maxwell (Cy Kendall), who wants to sell Norton's formula to the high bidder, has sent thugs McKenzie (Kenneth MacDonald) and Walters (Eddie Acuff) to waylay the inventor. The henchmen separate Norton from his briefcase and throw him off the train as it passes through a stretch of desert.

Rancher Joan Rutledge (Grace Gillern) and her foreman, Elmer (Emmett Lynn), rescue Norton, who finds himself stricken with amnesia. Memory or no memory, Norton and Joan fall in love.

Maxwell discovers the formula is worthless without an undocumented component known only to Norton. Later, a stranger arrives at the ranch, claiming to be searching for a lost friend; the visitor draws a gun at sight of Norton, but Elmer drives the intruder away. Sheriff Dixon (Sam Flint), summoned in the wake of the fracas, volunteers to help Norton. McKenzie and Walters arrive, posing as FBI agents, but carelessly give themselves away before they can abduct Norton. Norton and Joan flee, sending Elmer to summon the sheriff, but MacKenzie and Walters capture the sweethearts and take them to Maxwell's desert headquarters. Dissatisfied with the third-degree tactics of McKenzie and refusing to believe that Norton is suffering from amnesia, Maxwell administers a beating that causes Norton to regain his memory. Norton keeps mum.

Maxwell forces Norton and Joan into the desert, where his henchmen provide further torments. Meanwhile, Elmer and the sheriff have begun an airborne search. Norton digs a message for help into the sand. The plane arrives, buying Norton enough time to seize McKenzie's gun and shoot Maxwell. The gang is arrested. Norton's invention is hailed as a success when the A-bomb is dropped on Japan.

Richard Fraser makes a vigorous and determined scientist-hero, but he also conveys the character's addled disorientation to strong effect. Grace Gillern provides a more directly heroic and defiant presence as the no-nonsense cowgirl. Cy Kendall, as a crossbreed of spymaster and mad scientist, seems but a passive manipulator until the desperate finale, when he becomes disgusted with his inept flunkies and takes matters into his own fists. Lew Landers directs the proceedings with real urgency, and Jack Greenhalgh's cameras capture an essence of claustrophobia in the wide-open spaces of the Southwestern desert country.

CREDITS: Associate Producer: Jack D. Grant; Director: Lew Landers (Louis Friedlander); Screenplay: Arthur St. Claire; Story: Sheldon Leonard; Photographed by: Jack Greenhalgh; Art Director: Edward C. Jewell; Assistant Director: Lew Perlof; Editors: Roy Livingston and Carl Pierson; Settings: Glenn P. Thompson; Wardrobe: Mona Barry; Music: Karl Hajos; Sound: Max Hutchinson; Makeup: Bud Westmore; Production Manager: Raoul Pagel; Running Time: 64 Minutes; Released: November 5, 1945

CAST: Richard Fraser (Howard Norton); Grace Gillern (Joan Rutledge); Cy Kendall (Victor Maxwell); Emmett Lynn (Elmer); Kenneth MacDonald (McKenzie); Eddie Acuff (Walters); Sam Flint (Sheriff).

THE TIGER WOMAN
(Republic Pictures Corp.)

The film noir purists tend to snub the general such output of Republic, preferring to narrow their definitions of the idiom to such bigger recognized classics as *Double Indemnity* and *Murder, My Sweet*, and to such littler, more desperately nihilistic examples as *Detour* and *He Walked by Night*. Just as the music-lovers' community has its Blues Nazis—who hold as fast as Flat Earthers to such limiting denials as "White folks can't sing the blues" and "Blues can't have more than three chords"—so there are the Noir Nazis who refuse to accept the self-evident truth that this rip-snorting high-adventure studio contributed any respectable share to the emergence of film noir.

Not to suggest that *The Tiger Woman* is any sort of finery—it's a fair-to-middling muddle, derivative and overobvious—but all the same the picture boasts an erotically lethal performance from Adele Mara, disgraceful intrigues aplenty and a private-eye portrayal that moved *Variety* to proclaim Kane Richmond "another Alan Ladd."

CITY THEATRE
Today & Wednesday
Adele Mara
Kane Richmond
- In -
"TIGER WOMAN"
— ALSO —
Charles Starrett
Tex Harding
- In -
'Blazing the Western Trail'

Sharon Winslow (Miss Mara) is a cabaret singer, married to a nightclub's co-owner. Expressing concern that her husband is marked for death due to his gambling debts, Mrs. Winslow hires detective Jerry Devery (Richmond) to prevent a murder. She also admits to her affair with her husband's business partner, Stephen Mason (Richard Fraser), who is certain to be suspected if her fears should be realized.

Devery asks racketeer Joe Sapphire (Gregory Gay) to cancel a supposed contract on Fred Winslow. Sapphire says there is no such contract—that Winslow had paid him in full. Mrs. Winslow and Mason soon find the corpse of her husband, along with a suicide note that Mason destroys, lest it stymie an insurance settlement. Sapphire finds himself accused and, in turn, accuses Devery of a set-up. The purported suicide proves to have been murder, after all, and Mrs. Winslow is rather prematurely revealed to the audience as the killer. Devery's persistent sleuthing begins to prey on Mason, who finds himself defenestrated by Mrs. Winslow, lest he crack under pressure. The police are content to believe that Mason killed Winslow, then offed himself in remorse, but Devery pursues the case to the extent of pretending to romance Mrs. Winslow. Sensing entrapment, she draws a gun on Devery, only to be nabbed by the police, whom Devery had invited along just in case.

The title is rather misleading on a couple of counts: It is merely figurative, deriving from the name of the nightspot where Adele Mara holds forth. Miss Mara, incidentally, trades strikingly here upon her background as a singer and dancer with Xavier Cugat's orchestra. *The Tiger Woman* also is the name of an unrelated and much better-known Republic serial, from just the year previous. Nor is there any kinship, beyond studio pedigree, to *The Tiger Man*, which is the proxy title for *The Lady and the Monster*.

CREDITS: Executive Producer: William J. O'Sullivan; Associate Producers: Dorrell McGowan and Stuart McGowan; Director: Philip Ford; Screenplay: George Carleton Brown; Based upon: John A. Dunkel's Radio Play; Photographed by: Ernest Miller; Assistant Director: Leonard Kunody; Second Camera: Wallace Chewning; Special Effects: Howard Lydecker and Theodore Lydecker; Transparency Projection Shots: Gordon C. Schaefer; Art Director: Frank Hotaling; Editor: Fred Allen; Décor: Otto Seigel; Costumer: Adele Palmer; Music: Richard Cherwin; Song: "Who Am I?" by Jule Styne & Walter Bullock; Sound: Victor Appel; Re-Recording and Effects Mixers: Thomas A. Carman and Howard Wilson; Music Mixer: John Stransky, Jr.; Makeup: Bob Mark; Running Time: 58 Minutes; Released: November 16, 1945

CAST: Adele Mara (Sharon Winslow); Kane Richmond (Jerry Devery); Richard Fraser (Stephen Mason); Peggy Stewart (Phyllis Carrington); Cy Kendall (Inspector Henry Leggett); Gregory Gay (Joe Sapphire); John Kelly (Sylvester); Beverly Loyd (Constance Grey); Addison Richards (White); Donia Bussey (Rosie Gargan); Frank Reicher (Coroner); Garry Owen (Bartender); Jack O'Shea (Louie); Geraldine Farnum (Hat-Check Clerk); Maj. George C. McBride (Dealer); and Robert Strong

AN ANGEL COMES TO BROOKLYN
(Republic Pictures Corp.)

Considered here more for the record than for any sense of foreboding, Leslie Goodwins' *An Angel Comes to Brooklyn* is but a lightweight musical amusement that does indeed pivot on an element of supernatural fantasy.

The scene is Actors' Heaven, where *The Undersea Kingdom*'s C. Montague Shaw holds forth as the boss angel, Sir Henry Bushnell. Surveying the Earth, Sir Henry finds Karen James (Kaye Dowd) struggling to become a working actress. Sir Henry dispatches an inept angel named Phineas (Charles Kemper), who in life had been a stage magician, to help Karen. Convincing a reluctant producer (Wilton Graff) to audition Karen, Phineas inadvertently impresses the impresario with his magic tricks and finds himself courted as a featured attraction.

The picture dwells more rewardingly on Charles Kemper's misadventures than on the travails of Kaye Dowd and her youthful entourage of hopefuls. This focus curiously anticipates Valentine Davies' famous original-for-the-screen Christmas story, *Miracle on 34th Street* (filmed during 1946-47, but not published until 1967) with a subplot that finds Kemper's Phineas arrested on suspicion of theft—he has conjured up a huge sum of money-from-nowhere—and pronounced insane because of his insistence that he was born way back in 1832.

Much of the running time is given over to a soapy romantic situation between Miss Dowd and Robert Duke, as a struggling artist. Their playful wrestling match in a bedroom setting packs an erotic sub-charge that must have gone zooming over the heads of the more commonly vigilant Legion of Decency and Production Code Administration.

Lightweight show tunes abound. Several dwarf players grace the backup cast. All turns out unnaturally well, needless to say. The film ends on a peculiar gag where an escape artist (played by the bird-faced comedian Jimmy Conlin), whom Phineas had buried alive months before in a publicity stunt, is dug up alive and well—and fighting mad. Anything can happen in the movies.

CREDITS: Executive Producer: Armand Schaefer; Associate Producer: Leonard Sillman; Director: Leslie Goodwins; Screenplay: Stanley Paley and June Carroll, from Her Collaborative Story with Lee Wainer; Photographed by: Jack Marta; Assistant Director: Al Wood; Second Camera: Alfred Keller; Special Effects: Howard Lydecker and Theodore Lydecker; Matte Paintings: Lewis Physioc; Transparencies: Gordon C. Schaefer; Art Directors: Russell Kimball and Gano Chittenden; Editor: Tony Martinelli; Set Dresser: Otto Siegel; Costumer: Adele Palmer; Costume Designer: Travilla; Music: Morton Scott; Orchestral Arranger: Dale Butts; Choreography: Elsa Findlay; Songs: "Big Wide Wonderful World," by John Rox, "Gyp on the Nile," by Lawrence Harris & Buddy Harris, "You Better Go Now," by Bickley Reichner & Irvin Graham, "Love, Are You Raising Your Head Again?" by Lee Wainer & June Carroll, and Other Songs by Sanford Green & June Carroll; Makeup: Bob Mark; Running Time: 70 Minutes; Released: November 27, 1945

CAST: Kaye Dowd (Karen James); Robert Duke (David Randall); David Street (Paul Blake); Barbara Perry (Barbara); Charles Kemper (Phineas Aloyisus Higby); Marguerite D'Alvarez (Mme. Della); Bob Scheerer (Bob); Alice Tyrrell (Susie); June Carroll (Kay); Rodney Bell (Oscar); Betzi Beaton (Tiny); Jay Presson (Miss Johnson); Joe Cappo (Joe); Sherle North (Rosie); Billie Haywood (Theresa); Cliff Allen (Cliff); C. Montague Shaw (Sir Henry Bushnell); Eula Morgan (Olga Ashley); Gladys Gale (Sarah Gibbons); Harry Rose (Michael O'Day); Frank Scannell (Brian Hepplestone); Jack McClendon and Brant Hodges (Dancers); Wilton Graff (Rodney Lloyd); Jimmy Conlin (Cornelius Terwilliger); Ralph Dunn (Sgt. O'Rourke); Jack Daley (Cyrano); Beverly Loyd (Miss Dean); Sheila Stuart (Miss Haines); Monya André (Lady Teesdale); Frank Pharr (King Lear); Gertrude Astor (Eva Tanguay); Sandra Morgan (Theda Bara); Larry Steers (Matinee Idol); Jerry Maren (Dwarf Baby); Billy Curtis, John Bambury, Harry Monty and John Leal (Dwarf Musicians); A.B. Lane (Frankenstein); Ethel & Edward Shattuck (Jugglers); Madeline Grey (Matron)

DETOUR
(Producers Releasing Corp./Pathé Industries, Inc.)

The term *detour* in postwar America took on a dire cultural resonance of caution and, just as often, regret: It was the road not taken, the bridge toppled and burned, that would have led to that safe-and-sound brighter tomorrow. Call it Pop Existentialism, a despairing malaise felt on a grand social scale—if not articulated in so many words—amid what should have been a victorious long-term emergence from the globe-smothering shadow of Hitlerism. A crossover-hit honky-tonk tune of the  day, Paul Westmoreland's "Detour," offered a melodic primal scream from a born loser's vantage about the "muddy road ahead" that could have been avoided if only one had read the signs.

"Detour," the song, and *Detour*, the movie, have superficially only the title in common—and the music so crucial to the film is not the least bit countrified, but rather a raucously morose jazz leitmotif—but they are soulfully of a piece. The film's dominant song is the well-known "I Can't Believe That You're in Love with Me," a transitional piece in the decade's evolution from big-band swing to the nerve-jangling bop style. It is first heard issuing from the jukebox in a short-order eatery, where the melody so unnerves customer Al Roberts (Tom Neal) that he is forced into a nightmarish flashback:

Al, a New York club pianist, was keen on marrying singer Sue Harvey (*Face of Marble*'s Claudia Drake). Their favorite song was "I Can't Believe That You're in Love with Me." But Sue insisted upon pursuing a dream of stardom in Hollywood. Al impulsively telephoned her from New York—in those days when a long-distance call could land a guy in hock—and learned she had gotten only as far as a table-waiting job. So he set out on an impulse to join her in L.A. Al accepted a ride in Arizona from garrulous Charles Haskell (Edmund MacDonald), who explained a set of lacerations on his hand as the work of a woman to whom he had previously given a lift.

Haskell died of apparently natural causes while en route. Al, fearing arrest, dumped the body and drove onward with Haskell's wallet. Finally reaching California, Al offered a ride to Vera (Ann Savage), a hitchhiker—who accusingly demanded to know what he had done with Haskell. Vera, the rider who had scratched Haskell's hand, bullied Al into a scam to impersonate Haskell and claim an inheritance. After a drinking bout, Vera fell asleep in a locked bedroom, where she had taken the telephone out of Al's reach. Al, tugging at the phone from beyond the door, accidentally strangled Vera with the wrapped cord. Sneaking out of the city, Al had only his eventual capture to look forward to, a

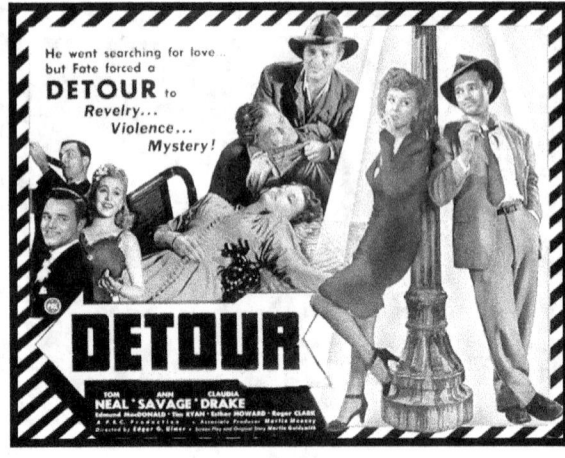

consequence of bad timing, circumstantial evidence and a chronic inability to defy temptation and/or manipulation.

Al muses at the fade-out: "Fate or some mysterious force can put the finger on you or me for no good reason at all." Blake Lucas, one of the more cogent interpreters of film noir, has noted that "such an understanding precludes the self-awareness that could reveal to him that his own [nature] has determined the twists of the road."

Tom Neal had become a B-movie regular by now, a busy but ill-distinguished tough-guy specialist whose fortunes were not changed appreciably by his splendid show of torment in *Detour*. He proceeded along this track into the early 1950s, when a brawl with fellow actor Franchot Tone over the attentions of actress Barbara Payton landed both men in the hospital and stymied Neal's career. Then in 1965, Neal found himself charged with the murder of his wife, Gail Evatt, but was convicted on a lesser count and spent six years in prison. He died in 1972, less than a year after his release.

Its Poverty Row origins, as Lucas points out, leave *Detour* unfettered by any "need to affirm conventional values," free to wallow in doomy nihilism. Which it does, to a coincidence-driven extent that would be absurd in the hands of any director more bound by bourgeois convention than Edgar G. Ulmer. That sense of ruination is passively well served in Neal's character, but it emerges more as an aggressive force of nature in B-pictures standby Ann Savage, as the malicious, unhealthy and shallowly conniving Vera. Even her fleeting attempts at cordiality feel tainted. It becomes patent that, although Al is trapped within Vera's web of bullying deceit, he'd as likely find himself attracted by her vile magnetism even if she didn't have the goods on him. Miss Savage's Vera is as monstrous a presence as the screen has known—but it is the viewer's deep identification with Neal's Al that renders the film an exercise in terror.

Detour suffered a prominent dismissal in its day, from the powerful trade-paper *Variety*, as being compromised by "a flat ending and its low-budgeted production mountings." The assigned critic was, in effect, championing the very conventionality that would have softened the story. But those same qualities have helped to earn the film a lasting regard as an essential example of film noir: That quote/unquote "flat ending" is readily understood as Al Roberts' own Sartre-like No-Exit sign, and the palpable cheapness—with a budget of around $30,000 and a shooting schedule of less than a week—becomes an asset to mood and attitude.

An ill-advised remake, bringing nothing to the table but the gimmicky casting of Tom Neal, Jr., was delivered in 1992 by Wade Williams

CREDITS: Producer: Leon Fromkess; Associate Producer: Martin Mooney; Director: Edgar G. Ulmer; Dialogue Director: Ben Coleman; Screenplay: Martin Goldsmith, from His 1939 Novel *Detour: An Extraordinary Tale*; Photography: Benjamin Kline; Assistant Director: William A. Calihan; Art Director: Edward C. Jewell; Editor: George McGuire; Décor: Glenn P. Thompson; Wardrobe: Mona Barry; Music: Leo Erdody; Song: "I Can't Believe That You're in Love with Me," by Jimmy McHugh & Clarence Gaskill; Makeup: Bud Westmore; Production Manager: Raoul Pagel; Running Time: 69 Minutes; Released: November 30, 1945

CAST: Tom Neal (Al Roberts); Ann Savage (Vera); Claudia Drake (Sue Harvey); Edmund MacDonald (Charles Haskell); Tim Ryan (Gus); Esther Howard (Hedy); and Pat Gleason, Roger Clark

THE ENCHANTED FOREST
(Jack Schwarz Productions/Producers Releasing Corp.)

"*The Enchanted Forest* is PRC's prestige picture," raved *Variety* following a preview screening, "undoubtedly the top production effort of this company. It's a colorful fantasy, in the Disney manner... a natural for the youngsters and should hold considerable charm for grown-ups."

The film is an ahead-of-its-time fable about conservation and nonviolence, centering upon a hermit, Old John (Harry Davenport), who purports to commune with nature and warns a party of loggers to lay off his redwood forest. The foreman, Gilson (Clancy Cooper), dismisses Old John as a crank, but suddenly a fresh-cut tree changes course in mid-fall and injures Gilson. Old John insists that a storm is due—this, according to a woodland frog—and sure enough, a downpour strikes, sweeping a baby away from its young-widow mother, Anne (Brenda Joyce), and washing him downriver. Old John rescues the tyke and takes him to safety, assuming an abandonment. Lumberman Ed Henderson (John Litel), the child's grandfather, abandons the search and closes the logging camp.

Three years later, Old John and the child, now called Jackie (Billy Severn), are enjoying a peaceable co-existence with the creatures of the wild. Dr. Steven Blaine (Edmund Lowe), a psychologist who lives in the nearby village, learns from Gilson that Henderson plans to sell the land to a timber company.

Dr. Blaine visits Henderson in San Francisco, hoping to persuade him to build a clinic instead, and learns that Anne has not yet come to terms with her loss. Blaine convinces Henderson to bring Anne back to the forest, certain that the setting will help her find serenity. Meanwhile, Gilson kills a woodland animal. Jackie swears vengeance, but Old John counsels the boy to let nature take its course.

While strolling through the woods with Blaine, Anne speaks of a recurring dream about a vain search for her son. Suddenly, she sees Jackie gazing at her from behind a waterfall. Jackie departs before Anne can point him out to Blaine, and the doctor concludes that she imagined the sighting. Other such near-miss encounters follow, and Henderson places enough stock in Anne's story that he posts a reward for the boy's discovery. Alerted to the search by the birds of the forest, Old John hides in a cave with his dog, Bruno, and Jackie. Gilson, prowling about, knocks Old John unconscious. Gilson is attacked by Bruno but opens fire on the dog and runs away. Taken to safety by friendlier loggers, Old John is counseled by the voices of the forest to help the searchers. Gilson, eager to claim the reward, nearly captures Jackie—who makes his way to Anne. The reunion finds Old John awarded a haven by a grateful Henderson, who also agrees to Dr. Blaine's idea about the clinic. Blaine and Anne have, of course, fallen in love.

The Enchanted Forest is indeed a wondrous film, a sweeping fantasy with just enough meanness, in the person of bad logger Clancy Cooper, to make a case for Harry Davenport's insistence upon standing one's peaceable ground in the face of cruelty. More significantly, the picture exults in robust adventure and a dreamlike texture. Moppet Billy Severn plays the rescued youngster with nary a trace of forcible cuteness. There is a mournfully weird quality of suspense in the sightings of the child by his distraught mother, and their reunion achieves poignance without trying too hard.

More amazing yet is the wealth of trained-animal activity, centering upon the heroic dog, a stealthy crow, a mountain lion, and a squirrel. The crow, a finely trained creature named Jim, figures in a dodgy extended passage involving the whereabouts of a piece of jewelry that had gone missing with the baby. Davenport's sense of oneness with the wildlife is thoroughly convincing, and camera chief Marcel Le Picard's examination of the lush environment captures an eerie serenity as Davenport retreats ever deeper into the forest before the onslaught of the logging company.

Le Picard's long involvement with the Poverty Row studios usually kept him working in black-and-white for budgetary reasons, but here he wields the Eastman Bi-Pack color palette with a painterly authority. PRC had launched *The Enchanted Forest* early in the spring of 1944, but pre-production dragged on for months as the studio puzzled over how to mount a color shoot with the greatest economy. It was decided to use 16-millimeter Eastman stock, then to blow up to theatrical 35mm in the Cinecolor process. Surviving prints vary in color quality, depending upon the care taken in preservation, but the better-maintained copies show a tonal delicacy that is lacking in most other Cinecolor features.

Edmund Lowe makes the village medico far more than a well-meaning interloper, revealing at one crucial point that he had suffered a breakdown but found himself healed by a sojourn in this endangered glade. Brenda Joyce, as the tormented mother, conveys a chin-up emotional strength that never lapses into the overacting one might expect. Her role originally had been assigned to the more genuinely tormented Frances Farmer, who hoped to make *Forest* her comeback following a three-year absence from the screen. No such luck—and Miss Farmer remained sidelined for the longer haul—but Miss Joyce is equally right.

The Enchanted Forest went over so well that producer Jack Schwarz developed a very similar, though more overtly sentimental, picture, *The Enchanted Valley*, three years later.

CREDITS: Executive Producer: Leon Fromkess; Producer: Jack Schwarz; Associate Producer: Lou Brock; Director: Lew Landers (Louis Friedlander); Screenplay: Robert Lee Johnson, John Lebar (from His Story) and Lou Brock; Adaptation: Sam Neuman and Lou Brock; Photographed by: Marcel Le Picard; Assistant Directors: Frank Fox, Lou Perloff and Arthur Hamburger; Color Supervisor: W.T. Crespinel; Art Director: Frank Sylos; Editor: Roy Livingston; Set Dresser: Harry Reif; Music: Albert Hay Malone; Sound: Max Hutchinson; Production Manager: Arthur Hammond; Animal Trainers: Curley Twiford and Earl Johnson; Running Time: 82 Minutes; Released: December 8, 1945

CAST: Edmund Lowe (Dr. Steven Blaine); Brenda Joyce (Anne); Billy Severn (Jackie); Harry Davenport (Old John); John Litel (Ed Henderson); Clancy Cooper (Gilson); Jim the Crow (Blackie)

THE WOMAN WHO CAME BACK
(Republic Pictures Corp.)

> Upon this mound in the Year of Our Lord Seventeen Hundred Forty-Five, the woman Jezebel Trister was burned to death for practicing sorcery and witchcraft. By order of Elder Elijah Webster, Judge of the Village of Eben.—Inscription upon an Ominous Monument in *The Woman Who Came Back*

"It's pure Hitchcock!" is a bit of archaic movie-hype lingo calculated to sell a suspense-laden picture from anyone *but* Alfred Hitchcock. By a kindred token, Walter Colmes' *The Woman Who Came Back* might be described as "pure Lewton." It might even be the best Val Lewton picture that Val Lewton *never* made, although Lewton doubtless would have demanded an ending more gracefully poetic than the overexplained mundane finale that mars *The Woman Who Came Back*.

Producer Lewton's understated and ominously lifelike approach to terror at RKO-Radio Pictures had emerged during the early 1940s as a moneymaking alternative to the more extravagantly lurid literalism of Universal Pictures' horror-movie franchises. In such poetic, Ecclesiastically *fated* works as *Cat People*, *The Leopard Man* and *I Walked with a Zombie*, the budget-bound Lewton unit had consistently implored the audience to work with these films to generate the ticket-selling thrills, freeing the viewers' imaginations to create illusions more unnerving than anything the camera could capture. That the Lewton style is inimitable is self-evident in a comparative lack of imitators.

Those few who tried, tried hard and memorably. Will Jason's *The Soul of a Monster*, a Columbia entry from 1944 (see the Price & Turner book *Human Monsters*), nails the philosophical pretensions of Lewton well enough and captures the right mood, but it proves lacking in the crucial narrative subtleties and finally retreats to an only-a-dream resolution. *The Woman Who Came Back* succeeds more strikingly on the psychological front, persuading the viewer to consider witchcraft as a fact of everyday existence as efficiently as it convinces its tormented heroine, played by Nancy Kelly, that she has been possessed by the spirit of a sorceress.

Lorna Webster (Miss Kelly) is returning by bus to her ancestral home near Eben Rock, Massachusetts, when a peculiar old woman (Elspeth Dudgeon), accompanied by an unfriendly dog, hails the vehicle and offers to pay her fare in pre-Revolutionary legal tender. The hitchhiker introduces herself as Jezebel Trister and claims to have known an ancestor of Lorna's, Judge Elijah Webster, 300 years previous.

The bus veers out of control and plunges into a river. Hours later, Lorna stumbles into a tavern owned by Ruth Gibson (Ruth Ford) and tells Dr. Matt

John Loder comforts Nancy Kelly during a lull between the torments in *The Woman Who Came Back*. The image is restored from a severely damaged lobby display from the George E. Turner collection.

Adams (John Loder)—Ruth's brother and Lorna's former sweetheart—enough to prompt a rescue mission. The old woman is nowhere to be found among the victims. Matt and Jim Stevens (Otto Kruger), a preacher and local historian, spot a menacing dog; Stevens has noticed that the bus driver's throat had been torn, as if by some animal.

Next day, Matt makes it plain he still loves Lorna. He hands her a black veil that she had carried when she entered the tavern. Lorna recognizes the veil as that worn by the old woman. A servant (Almira Sessions) recalls legends about women burned as witches under orders from Judge Webster. Lorna fancies herself transformed into the old woman when she gazes into a mirror. She receives a bouquet from Jim, but the flowers abruptly wither.

Wakened that night by a howling from the nearby cemetery, Lorna visits a crypt, where she finds a document, dated 1644, that suggests a pact between Jezebel Trister and Satan. Lorna becomes increasingly antisocial, and Ruth's daughter, Peggy (Jeanne Gail) falls mysteriously ill. The townspeople, including Ruth, peg Lorna as a returned witch—and Lorna cannot help but agree.

Meanwhile, Matt and Stevens find an account left by Judge Webster, explaining how he had forced Jezebel Trister to sign a false confession. Before the men can reach Lorna, the locals have taken vigilante action, pursuing her into a fall—if not a suicidal plunge—into the river. Matt rescues Lorna. The dog

The accusation was... WITCHCRAFT!

leads Stevens to where it has (apparently) dragged the flyblown corpse of the old woman, alongside a monument to the burning of Jezebel Trister. As Lorna and Peggy recover, we learn that the crone, who fancied herself a witch returned from Colonial times, escaped from an asylum.

The brooding, low-key unease of this little gem owes as much to the theatre-of-the-mind radio-drama background of producer-director Colmes as it does to the influence of Val Lewton. Colmes was no "one-shot director," as one authoritative genre reference declares he "appears to have been," and indeed he had a hand in more than 10 pictures during 1943-49. *The Woman Who Came Back* is a high point of this concentrated involvement in cinema, trading so cannily on the suggestion of hellborne possession that its more overtly hair-raising moments—most of them involving the dog, at large in a graveyard—pack a wallop beyond commonplace shock value. Miss Kelly is fine as the beleaguered prodigal whose hopeful homecoming becomes almost fatally sidetracked.

John Loder and Otto Kruger make robust and determined co-leading men, and the venerable Elspeth Dudgeon—a busy all-'round character player, best known to the weird-movie crowd for Universal's *The Old Dark House* and Warners' mind-boggling *Sh! The Octopus*—offers a brief appearance that casts a pall of morbidity over the entire picture.

CREDITS: Associate Producer and Director: Walter Colmes; Screenplay: Dennis Cooper and Lee Willis; Suggested by: Phillip Yordan; Story: John Kafka; Photographed by: Henry Sharp; Second Camera: Carl Wester; Assistant Director: Barton Adams; Miniature Effects: Ray Mercer; Projection Process Photography: Mario Castegnaro; Art Director: Frank Dexter; Editor: John F. Link; Décor: Jacque Mapes; Musical Director: Walter Scharf; Musical Score: Edward Plumb; Sound: Percy Townsend; Production Manager: Bartlett A. Carré; Running Time: 68 Minutes; Released: Dec. 13, 1945

CAST: John Loder (Dr. Matt Adams); Nancy Kelly (Lorna Webster); Otto Kruger (the Rev. Jim Stevens); Ruth Ford (Ruth Gibson); Harry Tyler (Noah); Jeanne Gail (Peggy Gibson); Almira Sessions (Bessie); J. Farrell MacDonald [Mis-Billed as Farrel] (Sheriff); Emmett Vogan (Dr. Peters)

THE STRANGE MR. GREGORY
(Monogram Pictures Corp.)

"An utterly fantastic murder mystery about a murder that was never committed," allowed *Variety*, whose assigned critic nonetheless found plenty to like about *The Strange Mr. Gregory*. The picture is one of the choicer oddities from director Phil Rosen, whose long stay on Poverty Row had already yielded such gems as *The Sphinx*, *Devil's Mate* and its remake *I Killed That Man*, and *Murder by Invitation*.

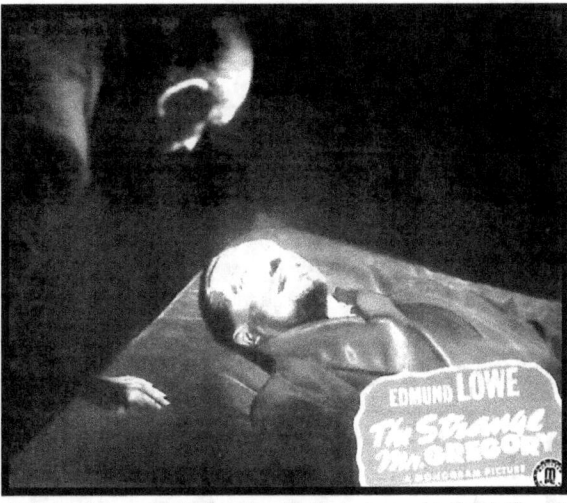

Edmund Lowe invokes the death-trance. At right: Frank Reicher

Suave Edmund Lowe has the title role, a stage magician and hypnotist who has perfected a trance that gives the impression of lifelessness. Gregory is hard-put to come up with the ideal use for his gimmick until he meets an eager amateur magician, John Randall (Donald Douglas), and develops an obsessive infatuation with Randall's wife, Ellen (Jean Rogers).

Convinced that there is more to his magic than mere illusion, Gregory contrives to obtain a drop of Ellen's blood and uses it to craft a Voodoo effigy. Ellen begins to sense that Gregory is working a sinister influence over her. Allowing himself to be caught in the act of embracing Ellen, Gregory stokes John's jealousy into a confrontational rage. Finally, Gregory uses the death trance to falsify his murder, leaving evidence that will incriminate John.

Once the coast is clear, Gregory's butler, Riker (Frank Reicher), releases Gregory from his crypt. Gregory wills Riker to write a letter that will further implicate John—and then kills the servant. John is arrested, but Gregory returns in the person of a fictitious brother, who testifies on John's behalf. Though the purported brother makes it plain to the court that Gregory "was" a madman, John is convicted.

His brotherly masquerade has endeared Gregory to Ellen, but she develops suspicions that force him to resume the trance and reoccupy his slab. Later, the vault is found empty. Gregory now intends to kill Ellen, but he is granted a genuine death by police officers dispatched by her worried friends. John is released from prison.

Lowe—the movies' original Chandu the Magician—makes a marvelously shameless, lust-driven misanthrope, whose vain megalomania proves his undoing. Jean Rogers, a beauty-pageant winner from Massachusetts who is forever to be remembered as Buster Crabbe's *Flash Gordon* leading lady, plays the object

of Lowe's affections and afflictions with a savvy combination of vulnerability and outraged determination. Donald Douglas is just right as the jealous husband who paints himself into a bad corner with a perfectly appropriate response to Lowe's shenanigans. *King Kong*'s Frank Reicher makes much of a pivotal small role as a paid accomplice whose loyalty is rewarded with a brutal demise. Jack Norton contributes his stock-in-trade impersonation of an observant lush.

CREDITS: Producer: Louis Berkoff; Associate Producer: Edward Kovacs; Director: Phil Rosen; Screenplay: Charles S. Belden; Story: Myles Connolly; Photographed by: Ira Morgan; Assistant Director: Seymour Roth; Editor: Seth Larsen; Set Dressers: Charles Thompson and Vin Taylor; Stylist: Lorraine McLean; Musical Director: Edward J. Kay; Sound: Tom Lambert; Production Manager: Glenn Cook; Technical Director: Ormind McGill; Running Time: 63 Minutes; Released: Dec. 13, 1945 (Some Sources Cite a January 1946 Release)

CAST: Edmund Lowe (Mr. Gregory); Jean Rogers (Ellen Randall); Donald Douglas (John Randall); Marjorie Hoshelle (Sheila Edwards); Jonathan Hale (Blair); Frank Reicher (Riker); Robert Emmett Keane (District Attorney); Frank Mayo (Inspector Hoskins); Fred A. Kelsey (Detective Lefert); Anita Turner (Maid); Jack Norton (Drunkard); Guy Pharis (Man at Graveyard); Brooks Benedict (Milkman); Felice Richmond (Society Matron); James Farley (Caretaker); Tom Leffingwell (Judge)

HOW DOOOO YOU DO!!!
(Producers Releasing Corp.)

Nobody, but *nobody*, could intone that clichéd greeting "How do you do?" with the style or the passion of Bert Gordon. In his radio-program guise of a character known as the Mad Russian, as a regular on Eddie Cantor's broadcasts from 1930 on through the '40s, Gordon transformed the offhanded question into the most emphatic of exclamations, worrying the first "do" into a sustained marvel of escalating double-O's that would move a studio audience to applause before he could complete the phrase. This indelible signature line was the most logical of titles for a Gordon-starring picture—and in fact the less imaginatively transcribed *How Do You Do?* had been the work-in-progress title of a 1942 Columbia comedy released as *Laugh Your Blues Away*, with Gordon and Jinx Falkenburg.

What a laff-riot of such origins is doing in a book of *Forgotten Horrors*' nature is a question that the film itself will answer in its own sweet time: *How Doooo You Do!!!* finds Gordon and fellow radio personality Harry von Zell—playing themselves, in broad strokes—in quest of some well-earned peace and quiet at a desert resort lodge. Two other members of their troupe, Cheryl Walker and Claire Windsor, arrive on a similar search for serenity. Each party is unaware of the other's presence until von Zell spots the women and panics: Von Zell's wife suspects that he and Miss Walker are romantically involved. Meanwhile, Gordon's over-amorous co-star, Ella Mae Morse, has tracked Gordon to the retreat.

That night, Miss Morse overhears a fracas in one of the suites. Next morning, the troupers find themselves held captive at the hotel, on orders from a grouchy sheriff (Charles Middleton) who is investigating the murder of another show-biz personage, a popularly well-despised agent named Thornton. The corpse goes missing, only to be rediscovered, lost again, found again and so forth. Miss Walker is accused in the killing, and von Zell supplies her with an alibi that can only mean trouble if-and-when his wife learns of it. Gordon has meanwhile sent telegrams summoning several actor chums, each of whom has impersonated crimebusters in moving pictures; they serve only to confuse the issue. Finally, the sheriff pegs the hotel manager (Francis Perliot)—who by the oddest irrelevant coincidence turns out to be Miss Windsor's father—as the killer, even as Miss Windsor comes forth with a confession.

The deliberately dingbat story peaks—or does it?—when the victim turns up, alive and well, accompanied by a phy-

> Aside from John Wooley: Damn! If there's a more perfect picture, I haven't found it. This thing is absolutely great, right down the wacky ending. Makes me wonder if Jerry Lewis didn't see *How Doooo You Do!!!* during his formative years—he sure seems to have copped a stroke or two from this picture, including the rubber-reality ending that serves to let us know that the characters know it's only a movie.
>
> But honestly, this is a great picture. It's all so weird, everything from the long conversation… at the beginning, to the introduction of the stars—and the insistence on explaining how they're "featured players"—to the old familiar faces who get called in to try and figure out whodunnit. I mean, obviously they were going for an audience familiar with the Mad Russian from radio, which was a potentially massive audience, and they felt they had to explain how things work in the radio business and in Hollywood. What a weird insider's picture; it's almost like you get to step into the minds of the Poverty Row studio heads as they struggle to try and figure out how to compete with the majors. Amazing.
>
> And while we're at it: PRC put another Eddie Cantor cast member in a '40s movie. Harry Einstein, better known as the Greek-dialect comic Parkyakarkus, co-starred with Walter Woolf King and H.B. Warner in 1942's *A Yank in Libya*—as an Arab merchant who secretly befriends the Americans. Einstein is the father of Albert Brooks, making Brooks' real name… yep.

sician (Sidney Marion) who attributes the seeming demise to an experimental drug. The doctor had been moving the comatose patient from place to place to keep the treatment a secret.

Here, the picture ends — or does it? — and the camera draws back to reveal that the entire misadventure has been a movie, being viewed by Gordon, von Zell and their producers. One of the studio executives declares that the film must never be released, arguing that the presumed victim should have proved genuinely dead. Gordon orders that the closing moments of the picture be re-screened. When the image of the revived Thornton reappears, Gordon leaps from his seat and guns down the on-screen character, thus rendering the film fit for distribution. Or not. Gordon's self-satisfied closing line is a gem of surreal nonsense.

Strange is too mild a descriptive term for *How Doooo You Do!!!* — even though the picture's engagingly bizarre awareness-of-self is hardly an innovation. Ole Olsen and Chic Johnson had long since covered similar film-within-a-film turf in *Hellzapoppin'* (1941), a drastically cinematic reworking of their like-titled Broadway revue, and even *How Doooo*'s aggressively romantic portrayal by the rural-bred Texan comedienne-singer Ella Mae Morse is patently derived from a role played by Martha Raye in *Hellzapoppin'*. But *How Doooo You Do!!!* allows vastly more time to elapse before it reveals itself as a movie that (according to the crackpot logic of the script) hasn't even been released yet. At 81 minutes in length, with nary a lapse into the doldrums, the picture is a good third of an hour longer than the typical PRC entry; a lengthy out-of-character prologue serves to acquaint the viewer with the radio milieu.

How Doooo You Do!!! proved an obscure marker for the end of Claire Windsor's movie career: The still-luminous silent-era star had lapsed to occasional appearances during the 1930s, and this assignment was her first time back on screen since *Barefoot Boy* (Monogram; 1938). Ella Mae Morse, who has a handful of knockout musical segments here, was bound for bigger and better things as a comically inclined jazz-pop singer—almost an ofay Ella Fitzgerald, though without the pretensions to diva-ism—at Johnny Mercer's Capitol Records. Charles Middleton was typecast for life as the intimidating authority figure, but he wears the stigma grandly. *Variety* noted that *How Doooo* "isn't [Bert] Gordon's first [*far from it*] but gives him one of his better efforts." This "better effort" proved to be the Mad Russian's last turn as a movie player.

Incidentally, *Variety*'s five-months-late review gave the title as *How Do You Do*—with neither the extravagant misspelling nor any over-assertive punctuation.

CREDITS: Producer: Harry Sauber; Director: Ralph Murphy; Screenplay: Harry Sauber (from His Story) and Joseph Carole; Photographed by: Benjamin H. Kline; Assistant Director: William H. Calihan, Jr.; Projection Process Photography: Ray Smallwood; Art Director: Edward C. Jewell; Editor: Thomas Neff; Décor: George Montgomery; Wardrobe: Mona Barry; Musical Director: Howard Jackson; Songs: "Boogie-Woogie Cindy," by Hal Borne, the Traditional "Drink to Me Only with Thine Eyes," Lyrics by Ben Jonson, and "I've Got a Twelve-Hour Pass," by Hal Borne & Paul Webster; Music-and-Effects Mixers: Joseph I. Kane and William H. Wilmarth; Makeup: Bud Westmore; Production Manager: Raoul Pagel; Running Time: 81 Minutes; Released: Dec. 24, 1945

CAST: Bert Gordon, the Mad Russian (Himself); Harry von Zell (Himself); Cheryl Walker (Herself); Frank Albertson (Tom Brandon); Ella Mae Morse (Herself); Claire Windsor (Herself); Keye Luke (Himself); Charles Middleton (Sheriff Hayworth); Thomas Jackson (Himself); James Burke (Himself); Fred Kelsey (Himself); Matt McHugh (Deputy McNeil); Leslie Denison (Himself); Francis Perliot (Manager); Sidney Marion (Dr. Kolmar)

1946

DIRTY GERTIE FROM HARLEM, U.S.A.
(Sack Amusement Enterprises)

W. Somerset Maugham's *Rain*, a sobering confrontation between the sacred and the profane, is patently the inspiration for *Dirty Gertie from Harlem, U.S.A.*, a gloomy pastiche capping the directing career of Spencer Williams, Jr. The film is scarcely a patch on Lewis Milestone's 1932 version of *Rain*, which boasts the volatile chemistry of Joan Crawford, as the free-spirited dancer Sadie Thompson, and Walter Huston, as an amen-corner hardshell missionary who cracks under the strain of sanctimony and lust. *Dirty Gertie from Harlem, U.S.A.* stops short of any spiritual showdown: This appropriation-of-plot reduces the preacher to merely an antagonistic plot device and leaves the grim resolution to an ordinary crime of pent-up passion.

American striptease artist Gertie LaRue (Francine Everette) receives a grand welcome in Trinidad, but her troupe is none too happy to have come. They all could have stayed in Harlem—a nicer place, in those days—if only Gertie had not provoked her lover, Al (John King), to a state of murderous jealousy. An evangelist, Jonathan Christian (Alfred Hawkins), schemes to have Gertie deported.

It appears that Al has followed Gertie. A derelict pianist mutters incoherently about Al's rage. Shaken by a glimpse of a lurking figure, Gertie collapses when Christian approaches her. She rallies to find Christian hovering, torn between the reformer's urge and plain old fleshly desire.

"Take your hands off me, you dirty, psalm-singing polecat!" she admonishes him. "If the truth were only known, you want me just like all the rest." Christian draws away, vowing: "You haven't heard the *last* from me!"

Gertie consults a conjure woman known as Old Hager

(director Williams), who tells her, "I see a man... Looks like he's comin' *after* you. I see blood! That's *bad*." (This, from the so-what-else-is-new? school of dialogue-writing.)

Backstage, Gertie chances to break a mirror. No sooner has she entered to begin her dance, than Christian intrudes, shouting: "I command you to stop!" The crowd riots, and Gertie retreats to the hotel, where Al is waiting: "I've come to *get* you, Gertie." She protests: "I've *always* loved you. Let's go a*way*... start all *over* again!" Al guns her down, then embraces the body as a trouper arrives with the police. "I killed her because I *loved* her," Al avers.

Gertie jazzes up the proceedings with an ominous element of Voodoo—and yes, that's Williams himself in drag, handling the crystal-gazer role in an instance of improvised casting—but an insurmountable problem is that screenwriter True T. Thompson, a distribution associate of backer Alfred N. Sack, simply did not steal enough from Maugham.

Though saddled with an indifferent-at-best script and a spur-of-the-moment directing assignment, Williams brought his customary enthusiasm and rough-hewn artistry to bear upon the project. *Gertie* is an anomaly among Williams' projects for the Dallas-based entrepreneur Sack, who since *Son of Ingagi* and *The Blood of Jesus* during 1940-41 had allowed the writer-director-actor a generally freer rein. On *Gertie*, however, Sack had summoned Williams to replace an assigned director who "just wasn't working out," as assistant cameraman Gordon Yoder told film preservationist G. William Jones in 1985. "Spencer came into town, he took over, and things were working *great*."

The salvage job lacks the bantering humor and earnest spirituality of Williams' more personally motivated pictures, but Williams draws a fine show of torment from Francine Everette as the high-strung, defiant Gertie. Alfred Hawkins makes more than is written of the preacher role, especially in scenes where he intimidates a flunky (played by David Boykin) into reinforcing his every condemnation of the heathens from Harlem. A Williams trademark, the extensive use of jazz-inspired dance numbers, is generously evident, especially in a show-stopping routine by the San Antonio hoofers Robert Orr (rechristened July Jones, by Williams) and Howard Galloway. The struggle between spiritual values and worldly diversions is stock-in-trade with Williams.

The artist's gruff portrayal of the fortune-telling woman was as much a case of last-minute urgency as the directing assignment itself.

"They couldn't find anybody just right [for the role]," Orr told Bill Jones. "So Spencer said, 'Give me a thousand dollars, and *I'll* do it.' Spencer found a great *big* ol' dress, and he put a bandana around his head, and he was somethin' *else*!"

The mock-West Indies setting is actually a combination of locations in Dallas, Fort Worth and San Antonio. The illusion is convincing enough, largely because Williams keeps things intimate between the camera and the players and confines much of the action to interiors and night exteriors. Like all the Sack-Williams productions, *Gertie* was circulated exclusively in its day among black neighborhood theatres and remained unknown to anything resembling a massed audience until the 1980s. The definitive print of *Gertie* is part of the Tyler, Texas, Black Film Collection, as rescued from a decrepit warehouse and preserved by the Southwest Film & Video Archive at Southern Methodist University in Dallas.

CREDITS: Producers: Alfred N. Sack and Bert Goldberg; Director: Spencer Williams, Jr.; Story and Screenplay: True T. Thompson, from *Rain* (Unattributed), by W. Somerset Maugham; Photographed by: John L. Herman; Assistant Cameraman: Gordon Yoder; Song: "Blues in the Night" (Excerpt), by Harold Arlen & Johnny Mercer; Sound Engineer: Dick Byers; Property Master: J.L. Bock; Art Director: Ted Solomon; Makeup Artist: Frillia; Running Time: 60 Minutes; Released: During 1946 on a State-by-State Basis

CAST: Francine Everette (Gertie LaRue); Don Wilson (Diamond Joe); Kathrine Moore (Stella Van Johnson); Alfred Hawkins (The Rev. Jonathan Christian); David Boykin (Ezra Crumm); L.E. Lewis (Papa Bridges); Inez Newell (Mama Bridges); Piano Frank (Larry); John King (Al); Shelly Ross (Big Boy); Hugh Watson (Tight Pants); Don Gilbert (Messenger); Spencer Williams, Jr. (Old Hager); and Robert Orr [a.k.a. July Jones]

STRANGLER OF THE SWAMP
(Producers Releasing Corp./Pathé Industries, Inc.)

> Old legends... never die in the lonely swampland... [T]he ferryman is a very important person... On his little barge ride the good and the evil; the friendly and the hostile; the superstitious and the enlightened; the living and — sometimes — the dead. — From the Prologue

A PRC remake of a German masterpiece is, in theory, enough to make one cringe at the prospect. In execution, the result is splendid. It helps that the original director and co-author, Frank Wisbar (*né* Franz Bentick Wysbar; 1899-1967), was responsible, and that he utilized the sparse resources at hand to convey a spiritual barrenness perfectly in keeping with the original.

Strangler of the Swamp derives from *Fahrmann Maria* (Pallas Film; 1936), Wysbar's finest accomplishment as a working artist in Germany. Then, as a fugitive-from-the-Reich arrival in America, altering his name slightly to Wisbar, the Prussian-born artist found himself associated categorically with pictures smaller by far than those he had made on his home turf: Wisbar's scenario for *Women*

Rosemary La Planche and Charles Middleton in *Strangler of the Swamp*

in Bondage (1944) graced a politically wide-awake picture that nonetheless was marketed with a bid for the cheap-thrills trade. Then there was *Secrets of a Sorority Girl* (1946).

But 1946 also found Wisbar helming the psychologically ambitious *Devil Bat's Daughter* and the righteously creepy *Strangler of the Swamp*. These transcend their shabby origins with sheer intellectual conceit, on the one hand, and a turbulent emotionalism on the other. (Wisbar later served as producer/host for the 1949 teleseries *Fireside Theatre*, during which period he directed a half-hour version of Poe's "The Tell-Tale Heart," among other acknowledged classics of the short-story idiom. Wisbar eventually would return to Germany as a working filmmaker, delivering such sparsely exported pictures as *Wet Asphalt* [1958] and *Marcia o Crepa/Commando* [1962].)

Fahrmann Maria, drawn from the same Northlands legend that figures in Carl Dreyer's *Vampyr* (Denmark; 1931), also features that dreamlike picture's female lead, the enigmatic, ethereally beautiful Sybille Schmitz. She plays a ferryboat operator who cheats the Grim Reaper of a victim, then lures the spirit into a quicksand bog. The film is beautiful yet ponderous, more a mood poem-in-*lederhosen* than a hair-raiser.

The cultural historian Phil Hardy has called *Strangler* "probably PRC's finest hour," and certainly the film ranks right up there with *Bluebeard*, *Detour* and *Strange Illusion*—those three being the work of director Edgar G. Ulmer—and the anomalously wholesome *The Enchanted Forest* as persuasive ballast in any argument for the studio's vindication. Rosemary La Planche, also of *Devil*

Bat's Daughter, serves *Strangler* in a more expressively earthy variation on the Sybille Schmitz role. Completing the Death-and-the-maiden *valse macabre* is gaunt Charles Middleton, who subdues his characteristic clipped voice here to emerge as a less cosmic, more personally motivated emissary of the Reaper. This version boasts both mood and thrills.

Slayings in the bayou country are chalked up to a menace the villagers call the Strangler, reckoned to be the ghost of former ferryman Douglas — hanged for a murder of which he had taken no part. Douglas (Middleton) had sworn vengeance upon all who condemned him, and upon their families, too. Only a voluntary sacrifice can break the curse. Maria (Miss La Planche), granddaughter of the actual murderer, comes home from a long absence to find herself inheriting the ferry operator's job along with the unwanted attentions of the Strangler. She falls in love with Chris Sanders (Blake Edwards), son of one of the jurymen (Robert Barratt) who had convicted Douglas. Sanders is injured by a hunter's trap, but before Maria can take him to safety, the Strangler arrives to claim the youth. Maria defies the wraith, only to realize that Chris is doomed unless she offers herself in his place. Which she does, putting the vengeful spirit to rest and surviving to marry Chris.

Strangler of the Swamp is the soul of simplicity, photographed indoors on an eerily dressed set garnished with a writhing ground-fog. Only an unsubtle symphonic underscoring, somehow inappropriate though tailored to the action, betrays the film's kinship to such overtly melodramatic pictures as *The Devil Bat* and *Fog Island*. Elaborate photographic effects are absent but not noticeably so. Middleton's dour, accusing presence becomes ghostly via an unaffected combination of attitude, shadowplay and stagecraft. Miss La Planche is herself an ethereal but gutsy presence, as would befit a self-exile whose homecoming carries an unwelcome responsibility for atonement. And yes, the Blake Edwards who plays the hapless almost-victim is the acclaimed screenwriter and director of years to come.

CREDITS: Associate Producer: Raoul Pagel; Director and Screenwriter: Frank Bentick Wisbar; Dialogue Director and Additional Dialogue: Harold Erickson; Story: Frank Wisbar and Leo McCarthy; Based upon: An Original Screenplay by Frank Wisbar and Hans Jeurgen Nierentz; Photographed by: James S. Brown, Jr.; Assistant Director: Harold Knox; Art Director: Edward C. Jewell; Editor: Hugh Winn: Décor: Glenn P. Thompson; Music: Alexander Steinert; Sound: Frank Webster; Makeup: Bud Westmore; Running Time: 60 Minutes; Released: January 1, 1946

CAST: Rosemary La Planche (Maria); Robert Barratt (Christian Sanders); Blake Edwards (Chris Sanders); Charles Middleton (the Strangler); and Effir Parnell, Nolan Leary, Frank Conlan

THE FACE OF MARBLE
(Monogram Pictures Corp.)

Last of the classic-manner Monogram mad-doctor chillers, *The Face of Marble* also marks a small transition in the career of John Carradine: His continued ascent in this narrow realm, decisively inheriting the shabby pre-eminence that had been Bela Lugosi's lot, would parallel Carradine's greater continuing rise as a favored character player of the bigger mainstream studios.

Classic is a relative term here, of course: It does not denote any grandiose qualities so much as it nails a style that Monogram practiced distinctively during most of the 1940s. *The Face of Marble*'s mingling of supernatural horrors with *Frankenstein*-derived science fiction is significant, but this quality serves more to provide a self-referential touchstone to its ancestors—the science-gone-awry implausibilities of *The Ape* and *The Ape Man*, for example, or the spectral shadings of a schizophrenic madness in *Invisible Ghost*—than to announce any shabbier surrealisms yet to come. As suddenly as the little studio's spigot of weird naïveté had begun gushing forth during the early war years, it dried up to barely a trickle: After *The Face of Marble*, Monogram would relegate such elements to mere window-dressing for its most famous comedy team, the Bowery Boys.

The seaside laboratory of Prof. Charles Randolph (Carradine) and his assistant, David Cochran (Robert Shayne), is the scene of an attempt to revive a shipwrecked sailor. The victim stirs faintly, but then his hair goes white and his features freeze into rigidity, earning for the film its ominous title. The scientists return the corpse to the beach; a coroner's inquest will prove the fatality a result of electrocution—not drowning.

Randolph is under siege at every hand: His housekeeper, Maria (Rosa Rey), is a Voodoo-styled priestess who fails in an attempt to cause Cochran to fall in love with Randolph's wife, Elaine (Claudia Drake). In frustration, Maria places the household under a curse. Elaine begs Cochran to halt her husband's research. Randolph kills Elaine's guard dog, Brutus (played by a magnificent Great Dane named General), then jolts the animal back to a menacing semblance of life. Brutus becomes a nocturnal predator, leaving livestock in the vicinity drained of blood. Randolph

Maria (Rosa Rey) is a Voodoo priestess/housekeeper in *The Face of Marble*.

General, as the ghostly and tragic Brutus, menaces John Carradine and Robert Shayne in *The Face of Marble*.

summons Cochran's fiancée, Linda Sinclair (Maris Wrixon), who proves a convenient near-victim.

A new attempt at spell-casting by Maria leaves Elaine in a ghostly state of her own; Maria orders her to kill Randolph—an act witnessed by the butler, Shadrach (Willie Best). Cochran rescues Linda from an attack by Elaine and the dog, and Maria is found dead, a casualty of her own bewitchments. The unholy case seals itself when two sets of footprints, one human and the other canine, are found leading into the ocean.

If not a fading echo of greatness—greatness, like classicism, being relative—then certainly *The Face of Marble* echoes the dire weirdness that had distinguished the studio's few memorably straight-faced spookers of the recent past. (*Invisible Ghost* and *Bowery at Midnight*, both from the Lugosi-at-Monogram period, spring to mind.) The diversified ensemble cast, dog included, radiates an immersion in character that renders the implausibilities at least persuasive. Carradine and Shayne (later of *The Neanderthal Man* and television's *The Adventures of Superman*) exhibit a properly tense camaraderie. Director William Beaudine makes unexpectedly efficient use of the longer-than-usual running time, and he paces the contrasting performances of Claudia Drake and the more spirited Maris Wrixon quite effectively.

As the ghostly, tragic Brutus, General leaves the film's most unnerving impression—and one that has yielded recurring nightmares for many postwar-generation movie buffs who first caught *The Face of Marble* on night-owl television during the 1950s and '60s. The sight of the huge phantom dog, entering the sanctity of a bedroom through solid barriers, is not only as chilling a moment as any such film has to offer but also a crystallization of a universal fear. Not to suggest that everyone harbors the literalized dread of a ghostly canine intrusion in the dead of night—but the figurative invasion is the very stuff of a half-waking nightmare.

Face of Marble is, for that matter, best viewed even today during those hours on the borderline of slumber, when the edge of intellect is dulled just enough to render one susceptible to the film's attitude of helplessness in the face of an implacable malignity.

CREDITS: Producer: Jeffery Bernerd; Director: William Beaudine; Screenplay: Michel Jacoby; Story: William Thiele and Edmund Hartmann; Photographed by: Harry Neumann; Assistant Director: Theodore Joos; Second Camera: Al Nicklin; Special Effects: Robert Clark; Special Optical Effects: Larry Glickman; Transparency Projection Shots: Mario Castegnaro; Editor: William Austin; Décor: Vin Taylor; Music: Edward Kay; Sound: Tom Lambert; Re-Recording and Effects Mixer: Joseph I. Kane; Music Mixer: William H. Wilmarth; Production Manager: Glenn Cook; Technical Director: David Milton; Running Time: 72 Minutes; Released: January 19, 1946
CAST: John Carradine (Prof. Charles Randolph); Claudia Drake (Elaine Randolph); Robert Shayne (David Cochran); Maris Wrixon (Linda Sinclair); Willie Best (Shadrach); Thomas E. Jackson (Norton); Rosa Rey (Maria); Neal Burns (Jeff); Donald Kern and Allan Ray (Photographers); General (Brutus); Clark Kuney (Fisherman and Corpse); Carl Wester (Cop)

THE MADONNA'S SECRET
(Republic Pictures Corp.)

The Madonna's Secret stands as the best of Republic's infrequent sorties into the European-styled art film. Director William Thiele is precisely right for the project: He had been a well-known filmmaker in pre-Hitler Germany and had known moderate success in England and America. Thiele treats this fairly conventional mystery-and-madness yarn in a manner that would do credit to Paul Wegener or Fritz Lang, building a brooding atmosphere through masterful chiaroscuro, lavish décor and a sustained concentration upon the sensitive, haunted features of Francis Lederer.

Drama editor John Earl (Edward Ashley), of the *New York Globe*, is touring an art gallery when he finds himself transfixed by a portrait by one James Harlan Corbin. Earl learns that the figure model was Helen North (Linda Stirling)—but the face is that of Madeleine Renard, a Parisienne who had drowned in the Seine under suspect circumstances. The face also appears in other works by Corbin

Francis Lederer and Ann Rutherford in *The Madonna's Secret*

(Lederer), an aloof chap with haunted eyes. Following Corbin, Earl informs the artist that he recognizes him as the long-vanished lover of Mlle. Renard. Earl suggests that Corbin knows more than he has revealed of the model's death. Corbin keeps silent.

Helen, who loves Corbin despite her engagement to another, complains about Corbin's use of the proxy face. He acquiesces, delivering a magnificent portrait that thrills Helen. Corbin's mother (Leona Roberts) seems possessive but cordial.

A premonition causes Corbin to break a dinner engagement with Helen. Next morning, she is found slain—drugged and then drowned, as Madeleine had been. Earl and Hunt Mason (Michael Hawks), Helen's fiancé, vowing to see Corbin hang, bring Helen's sister Linda (Ann Rutherford) into a plot of entrapment. Under an assumed name, Linda becomes Corbin's model. Her thirst for vengeance is tempered by a dawning affection for the melancholy artist.

Ella Randolph (Gail Patrick), a wealthy and predatory widow, commissions Corbin to paint her portrait, sidelining Linda's job. Mrs. Randolph conspires to marry Corbin, who angrily rejects her scheming. He confides to Linda that he fears he may have a dual personality. Linda is now certain of Corbin's innocence, but as the two declare their love for one another, the police break in and arrest Corbin. Mrs. Randolph has been murdered.

Mrs. Corbin invites Linda back to the studio, where she informs Linda that she "must go, like the others." Meanwhile, Corbin, under questioning, wises up to his mother's involvement and insists the police return to his studio. They arrive just as Mrs. Corbin is about to dispatch Linda. Fatally wounded, Mrs. Corbin tells her son that she felt compelled to kill the women who fell in love with him.

The story meanders at times, with some ponderous stretches of dialogue, and Edward Ashley's portrayal of a newspaper critic is annoyingly (though realistically) foppish. Hardly a flawless film, *The Madonna's Secret* is nonetheless a superior piece, rich in ideas and pictorial beauty—and handily a more personal film for Thiele than his hits *The Jungle Princess* (1937) and *Tarzan Triumphs* (1943). The elegant music is the work of Joseph Dubin, who performed most of his Hollywood scoring on animated cartoons from the Disney machine. The paintings integral to the story are by the Polish master, Alexander S. Keszthelyi, one of the 20th century's more affecting portraitists. Republic's in-house effects masters, the Lydecker Bros., provide perfectly realistic miniatures of a boat-house, a motorboat and the river. An unusual touch is a nightclub sequence where Tanis Chandler sings of love while a knife marksman outlines her in blades against a wall.

Gail Patrick, Old Hollywood's Other Woman incarnate, is fine as a voracious dilettante. Ann Rutherford is charming as the most sympathetic character. Linda Stirling shows abilities beyond what usually was demanded of her as Republic's serial queen. Leona Roberts' show of suffocating mom-ism and John Litel's efficient detective are strong assets.

Lederer assumes most of the burden, though, and gives it full measure: Whether skulking about his studio; exhibiting a strained gaiety in the face of deepening self-doubts; tossing off drinks in the Continental manner; or sharing an impassioned romantic scene, the Czech-born actor applies precisely the right ambiguity—leading the absorbed viewer at once to suspect him of being a crazed murderer, and to hope that he is not.

CREDITS: Associate Producer: Stephen Auer; Director and Co-Screenwriter: William Thiele; Co-Screenwriter: Bradbury Foote; Photographed by: John Alton; Assistant Director: Lee Luthaker; Second Camera: Herbert Kirkpatrick; Special Effects: Howard Lydecker and Theodore Lydecker; Matte Paintings: Lewis Physioc; Transparency Projection Shots: Gordon Schaefer; Art Director: Hilyard Brown; Editor: Fred Allen; Décor: John McCarthy, Jr., and George Suhr; Costumer: Adele Palmer; Gowns: Howard Greer; Music Director: Richard Cherwin; Musical Score: Joseph Dubin; Song: "C'est Vous," by Al Newman, Richard Cherwin & Ned Washington; Sound: Ed Borchell; Makeup: Bob Mark; Paintings: Alexander S. Keszthelyi; Running Time: 79 Minutes; Released: February 16, 1946

CAST: Francis Lederer (James Harlan Corbin); Gail Patrick (Ella Randolph); Ann Rutherford (Linda North); Edward Ashley (John Earl); Linda Stirling (Helen

North); John Litel (Lt. Roberts); Leona Roberts (Mrs. Corbin); Michael Hawks (Hunt Mason); Clifford Brooke (Hadley); Pierre Watkin (District Attorney); Will Wright (Riverman); Geraldine Wall (Joyce); John Hamilton (Lambert); Gino Corrado (Boucher); Lee Phelps (Detective); Alex Havier (Ling); Ann Chedister (Madonna); Edythe Elliott (Landlady); Harry Strang and George Magrill (Cops); Russ Whiteman (Intern); Pat Flaherty (Officer); James Carlisle (Doctor)

THE SHADOW REDACTUS: IMPERISHABLE CHARACTER, PERISHABLE SERIES

(Monogram Pictures Corp.)

The Shadow, pop-cultural icon though he be, has yet to meet with any self-perpetuating series of movies. Which is really more a matter of Hollywood's failure to get a handle on so complex a character. Not to suggest that the Shadow has not fascinated and tantalized Hollywood with the possibilities. From a short-subject series at Universal during the 1930s, to false starts, nice tries and dunderheaded misfires at intervals all along, the pulp-magazine and radio-network mystifier continues to tempt and thwart the society of high-adventure filmmakers. What the Shadow really needs is a Federico Fellini or a David Lynch; that is to say, an artist who understands the bizarre and absurd essential passions of the pulps.

After Rod La Rocque's starring series-in-miniature at Colony, Victor Jory toplined a 15-chapter serial, *The Shadow*, in 1940 for Columbia. Which brings us to Monogram Pictures' stab at the franchise, with Kane Richmond as the star of *The Shadow Returns* and *Behind the Mask* and *The Missing Lady*. A dozen years later, Republic would attempt to do the character justice with *Invisible Avenger* (1958). In 1994, Russell Mulcahy directed a big-budget *The Shadow*, overshadowing star player Alec Baldwin with an effects-laden style-over-substance muddle of a story.

Herewith, the Monogram *Shadow*s:

The Shadow Returns (1946): The object of a grave robbery is a cache of jewels interred with the corpse. Suspects abound, but they are murdered one by one as Inspector Cardona (Joseph Crehan) closes in on each new bogus solution. That mysterious crime-buster, the Shadow (Kane Richmond), ridicules the law for its inept handling of the matter. At length, the Shadow reveals that the jewels contain a greater treasure—a formula for a revolutionary plastic—and seals the case, casket and all.

As a bestselling series of pulp-magazine yarns, *The Shadow* helped mightily to define the Great American Monomyth, the notion of a maverick who upholds law-and-order by defying the very processes that define law-and-order.

Most such mystery-man heroes have fared better in the pulps and the funny-books than they have in the movies—Clint Eastwood's grimmer characters, as in 1985's *Pale Rider*, to the contrary—and the Shadow is no exception.

The Shadow Returns, a desultory opener in Monogram's attempt at a series, suffers from the usual ailments of melodramatic hackery: A sinister conspiracy proves only superficially complex; a police force exists primarily to be shown up by the outlaw hero; and heavy-duty villainy is lacking. The Shadow is reduced from the pulps' formidable shape-shifter and mind-clouder to merely a bright dilettante detective leading a double life.

The Shadow (Kane Richmond) investigates a graveyard in *The Shadow Returns*.

Kane Richmond is better than the material, and Tom Dugan accounts for some welcome brusque comedy. Joseph Crehan makes a convincing Lestrade to the Shadow's masked equivalent of a Holmes. Barbara Reed is scarcely more than window-dressing as the Shadow's Gal Friday; director Phil Rosen usually put his leading ladies to sharper use.

CREDITS: Producer: Joe Kaufman; Associate Producer: Lou Brock; Director: Phil Rosen; Screenplay by: George Callahan; Based upon: The *Shadow* Magazine Stories; Photographed by: William Sickner; Assistant Director: Eddie Davis; Art Director: E.R. Hickson; Technical Director: Dave Milton; Editor: Ace Herman; Décor: Charles Thompson; Music: Edward Kay; Sound: Tom Lambert; Production Manager: Glenn Cook; Running Time: 61 Minutes; Released: February 19, 1946

CAST: Kane Richmond (Lamont Cranston/the Shadow); Barbara Reed (Margo Lane); Tom Dugan (Shrevvie); Joseph Crehan (Inspector Cardona); Pierre Watkin (Commisioner Weston); Robert Emmett Keane (Charles Frobay); Frank Reicher (Michael Hasdon); Lester Dore (William Monk); Rebel Randall (Lenore Jessup); Emmett Vogan (Breck and Yomans); Sherry Hall (Robert Buell)

Behind the Mask (1946): A masked killer frames the Shadow for the slaying of a newspaper reporter. Seems the victim had been a blackmailer. Lamont "the

Shadow" Cranston (Kane Richmond) juggles his impending marriage to Margo Lane (Barbara Reed) with a campaign to crack the case and clear himself of suspicion. The clues, and an escalating trail of corpses, lead to a shady nightclub operator (Lou Crosby) running a separate blackmail scam; to a dive whose jukebox has been cleverly rigged to register gambling bets—and right back to the newsroom, where another journalist (Robert Shayne) turns out to be the perpetrator. The instrument of murder proves to have been a hypodermic injection of air, which works fine in the lungs but has no business entering the bloodstream.

An improvement over *The Shadow Returns* in terms of suspenseful ferocity, *Behind the Mask* nonetheless compromises itself with an indulgence in lowbrow comedy, which is poorly integrated with the more nearly serious business. This stylistic unevenness betrays the unbilled contributions of William Beaudine, who subbed briefly for director-of-record Phil Karlson while the latter was recovering from a case of ptomaine poisoning. The work-in-progress title was *The Shadow's Shadow*, which sounds about as redundant as the series itself.

CREDITS: Producer: Joe Kaufman; Supervising Producer: Glenn Cook; Associate Producer: Lou Brock; Directors: Phil Karlson and William Beaudine; Screenplay by: George Callahan; Story: Arthur Hoerl; Based upon: The *Shadow* Magazine Stories; Photographed by: William Sickner; Second Camera: William Clothier; Special Effects: Ray Mercer and Vernon L. Walker; Special Optical Effects: Larry Glickman and Linwood Dunn; Transparency Projection Shots: Mario Castegnaro and Russell A. Cully; Matte Paintings: Al Simpson; Technical Director: Dave Milton; Editor: Ace Herman; Décor: George Mitchell; Music: Edward Kay; Sound: Tom Lambert and George Mitchell; Re-Recording and Effects Mixers: Joseph I. Kane and James G. Stewart; Music Mixers: William H. Wilmarth and Earl B. Mounce; Production Manager: Charles Kerr; Running Time: 67 Minutes; Released: May 25, 1946

CAST: Kane Richmond (Lamont Cranston/the Shadow); Barbara Reed (Margo Lane); George Chandler (Shrevvie); Dorothea Kent (Jennie); Joseph Crehan (Inspector Cardona); Pierre Watkin (Commisioner Weston); Robert Shayne (Brad Thomas); June Clyde (Edie Merrill); James Cardwell (Jeff Mann);

Marjorie Hoshelle (Mae Bishop); Joyce Compton (Lulu); Ed Gargan (Dixon); Lou Crosby (Marty Greane); Bill Christy (Copy Boy); Nancy Bronkman (Susan); Dewey Robinson (Headwaiter); Jean Carlin (Cigarette Girl); Laura Stevens (Hazel); Ruth Cherrington (Society Matron); Ralph Brooks and James Nataro (Reporters); Bill Ruhl (Detective); Marie Harmon and Lois Fields (Operators)

The Missing Lady **(1946)**: The title refers not to a character, but to a statue of jade, nabbed following the slaying of its owner. Murder piles upon murder as the underworld conspires to claim the object, and Lamont "the Shadow" Cranston is once again mis-labeled a killer. Cranston skips jail through the convenience of having an uncle who happens to be the police commissioner (Pierre Watkin). Cranston's accuser, an artist's model named Gilda Marsh (Jo Carroll Dennison), lends the flagging series a welcome fatal-lady presence, and indeed proves responsible for a majority of the slayings. The film rewards Miss Dennison's show of conniving malice with a brief "gotcha" scene but denies her any showy comeuppance, settling instead for the letdown of a simple arrest.

CREDITS: Producer: Joe Kaufman; Associate Producer and Screenwriter: George Callahan; Director: Phil Karlson; Photographed by: William Sickner; Assistant Director: Theodore Joos; Second Camera: William Margulies; Special Optical Effects: Larry Glickman; Transparency Projection Shots: Mario Castegnaro; Technical Director: Dave Milton; Editor: Ace Herman; Décor: Ray Boltz; Music: Edward J. Kay; Sound: Tom Lambert and George Mitchell; Re-Recording and Effects Mixer: Joseph I. Kane; Music Mixer: William H. Wilmarth; Production Manager: Glenn Cook; Running Time: 60 Minutes; Released: August 17, 1946

CAST: Kane Richmond (Lamont Cranston/the Shadow); Barbara Reed (Margo Lane); George Chandler (Shrevvie); James Flavin (Inspector Cardona); Pierre Watkin (Commisioner Weston); Dorothea Kent (Jennie); James Cardwell (Terry Blake); Claire Carleton (Rose Dawson); Jack Overman (Ox Welsh); Jo Carroll Dennison (Gilda Marsh); Frances Robinson (Anne Walsh); Almira Sessions (Effie); Nora Cecil (Millie); George Lewis (Jon Field); Dewey Robinson (Barkeep);

Anthony Warde (Lefty); Bert Roach (Waldo); Gary Owen (Johnson); Ray Teal (Slater); Douglas Wood (Alfred Kester); Ralph Dunn (Clark)

THE FLYING SERPENT
(Producers Releasing Corp.)

"Horror stuff that may get the kids but n.g. [no good, *i.e.*] for adults," declared *Variety* in appraising the box office prospects of *The Flying Serpent*. A good day's trudge through the back issues of *Variety* is invariably enlightening—for those brittle newspulp pages yield, along with airborne allergens and paper mites, a wealth of on-the-spot first-blush reactions from critics trained to address the concerns of theatre operators. The experience is, however, seldom fulfilling in any aesthetic sense. Even so, this anonymous reviewer's point is well taken that the picture "could have been the curdling meller [melodrama] it set out to be if its instrument of horror... did not resemble an oversized hawk rather than the lethal, blood-sucking monster intended." And suspense is, indeed, "fatally lacking."

And yet George Zucco serves well the role of Prof. Andrew Forbes, who while exploring the Indian ruins around San Juan, New Mexico, finds an ancient treasure and its guardian. This creature would be an airborne reptile, which Forbes christens Quetzalcoatl, after an Aztec deity. Imprisoning the creature within a hidden chamber, Forbes grows ever more resentful of the efforts of a rival (James Metcalf), whose published writings are likely to attract gawkers

The Flying Serpent **is a remake of** *The Devil Bat.*

and fortune-hunters. The victims begin accumulating. A visiting radio journalist (Ralph Lewis) intrudes, and he and Forbes' stepdaughter (Hope Kramer) ferret out the truth. The tale peaks with the stepdaughter's near-murder, which the writer thwarts, leaving the creature to make a meal of Forbes.

If it all sounds familiar to the follower of Poverty Row's Depression-into-wartime pageant of shockers, that can only be because *The Flying Serpent* is a remake of 1940's *The Devil Bat*, as superficially jockeyed about by the original screenwriter, John Thomas Neville. Neville also is assigned credit for the source-story on this refried-beans version, elbowing aside *The Devil Bat*'s pre-screenplay scenarist, George Bricker. Where *Bat*'s star player, Bela Lugosi, has vengeful motivations out the wazoo and breeds his own strain of monster to perpetrate the mayhem, *Serpent*'s Zucco is merely a resentful glory-hog who deploys a creature that he has chanced to find. The distinction is significantly damning to *Serpent*. (For evidence of additional tampering, albeit on comparatively higher moral and intellectual planes, see *Devil Bat's Daughter*.)

The myth of Quetzalcoatal would receive a more satisfying exploration in *Q—the Winged Serpent* (1982), Larry Cohen's audacious mingling of monster-movie and film noir narrative elements.

CREDITS: Producer: Sigmund Neufeld; Director: Sherman Scott [Sam Newfield]; Screenplay and Story: John T. Neville; Story (Unattributed): George Bricker; Photographed by: Jack Greenhalgh; Assistant Director: William O'Connor; Art Director: Edward C. Jewell; Editor: Holbrook N. Todd; Set Dresser: Syd Moore; Props: Eugene C. Stone; Music: Leo Erdody; Sound: Frank McWhorter; Makeup: Bud Westmore; Production Manager: Bert Sternbach; Running Time: 59 Minutes; Released: February 20, 1946

CAST: George Zucco (Prof. Andrew Forbes); Ralph Lewis (Richard Thorpe); Home Kramer (Mary Forbes); Eddie Acuff (Jerry Jones); Wheaton Chambers (Lewis Havener); James Metcalf (Dr. John Lambert); Henry Hall (Billy Hayes); Milton Kibbee (Hastings); Budd Buster (Coroner); Terry Frost (Vance Bennett)

THE HAUNTED MINE
(Great Western Productions, Inc./Monogram Pictures Corp.)

All the barbers we've ever known—from coiffeurists-turned-entertainers like Bob Wills, Chuck Carbo and Perry Como, to the neighborhood razor artist—have been all-'round okay chaps, well worth trusting with the care and handling of one's hairline and whiskers. Say, even George Turner's father was a barber, and a mighty fine one at that. So we mean it in the nicest way possible when we say that a barber's chair can be the creepiest place this side of a bathroom in the Bates Motel.

Blame the image upon the English playwright George Dibdin-Pitt, whose *The String of Pearls*, from 1847, codified the legend of Sweeney Todd, the murderous barber with a cannibalistic entrepreneurial sideline, and thus paved the way for an internationally popular British film of 1936, *Sweeney Todd, the Demon Barber of Fleet Street*, starring Tod Slaughter. Sweeney's delighted mutterings about "throats... rich, and mellow to the razor," even as he plots to send another client tumbling into an appointment with murder, have caused generations of moviegoers to experience spasms of unease as the time approaches for a trim. Even W.C. Fields had contributed to the slander with a hilariously queasy sequence in a 1933 two-reeler, "The Barber Shop," and American movies from this volume's *Code of the Prairie* to, elsewhere, *Dr. Renault's Secret* (1942) and *Showdown at Boot Hill* (1958), have tapped that jugular-deep potential for tonsorial trepidation.

Derwin M. Abrahams' *The Haunted Mine* comes particularly close to recapturing the predatory ferocity of *Sweeney Todd*, lacking only the playfully grim relish that Tod Slaughter brought to his many portrayals of Evil for Evil's Sake. That lack, in fact, may make *The Haunted Mine* the more terrifying experience.

Johnny Mack Brown, who made some of the weirdest Westerns of all over the long stretch, stars as Jack "Nevada" McKenzie, a U.S. marshal investigating the drowning of one Frank Durant in a supposedly haunted mine. En route, Nevada finds the corpse of Rusty Stewart, an employee of secretive mob boss Steve Twining (John Merton), alongside a cache of gold nuggets and a knife. Twining is conspiring to take ownership of the Durant mine, where he has discovered a fresh lode. Nevada, framed by the Twining gang in connection with Stewart's murder, is granted the last request of a shave. Fellow lawman Sandy Hopkins (Raymond Hatton) has already infiltrated the town as its new barber.

Nevada tells Sandy that he believes Stewart's wounds were caused by a razor, not a knife. A shadowy figure prowls about. Sandy takes Nevada to safety through a hidden passageway. Nevada steals the deed to the mine before Twining can finagle it away from Durant's widow and her daughter (Claire Whitney and Linda Johnson), but then the mystery man knocks Nevada cold and prepares to treat him to a throat-slitting. Saved by the arrival of Sandy, Nevada proceeds to a deal-cutting appointment with Twining. En route, he and Dan McLeod (Riley Hill), Miss Durant's sweetheart, exchange gunfire with one of the outlaws (Marshall Reed)—who turns up with his throat slashed. Dan survives a similar attack, and Sandy captures the razor-wielding assailant and hears his confession. Seems this hermit (Raphael Bennett) had been a barber whose son was killed while working in the mine. Maddened by the tragedy, he has lurked about the mine ever since, slicing up anyone who would venture too near. Twining, however, proves to have killed Durant, by flooding the mine to hide the new gold strike.

The Haunted Mine, reminiscent of Ken Maynard's 1932 *Tombstone Canyon*, marks the end of the *Nevada McKenzie* series.

CREDITS: Producer: Scott R. Dunlap; Director: Derwin M. Abrahams; Screenplay: Frank H. Young; Story: Elizabeth Burbidge; Photographed by: Harry Neumann; Editor: Fred Maguire; Music: Edward Kay; Running Time: 52 Minutes; Released: February 23, 1946

CAST: Johnny Mack Brown (Jack "Nevada" McKenzie); Raymond Hatton (Sandy Hopkins); Linda Johnson (Jenny Durant); Riley Hill (Dan McLeod); John Merton (Steve Twining); Raphael Bennett (Hermit); Claire Whitney (Mrs. Durant); Marshall Reed (Blackie); Bob Butt (Tracy)

I RING DOORBELLS
(Producers Releasing Corp./Pathé Industries, Inc.)

Yes, and it can't be the postman, because he always rings twice. Not to mention this film's assistant director: Harold *Knox*.

Anne Gwynne, that ethereally beautiful B-pictures leading lady from Texas, found her limited stardom defined largely by Universal Pictures' horror-movie factory, where she registered impressively in the likes of *The Strange Case of Dr. Rx* (1942), *Weird Woman* (1944) and *House of Frankenstein* (1944-45). Miss Gwynne was possessed of a brighter range, however, and it shows to striking advantage in this forgotten romance-comedy-thriller.

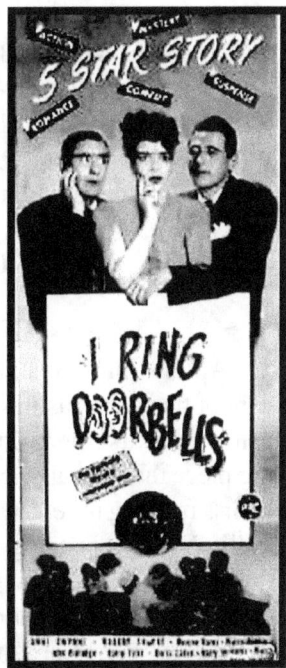

Miss Gwynne serves *I Ring Doorbells* as rural schoolteacher Brooke Peters, who gets cozy with Los Angeles newspaperman Dick Meadows (Robert Shayne) just in time to find herself caught up in the murder of the fiancée (Jan Wiley) of the publisher's son (Joel McGinnis). Miss Gwynne's is a delightful performance, wavering between insecure jealousy and confident resourcefulness in the face of terror. The victim proves to have been slipping around with an ill-tempered drama critic (John Eldredge), who admits readily to having struck her when he knows that an autopsy will reveal poison. The critic is revealed, too, as the poisoner, thanks to a hidden camera rigged by Meadows' photographer chum (Roscoe Karns).

Robert Shayne's brusque manner hardly fits his character, but he pairs nicely with Miss Gwynne. Shayne's Dick Meadows—a failed playwright, glib enough to schmooze his way back into the newspaper racket he had abandoned—is obviously though broadly patterned after the acclaimed journalist Ben Hecht (of *The Specter of the Rose*), who retrenched time and again into the newspaper racket despite his grander successes as a playwright and filmmaker.

Miss Gwynne's top-billed assignment could scarcely have been a strategic move, given PRC's low station within the industry, but she carries the picture with a brisk authority. The director is Frank Strayer, of such *Forgotten Horrors* linchpins as *The Monster Walks* and *The Vampire Bat*. Strayer had spent much of the late-Depression/early-wartime period handling many of Columbia's funnypapers-into-film *Blondie* pictures.

CREDITS: Producer: Martin Mooney; Director: Frank Strayer; Dialogue Director: Ben Irving Coleman; Shooting Script: Dick Irving Hyland; Adaptation: Dick Irving Hyland and Raymond L. Schrock; Based upon: Russell Birdwell's 1939 Novel, *I Ring Doorbells*; Photographed by: Benjamin H. Kline; Assistant Director: Harold Knox; Special Effects: Ray Smallwood; Art Director: Edward C. Jewell; Editor: George McGuire; Décor: Glenn T. Thompson; Music: Leo Erdody; Sound: Ben Winkler; Re-Recording and Effects Mixer: Joseph I. Kane; Music Mixer: William Wilmarth; Makeup: Bud Westmore; Production Manager: Raoul Pagel; Running Time: 67 Minutes; Released: February 25, 1946

CAST: Anne Gwynne (Brooke Peters); Robert Shayne (Dick Meadows); Roscoe Karns (Stubby); Pierre Watkin (G.B. Barton); Harry Shannon (Shannon); John Eldredge (Ransome); Harry Tyler (Tippy Miller); Doria Caron (Yvette); Jan Wiley (Helen Carter); Joel McGinnis (Clyde Barton); Charles Wilson (Inspector); Hank Patterson (Bradley); Eugene Stutenroth (O'Halloran)

CRIME OF THE CENTURY
(Republic Pictures Corp.)

An outwardly conventional journalism-exposé melodrama with a helpful core of macabre business, *Crime of the Century* comes nowhere near being the epic thriller its title promises. It is, however, a respectably brisk and entertaining piece that actually leaves the viewer wanting more. Clocking in at under an hour's running time, the picture may be less a case of efficient direction (though Philip Ford keeps things cracking right along) than of a merciless treatment in the cutting room. In the present day's receptive climate for director's-cut video editions of any number of films, it is tantalizing to imagine a more generously fleshed-out version of this strange entry. Fat chance.

Andrew Madison (Paul Stanton), a crooked captain of industry, plots to keep secret the death of a business partner until he can sway a vote by the board of directors. The conspiracy gets found out by newspaperman Jim Rogers (Ray Walker), but Rogers is abducted and imprisoned before he can file a story. Hank Rogers (Michael Browne), brother of the missing newshound, picks up the trail for reasons more personal than journalistic, only to run afoul of Madison's treacherous circle—and to fall in love with the equally dangerous Audrey Brandon (Stephanie Bachelor), an employee of the big shot. The case is cracked, and the plot foiled, when the dead tycoon's embittered daughter leads Hank to where Madison has hidden the corpse.

Crime of the Century made a late show appearance with *Marshal of Laredo* at the Lyric movie house.

The greater appeal for the horror-film audience lies in an iced-down bathtub containing the missing stiff. More than just literally chilling, the scene illustrates vividly the lengths to which the conspirators will go to ice-o-late the *corpus delecti*. There is also the payoff of a typically creepy performance from Martin Kosleck—a less painstakingly developed variant on his role as a fawning but irritable henchman in Paramount's *The Mad Doctor* (1940)—and a nice show of romanticized villainy from top-billed Stephanie Bachelor. Paul Stanton seems the very stuff of pompous dignity as the crooked pillar of society.

This *Crime of the Century* is unrelated to a like-titled Paramount production of 1933, which offers Jean Hersholt as a physician using hypnosis to counteract sociopathic tendencies.

CREDITS: Executive Producer: William J. Sullivan; Associate Producer: Walter H. Goetz; Director: Philip Ford; Screenplay: O'Leta Rhinehart, William Hagens (from Their Story) and Gertrude Walker; Photographed by: Reggie Hagens; Assistant Director: Allen Wood; Second Camera: Robert Tobey; Matte Paintings: Lewis Physioc; Miniatures and Special Optical Effects: Howard C. Lydecker and Theodore J. Lydecker; Transparency Projection Shots: Gordon Schaefer; Art Director: Gano Chittenden; Editor: William P. Thompson; Décor: John McCarthy, Jr., and James Redd; Costumer: Adele Palmer; Music: Richard Cherwin; Sound: Ed Borchell; Makeup: Bob Mark; Running Time: 57 Minutes; Released: February 28, 1946

CAST: Stephanie Bachelor (Audrey Brandon); Michael Browne (Hank Rogers); Martin Kosleck (Paul); Betty Shaw (Margaret Waldham); Paul Stanton (Andrew Madison); Mary Currier (Agatha Waldham); Ray Walker (Jim Rogers);

Tom London (Dr. Jackson); Don Costello (Bartender); Earle Hodgins (Eddie); Garry Owen (Cabbie); Charles Cane (Ed Harris); Charles Wilson (Lieutenant); Frances Morris (Nurse); Frederick Howard (Richard Waldham); David Fresco (Clerk); Donald Kerr (Reporter)

SWING COWBOY, SWING
a.k.a.: BAD MAN FROM BIG BEND
(Wells-Shrum Productions/Westernair Pictures/Astor Pictures)

Any swinging done here by any masked-phantom killer is likely as not to take place at the end of a rope. This music-hating badman struggles throughout to steal *Swing, Cowboy, Swing* away from a tuneful pageant of Western Swing, as performed by Cal Shrum's Rhythm Rangers, Walt Shrum & His Colorado Hillbillies and Alta Lee, the Yodelling Rangerette. Good ol' Max "Alibi" Terhune, the popular ventriloquist and scene-stealing loudmouth of the *Three Mesquiteers* and *Range Busters* matinee-Western series, also does his share of scene-snatching.

The larger struggle here lies in the futility of trying to make sense of a muddle of confused documentation on the film itself: If not for the compelling evidence of a 1949 reissue print bearing the proxy title of *Bad Man from Big Bend*, it might be more convenient to assume that *Swing, Cowboy, Swing* had never existed. The Motion Picture Academy's archives show that the Production Code Administration issued its Purity Seal to producer-and-star Cal Shrum on March 20, 1946, just a week after a screening. *The Hollywood Reporter* for that same week allowed as how Cal Shrum was touring Northern California with his Rhythm Rangers on behalf of the film. But then, a June-of-'46 announcement from that same *Hollywood Reporter* announces the start of principal photography. No formal release date has come to light, and various genre histories of times more recent list the picture as a *1944* entry.

Whatever and whenever, *Swing, Cowboy, Swing* is a ragged-but-right delight. Patently conceived as a D-I-Y promotional vehicle, the film could have settled for mere adventure as a setting for its music and comedy. Old-time director Elmer Clifton's original scenario, however, veers into the more troubling orbit of a serial killer who specializes in dispatching musicians.

Cal Shrum and his band are en route to a gig when they find themselves under fire from a conspicuously annoying sniper. They hook up safely with Shrum's bandleader brother, Walt, but Walt balks when he learns that Cal is bound for Big Bend, where entertainers are an endangered genus-and-species. Cal persists, and in Big Bend he finds his bunch barred from the local hotel. At their concert venue, a sinister stage manager named Beeton (I. Stanford Jolley, that perfect conniving presence of the B-movies) warns them that no one will attend the show lest mayhem erupt. Cal starts his program, anyhow, throwing the doors wide open so that the whole town can hear. The phantom gunman opens fire. One trouper, Alibi Terhune, pegs Beeton as the menace; it seems the manager's daughter, Mary, has run off with a magician (Tom Hubbard). To complicate matters, the sheriff is away.

Ordered to leave Big Bend by Beeton's vigilante group, Cal conspires to stick close and investigate. He determines that the phantom's weapon is an antique Sharp's Rifle, which would bespeak a more gentlemanly grade of assassin. Mary (Ann Roberts) returns but finds herself kidnapped by the masked man. Cal engineers a rescue and stakes out the villain's shack, revealing the killer as a prominent citizen (Frank Ellis) who had hoped to wreck Beeton's business so he could buy the theater—cheap. Cal parlays his sleuthing skills into ever greater acclaim for his band.

It's all pretty silly, in its delightful way, and *Swing, Cowboy, Swing* actually manages to have it *both* ways: The music is generously deployed, and the threat is both mysterious and urgent. Cal Shrum is no actor, but he seems to believe that he is, and that confidence goes a long way toward elevating the picture beyond vanity.

Elmer Clifton (1892-1949) had long since lapsed from his glory days as an actor-turned-director, starting with the D.W. Griffith company in the 1910s. Clifton's talkie-era low-budgeters are amply well represented in the *Forgotten Horrors* collections, including 1935's *Captured in Chinatown*, 1936's *Death in the Air* and 1938's *Wolves of the Sea*. The war years saw such striking signature pieces from Clifton as the *Captain America* serial (co-directed with John English) and *Seven Doors to Death*.

Cal Shrum and Walt Shrum were key players in the West Coast's Western Swing community of the 1940s, and indeed both were first-generation cowjazz artists with credentials dating from the latter 1930s, coming up amid the long shadows cast by Bob Wills, Milton Brown, the Light Crust Doughboys and other such first-generation masters. The Shrum boys learned early on how to reach a vaster audience by broadcasting from the unregulated flamethrower radio stations below the Mexican border. Cal's short-lived Westernair movie company was an offshoot of his Westernair record label, for which even the major-league entertainer Tex Williams once recorded. The brothers' 78-r.p.m. platters are elusive nowadays, but each artist is represented on a fine compact-disc anthology called *Swinging West* (Krazy Kat Records; 1998).

CREDITS: Producer: Cal Shrum; Director and Writer: Elmer Clifton: Photographed by: Robert Cline; Special Photographic Effects: Ray Mercer; Editor: George M. Merrick; Assistant Director: Bobby Ray; Music: Frank Sanucci; Songs: "Rhythm Rangers Waltz," by Cal Shrum, "End of Rainbow Trail," "Trying To Forget" and "Who's Lonesome Now?" by Don Weston; "Do You Miss Me?" and "Come Be My Sunshine," by Walt Shrum & Bob Hoag, "Oh! Susannah," by Stephen Foster, and the Traditional "Old Chisholm Trail"; Sound: Lyle Willey; Production Manager: William L. Nolte; Released: Following Previews in March of 1946; Reissued: 1949 by Astor Pictures as *Bad Man from Big Bend*

CAST: Cal Shrum (Himself); Don Weston (Himself); Max "Alibi" Terhune (Himself); Alta Lee the Yodelling Cowgirl (Herself); Walt Shrum (Himself); Robert Hoag, Rusty Cline, Jeannie Akers and Chuck Peters (Walt Shrum's Colorado Hillbillies); I. Stanford Jolley (Beeton); Ann Roberts (Mary); Frank Ellis (Frank Lawson); Ed Cassidy (Sheriff); Phil Dunham (Wells Fargo Agent); Ted Adams (Gun Hand); Tom Hubbard (Tom); and Al Winter, Shorty Woodward, Ace Dehne, Judy Barnes

FIGHT THAT GHOST
(Toddy Pictures Co.)

Dewey "Pigmeat" Markham (1905-1981) was born in Durham, North Carolina, and found his calling as an entertainer while a child. "Just seems like I had a talent for being funny," Markham told *The Jazz Record* during a particularly busy spell of stage, screen and recording-studio activity. The recently issued *Fight That Ghost*—Markham's first starring film, following an appearance in Republic's 1944 musical-comedy revue *That's My Baby*—was a latecomer in the cycle of nostalgically corny, minstrel-style scare-comedies that Mantan Moreland and Flournoy E. Miller had launched as a team earlier in the decade.

Markham also starred in *House-Rent Party* (1946; made back-to-back for Toddy Pictures with *Fight That Ghost* and boasting its own eerie grace-notes) and *Swanee Showboat* (1946-47). The latter, an Ajax Pictures production, provoked various censorship groups to invoke a favorite term—*lascivious*—while en route to a severely limited release. These films' booking pattern of black-neighborhood theatres contrasted strikingly with a new phase in Markham's larger career as an in-person showman: For the first time, now, he was touring big-city mainstream theatres, sharing playbills with the Andrews Sisters' whitebread jazz-pop harmonizing act, and convulsing audiences of the Caucasian persuasion with his broad-stroke clowning and freewheeling dance steps.

"Pigmeat" Markham and "Rastus" Murray meet a ghost in *Fight That Ghost*.

"All of my jokes are mostly ad-lib, and I originate all my own dancing," Markham said. Of his famous nickname, he revealed: "[It] came about in a funny way. On my early theatre dates, I used to say, 'I'm a sweet papa Pigmeat with the River Jordan in my hips, and all the women run to be baptized.' When I came out of the theatre, all the people hanging around used to say, 'That's Pigmeat—there goes Pigmeat,' and so the name stuck." A secondary monicker, "Alamo," went unexplained.

The Jazz Record's interviewer, Alison Blair, detailed finer, unspoken points that strike a telling contrast with Markham's exaggerated stage presence, which often included deliberately over-sized clothing and shoes and, occasionally, even the lily-gilding of black-on-black grease-paint makeup. (This archaic phenomenon would resurface to inform Spike Lee's embittered comedy of 2000, *Bamboozled*.) In the dressing-room, the article continued, "a tall, well-built, serious-looking man greeted me, and outside of an engaging smile, there was nothing of the comedian about him... [He displayed] the subtle plasticity of a dancer... Pigmeat gazed thoughtfully at his hands as he spoke. His fingers were long and sensitive, and he gestured with them gracefully." Among his tales of earlier times, Markham dropped the intriguing title of one of his schoolboy plays: "Twenty Minutes in Hell."

Markham evidently did not discuss his films during this session—except to mention, "I made three movies in California, and I wrote two of them myself." Although only producer Ted Toddy and director Sam Newfield receive screenwriting credit on *Fight That Ghost*, there is clearly some better writing going on in the comedy routines of Markham and his equally amusing cohort, John "Rastus" Murray, than in the hackneyed and dramatically incoherent excuse for a plot.

Pigmeat and Shorty (Murray) have run their tailoring shop into ruin, and suicide seems the only way out. A telegram arrives with hopeful news: The pals

stand to inherit $5,000 and a house—on condition that they spend a night in their dead benefactor's room. Locked inside the darkened bedchamber, they are startled by the appearance of disembodied hands holding a candle. Voices, seemingly from nowhere, assail them, and a face in a framed portrait suddenly grows a beard. Or so it might seem.

But no—the haunting is the work of a crooked mob that has been using the place as a hideout and hopes to scare the heirs into leaving. Pigmeat and Shorty turn the tables on the hoods. And now that that's all settled, a new barrage of eerie noises causes the pals to light a shuck out of the premises.

One expects a certain raggedy quality from such pictures as *Fight That Ghost*, which looks threadbare by even this subgenre's standards. Even so, the point is the comedy, and Markham and Murray give it full ribald measure, with Murray displaying an out-and-out crooked streak and Markham ogling the ladies so aggressively as to make Mantan Moreland's occasional flirtations, as in 1941's *King of the Zombies*, look almost bashful. Markham deserved—and got—much better during this period from his stage tours, and from a Blue Note Records session that allowed him to hold forth as a singer, freed briefly of the laughmaking imperative. Before the decade ran out, he made another film, *Junction 88*, sparsely released during 1948. Markham's work over the longer haul was distinguished by several comedy albums for Chicago's Chess Records. His bluesy proto-rap, "Here Come de Judge," became a rock-and-roll crossover sensation during the soul-music craze of the waning 1960s and supplied the popular culture with a done-to-death catch-phrase.

Fight That Ghost unwittingly provoked a regional outcry over "Rastus" Murray's ram-bunctiously suggestive song, "A Brown Skin Gal Is the Best of All." The provincial censors in Maryland compromised the ethnic integrity, and the rhythm, of the tune by removing snippets of footage containing the phrase, "yellow gal."

CREDITS: Producer: Ted Toddy; Director: Sam Newfield; Story & Screen Treatment: Ted Toddy and Sam Newfield; Photographed by: Jack Etra; Assistant

Photographer: Sol Wichuall; Special Photography: Richard Marks; Assistant Director: Thomas Darby; Film Editor: Elmer J. McGovern; Sound Engineer: Nelson Minnerly; Assistant Sound Engineer: J. Burgi Contner; Makeup: R.J. Liszt; Production Manager: S. Hickman; Script Editor: Violet Neufeld; Effects Engineer: John Allstedt; Songs: "Take Me," by Porter Grainger, and "Hard Luck Blues" and "A Brown Skin Gal Is the Best of All," by John "Rastus" Murray; Running Time: 45-50 Minutes; Submitted for New York State Censors' Consideration: During April of 1946

CAST: Dewey "Pigmeat"/"Alamo" Markham (Pigmeat); John "Rastus" Murray (Shorty); Percy Verwayne (Moneybags Jim); David Bethea (Mr. Cook); Alberta Payne (Sweet Sue); Claire Leyba (Honeychile Polly); Bill Dillard (Jim Brown); George Wiltshire (Lawyer Smith); Wen Talbert (James Henry); Clarice Graham (Georgia Brown); Ray Allen (Fast Delivery Bill); Rudolph Toombs (John Mugger); Milton Woods (Bill White); Sid Easton (Spooky Lightnin')

FEAR
(Monogram Pictures Corp.)

Anne Gwynne, like Evelyn Ankers a favored but typically over-objectified leading lady of the Universal chillers, was allowed to display a greater range in her turns at the low-budget studios. She lends a thoroughly romantic, stabilizing presence to Alfred Zeisler's *Fear*, a free-handed reworking of Fyodor Dostoyevsky's *Crime and Punishment* in a noir-ified context, compromised by an awkwardly dishonest finale.

The picture belongs more rightly to Peter Cookson, who plays a hard-luck student named Larry Crain. Stripped of his scholarship, Crain places himself in hock to one of his professors, Morton Stanley (Francis Perliot), who runs a cottage-industry pawnbroker racket on the side.

After befriending a penniless young woman (Miss Gwynne) at a restaurant, Crain returns to Stanley's apartment, hiding until a housepainter (Ernie Adams) finishes working nearby, and then killing Stanley in an intended act of robbery. Spooked by the arrival of two other customers, Crain leaves empty-handed.

Crain is ill-prepared for a visit from the police, but the call is purely a courtesy extended to Prof. Stanley's clients to reclaim their belongings. A letter informs Crain that a magazine has accepted one of his articles, "Men above the Law." Crain finds his scholarship renewed, after all. Crain, who has become chummy enough with the woman from the restaurant to call her Eileen, is at once reassured and shaken by these developments. He reveals his guilt to Eileen, who seems altogether too understanding. The painter has surrendered in connection with the slaying. But a friendly, relentless police captain (Warren William) stays

on the case, mentioning offhandedly that innocent people sometimes admit to the crimes of others. Rushing to meet Eileen for an impulsive getaway, Crain is run down in traffic.

At this point, Crain wakes from a dream, which presumably had begun after the encounter at the café. Prof. Stanley arrives with a more generous loan, Crain receives word that his scholarship is back in force—and the dream-girl proves to be Crain's new neighbor in his rooming-house. Life can be sweet, even for an arrogant twit capable of such resentful, self-pitying dreams.

Cookson, of those aggressively mediocre *Kitty O'Day* pictures, fares better here as the dreamer. Francis Perliot is fittingly irritable as the professor, and Warren William is in his element as the insistent lawman. The photography is appropriately somber, brightening when Miss Gwynne graces the screen, and the pacing of Cookson's extended stalk-kill-and-flee scene is pleasantly unnerving. The whew-just-a-dream resolution is a cheat, probably nothing more than a pre-emptive sop to the censors, although it inadvertently sheds a revealing light on Cookson's character.

CREDITS: Producer: Lindsley Parsons; Director: Alfred Zeisler; Dialogue Director: Leonard Zurit; Screenplay: Dennis Cooper and Alfred Zeisler; Based upon: Dostoyevsky's *Crime and Punishment*; Photographed by: Jackson Rose; Special Effects: Bob Clark; Art Director: F. Paul Sylos; Technical Director: Dave Milton; Editor: Ace Herman; Décor: Charles Thompson and Vin Taylor; Music: Edward J. Kay; Sound: Tom Lambert; Running Time: 68 Minutes; Released: March 2, 1946

CAST: Peter Cookson (Larry Crain); Warren William (Capt. Burke); Anne Gwynne (Eileen/Cathy); Francis Perliot (Prof. Morton Stanley); Nestor Paiva (Schaefer); James Cardwell (Ben); Almira Sessions (Mrs. Williams); William Moss (Al); Harry Clay (Steve); Johnny Strong (John); Ernie Adams (Painter); Charles Calvert (Doc); Darren McGavin (Chuck); Fairfax Burger (Magician); Lee "Lasses" White (Janitor); Ken Broeker and Brick Sullivan (Cops); Carl Leviness (Tailor); Dewey Robinson (Bartender); Jack Richardson, Winnie Nard, Phyllis Ayres and Hy Jason (Bystanders)

THE MASK OF DIIJON
(Producers Releasing Corp.)

As Erich von Stroheim's lesser star vehicles go, *The Mask of Diijon* cuts the mustard quite nicely. The film is a singularly morbid variation upon a theme of show-biz paranoia that Stroheim had been exploring off and on since his first talking picture, 1929's *The Great Gabbo*. Our present period's *The Great Flamarion* covers similar ground with both repetition and innovation, and *Diijon* raises the stakes considerably. The picture feels more like some European art film than anything one would expect from Hollywood's Poverty Row.

Diijon (Stroheim) is a once-great magician who has abandoned his stagecraft to study the crackpot science of mind control. His wife, Victoria (Jeanne Bates), attempting to lure Diijon back to the arena of his moneymaking talent, works with a magic-trick inventor (Edward Van Sloan, in fine grandfatherly form) to develop a potentially crowd-pleasing guillotine routine; the charm of the device is that it is genuinely deadly if not properly operated. Diijon will have no part of it, and his refusal to accept work drives Victoria to distraction. A newly arrived friend of Victoria's, musician Tony Holiday (William Wright), offers Diijon a spot in a nightclub's floor show, and Diijon surprisingly accepts. His performance proves a fiasco, and Diijon accuses Tony of sabotaging the routine to impress Victoria.

During a visit to a late-hours eatery, Diijon chances to foil a robbery by means of hypnosis—a breakthrough that leaves him elated until he returns home to find Victoria and Tony visiting over breakfast. Drawing all the wrong conclusions, Diijon now begins plotting a murder-by-hypnosis. He tests the method on a hapless colleague (Mauritz Hugo), with harrowing results. Diijon mesmerizes Victoria, leaving her with orders to gun down Tony during a performance; the ploy works, except that her weapon proves to contain blanks. Tony, suspecting Diijon, summons the police, who trap Diijon in the inventor's shop. Diijon topples into the trick guillotine and is beheaded.

Stroheim has never seemed quite so sour as in *The Mask of Diijon*, which of course allows his character little about which to be happy. Even his success at preventing a crime becomes

Erich von Stroheim goes over the edge in *The Mask of Diijon*.

a stepping-stone to his own criminal acts, which lead to one of the more bewildering small tragedies in the long haul of cinema. Even the nightclub setting's musical numbers bear out Lew Landers' somber telling of this elemental account of misguided revenge. Edward Van Sloan contributes a gentle garnish of bemused humor, and William Wright and Hope Landin lighten things a bit with an Irish-dialect routine.

A prematurely published *Variety* review declared that *Diijon* "aims for deep dramatics which fail to register [but] could pass as a so-so horror meller." *Meller* is archaic show-speak for *melodrama*.

CREDITS: Producers: Max Alexander and Arthur Stern; Director: Lew Landers (Louis Friedlander); Screenplay: Arthur St. Claire (from His Story) and Griffin Jay; Photographed by: Jack Greenhalgh; Assistant Director: Lou Perlof; Special Effects: Ray Mercer; Editor: Roy Livingston; Music: Karl Hajos; Songs: "White Rose," by Carroll K. Cooper & Lee Zahler, and "Disillusion," by Lou E. Zoeller & Billy Austin; Sound: Ben Winkler; Running Time: 73 Minutes; Released: March 7, 1946

CAST: Erich von Stroheim (Diijon); Jeanne Bates (Victoria); William Wright (Tony Holiday); Denise Vernac (Denise); Edward Van Sloan (Sheffield); Hope Landin (Mrs. McGaffey); Mauritz Hugo (Danton); Shimen Ruskin (Guzzo)

STRANGE IMPERSONATION
(Republic Pictures Corp./William Wilder Productions, Inc.)

"Betrayal. Chemists. Disfiguration. Impersonation & Imposture. Medicine—Research. Nightmares. Accidental Death. Anesthesia. Attempted Murder. Drunkenness... Falls from Heights. Fires... Plastic Surgery. Scientific Apparatus & Instruments. Vocational Obsession." So reads the American Film Institute's subject-matter index of bases covered in Anthony Mann's *Strange Impersonation.* Having helped to assemble these monumentally well-organized indexes, which have come a long way toward detailing every film ever made in these United States from Day One onward, we could scarcely agree more with the inventory: *Strange Impersonation* is a veritable smorgasbord of ghastly clinical delights—until a sorry excuse for a denouement kicks in.

Here is another formative film in the impressive career of director Anthony Mann. The film starts out like some proto-Lifetime Network angst-opera—heroine, torn between romance and her imminent breakthroughs as a brilliant maverick scientist—but veers straightaway into outlaw medicine and horrific tragedy.

Nora Goodrich (Brenda Marshall) balks at the marriage-bound insistence of Dr. Stephan Lindstrom (William Gargan), preferring to concentrate on the development of a revolutionary anesthetic. A treacherous assistant, Arline Cole (Hillary Brooke), sets Nora's apartment/laboratory ablaze, and Nora is hideously scarred.

Arline uses the situation to settle in with Dr. Lindstrom. Nora finds herself under threat of a lawsuit from Jane Karaski (Ruth Ford), a boozer whom Nora had injured in an auto accident some length of time before the fire. Jane, pressing the shakedown too far, is killed in a struggle with Nora for control of a gun. A convenient fall disfigures Jane beyond recognition, and her corpse is identified as that of Nora. Nora steals away, indulges in reconstructive surgery to make herself resemble Jane, and returns to undermine the marriage of Arline and Dr. Lindstrom. Which she does, meanwhile coaxing Arline's confession that the fire was something more sinister than sabotage. Nora/Jane is content with the results until her fingerprints on a passport application are linked with the death of the real Jane Karaski. Nora conks out during an interrogation—and wakes to find everything perfectly normal. She abruptly asks Lindstrom to marry her.

And yes, of course, the whole thing was starting to feel like somebody's whacked-out nightmare somewhere along the way, anyhow. The pageant of torments is as absurd as it is cruel, but Mann plays the works with a straight face and a brooding sense of mounting disaster. Brenda Marshall and Ruth Ford are quite good as the antagonists forced by Fate and/or Freud into a life-swap scheme, and Hillary Brooke makes a convincing interloper. Token leading man William Gargan (1905-1979), who had landed an Oscar nomination for *They Knew What They Wanted* (1940), also is well remembered for *I Wake Up Screaming* (1941), a title-role turn in *Enemy Agents Meet Ellery Queen* (1942), and *The Canterville Ghost* (1944). A late-'50s television breakthrough, via the *Martin Kane* crime series, fell apart abruptly when a bout with cancer forced Gargan's retirement. He later became a spokesman for the American Cancer Society.

CREDITS: Producer: William Lee Wilder; Director: Anthony Mann; Screenplay: Mindret Lord; Story: Anne Wigton and Lewis Herman; Photographed by: Robert W. Pittack; Assistant Director: George Lopez; Art Director: Edward Jewell; Editor: John F. Link; Décor: Sydney Moore; Music: Alexander Laszlo; Sound: Earl Crain, Sr.; Makeup: Bud Westmore; Production Manager: Bartlett A. Carré; Running Time: 68 Minutes; Released: March 16, 1946

CAST: Brenda Marshall (Nora Goodrich); William Gargan (Dr. Stephan Lindstrom); Hillary Brooke (Arline Cole); George Chandler (Jeremiah Wilkins Rinse); Ruth Ford (Jane Karaski); H.B. Warner (Dr. Mansfield); Lyle Talbot (Inspector Malloy); Mary Treen (Nurse); Cay Forester (Miss Roper)

DEVIL BAT'S DAUGHTER
(Producers Releasing Corp.)

All these years later, and the merest mention of the old Carruthers place around this quaint Yankee village will still drive the locals to shivering fits. All these years later—actually, only six—and PRC has as good as forgotten the crucial particulars of its own seminal gallows comedy, *The Devil Bat* (1940). Was Dr. Paul Carruthers a vampire? No, actually, he was a vengeful scientist who bred a mutant species of bat to kill off his perceived enemies. But his hometown seems to remember him as more the Dracula type. Did he have a daughter? None that he mentioned, but here she comes, anyhow. Otherwise, why call the picture *Devil Bat's Daughter*?

Said title character (the wondrously vulnerable but resilient Rosemary La Planche) shows up to inspect the abandoned Carruthers mansion and falls abruptly into a trance-like state. She is placed under the care of Dr. Elliott (Nolan Leary), who calls in a psychiatrist, Dr. Cliff Morris (Michael Hale). Exploring the Carruthers place, Elliott and the sheriff (Edward Cassidy) find a weathered newspaper bannering an end to the town's so-called Devil Bat murder case, alongside a suitcase and a passport identifying the young woman as Nina McCarron, daughter of the long-defunct Dr. Carruthers.

Anyone looking for a *bona fide* sequel to *The Devil Bat* might as well give up here and turn instead to *Wild Horse Phantom*, a ripsnorting horse opera that unwittingly suggests one of Carruthers' bats might have gone maverick and headed way out West. Continuity is the overriding problem—if problem it be—beginning with the simple fact that the headline on that long-ago newspaper declares a trial and conviction for the vengeful Paul Carruthers, when in fact the finale of *The Devil Bat* had found

Carruthers done in by his own creation. The locale, called Heathville in the source-picture, becomes Wardsley here. Bela Lugosi, whose juicy portrayal of Carruthers in the original film had pretty well cinched a final exile into leading roles in lesser pictures, is nowhere to be found in *Devil Bat's Daughter*, which at least could have used a flashback or two. (The nearest thing to a flashback is the recycling of footage, in a dream-state context.)

But then, a flashback would have bound *Devil Bat's Daughter* more emphatically to the source-film—and all PRC really wanted from the kinship was an exploitable title. Saddling the immigrant director Frank Bentick Wisbar with the project was merely a matter of assigning him the title and allowing him to take it from there, rather like RKO-Radio Pictures had done in ordering Val Lewton to turn such inflexibly lurid titles as *I Walked with a Zombie* and *Curse of the Cat People* into what stories he would. (And yes, *Curse of the Cat People* is itself more fugue than sequel in relation to Lewton's original *Cat People*.)

Wisbar had worked wonders for PRC with a seriously artistic remake of his own German masterwork, *Fahrmann Maria*, under the sensationalized title *Strangler of the Swamp*. He and scenarist Griffin Jay drastically reworked the postulation of *The Devil Bat*—which had came from other talents entirely—into a forward-thinking terrors-of-the-mind scenario. And Wisbar strategically positioned Rosemary La Planche as a focus for psychological torments, implanted by a wicked shrink who'd have her believe herself descended from a madman, if not an out-and-out vampire.

Michael Hale's Dr. Morris is plotting to do away with his wealthy wife, Ellen (Molly Lamont). The arrival of Ted Masters (John James), Ellen's son from a prior marriage, complicates matters more than somewhat. Morris intends to frame Nina, with her vampire fixation, in the inevitable slaying of Ellen. Ted, who has never particularly liked Morris, falls in love with Nina. Such a rotter is Morris that he kills Ted's pet dog and allows Nina to accept the blame. This frame-up scenario is replayed with the death of Ellen. Ted still suspects his stepfather and sets out to crack the case.

A subplot involving the missing research papers of Dr. Carruthers turns up proof that Nina's father wasn't such a bad sort, after all—merely a misunderstood genius, whose ambitions to improve the lot of humankind had gone tragically awry. Try telling that to Bela Lugosi, who had given his all to make *The Devil Bat*'s leading character as calculating a Grand Manner menace as ever stalked the screen.

And so it is with admiring but mixed feelings that we consign *Devil Bat's Daughter* to the ranks of *Forgotten Horrors* in the hope of rendering it less thoroughly forgotten. The tampering with the source's bitterly droll premise is nothing that will either vindicate the 1940 film in the eyes of its detractors or ruin it for its devotees. And *Daughter* stands on its own as a study of progressive medicine applied for purely wicked purposes.

PRC formally remade *The Devil Bat*, also in 1946, as *The Flying Serpent*, with George Zucco.

CREDITS: Producer and Director: Frank Bentick Wisbar; Associate Producer: Carl Pierson; Dialogue Director: Harold Erickson; Screenplay; Griffin Jay; Story: Leo J. McCarthy and Ernst Jaeger; Photographed by: James S. Brown, Jr.; Assistant Director: Louis Germonprez; Special Effects: Ray Mercer; Art Director: Edward C. Jewell; Editor: Douglas W. Bagier; Décor: Glenn P. Thompson; Wardrobe: Karlice; Music: Alexander Steinert; Sound: Earl Sitar; Production Manager: Norman Cook; Running Time: 67 Minutes; Released: April 15, 1946

CAST: Rosemary La Planche (Nina MacCarron); John James (Ted Masters); Michael Hale (Cliff Morris); Molly Lamont (Ellen Morris); Nolan Leary (Dr. Elliott); Monica Mars (Myra Arnold); Edward Cassidy (Sheriff)

THE CATMAN OF PARIS
(Republic Pictures Corp.)

Seldom did Republic trespass on the ersatz-European turf of Universal Pictures' horror-movie factory. Although the ambitious littler studio came admirably well equipped to recapture an Old World ambiance, it generally went its own way in forging a Gothic chiller style. *The Catman of Paris*, that rare stab at a Universal-type piece, crucially flubs the creature design and makeup. Where *Variety* lauded the appearance of the title menace as certain "to earn balcony shrieks," a comparison of the monster's aspect with the finely realized bogeymen of Universal's *Wolf Man*, *Mummy* &c. series finds Republic's makeup chief, Bob Mark, thoroughly lacking.

Director Lesley Selander finds a more assured pace here than he had on 1945's *The Vampire's Ghost*. His greater confidence with an outlandish premise allows the homicidal impulses of Douglass Dumbrille to account for a loping narrative rhythm. The title character is not the leading character, which makes for an interesting twist, and the hero turns out to be a hapless if courageous sort who finds himself suspected of being a superhuman killer.

Author Charles Regnier (Carl Esmond), pronounced an enemy of the state for his inflammatory writings about a corrupt judiciary, is dining with a friend, Borchard (Dumbrille), when suddenly afflicted with hallucinations involving a cat. That night, a government fink (Francis McDonald), seeking to implicate Regnier in a conspiracy, is slashed to death. Regnier begins to wonder whether he might be the killer.

Though engaged to marry Marguerite Duval (Adele Mara), Regnier takes up with Marie Audet (Lenore Aubert), daughter of his publisher. Marguerite

The Catman of Paris works on all counts but that blasted monster get-up.

complains to Borchard; later, she is killed by a catlike attacker. Marie prevents Regnier from turning himself in to the law. Regnier believes that Marie will be the next victim—and sure enough, she *nearly* is. The police gun down the catman just in time and find him to be a transformed Borchard, who had appointed himself rather a guardian demon to Regnier. Borchard announces that this death puts the wraps on his ninth and final incarnation as the catman.

On *Variety*'s condition that credulity be duly indulged, *The Catman of Paris* works on all counts but that blasted monster get-up, which looks like some schoolkid's idea of a really scary Halloween costume—pointed ears, an inflexible scowl and an opera topper. The performances are across-the-board redeeming, however, and the film's refusal to over-explain the existence of the were-cat is a welcome bit of restraint.

The Catman of Paris is a companion production of *Valley of the Zombies*, with shooting schedules and a marketing campaign in common.

CREDITS: Associate Producer: Marek M. Libkov; Director: Lesley Selander; Screenplay: Sherman L. Lowe; Photographed by: Reggie Lanning; Assistant Director: John Grubbs; Second Camera: Herbert Kilpatrick; Special Effects: Howard Lydecker and Theodore Lydecker; Matte Paintings: Lewis Physioc; Transparency Projection Shots: Gordon Schaefer; Art Director: Gano Chittenden; Editor: Harry Keller; Set Dresser: John McCarthy, Jr.; Music: Dale Butts; Dance Director: Larry Ceballos; Sound: Fred Stahl; Re-Recording and

Effects Mixers: Thomas A. Carman and Howard Wilson; Music Mixer: John Stransky, Jr.; Makeup: Bob Mark; Running Time: 65 Minutes; Released: April 20, 1946

CAST: Carl Esmond (Charles Regnier); Lenore Aubert (Marie Audet); Adele Mara (Marguerite Duval); Douglass Dumbrille (Henry Borchard); Gerald Mohr (Inspector Severen); Fritz Feld (Prefect of Police); Francis Perliot (Paul Audet); George Renavent (Guillard); Francis McDonald (Devereaux); Maurice Cass (Paul deRoche); Alphonse Martell (Maurice Cavaignac); Paul Marion (Jules); John Dehner (Georges); Anthony Caruso (Raoul); Carl Neubert (Philippe); Elaine Lange (Blanche de Clermont); Tanis Chandler (Yvette); George Davis (Concierge); Albert Petit and Gino Corrado (Policeman); Jean de Briac (Butler); Louis Mercier (Old Man); Eugene Borden (Porter); Steve Darrell (Driver)

THE GLASS ALIBI
(Republic Pictures Corp.)

William Lee Wilder, already promisingly established as a producer, weighed in as a director with this tale of journalistic corruption an overconfident sneak-attack killer and an ironic outcropping of damning circumstantial evidence. Wilder's impressive grasp of suspense here foreshadows no particular greatness to come, and within a decade his name would become more indelibly associated with such tedious fare as *Snow Creature* (1954) and *Spell of the Hypnotist* (1956).

While holding ailing heiress Linda Vale (Maris Wrixon) hostage in her home at Malibu, fugitive convict Red Hogan (Cy Kendall) telephones his mistress, Belle Marlin (Anne Gwynne). Belle happens to be entertaining news reporter Joe Eykner (Douglas Fowley) at the moment, and Eykner engineers a scoop by alerting his pal Max Anderson (Paul Kelly), a police lieutenant, to Hogan's whereabouts. The resulting bust also serves to acquaint Eykner with Linda, who proves to have not only a fortune at her disposal but also a life expectancy of mere months. Eykner conspires to marry Linda, meanwhile allowing Belle to support him in style with Hogan's money.

Linda rallies and flourishes as the engineered romance progresses to marriage. Desperate to see Linda dead, Eykner resorts to substituting aspirin for her heart medication, then escalates to measures more direct. Sending the impatient Belle to Palm Springs, Eykner visits her hotel suite and makes a point of leaving fingerprints on every polished surface. Then he rushes back home to Malibu and empties a gun into Linda as she lies abed.

Lt. Anderson, who has followed the situation with concern, suspects Eykner despite his show of bereavement and that convenient "glass alibi." The coroner (Walter Soderling) determines that Linda had already died of heart failure before the shooting. Meanwhile, Belle has been murdered—no doubt by a vengeful Red, who has escaped all over again. Eykner's fingerprints in Belle's hotel room, however, make him the likelier candidate for a murder rap. Red and his henchman, Benny (Jack Conrad), might clear Eykner, but they have been killed in a showdown with the law.

LIBERTY 4th Street Palace
Sunset Carson in
"Rough Riders of Cheyenne"
Also Paul Kelly and Anne Gwynne in
"The Glass Alibi"

The production values are substantial, with the contrasting settings of underworld and upper crust providing a vivid backdrop for Douglas Fowley's conniving progress. Extensive Southern California location work is a big help toward grounding the tale in a recognizable reality. Anne Gwynne is at once seductive and creepy as the gang moll who underwrites Fowley's infiltration of Maris Wrixon's shaky orbit, demanding a great deal more in return than she winds up receiving. Miss Wrixon is more emotionally than physically convincing as the doomed heiress, with a vibrant presence better suited to the character's seeming recovery; her supposed slaying is a shocker that is soon compounded by a yet grimmer autopsy report. Top-billed Paul Kelly is quite good as the determined plainclothesman who is chagrined to watch a friend degenerate into a career of murder, but Fowley carries the picture as the crooked news-hack. Cy Kendall is rightly formidable as the cuckolded gangster, and Jack Conrad contributes a fair measure of brutish menace as Kendall's chief enforcer.

CREDITS: Producer and Director: W. Lee Wilder; Screenplay; Mindret Lord; Photographed by: Henry Sharp; Editors: John F. Link and Asa Clark; Wardrobe: Lucille Sothern; Music: Alexander Laszlo; Sound: Ferol Redd; Makeup: Jack Casey; Running Time: 68 Minutes; Released: April 27, 1946

CAST: Paul Kelly (Max Anderson); Douglas Fowley (Joe Eykner); Anne Gwynne (Belle Marlin); Maris Wrixon (Linda Vale); Selmer Jackson (Dr. John F. Lawson); Cyril Thornton (Riggs); Cy Kendall (Red Hogan); Walter Soderling (Coroner); Vic Potel (Gas Station Attendant); George Chandler (Bartender); Phyllis Adair (Nurse); Ted Stanhope (Pharmacy Clerk); Dick Scott (Frank)

PASSKEY TO DANGER
(Republic Pictures Corp.)

Gregory Gay heads up a fine mob of sorehead paranoid heavies in Lesley Selander's *Passkey to Danger*, an unusual attempt to extract weird menace from the contrived mystique of the advertising industry. Adman Tex Hanlon (Kane Richmond) is the brains behind a high-fashion campaign calculated to keep the public guessing: He calls this campaign "Three Springs," and veils it with such secrecy that even his client, couturier Malcolm Tauber (Gerald Mohr), is in the dark. Hanlon's big surprise is that the final installment of his ad blitz will reveal three models, labeled "Palm Springs," "Sarasota Springs" and "Colorado Springs." Only Gwen Hughes (Stephanie Bachelor), Taubert's assistant and Hanlon's fiancée, is in on the secret—which has already begun to attract snoopers.

Hanlon laughs off a warning note. An alluring stranger named Renée Beauchamps (Adele Mara) approaches Hanlon to seek a job and then tries to steal his production sketches. A rival fashion designer named Warren (Gay) demands to know the lowdown on the "Three Springs" pitch, and when Hanlon refuses to talk Warren unleashes a brutal flunky (Fred Graham). Gwen tries a new approach, offering to help Hanlon. Then a meat-packing executive, Leighton (George J. Lewis), offers a hefty sum on condition that Hanlon abandon the campaign. Another caller, Cardovsky (John Eldredge), ups the offer considerably. An astrologer (Donia Bussey) attempts to warn Hanlon and gets murdered for her trouble. Renee plots to marry Hanlon and thus obtain his big secret—but then is forced to admit that she is in cahoots with his persecutors.

The underworld connection is borne out when a notorious family of crooks known as the Spring Bros. proves to have sensed a shakedown attempt in the innocuous "Three Springs" promotion. The Springs are fugitives, moving about under assumed names, and the last thing they want is attention. Hanlon, indignant at the intrusion, hooks up with an investigator (Tom London) to trap the Springs, who retaliate by ordering Renée's murder. The brothers, hiding in more-or-less plain sight, prove to be designer Tauber, meat packer Leighton and the elusive Cardovsky. Warren, revealed as the brothers' prison-break connection, loses patience with his accomplices and has begun to kill them off before the police can make the scene.

The gimmicky plot is a tangle of stretches, but Selander gives it a brisk pace and terse, meaningful characterizations, especially from Gay, Adele Mara and Gerald Mohr. Kane Richmond is likably flustered as the marketing whiz who

is forced into a sleuthing job of which he wants no part. Similarly innocent bursts of creativity have triggered the killing urge in Real World grouches who, like these Spring Bros., have no sense of humor and no desire to develop one.

CREDITS: Associate Producer: William J. O'Sullivan; Director: Lesley Selander; Screenplay:

O'Leta Rhinehart and William Hagens; Photographed by: William Bradford; Assistant Director: Don Verk; Second Camera: Joseph Novak; Matte Paintings: Lewis Physioc; Miniatures and Special Optical Effects: Howard Lydecker and Theodore Lydecker; Editor: Harry Keller; Music: Richard Cherwin; Sound: Victor Appel; Makeup: Bob Mark; Running Time: 58 Minutes; Released: May 11, 1946

CAST: Kane Richmond (Tex Hanlon); Stephanie Bachelor (Gwen Hughes); Adele Mara (Renée Beauchamps); Gregory Gay (Warren); Gerald Mohr (Malcolm Tauber); John Eldredge (Alex Cardovsky); George H. Lewis (Julian Leighton); Fred Graham (Bert); Tom London (Gerald Bates); Donia Bussey (Jenny); Charles Williams (Williams); Charles Wilson and Bob Wilke (Sergeants)

JUNGLE TERROR
(Favorite Films, Inc.)

This erratically distributed feature-lengther is a condensation of the Weiss Bros.' 1937 serial *Jungle Menace*, itself a star vehicle for the expeditioner Frank Buck. Buck had closed out his moviemaking career—barring an appearance in the Abbott & Costello spoof *Africa Screams* (1949)—with 1943's *Tiger Fangs*.

Jungle Terror is distanced from its chapter-play origins by a separate production-and-distribution company and a shoddy job of archival preservation. Documents filed in 1946 by Favorite Films, Inc., with the New York Board of Censors neglect to link *Jungle Terror* with its Weiss-company pedigree (Adventure Serials, Inc.) and supply only the characters' names without the players' identities.

Ascribe the solution to film enthusiast Rich Wannen, who pegged the hidden connection shortly after the arrival of the first edition of *Forgotten Horrors 3* in 2003. We had cited *Jungle Terror* as a more elusive entry. Wannen provided the information in time for an update in *Forgotten Horrors 4* (2007).

The story, as streamlined from *Jungle Menace*, concerns a campaign of murder stemming from a rubber-smuggling racket in Malaysia. The menace stems as much from tribal unrest and rampant tigers as from colonial villainy.

Favorite Films officed in New York at 630 Ninth Avenue and, later, at 151 W. 46th Street. The company was headed by Moe Kerman as president, J.J. Felder as vice president, and Leo Seligman as comptroller. The little company advertised fairly prominently in the show industry's almanacs, but even the near-comprehensive *Film Daily Year Book of Motion Pictures* neglects to mention *Jungle Terror* among its "Titles Released since 1915" inventories.

CREDITS: Executive Producer: Robert Mintz; Producer: Louis Weiss; Directors: Harry L. Fraser and George Melford; Story and Screenplay: George M. Merrick, Sherman L. Lowe, Harry O. Hoyt, George Melford, George Rosener, Arthur Hoerl, Dallas M. Fitzgerald, and Gordon Griffith; Photographed by: Edward Linden and Herman Schopp; Editor: Earl Turner; Running Time: 70 Minutes; Feature Version of 1937 Serial *Jungle Menace*, Submitted in this Version for New York Censors' Consideration on May 16, 1946; Released: Sporadic Distribution, Beginning in June 1946

CAST: Frank Buck (Frank Hardy); Charlotte Henry (Dorothy Elliott); LeRoy Mason (Murphy); Duncan Renaldo (Rogét); Richard Tucker (Robert Banning); Sasha Siemel (Tiger Van Dorn); John Davidson (Dr. Coleman); George Rosener (Professor); William Bakewell (Tom Banning); Matthew Betz (Lt. Starrett); Robert Warwick (Inspector Angus MacLeod); Dirk Thane (Joe Nolan); Willie Fung (Chang); Gertrude Sutton (Mrs. Maitland); Clarence Muse (Shuffle); John St. Polis (Edward Elliott); Reginald Denny (Ralph Marshall)

VALLEY OF THE ZOMBIES
(Republic Pictures Corp.)

There are degrees of forgotten-ness, of course, among the blurred genres of the *Forgotten Horrors* selections. A majority will have been forgotten outright, popularly unseen for generations and probably just vaguely recollected by even those hellbent-for-completism souls who stake out the obscure-video Web sites and Xerocopy catalogs and the late-night one-lung TV stations. Other features, such as *Valley of the Zombies*, remain vaguely familiar, their chief function now retooled to that of provoking fashionable sneers from people who take the more forcibly snarky published accounts at their word that these pictures are merely laughable stinkeroos.

What lies forgotten for the most part about *Valley of the Zombies* is that it's a respectable stab at innovation in an overworked walking-dead subgenre, with a righteously creepy show of surly malice from dependable Ian Keith. One 20th-century reference cites "a total lack of zombies," and another snipes that "the script seems to have exhausted its supply of wit in finding the name Ormand Murks" for Keith's character. And yes, perhaps the chap bearing that Dickensian monicker is more vampire than zombie—but he is withal a sure-enough ambulatory stiff, with a death-certificate pedigree from the very clinic where he had croaked on the operating table. And he seems dead-set, you should forgive the expression, upon administering a dose of embalming fluid to anyone who crosses him.

Not to put too fine a point on it, but *Variety* in 1946 called Keith "an un-zombielike zombie [in] a fairly horrorless story." Those perceived debits may, in fact, be the greater strength of the picture—a defiance of convention in the portrayal of a soulless monster who does more lurking than lurching: The mood is the menace. The anonymous *Variety* reviewer kvetched further that "the zombie... looks more like a mean college professor" but allowed as how the picture "[is] pretty fair Saturday matinee stuff," with seasoned ensemble acting at "a good B level." Damnation by faint praise, in other words.

Robert Livingston and Adrian Booth meet no zombies in *Valley of the Zombies*.

We are not here to suggest that *Valley of the Zombies* is any rediscovered classic, but the film bears a more thoughtful consideration within the layered contexts of its genre, its studio and its day and age.

The picture opens with an eerily photographed twilight townscape. A gaunt figure creeps across the rooftops toward the office of Dr. Rufus Maynard (Charles Trowbridge). Maynard's laboratory has experienced a rash of blood thefts, and now fresher plasma is sought—from the doctor himself. But first, the intruder reintroduces himself as Ormond Murks, whom Maynard had consigned five years ago to an asylum. Murks' mania had caused him to believe that a regimen of transfusions would render him immortal, and when Maynard had later attempted to treat him Murks had died of no obvious cause. Murks speaks of some "valley of the zombies," where he has discovered a state of existence between life and death. As if to dramatize his point, Murks strangles the doctor, then drains him of blood and embalms the corpse.

The case provokes an investigation by Dr. Terry Evans (Robert Livingston) and nurse Susan Drake (Adrian Booth), who go prowling about the Murks estate and find the crypt empty. Dr. Garland (Wilton Graff), who had treated Murks at the asylum, turns up slain. Murks hypnotizes Susan into carrying out his orders, only to run afoul of Dr. Evans and a detective (Thomas Jackson), who dispatches the supernatural fiend with an ordinary bullet.

Keith's persuasive portrayal goes a long way toward lifting *Valley* above the clichés of the genre, which persist despite the inventive characterization. Bob

Livingston is as heroic here as in his better-known Western assignments, and Adrian Booth makes a winning sleuth-become-pawn, who at one point turns as numbly menacing as Keith.

Valley's companion film, produced simultaneously for a cross-marketing strategy, is Lesley Selander's *The Catman of Paris*.

CREDITS: Associate Producers and Screenwriters: Dorrell McGowan and Stuart McGowan; Director: Philip Ford; Story: Royal K. Cole and Sherman L. Lowe; Photographed by: Reggie Lanning; Assistant Director: Joe Dill; Second Camera: Herbert Kirkpatrick; Special Effects: Howard Lydecker and Theodore Lydecker; Matte Paintings: Lewis Physioc; Transparency Projection Shots: Gordon Schaefer; Art Director: Hilyard Brown; Editor: William P. Thompson; Music: Richard Cherwin; Sound: Fred Stahl; Makeup: Bob Mark; Running Time: 56 Minutes; Released: May 24, 1946

CAST: Robert Livingston (Dr. Terry Evans); Adrian Booth (Susan Drake); Ian Keith (Ormand Murks); Thomas Jackson (Blair); Charles Trowbridge (Dr. Rufus Maynard); Earle Hodgins (Fred Mays); LeRoy Mason (Hendricks); William Haade (Tiny); Wilton Graff (Dr. Garland)

GHOST OF HIDDEN VALLEY
(Sigmund Neufeld Productions, Inc./Producers Releasing Corp.)

Another spook-decoyed entry in the *Billy Carson* series, *Ghost of Hidden Valley* makes far less of the element of superstition than *His Brother's Ghost*. It is curious that Al "Fuzzy" St. John, who had derived such glee from pretending to be a vengeful revenant in the earlier film, should portray that same Fuzzy Q. Jones here as a chap with a healthy fear of ghosts.

Cattle rustler Ed Dawson (Charles King) makes a practice of gunning down anyone who gets in his way, certain that each new killing will be blamed upon a spirit supposed to haunt the long-abandoned Hidden Valley. So since when does a ghost pack a shootin'-iron? Anyhow, meanwhile, Billy Carson (Buster Crabbe) and Fuzzy Jones greet a new arrival from England, Henry Trenton (John Meredith), heir to a ranch. Assigning themselves as protectors of Trenton and his butler

(Jimmy Aubrey), Billy and Fuzzy determine that the mob has been hiding stolen cattle at the Trenton ranch.

Dawson, whose conscience has begun nagging him, decides he wants out of the racket. Henchman Arnold (Zon Murray) kills Dawson and declares himself the new boss, then attempts to frame Billy for Dawson's murder. No such luck, of course, and the rangeland is rendered safe once again without any sustained delivery on the title's promise of ghostly delights. John Meredith and Jimmy Aubrey, as the tenderfoot Englanders, provide little more than a distraction from Buster Crabbe's heroism and Fuzzy St. John's crochety antics.

CREDITS: Producer: Sigmund Neufeld; Director: Sam Newfield; Story and Screenplay: Ellen Coyle; Photographed by: Art Reed; Assistant Director: Stanley Neufeld; Second Camera: Ralph Ash; Special Effects: Ray Mercer and Ray Smallwood; Art Director: Edward C. Jewell; Editor: Holbrook N. Todd; Music: Lee Zahler; Sound: Glen Glenn; Re-Recording and Effects Mixer: Joseph I. Kane; Music Mixer: William Wilmarth; Production Manager: Bert Sternbach; Running Time: 57 Minutes; Released: June 3, 1946

CAST: Buster Crabbe (Billy Carson); Al "Fuzzy" St. John (Fuzzy Q. Jones); Jean Carlin (Kaye); John Meredith (Henry Trenton); Charles King (Ed Dawson); Jimmy Aubrey (Tweedle); Karl Hackett (Zed); John L. Carson (Sweeney); Silver Harr (Stage Gunner); Zon Murray (Arnold)

SUSPENSE
(King Bros. Productions/Monogram Pictures Corp.)

Maurice and Franklin King assembled an ensemble cast of bigger names than usual for this first million-dollar extravaganza from a striving little studio. Monogram Pictures, of course, would stay small and soft-pedal the striving over the longer haul. Both literally and figuratively a chiller, *Suspense* is at once a ballet-on-ice musical and a grim crime melodrama, with keen production numbers showcasing the lovely skating star Belita and a missing-corpse situation that leads to a rewardingly honest downbeat ending.

Barry Sullivan is Joe Morgan, a charming sneak who takes a job with ice-follies impresario Frank Leonard (Albert Dekker). Finding himself lusting after Leonard's wife, exhibition skater Roberta Elva (Belita), Morgan implements refinements that will render her performances more thrilling; these win him a promotion. Ronnie (Bonita Granville), Joe's former sweetheart, tracks him from New York in an attempt to reclaim his affections. Following Frank and Roberta to their mountainside hunting lodge, Joe makes a sufficient nuisance of himself to provoke Frank into a murder attempt. Frank disappears after a blast from his gun triggers an avalanche.

Roberta and Joe return to Los Angeles, where Roberta insists she believes Frank has survived. During a party, Joe is unnerved to find in his champagne glass a piece of Frank's jewelry. At the ice show's offices, Roberta observes Joe securing a desk that is usually kept unlocked; next day, the desk has vanished. Confronted by Roberta, Joe admits he killed Frank and hid the body in the desk, which he then ordered trashed and burned. Roberta leaves it up to Joe's conscience to surrender to the police.

Ronnie, meanwhile, has dug up sufficient dirt from Joe's secretive past to threaten him with blackmail if he will not marry her; he retaliates brutally. Just before the next show, Joe sabotages Roberta's stage riggings; he reconsiders, then, and stops the presentation until he can disable the death-trap. Joe exits the ice pavilion. Ronnie, waiting outside, guns him down in cold blood.

Director Frank Tuttle maneuvers the glitzy musical segments and the murderous treacheries into a seamlessly well-integrated whole, with nary a wasted moment in an extraordinarily lengthy 103 minutes. Philip Yordan's screenplay refers wittily to a legend fundamental to the film noir movement, the Southern folk-tale and ballad of "Frankie and Johnnie," in a secondary plot about the scorned lover who resorts to blood vengeance after all else has failed. Yordan's central concern, however, is with the cunning and ruthless young up-and-comer.

Sullivan's display of brash overconfidence recalls that of the novelist Budd Schulberg's most celebrated fictional character, the show-biz schemer Sammy Glickstein of *What Makes Sammy Run?*—published in 1941, and long a daunting challenge to everyone who has tried and failed to make a film of it. Of course, Sammy Glickstein's rottenness is more of the lapsed-ethics variety and Sammy survives to keep running at the novel's end, but the resemblance is patent, from the extraordinary secrecy to the relentlessly underhanded deeds. (There have been successful versions of *Sammy* for the stage and early-day television, which once was a more risk-prone medium. But in times more recent, such prominent screen actors as Michael J. Fox and Ben Stiller have been thwarted in their ambitions to tackle *Sammy* for the big screen. The sticking point, in skittish corporate Hollywood, is the character's loathsome essence as an anti-Semitic Jew. Schulberg himself, with director Elia Kazan, mounted a highly satisfactory variant of *Sammy* with 1957's *A Face in the Crowd*, starring Andy Griffith as a redneck vagrant who finagles his way into a station of influence.) *Suspense* lacks the timeless cultural resonance of *Sammy*, but Sullivan's nuanced yet forceful portrayal of a richly written character elevates the film.

Ice ballet was second-nature to Belita (*née* Gladys Lyne Jepson-Turner), who starred at age 14 in the 1937 London production of *Opera on Ice* and then toured extensively with the *Ice Capades* revues. Exploiting this talent as an intro to Hollywood in 1941, she proved herself along the way a capable leading lady and character player. Her production numbers here, including a hair-raising leap through a ring of flashing blades, are staged by Nick Castle.

As Belita's showman husband, Albert Dekker seems both genial and formidable. The husky Dekker—often typecast as a threatening sort, thanks to his popular impact in *Dr. Cyclops* and *Among the Living*—was in the midst of a term of office in the California State Legislature when he made *Suspense*. Bonita Granville, a former child star whose vivacious presence often disqualified her for more serious roles, is vulnerably indignant as the jilted sweetheart who accounts for the bracing finale. Gruff Eugene Pallette contributes another winning turn, as Dekker's right-hand man.

CREDITS: Producers: Maurice King and Franklin King; Director: Frank Tuttle; Screenplay: Frank Yordan; Photographed by: Karl Struss; Assistant Director; Frank S. Heath; Second Camera: Fleet Southcott; Special Effects: Jack Shaw, Ray Mercer, Larry Glickman and Mario Castegnaro; Art Director: F. Paul Sylos; Editor: Otho Lovering and Richard Heermance; Décor: George James Hopkins; Costumer: Robert Kalloch; Music: Daniele Amfitheatrof; Music Editor: Al Teeter; Songs: "East Side Boogie," by Tommy Reilly, "With You in My Arms," by Alexander & Dunham, and "Cabildo," by Miguelito Valdes; Sound: Tom Lambert; Running Time: 103 Minutes; Released: June 15, 1946

CAST: Belita (Roberta Elva); Barry Sullivan (Joe Morgan); Bonita Granville (Ronnie); Albert Dekker (Frank Leonard); Eugene Pallette (Harry Wheeler); George E. Stone (Max); Edit Angold (Nora); Leon Belasco (Pierre); Miguelito Valdes, Bobby Ramos, Billy Nelson, Robert Middlemass and Lee "Lasses" White (Woodsmen); Byron Foulger (Cabbie); Nestor Paiva and Dewey Robinson (Men with Blonde); Marian Martin (Blonde); George Chandler (Louie); Frank Scannell (Monk); Sidney Melton (Smiles)

AVALANCHE
(Imperial Productions/Producers Releasing Corp.)

Bruce Cabot's early years in Hollywood were demarcated by the exquisitely robust extremes of *King Kong* (1933) and, on the villainous side, *Let 'Em Have It* and *Show Them No Mercy!* (both from 1935). Cabot, scion of an aristocratic French-Indian family of New Mexico, was handicapped by a lack of acting experience when he made *Kong*, during whose production, as he told us in 1969, "I just did what I was told and collected my weekly paycheck." He soon overcame that deficiency, however, and by 1935 the *New York Times* would hail Cabot's performance in *Show Them No Mercy!* as one of the year's finest, citing a presence of "cold brutality and macabre humor" in counterpoint to the heroic resourcefulness Cabot had shown in *Kong*. Cabot proved equally memorable as Magua in *The Last of the Mohicans* (1936).

For four decades, the six-foot-two Cabot kept alternating between heroism and villainy, taking time out for Army Intelligence duty during World War II and overall pursuing an off-screen life as adventurous as the roles he played. When Cabot died in 1972 at age 68, most of the obituary notices led off with the headline-friendly phrase "*King Kong* hero," despite his scores of other roles.

Perhaps the most obscure of those other roles is that of U.S. Treasury Agent Steve Batchellor in Irving Allen's *Avalanche*. This unprepossessing production suffers from a too-loquacious script, an absence of spectacle—the title's payoff is late and lacking—and a willingness to allow some magnificent scenery and a wealth of stunt-skiing routines to fill in for a more involving story. Cabot is quite good, under the circumstances, as is comic-relief specialist Roscoe Karns, who plays a fellow agent.

Believing crooked industrialist Giles Gilby to be hiding out in a mountainous region, T-Men Batchellor and Red Kelly (Karns) visit a ski lodge, where they are welcomed by Ann Watson (Helen Mowery) and skiing pro Sven Worden (John Good). Kelly notices that one guest, Malone (Philip Van Zandt), is packing a gun. Gilby is indeed known here, but he is overdue to return from an excursion. A report of snow-slides prompts a search mission. An eccentric mountain-dweller (Eddy Waller) leads the party to a corpse whose face has been blasted away. Worden identifies the victim as Gilby.

Returning to the lodge, the searchers find themselves trapped by intensifying slides. Ann reveals that Gilby had strongarmed his way into ownership of the resort. Batchellor, recovering from an ambush suffered while investigating Gilby's rooms, learns that Malone had come here to collect a gambling debt from Gilby. It develops that the murdered man was in fact one of Malone's thugs. Another guest turns up dead. Then, outside, Gilby's body is found—impaled upon a ski pole. Batchellor pegs Worden as the killer, who at first was working on Gilby's orders but finally murdered Gilby out of greed. Worden, attempting to escape, is buried alive in a collapsing wall of snow.

Cabot offers his usual commanding presence, but the overwritten yarn makes it a strain; Cabot fared best in understated situations. John Good tries a bit too hard as the murderer. Veda Ann Borg stands out as a troublemaking guest. The real scene-stealer is a trained raven named Joe, in the service of comical bartender Syd Saylor. The production manager is Albert R. Broccoli, later the mastermind of the *James Bond* series.

CREDITS: Producer: Pat Di Cicco; Director: Irving Allen; Screenplay: Andrew Holt; Photographed by: Jack Greenhalgh; Assistant Director: Louis Germonprez; Special Effects: Ray Mercer; Art Director: Edward C. Jewell; Editor: Louis Sackin; Sets: Glenn P. Thompson; Costumer: Karlice; Musical Director: Lud Gluskin; Musical Score: Lucien Moraweck and René Garriguenc; Sound: Percy Townsend and W.N. Dalgleish; Makeup: Bud Westmore; Production Manager: Albert R. Broccoli; Puppetry: Russ Clark; Running Time: 70 Minutes; Released: June 20, 1946

CAST: Bruce Cabot: Steve Batchellor; Roscoe Karns (Red Kelly); Helen Mowery (Ann Watson); Veda Ann Borg (Claire Jeremy); Regina Morris (Eva Morris); John Good (Sven Worden); Philip Van Zandt (Malone); Eddie Parks (Carlton Morris); Wilton Graff (Austin Jeremy); Henry Hays Morgan (Duncan); Eddie Hyams (Jean); Eddy Waller (Sam); Syd Saylor (Bartender); Joe (Raven)

GO DOWN, DEATH!
(Sack Amusements Enterprises)

The pioneering black filmmaker Spencer Williams, Jr., is a key figure in the *Forgotten Horrors* canon and beyond. *Son of Ingagi* and *The Blood of Jesus* are enough in themselves to establish Williams as a force with whom to reckon in independent filmmaking as a class.

Williams' 1946 film *Dirty Gertie from Harlem, U.S.A.* likewise fits *Forgotten Horrors'* criteria of prevailing doom and an ineffable eccentricity. *Go*

Down, Death! is a tougher call, for it is primarily a religious film—nowhere near as relentlessly weird as *The Blood of Jesus*, but nonetheless suffused with a ghostly presence and a sense of hellborne desperation, to say nothing of its own palpable orientation between the holy and the profane.

Williams plays underworld honcho Big Jim Bottom, who frames a reform-minded preacher on a morals rap. The incriminating photograph that results is destroyed with help from the ghost of Jim's uncle. Jim angrily strikes the righteous aunt who had raised him from orphanhood—killing her. Tormented by conscience, Big Jim takes flight, imagining himself dragged into Hades. Next day, Jim's body is found in a desolate ravine.

Dr. G. William Jones, the Dallas film archivist who spearheaded a restoration campaign for a number of Williams' movies, pegged *Go Down, Death!* as a 1944 release, relying on preproduction notes dating from that year. The Motion Picture Association's Production Code archives, however, show the movie to have been submitted for approval in July of 1946. Regional censorship hassles stalled distribution to as late as 1947—there were problems with what the bluenoses termed lascivious content, including flashes of nudity—and Ohio's censors in 1948 demanded the removal of a scene where a demon chomps down on a human figure.

The picture takes its title and its message from James Weldon Johnson's famed narrative poem, "Go Down, Death!" whose soul-harvesting scenario figures in a funeral scene. Publicity materials refer to the film as *Go Down, Death! The Story of Jesus and the Devil*. Williams is quite affecting as the remorseless mob boss who wises up rather a bit too late to save his snakebit soul.

The crucial films of Spencer Williams are *Son of Ingagi* (1940); *The Blood of Jesus* (1941); *Brother Martin* (1942); *Marchin' On*, a.k.a. *Where's My Man Tonight?* (1943); *Of One Blood* (1944); *Dirty Gertie from Harlem, U.S.A.*, *The Girl in Room 20*, *Go Down, Death!* and *Beale Street Mama* (1946); and *Juke Joint* (1947). The Texas filmmaker Walid Khaldi delivered a documentary survey, *Spencer Williams: Reminiscences of a Black Film Pioneer*, in 1996.

CREDITS: Presented by: Alfred N. Sack; Director: Spencer Williams; Dialogue

Director: Robert M. Moscow; Screenplay: Sam Elljay; Story Idea: Jean Roddy; After the Poem by: James Weldon Johnson; Photographed by: H.W. Keir; Editor: I.J. Powell; Sound: Bruce Jamieson; Running Time: 56 Minutes; Submitted for Production Code Certification: During July of 1946

CAST: Spencer Williams, Jr. (Big Jim Bottom); and Myra D. Hemmings, Samuel H. James, Eddye L. Houston, Amos Droughan, Walter McMillion, Irene Campbell, Charlie Washington, Helen Butler, Dolly Jones, the Heavenly Choir, Jimmie Green's Orchestra

THE SPECTER OF THE ROSE
(Republic Pictures Corp.)

"Ben Hecht, to say the least, has done the expected by coming up with the unusual," *Variety* reported in an enthusiastic pre-release review of *The Specter of the Rose*. Hecht had long since staked out a position along the more progressive fringes of studio-system filmmaking, starting with a Depression-era deal at Paramount Pictures with fellow dramatist Charles MacArthur. Their partnership, an extension of the Broadway blitz that had yielded such hit plays as *The Front Page* and *Twentieth Century*, was a prestigious money pit whose projects ranged from the triumph of *Crime Without Passion* (1934) to the disaster of a long-unproduced *The Monster*, which Paramount finally appropriated in a last-straw buy-out and belatedly delivered as *The Mad Doctor* in 1940—without screen credit to the authors.

Hecht explained in his 1954 autobiography, *A Child of the Century*, that he deplored the Hollywood establishment; usually cranked out a script in a couple of weeks; and accepted movie gigs only when he ran low on cash. *The Hollywood Reporter* described Hecht's affiliation with Republic Pictures as "an exclusive writer-producer contract" that called for six pictures in three years.

"All I want is a pinch of the profits and no interference," Hecht recalled telling Republic's founding honcho, Herbert J. Yates.

"All right," replied Yates, "but when you've finished it, I hope I can understand it."

The Specter of the Rose proved to be Hecht's only turn at Republic, although he remained in demand for other studios' postwar projects. In lieu of a flat salary, Republic wound up paying Hecht 50 percent of *Specter*'s long-term profit. Hecht praised Yates for "a miraculous lack of interference." The budget was generous for Republic, reported at between $160,000 and $200,000 on a three-week shooting schedule. Hecht stretched these resources with detailed planning and extensive rehearsals. He assigned co-producer and co-director credit to ace photographer Lee C. Garmes, who took up the slack from Hecht's admittedly incomplete knowledge of camera technique.

Hecht had written the source-story, "The Spectre of the Rose" (using the Old World spelling), after sitting through a 1936 staging of the like-titled one-act ballet by Carl Maria von Weber and Jean-Louis Vaudoyer, with choreography by Michael Fokine. The ballet, inspired by a poem by Théophile Gautier, had originated in 1911 as a vehicle for the extraordinary leaps of Vaslav Nijinsky. All of which amounted to some mighty high-falutin' source-material for a studio whose general run of product was such that, as *Variety* put it, "the [theater operator] opens the can and expects horses to come galloping out."

Any galloping here is balletic, not equestrian. Dancer Ivan Kirow ramrods the ensemble cast as the brilliant André Sanine, who had cracked up after the death of his wife, Nina, during a staging of their starring ballet, *Le Spectre de la Rose*. Struggling producer Max Polikoff (Michael Chekhov) means to regain a shred of respect by luring Sanine back to performing, over the objections of Sanine's former mentor, Mme. La Sylph (Judith Anderson), who has seen her own better days as a dancer and now operates a rather dreary studio. A young ballerina, Haidi (Viola Essen), has helped Sanine regain his mental balance and now aspires to inherit the *Spectre* role.

Rehearsals progress well enough, but Sanine falls prey to an intermittent fancy that he is possessed by the ballet's murderous revenant. Haidi and Sanine decide that their marriage will cure him of the delusion. Mme. La Sylph confides her greater fears to Haidi, declaring that Nina's death was caused not by heart failure—the official story—but by well-hidden wounds dealt by Sanine. As the production commences, Sanine inflicts minor damage upon Haidi, who covers the abrasions and proceeds with a successful début. While on tour, Sanine's madness kicks into overdrive, and at length he comprehends that he must kill himself before he loses all control and kills Haidi. Calling upon his fabulous skills as a dancer, Sanine leaps out a high window to his death. Haidi, in perpetual mourning for the jerk, moves along to lesser acclaim as a teacher in Mme. La Sylph's ballet studio.

A beautifully mounted production, with passionate portrayals from its charismatic dancing-and-acting leads, *The Specter of the Rose* also takes the palm for one of the English language's sappier I'm-such-a-sensitive-brute yarns. Hecht's own arch wordsmithery gets in the way of his born-journalist storytelling, with altogether too much florid dialogue—although this very dialogue bespeaks a passionate love of the language, and even at his most rococo Hecht never becomes incoherent. One backup character, a scruffy womanizing poet played in high Greenwich Village bohemian style by gruff-voiced Lionel Stander, seems to exist merely as a mouthpiece for Hecht's baroque cynicism. To Stander's Lionel Gans, Mme. La Sylph is not merely a has-been, but "the remains of a pirouette... knitting a shroud for yesterday." As to Polikoff: "a wilted carnation in the Broadway buttonhole." Gans regards Haidi as not only a potential conquest but also "an exclamation point after the word *beauty*." Gans will not even spare himself: "[I am] a gargoyle in love with a goddess... I live 'til morning on the delusion that I am not a monster but a poet." The marriage of Haidi and Sanine drives Gans to this outpouring: "My grief added a little bouquet to the drab ceremony... My heart performed a minuet in an ashcan." The poet is of a piece with such Hecht-on-Hecht surrogates as the hell-bent-for-contempt boss-journalist of *The Front Page*, ever at the ready with "a wild barbaric yawp at life," and the Times Square gadabout of *Angels over Broadway*. And God bless Ben Hecht.

A sardonic compassion toward its crucial underdog characters helps *Specter* greatly, with Judith Anderson providing a stabilizing presence of ill-heeded authority (and shadings of a repressed-lesbian interest in Viola Essen's Haidi); and Leningrad-born Michael Chekhov offering a richly drawn caricature of a (stereo)typical New York impresario whose strivings seem at once ambitious and pathetic. (The *Variety* review, in an inadvertently laughable error, gave the actor's name as Anton Chekhov. Michael was a nephew of the famed playwright Anton.)

The mass-media reviewers weighed in with generally favorable notices. "Totally absorbing," gushed *Look* magazine, adding: "[Y]ou'll find its structure perfect." *Look*'s better-heeled rival, *Life*, on the other hand, called the film "arty, bombastic and never worthy of its exciting climactic scene."

Hecht despised critics. After St. John Ervine weighed in unfavorably on Hecht & MacArthur's *The Front Page* in 1928, Hecht cajoled the journalist into taking a second look—then had a set builder rig Ervine's seat to collapse under his weight. Hecht once published a "Sonnet to the Critics," characterizing that lot as "theatre moles with inattentive ears…/Who come to drama not to drink or sup/But more to shine your little egos up." As to *The Specter of the Rose*, the author summed up his satisfaction in these mordant words: "All its mistakes are mine."

Scarcely two years later, Michael Powell and Emeric Pressburger would offer a more sunnily conceived take on a similar tale of mad obsession, with *The Red Shoes* (England; 1948). The overt glamour of *The Red Shoes* has made it the more famous such film over the long haul, but *The Specter of the Rose* boasts the more satisfying combination of streetwise naturalism—highfalutin' language and all—and breezy defiance in the face of crushing disappointments.

The network-radio series *Inner Sanctum* later dramatized *The Specter of the Rose*, with Hecht as narrator. Then in 1963, about a year before his death at age 71, Hecht re-sold the source-story to the composer Louis Adelson for an intended Broadway musical.

CREDITS: Producer, Director and Source-Author/Screenwriter: Ben Hecht; Co-Producer, Co-Director and Director of Photography: Lee Garmes; Dialogue Director: Serene Kassapian; Assistant Directors: Harold Godsoe and Al Wood; Second Camera: Harry Webb; Special Optical Effects: Howard C. Lydecker and Theodore J. Lydecker; Editor: Harry Keller; Décor: John McCarthy, Jr., and Otto Seigel; Costumer: Adele Palmer; Musical Score: George Anthiel; Music Director: Morton Scott; Showcased Composition: "Invitation to the Dance," by Carl Maria von Weber; Song: "She's Only Partly Human," Writer Unacknowledged; Choreography: Tamara Geva; Sound: Ferol Redd; Makeup: Bob Mark; Hair Stylist: Peggy Gray; Running Time: 90 Minutes; Released: July 5, 1946

CAST: Judith Anderson (Mme. La Sylph); Michael Chekhov (Max Polikoff); Ivan Kirov (André Sanine); Viola Essen (Haidi); Lionel Stander (Lionel Gans); Charles "Red" Marshall (Specs McFarlan); George Shdanoff (Kropotkin); Billy Gray (Jack Jones); Juan Panalle (Jibby); Lou Hearn (Fred Lyons); Ferike Boros (Mamochka); Bert Hanlon (Margolies); Constantine (Alexis); Ferdinand Pollina (Giovanni); Polly Rose (Olga); Jim Moran (Jimmy); Ben Hecht (Waiter)

STRANGE VOYAGE
(Signal Pictures/Monogram Distributing Corp.)

Variety reviewed *Strange Voyage* late in 1945 as an unattached fresh production of Signal Pictures, an upstart studio organized by former servicemen who had worked in the industry prior to World War II. The executives of Signal also were the hands-on makers of *Strange Voyage*: producer L.B. Appleton, Jr., director Irving Allen, star player Eddie Albert, screenwriter Andrew Holt and assistant director Harold Knox.

The straightforward, somewhat documentary-like *Strange Voyage* is related in flashback, as told by Forrest Taylor, playing the owner of an oddly fated ketch: Sportsman Chris Thompson (Albert) had accrued a crew for a voyage to Mexico. En route, the men discovered a stowaway, young Jimmy Trask (Bobby Cooper), and Jimmy's pet monkey. Bad omens heralded a shark attack. Chris revealed his search for buried treasure, which he intended to donate to charity in gratitude for past kindnesses. Once ashore—despite warnings from a local beauty named Carmelita Lopez (Elena Verdugo)—the party forged onward, only to be split up by greed, superstitious fears and disease. There followed a shoot-out and a slugfest, during which a mighty wind arose to re-bury the unearthed treasure.

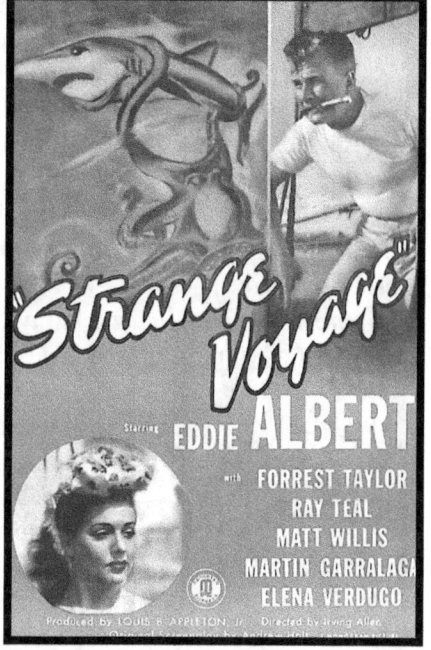

Taylor's yarn is now told, and his listener (Clyde Fillmore) scoffs. Just then, Chris, Jimmy and the monkey come aboard. The monkey wears a necklace of gold coins.

Realistic stagings and some gripping underwater encounters keep the interest stoked, and Matt Willis and Ray Teal, as cunning mutineers, lend a welcome tension. Albert's robust intelligence makes for a winning heroic presence. Jack Greenhalgh's camerawork captures ideally the clash of high adventure and low treachery, particularly in the seascapes.

Despite the favorable notice in *Variety*, the offbeat little show proved to be the one-and-only production of Signal Pictures.

CREDITS: Producer: L.B. Appleton, Jr.; Director: Irving Allen; Screenplay: Andrew Holt; Photographed by: Jack H. Greenhalgh, Jr.; Assistant Director: Harold Knox; Special Effects: Larry Glickman and Mario Castegnaro; Art Director: Ralph Berger; Editor: Irving A. Applebaum; Décor: Sydney A. Moore and Tommy Thompson; Music Director: Lud Gluskin; Musical Score: Lucien Moraweck; Sound: Percy J. Townsend; Running Time: 70 Minutes; Released: July 6, 1946

CAST: Eddie Albert (Chris Thompson); Forrest Taylor (Skipper); Ray Teal (Capt. Andrews); Matt Willis (Hammer); Martin Garralaga (Manuel); Elena Verdugo (Carmelita Lopez); Bobby Cooper (Jimmy Trask); Clyde Fillmore (Barrier); Daniel Kerry (Ben); Henry Orosco (Father); Junior (Monkey)

LARCENY IN HER HEART
(Producers Releasing Corp.)

The best of quite a few attempts to picturize Brett Halliday's glib private-eye character, Michael Shayne, is... —well, it's a far cry from *Larceny in Her Heart*, a muddled entry in a PRC series. For Michael Shayne had, like Earl Biggers' Charlie Chan, known better days, beyond his published origins, in a 20th Century-Fox series. Lloyd Nolan launched the impersonation in 1941 with *Michael Shayne, Private Detective* at Sol Wurtzel's Fox B-picture unit, whose dependable output helped the big studio overcome the inevitable losses incurred by big-budget flops.

Of Wurtzel's seven Nolan-as-Shane mysteries, the best is, hands-down, 1942's *The Man Who Wouldn't Die*, in which an intruder with glowing eyes makes life miserable for a wealthy household. PRC's *Shayne*s hadn't a chance of living up to the high gloss and cracking pace of the Foxes, what with Sigmund Neufeld riding herd on the pinch-penny budgets and his brother, Sam Newfield, hiding his greater light as a sometimes-visionary director under a bushel-basket of hackwork.

Larceny in Her Heart is stray-corpse fare of a stale vintage, with Hugh Beaumont a winning presence despite the absence of material to stoke either

his easygoing wit or Shayne's deductive intelligence. Beaumont's Shayne suffers indignities that Nolan's Shayne would not have brooked, including the heave-ho from a high-tone nightclub whose dress code exceeds his wardrobe. The missing body, victim of a strangler-at-large, would appear to belong to Helen Stallings (Marie Harmon). A trail of shameful (not to say Shayne-ful) family secrets leads the detective to an asylum for alcoholics—this, in a day before it became fashionable to announce oneself to polite society as a supposedly recovering dipsomaniac—where the dead woman proves to have been somebody else entirely (but also played by Marie Harmon). Shayne cracks the case without particularly enlightening anyone in the audience as to any deeper whys or wherefores.

This outbreak of *Shayne*s also includes *Blonde for a Day*, *Murder Is My Business*, *Three on a Ticket* and *Too Many Witnesses*, all from 1946-47. And just for the record, the Fox *Michael Shayne*s: from 1941, *Dressed To Kill* and *Sleepers West*, in addition to *Michael Shayne, Private Detective*; from 1942, *Blue, White and Perfect* and *Just off Broadway*, in addition to *The Man Who Wouldn't Die*; and from 1943, *Time To Kill*.

CREDITS: Producer: Sigmund Neufeld; Director: Sam Newfield; Screenplay: Raymond L. Schrock; Based upon Characters Created by: Brett Halliday; Photographed by: Jack Greenhalgh; Assistant Director: Stanley Neufeld; Second Camera: Ben Colman; Special Effects: Ray Mercer and Ray Smallwood; Art Director: Edwqard C. Jewell; Editor: Holbrook N. Todd; Settings: Elias H. Reif; Music: Leo Erdody; Sound: Earl Sitar; Makeup: Bud Westmore; Running Time: 68 Minutes; Released: July 10, 1946

CAST: Hugh Beaumont (Michael Shayne); Cheryl Walker (Phyllis Hamilton); Ralph Dunn (Sgt. Pete Rafferty); Paul Bryar (Tim Rourke); Charles Wilson (Chief Gentry); Douglas Fowley (Doc Patterson); Gordon Richards (Burton Stallings); Charles Quigley (Arch Dubler); Julia McMillan (Lucille); Marie Harmon (Helen Stallings and Barbara Brett); Lee Bennett (Whit Marlow); Henry Hall (Dr. Porter)

NIGHT TRAIN TO MEMPHIS
(Republic Pictures Corp.)

Grand Ole Opry mainstay Roy Acuff not only made two of the scariest phonograph records in the history of hillbilly gospel music—those would be the righteously ominous "Great Speckled Bird" and its imaginatively titled sequel, "Great Specked Bird No. 2"—but he also mounted a short-order movie career that yielded this upsetting study of inflicted madness and inbred degeneracy within a backwoods settlement. Ostensibly a down-home piece of tuneful rusticity, *Night Train to Memphis* serves more strikingly to showcase the bad-brother act of Republic's reigning chapter-play villain, Roy Barcroft, and dependable Kenne Duncan, who was fated eventually to wind up among the hardscrabble stock company of Edward D. Wood, Jr.

Acuff plays himself, more or less, as a farmer-turned-stationmaster in a whistle-stop mountain village, where a (purely fictional) brother, Danny Acuff (played by Allan Lane), comes sneaking back home after a hitch in prison. Danny is angered to learn that Roy works for the very railroad that Danny blames for

having framed him in a holdup. Danny settles in with moonshiners Chad and Asa Morgan (Barcroft and Duncan), who actually had committed the robbery. Citified newcomers John Stevenson (Joseph Crehan) and his daughter, Constance (that glamorous dependable of the B-movie mysteries, Adele Mara), supposedly on a fishing trip, turn out to be railroad owners. Stevenson seeks to uproot the villagers with a new wayside development. Danny Acuff becomes romantically involved with Constance despite Roy's own, more bashful, attraction to her. Danny inadvertently provokes Constance into shooting at Chad. A conspiracy to fake Chad's death causes Constance to suffer a mental breakdown, and she seems beyond recovery unless Roy can force Chad to turn up alive and well. A fight between the Morgan boys finds Asa inadvertently revealing himself as the party who had framed Danny. Asa kills Chad, and in the aftermath Constance is jolted out of her crack-up. Stevenson, who has by now obtained the deeds to the surrounding lands, is so grateful that he abandons his scheme.

The spiritual darkness and prevailing lawlessness inherent in the Southern mountain country translate well to this telling, which director Lesley Selander treats more as a local-yokel noir than as the lilting backwoodser that the studio must have intended. The clash of storytelling imperatives causes an unfortunate lurching in the narrative rhythm. Roy Acuff stretches beyond his natural tunesmithing showmanship to deliver a fairly credible show of stable heroism, and Adele Mara seems more delicately vulnerable than usual. Allan "Rocky" Lane's portrayal suggests the dashing Western-hero star had been studying up on Henry Fonda's work in *The Trail of the Lonesome Pine* (1936) and *The Grapes of Wrath* (1940). Black players Nicodemus Stewart and Nina Mae McKinney supply welcome comic-relief bits. The zippy title tune wears out its welcome through overuse. Barcroft and Duncan account for the more memorable moments, overall.

CREDITS: Associate Producers and Screenwriters: Dorrell McGowan and Stuart McGowan; Director: Lesley Selander; Photographed by: William Bradford; Assistant Director: Don Verk; Special Effects: Howard Lydecker and Theodore Lydecker; Art Director: Fred A. Ritter; Editor: Tony Martinelli; Décor: John McCarthy, Jr., and George Milo; Costumer: Adele Palmer; Music Director: Morton Scott; Songs: "Night Train to Memphis," by Beasley Smith, Marvin Hughes &

Owen Bradley, the Traditional "Sally Goodin'," adapted by Mel Foree & Fred Rose, and "That Glory Bound Train," by Roy Acuff & Odell McLeod; Makeup: Bob Mark; Running Time: 67 Minutes; Released: July 12, 1946

CAST: Roy Acuff (Himself) & His Smoky Mountain Boys; Allan Lane (Danny Acuff); Adele Mara (Constance Stevenson); Irving Bacon (Rainbow); Joseph Crehan (John Stevenson); Emma Dunn (Ma Acuff); Roy Barcroft (Chad Morgan); Kenne Duncan (Asa Morgan); LeRoy Mason (Wilson)

QUEEN OF BURLESQUE
(Sigmund Neufeld Productions, Inc./Producers Releasing Corp./ Pathé Industries, Inc.)

The prospect of an escape from her prominent typecasting as Universal Pictures' "Queen of the Horror Movies" must have been appealing to Evelyn Ankers, although her star turn in Sam Newfield's *Queen of Burlesque* requires as much peeling as it calls for movie-star appeal. This titillating little chiller is more *tease* than outright *strip*, but it allows Miss Ankers a pleasing display of range and epidermis as a burley-cue artiste who becomes embroiled in a case of serial murder.

Crystal McCoy (Ankers) is torn between the underhanded intrigues of her profession and a proposal of marriage from her news-columnist boyfriend, Steve Hurley (Carleton Young). Crystal's headliner status with a burlesque revue is threatened by Dolly Devoe (Jacqueline Dalya) and Blossom Terraine (real-life stripper Rose La Rose). Lola Cassell (Marian Martin), another dancer, accuses Dolly of murder in a long-unresolved case. Which becomes an academic matter when Dolly's strangled corpse is discovered by Annie Morris (Alice Fleming), a matronly wardrobe-mistress. Then, the slayings of Blossom and Lola cast suspicion upon Crystal. Annie, whose behavior has become more peculiar with each new murder, at last reveals herself as a possessive, overprotective psychopath who believes Crystal must be her long-lost daughter. Once the menace has been put down, Crystal decides she has enjoyed all of this corruption she can tolerate and decides to marry Steve, after all.

Evelyn Ankers and Carleton Young in *Queen of Burlesque*

The staging of routines from a then-current but since-collapsed substratum of show business renders *Queen of Burlesque* as vivid a cultural document as it is a thriller. The strip joints didn't exactly become extinct, but as soon thereafter as the 1960s they had begun to mutate into grim, humorless places, leaving increasingly little to the imagination and lacking in the redeeming suggestiveness and hambone comedy of classic-manner burlesque. Murray Leonard represents that comical style well, playing a character whose amusing on-stage routines give way to a near-menacing, secretive presence beyond the range of the spotlight Alice Fleming proves effective throughout as the killer within, conveying a suffocating attitude of mom-ism even in her more nearly stabilized moments. Miss Ankers radiates a brash vivacity that is scarcely to be found in her more famous roles. The dialogue is witty and insinuative, indulging in *double-entendre* lines that served in 1946 to put across the meaning without red-flagging the censors. Carleton Young makes an insistent, somewhat conflicted, romantic lead—earnestly wooing Miss Ankers even as he uses her stardom in the racket as leverage to research a book about the burlesque scene.

Backup player Rose La Rose once was cited by a French film critic as a contributing author of 1933's *King Kong*—more than merely an error, and in effect a laughably pompous attempt to explain *Kong*'s erotic undercurrents in terms of Miss La Rose's striptease credentials. That full-of-it Gallic theorist in fact had confused Rose La Rose with *Kong*'s actual screenwriter, Ruth Rose.

CREDITS: Executive Producer: Sigmund Neufeld; Producers: Arthur Alexander and Alfred Stern; Director: Sam Newfield; Screenplay: David Lang; Additional Dialogue: Arthur St. Clair; Photographed by: Vincent J. Farrar; Assistant Director: Louis Germonprez; Special Effects: Ray Mercer; Art Director: Edward C. Jewell; Editor: Jack W. Ogilvie; Décor: E.H. Reif; Music: Karl Hajos; Songwriters: Al Stewart and Gene Lucas; Sound: John Carter; Running Time: 68 Minutes; Released: July 24, 1946

CAST: Evelyn Ankers (Crystal McCoy); Carleton Young (Steve Hurley); Marian Martin (Lola Cassell); Craig Reynolds (Joe Nolan); Rose La Rose (Blossom Terraine); Emory Parnell (Inspector Crowley); Alice Fleming (Annie Morris); Murray Leonard (Chick Malloy); Jacqueline Dalya (Dolly Devoe)

THE INNER CIRCLE
(Republic Pictures Corp.)

Adele Mara pulls off a curious twist on *femme fatale* form in Phil Ford's *The Inner Circle*. Miss Mara commandeers the ill-handled yarn right off the bat as a nervy secretary named Geraldine Smith, who insinuates herself into a job with private eye Johnny Strange (Warren Douglas). Johnny may be Strange, but Geraldine is even more so—ordering him straightaway to consult with a mystery-woman client who wants him to help her hide a corpse. Strange balks at the assignment, whereupon the veiled woman konks him a good one and then sets things up to look as though Strange had killed an assailant in self-defense.

Before Strange can revive, the woman unveils herself: She is Geraldine Smith. The police nab Strange before he can comprehend what is going on, but Geraldine comes to his assistance, sort of, by insisting she had seen him commit a justifiable homicide. The victim proves to be a celebrity-gossip radio personality named Anthony Fitch. Strange is befuddled by Gerry's insistence that he killed the jerk, but her testimony clears him in the eyes of coroner's jury.

Gerry insists that the resulting publicity will bring Strange more business than he can handle, but he obsessively begins digging into the sordid past of Fitch, who proves to have been running a blackmail racket. Meanwhile, a gardener named Boggs (Will Wright), who had witnessed Gerry's removal of her disguise, decides to try a little blackmail of his own. (Although Boggs exacts a payoff, this subplot is one that goes but ill-resolved in the three surviving prints we have found.) Strange's snooping leads to nightclub singer Rhoda Roberts (Virginia Christine), whose gangster sweetheart, Duke York (Ricardo Cortez), abducts Johnny for an underworld interrogation session. Rescued by a grouchy police detective (William Frawley, playing precisely to type), Johnny determines that Fitch was about to go public with a spot of ruinous information about a certain high-society woman.

Confronting Gerry, Strange learns her sister Anne Lowe (Martha Montgomery), is the endangered woman—and Gerry fears Anne had murdered Fitch lest Anne's politician husband be scandalized.

In a development that resolves absolutely nothing to the viewer's satisfaction, Strange decides he must re-enact the crime in an on-the-spot broadcast from Fitch's residence. This urgently silly parlor game reveals the killer to be Rhoda Roberts, whose motivation had been mere anger over Fitch's unwillingness to pay her for digging up dirt for his program. Strange seals the case by planting a passionate smooch on Geraldine.

William Frawley, already a veteran character man with his *I Love Lucy* fame yet to come, is a real scene-stealer as the impatient lawman. Ricardo

Cortez, whose splendid career was winding down, is a big asset as the suave, indignant mobster.

CREDITS: Associate Producer: William J. O'Sullivan; Director: Phil Ford; Screenplay: Dorrell McGowan and Stuart McGowan; Based upon: A Radio Play by Leonard St. Clair and Lawrence Taylor; Photographed by: Reggie Lanning; Assistant Directors: Roy Wade and Virgil Hart; Second Camera: Herbert Kilpatrick; Matte Paintings: Lewis Physioc; Miniatures and Special Optical Effects: Howard C. Lydecker and Theodore J. Lydecker; Transparency Projection Shots: Gordon Schaefer; Art Director: Fred A. Ritter; Editor: Tony Martinelli; Music: Mort Glickman; Sound: William E. Clark; Makeup: Bob Mark; Running Time: 57 Minutes (Some Sources Cite 65 Minutes); Released: August 7, 1946

CAST: Adele Palmer (Geraldine Smith); Warren Douglas (Johnny Strange); William Frawley (Webb); Ricardo Cortez (Duke York); Virginia Christine (Rhoda Roberts); Ken Niles (Announcer); Will Wright (Henry Boggs); Dorothy Adams (Mrs. Wilson); Martha Montgomery (Anne Lowe)

DEATH VALLEY
(Golden Gate Pictures, Inc./Screen Guild Productions, Inc.)

The crushing vastness of California's Death Valley had provided the setting for the climax of Erich von Stroheim's troubled masterwork, *Greed*, a generation before the theatre operator and ascending Poverty Row producer Robert L. Lippert gave that forbidding region its own marquee billing in this similarly ominous—though hardly similarly grandiose—study of greed-driven madness. *Death Valley*, directed with an implacable severity by Lew Landers, pivots on a rich portrayal of rancid anti-heroism by 51-year-old Nat Pendleton, as a greenhorn prospector whose big strike seems always to lie just beyond the next desolate horizon.

Cowhand Jim Ward (Pendleton), while searching for a fabled gold mine, befriends an injured miner, Silas Bagley (Russell Simpson)—only to learn that the map in which he has invested is identical to a bogus map that Bagley had once bought. Bagley insists, all the same, that there must be gold hereabouts. Bagley's daughter, Joan (Helen Gilbert), warms but gradually to Ward.

A claim by the Bagleys proves of low grade, but it still nets Joan a quick $5,000 from a mining syndicate. Ward's own strike assays out as only fool's gold. While visiting a barroom with Joan, Ward urges her to marry him, then grows ever more obnoxious. A sailor named Steve (Robert Lowery) intrudes well-meaningly, but Joan rebuffs him. Ward, wandering drunkenly, is robbed of the money Joan had entrusted to him; he trails the woman who had taken it—and kills her. He keeps the loot but reports it stolen.

Steve, who blames himself for provoking the situation, insists upon following the miners into the desert to make amends with plain hard work. A peculiar triangle among Ward, Steve and Joan grows increasingly tense when Steve makes a rich strike and, meanwhile, learns that Ward has the Bagleys' grubstake. Ward has now come under suspicion in the slaying of the thief. Ward  flees with gold from Steve's strike, and Steve follows, only to be overcome in the resulting struggle. Ward wanders ever deeper into the desert, eluding the law—but dying from a snake's bite.

It's no *Treasure of the Sierra Madre*, and most assuredly no *Greed*, but *Death Valley* packs its own morbid charms, thanks largely to Pendleton's show of predatory, however pathetic and cowardly, viciousness. The former Olympian-turned-professional wrestler had long since become a familiar face on screen, but his popular image was that of a comical oaf—fondly remembered as a self-important stooge for the antics of Bud Abbott and Lou Costello, and ever better known in those days as a dufus ambulance driver in the *Dr. Kildare* features. Pendleton's *Death Valley* portrayal is a revelation, though it led merely to a return-to-form, with 1947's *Buck Privates Come Home* and *Scared to Death*.

The supporting cast efficiently points up Pendleton's self-pitying monomania, with Helen Gilbert in fine tart form as a might-be romantic interest; whispery-voiced Sterling Holloway as a cohort in the quest; and Russell Simpson as a trusting miner who has been struggling long enough that he ought to know better. Robert Lowery presents a robust opposite number to Pendleton's raging conflicts.

CREDITS: Executive Producer: Robert L. Lippert; Producer: William B. David; Production Supervisor: Walt Mattox; Director Lew Landers (Louis Friedlander); Dialogue Director: Irvin Berwick; Story and Screenplay: Doris Schroeder; Photographed by: Marcel Le Picard; Assistant Director: Lou Perloff; Art Director: Harri Reif; Editor: George McGuire; Music: Carl Hoefle; Sound: Glen Glenn; Makeup: John Sweeney; Running Time: 67 Minutes; Released: August 15, 1946

CAST: Nat Pendleton (Jim Ward); Helen Gilbert (Joan Bagley); Robert Lowery (Steve); Sterling Holloway (Slim); Russell Simpson (Silas Bagley); and Barbara Reed, Paul Hurst, Dick Scott

THE INVISIBLE INFORMER
(Republic Pictures Corp.)

In the haunted bayou country of Louisiana, insurance detectives Eve Rogers (Linda Stirling) and Mike Reagan (William Henry) have a case and a half on their hands in pursuing the truth behind a $100,000 claim on a missing necklace. Suave Eric Baylor (Gerald Mohr), scion of a disreputable old-money clan, seems to know more than he or his family is willing to reveal, and nosy associates tend to turn up dead—some strangled, one by apparent suicide, others torn apart by a wolflike beast.

At length, Eve and Mike catch Baylor off guard, revealing him as the thief, fraud artist and murderer. Baylor's accomplice is a German Shepherd that will attack on command. Baylor is beaten to death in a climactic slugfest with Reagan, and all ends agreeably for the sleuthing couple.

Fourth-billed Gerald Mohr, heavy of brow and brusque of manner, walks away with this slight production, stealing the show right out from under the noses of its ill-cast heroic-romantic stars. Linda Stirling and William Henry fared better in separate assignments elsewhere, and together in 1946's *Mysterious Mr. Valentine*—also at Republic. *The Invisible Informer* leaves, withal, an indelible impression of calculating, remorseless menace. That traffic-stopping looker Adele Mara fares nicely as a hotel desk-clerk who becomes tensely involved with Mohr, but her role is nowhere near the tragically bravura *femme fatale* part she had enjoyed in Lesley Selander's *Passkey to Danger*.

The Invisible Informer is fairly conventional whodunnit stuff except for Mohr's seething bad-guy turn and a generous slathering of weirdness. Tom London and Donia Bussey are especially memorable as members of an eccentric clan bearing the name of Shroud.

CREDITS: Associate Producer: William J. O'Sullivan; Director: Philip Ford; Screenplay: Sherman L. Lowe; Story: Gerald Drayson Adams; Photographed by: William Bradford; Assistant Director: Don Verk; Second Camera: Jack Warren; Matte Paintings: Lewis Physioc; Miniatures and Optical Effects: Howard Lydecker and Theodore Lydecker; Transparency

Projection Shots: Gordon Schaefer; Art Director: James Sullivan; Supervising Art Director: Russell Kimball; Editor: Richard L. Van Enger; Décor: John McCarthy, Jr., and Otto Seigel; Music: Mort Glickman and Richard Cherwin; Sound: Ferrol Redd; Running Time: 57 Minutes; Released: August 19, 1946

CAST: Linda Stirling (Eve Rogers); William Henry (Mike Reagan); Adele Mara (Marie Ravelle); Gerald Mohr (Eric Baylor); Peggy Stewart (Rosalind Baylor); Tom London (Eph Shroud); Donia Bussey (Grandma Shroud); Claire DuBrey (Martha Baylor); Tristram Coffin (David Baylor); Charles Lane (Nick Steele); Cy Kendall (Sheriff Ladeau); Francis McDonald (Jules Ravelle)

SPOOK BUSTERS
(Monogram Pictures Corp.)

There is the ever-present feeling of having seen all this somewhere before.
—*Variety*

Contrary to popular assumptions, the 1984 smash *Ghostbusters* represented no particular innovations, except perhaps in the special-effects department. Nor did a key ancestor of *Ghostbusters*, William Beaudine's *Spook Busters*, set any revolutions in motion. Even in its own day, *Spook Busters* was merely a continuation of a long horror-spoofing tradition, tainted perhaps by rote genre-fication, but never by shallow trendiness. This early volley in the transformation of the *East Side Kids* series into the *Bowery Boys* franchise does, however, explicitly prefigure *Ghostbusters* in its premise of an exterminating service dedicated to the removal of hauntings.

The haunting here is not explicitly ectoplasmic. The Bowery Boys—Leo "Slip" Gorcey, Huntz "Sach" Hall, Bobby Jordan, Billy "Whitey" Benedict, David "Chuck" Gorcey and Gabriel

"Gabe" Dell—have landed in a purportedly haunted mansion, where a squatter's-rights mad doctor named Coslow (Douglass Dumbrille) and his captive assistant (Maurice Cass) are preparing to equip a gorilla with a human brain. The ghostly trappings of the place, which comes complete with graveyard, are calculated to discourage intruders.

All the fellows but Gabe are new graduates of an exterminators' academy, hired by a realty firm to de-bug the house. The bugs are chiefly of the electronic-surveillance variety, including an unaccountably elaborate television system. Gabe, returning from Navy service with his war bride, Mignon (Tanis Chandler), stumbles in to lend a hand. (The picture marks Dell's return to the team; he had been aboard from the formative *Dead End*-based pictures, on into the *Little Tough Guys* and *East Side Kids* spin-offs.) The plot reaches its crisis of urgency when Coslow pegs the numbskulled Sach as an ideal brain donor. The police arrive just in time, although Slip has offered wisecracking resistance.

Among the Poverty Row studios, the familiar initials *W.B.* stood not for Warner Bros., but rather for William Beaudine, that pioneering director who, after a lengthy stay in England, had become a mainstay of the stepchild-of-Hollywood independent studios. Beaudine's prolific efficiency seldom rose above competence, but he characteristically delivered the basic goods of any genre in which he happened to be working. The *Variety* review of *Spook Busters* lamented the story's over-padding of easy gags and bogus scares but declared, "That the pacing holds up at all... is a credit to editor Richard Currier and director William Beaudine." Shortly before Beaudine's death at age 78 in 1970, the Directors Guild acknowledged him as its oldest active helmsman.

Variety's chief delight with *Spook Busters* lay merely in having found such an easy target. The anonymous critic sniped about the film's lacking appeal "except to the grammar-school level and weekend matinee business."

The *Bowery Boys* playlist for 1946 includes a couple of other weirdly conceived entries: *Bowery Bombshell*, in which an experimental explosive leads to the creation of a "human bomb," if not a cinematic bomb; and *Mr. Hex*, a prizefighting opus in which a hypnotized Huntz Hall falls under the spell of a crook known as Evil Eye.

CREDITS: Producer: Jan Grippo; Director: William Beaudine; Screenplay: Edmond Seward and Tim Ryan; Photographed by: Harry Neumann; Assistant Director: Eddie Davis; Technical Director: Dave Milton; Editors: Richard Currier and William Austin; Music: Edward J. Kay; Sound: Tom Lambert; Makeup: Harry Ross; Production Manager: Glenn Cook; Running Time: 68 Minutes; Released: August 24, 1946

CAST: Leo Gorcey (Slip); Huntz Hall (Sach); Douglass Dumbrille (Dr. Coslow); Bobby Jordan (Bobby); Gabriel Dell (Gabe); Billy Benedict (Whitey);

David Gorcey (Chuck); Tanis Chandler (Mignon); Maurice Cass (Dr. Bender); Vera Lewis (Mrs. Grimm); Charles Middleton (Stiles); Chester Clute (Brown); Richard Alexander (Ivan); Bernard Gorcey (Louie); Charles Millsfield (Dean Pettyboff); Arthur Miles (Herman); Tom Coleman (Police Captain)

ACCOMPLICE
(Producers Releasing Corp.)

Frank Gruber's novel *Simon Lash, Private Detective* is a regular jewel of the hard-boiled school. It was so popular in its day that it led Gruber to Hollywood to develop this screen version, *Accomplice*, with scenarist Irving Elman. PRC's no-frills/no-nonsense approach to filmmaking proved ideal for the book's roughhouse primitivism. A wealth of rigorous action—including a spectacular chase that provoked chief cameraman Arthur "Jockey" Feindel to declare, "No more action pictures for me!"—is enough to make *Accomplice* a well-spent hour-and-change, but the film also boasts crisp characterizations of the doomed variety and a tense undercurrent of embittered romantic longings.

Former silent-era leading man Richard Arlen plays attorney-turned-investigator Simon Lash, who is approached by a bygone lover, the icily beautiful Joyce Bonniwell (Veda Ann Borg), with a plea to find her missing husband. There seems no trace of Los Angeles banker Jim Bonniwell, but after a murder in nearby Palmdale, Joyce identifies the victim as her husband.

Unwilling to close the matter here, Lash finds himself under surveillance and obliged to look into a second murder. He pursues a vague clue as far as New Mexico, where he is taken captive in a forbidding place known as Connors' Castle. He breaks free and encounters Joyce Bonniwell.

Suddenly, Lash hears the voice of Jim Bonniwell, proposing a bribe that Lash rejects. A motor car speeds away from the castle, but Lash disables the vehicle with two gunshots. The occupant proves to be Bonniwell (Edward Earle), who had faked his death with a proxy victim to cover a secretive criminal career. In a wild gun battle, the treacherous Joyce is killed by a stray bullet from her husband's pistol. Bonniwell commits suicide.

The centerpiece of *Accomplice* is that jaw-dropping road chase, which begins when Arlen, on learning that an elusive woman is implicated in two slayings, heads out hellbent for the Mojave. The pursuit sustains a breakneck pace over mountain passes, desert trails and any number of deadly obstacles. Cinematographer Feindel said later, "Following those

two speeding vehicles in an open truck and worrying about a $10,000 camera falling over the side is more than I can stand."

The Virginia-born Arlen had reached his peak of stardom in the William Wellman films *Wings* and *Beggars of Life*, and in Victor Fleming's *The Virginian* (1929). He kept working relentlessly, however, as talking pictures edged out the silents, scoring such coups as *Island of Lost Souls* (1933), *Submarine Alert* (1943) and *The Lady and the Monster* (1944), and gradually struck a balance between leading roles in the B-movie realm and supporting character parts in bigger pictures. A vigorous 47 at the time of *Accomplice*, Arlen carries the show with a gruff vulnerability—a hero whose stubborn streak and romantic longings lead him to stay on a case well past the point of diminishing returns.

Veda Ann Borg is an ideal *femme* noir, as it were, an irresistibly striking beauty who is at once alluring and foreboding. Tom Dugan supplies expert comedy relief as Arlen's assistant. The venerable Francis Ford, estranged but paradoxically still collaborative brother of the major-league director John Ford, has a nice bit as a desert-dweller in cahoots with the schemers. Ominous musical cues by Alexander Laszlo, a gifted and inventive composer who usually delivered scores better than the films they would grace, contribute immeasurably to the dark and desperate charm of *Accomplice*.

CREDITS: Producer: John K. Teaford; Director: Walter Colmes; Screenplay by Irving Elman and Frank Gruber; from the Novel, *Simon Lash, Private Detective*, by Frank Gruber; Photographed by Arthur "Jockey" Feindel; Musical Score: Alexander Laszlo; Film Editor: Robert Jahns; Sound: Frank Webster; Running Time: 68 Minutes; Released: September 12, 1946

CAST: Richard Arlen (Simon Lash); Veda Ann Borg (Joyce Bonniwell); Tom Dugan (Eddie Slocum); Michael Branden (Sheriff Rucker); Marjorie Manners (Evelyn Price); Earl Hodgins (Jeff Bailey); Francis Ford (Pete Connors); Edward Earle (Jim Bonniwell); Herbert Rawlinson (Vincent Springer)

MYSTERIOUS MR. VALENTINE
(Republic Pictures Corp.)

Milton Raison's original screenplay for *Mysterious Mr. Valentine* almost could pass for one of Seabury Quinn's brilliant stream-of-consciousness hair-raisers from the long-running *Jules de Grandin* series in *Weird Tales* magazine. About all that is missing is the case-cracking team of that great French detective, Jules de Grandin of the Sureté, and his bucolic Yankee Watson, Dr. Trowbridge. That, and of course the element of perverted science and/or supernatural intrusion that was a Quinn hallmark; lethal scheming suffices here. The establishing mood is precisely right, though, what with a desolate roadway; a forbidding factory and its proprietor, who hides a ghastly secret; a vulnerable young-lady motorist with a disabled vehicle; and a corpse that goes missing before anyone can figure out how to dispense with it.

The menaced woman is Republic's dependable Linda Stirling, who plays Janet Spencer, visitor-by-inconvenience to a chemical plant. Co-owner John Armstrong (Tristram Coffin), nervously welcoming her, points Janet toward a telephone while he fidgets, with good reason: Armstrong has just killed a man. The body vanishes. Armstrong's antagonistic wife, Rita (Barbara Woodell), barges in.

Janet does the sensible thing under the circumstances and steals Rita's car for a quick getaway. Swerving to avoid an oncoming vehicle, Janet strikes a pedestrian—or so it is made to appear to her. Two men from the other car, pretending helpfulness, make ready to frame Janet for a hit-and-run killing. En route home, she collides with another vehicle but speeds onward. The driver of the smashed car, private eye Steve Morgan (William Henry), trails Janet and offers his services. The corpse from the faked accident proves to be that of Ralph Doane, Armstrong's business partner. Janet finds herself under threat of blackmail by one Mr. Valentine.

Steve determines that Doane and his mistress, Lola Carson (Virginia Christine), had been plotting a life-insurance scam, and that Doane was already dead before he was placed in Janet's path. The elusive Mr. Valentine attacks Steve. Armstrong is found slain, and his estranged wife finds herself under arrest. The underlying culprits are finally revealed as Lola and Armstrong and insurance agent Sam Priestly (Kenne Duncan), who had posed as Mr. Valentine.

The story gradually gives way to a gathering romantic attraction between Miss Stirling and William Henry, but it is that ominous first reel—echoed in the escalating dirty deeds of Virginia Christine—that leaves the overriding impression.

CREDITS: Associate Producer: Donald H. Brown; Director: Philip Ford; Screenplay: Milton Raison; Photographed by: Alfred Keller; Assistant Director: Jack Lacey; Second Camera: Herbert Kirkpatrick; Matte Paintings: Lewis Physioc; Miniatures and Special Optical Effects: Howard C. Lydecker and Theodore J. Lydecker; Transparency Projection Shots: Gordon Schaefer; Art Director: Hilyard Brown; Editor: Richard L. Van Enger; Décor: John McCarthy, Jr., and

George Milo; Costumer: Adele Palmer; Music: Mort Glickman; Sound: Richard Tyler; Music Mixer: John Stransky, Jr.; Makeup: Bob Mark; Running Time: 60 Minutes; Released: September 3, 1946

CAST: William Henry (Steve Morgan); Linda Stirling (Janet Spencer); Virginia Christine (Lola Carson); Thomas Jackson (Det. Lt. Milo Jones); Barbara Woodell (Rita Armstrong); Kenne Duncan (Sam Priestly); Virginia Brissac (Martha); Lyle Latell (Peter Musso); Ernie Adams (Frank Gary); Tristam Coffin (John Armstrong); Arthur Space (Coroner); Robert Bice (Doctor)

DECOY
(Monogram Productions, Inc.)

One of the finer postwar entries from Monogram Pictures is Jack Bernhard's *Decoy*, a life-beyond-death revenge melodrama of which *Variety* raved: "It's not plausible, but it doesn't have to be." The usually crochety tradepaper added that "canny direction whips *Decoy* along at a jet-propelled pace so fast that the customers can't take time out for wondering."

Alive only through grim determination, Dr. Lloyd Craig (Herbert Rudley) staggers into the apartment of beautiful Margot Shelby (Jean Gillie) and opens fire on her. Detective Joe Portugal (Sheldon Leonard) arrives to find Craig dead and Margot gravely wounded. She tells of how she caused four deaths:

Frankie Olins (Robert Armstrong), Margot's lover, hid $400,000 taken in a bank heist before his death sentence for killing a guard. Margot feigned affection for gangster Jim Vincent (Edward Norris) and lured him into a scheme to remove Olins' body just after the execution. She also seduced the prison medico, Craig, into playing along. The hearse driver was murdered during the body-napping. Craig administered a treatment to restore Olins to life. Treacheries piled up from there, with a proportionate body count, en route to the retrieval of a strongbox.

The money box is at Margot's side as she finishes her story. After she dies, Portugal opens the box to find a dollar bill — Olins' joke from beyond the grave.

Jean Gillie, a British-born dancer-turned-actress for whom great things were predicted, holds the audience and the male-ensemble cast in thrall. She comes as close to an incarnation of sexual sadism as the censors would allow. Despite acclaim for this brilliant interpretation of a poisonous woman, the red-haired beauty remained largely overlooked in Hollywood. Miss Gillie returned to England, where she died in 1949 without having achieved the prominence her abilities merited.

Decoy's misguided menfolk are well represented by Robert Armstrong, Edward Norris and Herbert Rudley. The gorgeous Marjorie Woodworth plays a nurse whom Rudley casts aside in favor of Miss Gillie.

The photographic and technical expertise illustrates the maturation of Monogram from its fast-and-cheap essence. *Decoy* boasts a most striking build-up, with Rudley resembling a walking corpse (in an overdone but effective-in-context makeup) as he staggers into a filthy service station and sees his ravaged face in a cracked mirror. This scene was acknowledged by E.C. Comics publisher Bill Gaines as a springboard for the memorable "Reflection of Death," first published in a 1951 issue of *Tales from the Crypt*.

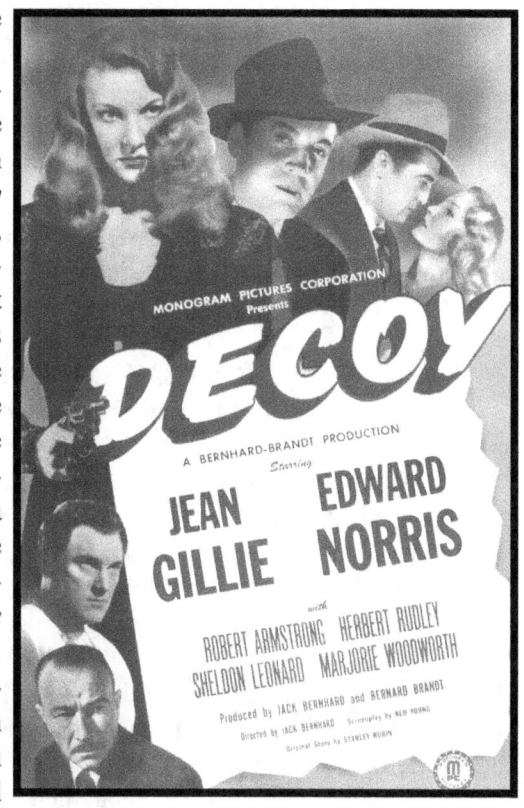

The resurrection of Armstrong is rather an outlandish premise on which to hang such a hard-boiled yarn; the idea had gained some credence via experimentation with laboratory animals (see *Life Returns* in *Forgotten Horrors 2*), and in rumors that a big-time mobster had been revived after a Real World execution.

Jack Bernhard, the director and co-producer, had done some work at Universal, including the popular *Man Made Monster* (1941), before a hitch in uniform during the war. His success with *Decoy*, which drew favorable reviews and respectable box office numbers, led to little else of note. Actor-turned-screenwriter Nedrick Young found his career blighted in the blacklisting that followed the Congressional hearings on Communist influences in Hollywood. Scenarist Stanley Rubin and actor Sheldon Leonard, on the other hand, kept rising as movie and television producers. So did actor Bill Self, seen here in a small role.

CREDITS: Producers: Jack Bernhard and Bernard Brandt; Director: Jack Bernhard; Dialogue Director: Escha Bledsoe; Screenplay: Nedrick Young; Story: Stanley Rubin; Photographed by: L.W. O'Connell; Assistant Directors: William Calihan and Kenny Kessler; Second Camera: Ed Kearns; Special Effects: Augie Lohman; Special Optical Effects: Larry Glickman and Mario Castegnaro; Art

Director: Dave Milton; Editor: Jason Bernie; Set Dresser: Ray Boltz; Music: Edward J. Kay; Sound: Tom Lambert; Production Supervisor: Glenn Cook; Running Time: 77 Minutes; Released: September 14, 1946
CAST: Jean Gillie (Margot Shelby); Edward Norris (Jim Vincent); Herbert Rudley (Dr. Lloyd Craig); Robert Armstrong (Frankie Olins); Sheldon Leonard (Joe Portugal); Marjorie Woodworth (Nurse); Phil Van Zandt (Tommy); John Shay (Al); Bill Self (Station Attendant); Betty Lou Head (Visitor); Jody Gilbert (Mrs. Noonan); Louis Mason (Mack); Ferris Taylor (Benny); Donald Kerr (Elevator Man); William Ruhl (Guard); Franck Corsaro (Kelsey)

OUTLAWS OF THE PLAINS
(Producers Releasing Corp.)

Ghostly masquerades were a standby of the *Billy Carson* shoot-'em-up series. In the generically christened *Outlaws of the Plains*, Al "Fuzzy" St. John—having posed as a spook in *His Brother's Ghost* and professed an aversion to hauntings in *Ghost of Hidden Valley*—now accepts the purported spirit of an Indian chief as his own personal financial advisor.

Fuzzy Q. Jones (St. John) has it on the ghostly authority of Chief Standing Pine (voiced off-camera by John L. Cason) that a vein of gold lies within grabbing range. Sure enough, Fuzzy finds a batch of nuggets, which just happen to lie on a staked claim whose owner, Nord Finners (Charles King, Jr.), first accuses Fuzzy of trespassing but then offers to sell out. Fuzzy consults the (perceived) ghost, who suggests a group investment. The voice warns Fuzzy against involving his chum, Billy Carson (Buster Crabbe), who is "bad medicine"—which is to say, someone with enough good horse sense to see through the scam.

The ranchers mortgage their properties to buy into Fuzzy's stake, but one landowner (Karl Hackett) gets wise to the game and is murdered. Billy recovers from an attack in time to attend to the gang's capture. Fuzzy's dreams of wealth seem punctured until a railroad company shows up with a generous offer to buy the land. The picture is scarcely more than pageantry, but Buster Crabbe and Fuzzy St. John are invariably a delight.

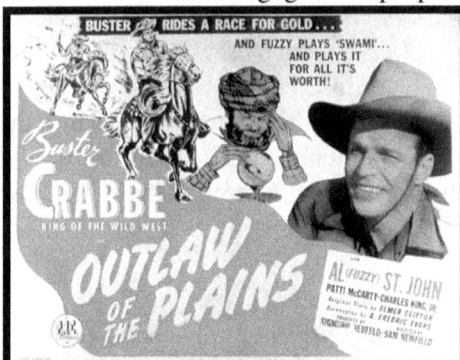

CREDITS: Producer: Sigmund Neufeld; Director: Sam Neufeld; Screenplay: A. Fredric Evans; Story: Elmer Clifton; Photographed by: Jack Greenhalgh; Assistant Director: Snatley Neufeld; Special Effects: Ray Mercer; Editor: Holbrook N. Todd; Music: Lee Zahler; Sound: Elden Ruberg; Production Manager: Bert Sternbach; Running Time: 56 Minutes; Released: September 22, 1946

CAST: Buster Crabbe (Billy Carson); Al "Fuzzy" St. John (Fuzzy Q. Jones); Charles King, Jr. (Nord Finners); Karl Hackett (Reed); Bud Osborne (Sheriff); John L. Cason (Impersonator of Chief Standing Pine); and Patti McCarty, Jack O'Shea, Budd Buster, Roy Brent, Slim Whitaker

THE BRUTE MAN
(Universal Pictures Co., Inc./Producers Releasing Corp./ Pathé Industries, Inc.)

...think about [Rondo] Hatton, not as an actor, or as a monster, but rather as a person... who had really paid some heavy dues. He never even enjoyed the brief fame that was his...
—Fred Olen Ray *Midnight Marquee 25th Anniversary* Volume; 1988

Much as PRC would strive to outdistance its impoverished origins, so bigtime Universal Pictures would vow repeatedly to axe its lucrative B-pictures unit and concentrate on more prestigious fare. Neither ambition was particularly well grounded in reality, for it was the budget-bound genre pictures whose modest investments and loyal audiences helped to underwrite the classier big-movie risks at Universal—and it was the cheap shockers and Westerns that kept PRC solvent enough to entertain its escalating pretensions to finery.

The companies found a shaky common ground early in 1946 with Universal's opening of *House of Horrors* and its balky preparations to release *The Brute Man*, a rapid-fire companion picture. Both had been filmed during the autumn of 1945 as an extended showcase for the extravagantly menacing presence of Rondo Hatton.

> Aside from Mike Price: As a movie-struck schoolboy during the early 1960s, I undertook to shoot the occasional picture, usually in collaboration with a down-the-block chum named Richard Love. One of these projects was a short we called "Return of the Brute Man." Richard, being the tallest kid on the block, was our inheritor of the Rondo Hatton role—rendered more Hatton-esque via under-sized costuming and a makeup whose basic ingredient was chilled axle grease. We crowd-tested the makeup with a visit to the neighborhood grocery store, where the popular response leaned more toward annoyance than toward anything resembling terror.
>
> Richard and I shot quite a bit of footage, mostly showing the Brute Man lurking among the backyard zucchini vines, until other distractions kicked in and we left the film stock developed but unedited. Months later, I had driven to my younger brother's schoolhouse to give him a lift home. I noticed a girl leaving the building: She had the very aspect, the jawline and elongated hands, of Rondo Hatton. Now, my brother wasn't particularly keen on horror movies and wouldn't have known Rondo Hatton from Adam's Off Ox. I asked him about the child I had just sighted. He replied off-handedly: "Oh, yeah. That's Rhonda Hutton." I can still hear the malign laughter of some Cosmic Prankster.

Dr. Turner's House of Horrors

Hatton, a character player of extraordinary aspect, had caused a popular sensation as a backbreaking serial murderer called the Hoxton Creeper in *The Pearl of Death* (1944), one of the better entries in Universal's *Sherlock Holmes* series. Although *House of Horrors* presumed to introduce Hatton, the former newspaperman and publicist from Florida had been handling small featured parts since the early 1930s and already had become a dependable standby in Universal's lesser horror pictures of the 1940s.

The prospect of stardom, however narrow, was quite another matter. Hatton was by now in his early 50s, and the chronic illness that had distended his face and limbs also had lessened his life expectancy to an any-day-now proposition. His ailment was acromegaly, a glandular disorder, which seems to have stemmed from—or been aggravated by—a chemical-combat attack during a tour of uniformed service in the First World War. (This, according to a devoted fact-finding project undertaken by the filmmaker and cultural historian Fred Olen Ray.) In those less enlightened days for medical science, Hatton philosophically turned an intimate tragedy into an attention-getting career device and eventually wound up atop Universal's eroding heap of ticket-selling matinee monsters. Today, a sufferer would be likelier to parlay such a misery into a momentary recognition via tabloid television; Hatton's approach seems the more constructively entertaining, if not necessarily the more dignified.

His brush with fame was more a matter of reach than of grasp, beyond the self-evident fact that Hatton got to star in two movies—three, if one counts his small but showy role in *The Pearl of Death*—of an ill-defined *Creeper* series. Hatton died on February 2, 1946, just weeks before the release of *House of Horrors*. *The Brute Man*, which had been poised for a prompt follow-through, languished until the late summer of 1946, when Universal sold the film to PRC. This move, as reported by *Variety*, was "in line with U's [Universal's] policy of no more B's." Which in the long-term perspective can only fall under the heading of Yeah, Right, Whatever You Say, Boss.

House of Horrors, directed by Jean Yarbrough and toplining Robert Lowery, Virginia Grey and Bill Goodwin, is the story of an embittered sculptor (Martin Kosleck) who rescues a deformed hulk (Hatton) from drowning—only to find him the ideal model for a study of primitive man. The artist's new friend proves to be a presumed-defunct marauder known as the Creeper, who is sufficiently grateful for the life-saving routine that he will perform acts of murder on command, or even on mere suggestion. The yarn conveniently ignores the Creeper's demise at the hands of Sherlock Holmes (Basil Rathbone) at the finale of *The Pearl of Death*—if indeed this is even that same Hoxton Creeper. At any rate, Hatton takes a one-presumes-fatal bullet at the climax of *House of Horrors*.

Yarbrough's *The Brute Man* sidesteps such pitfalls of continuity, as if that had mattered to begin with, via a story whose events occur before the ordeals of *House of Horrors*. The cinematic vocabulary of the day had not yet been afflicted

The Creeper (Rondo Hatton) creeps up on Virginia (Jan Wiley) in *The Brute Man*.

with the fatuous term *prequel*. In light of Fred Ray's research into the Hatton lineage, *The Brute Man* becomes far and away the more disturbing picture: It deals all but autobiographically with a handsome athlete (Fred Coby) whose transformation into the Creeper (Hatton) is the result of a chemical accident. The Creeper's killing urge here is more along grudging lines; he also strikes up a touching friendship with a blind woman (Jane Adams), who innocently shelters him. The film is Universal's most overtly sentimentalized chiller since *Man Made Monster* (1941), and although Hatton was no master of range or delivery, still he conveys a certain pathos with a soulfully wounded gaze and a guttural delivery, inflected with a childlike resentment.

"Everyone kept asking me," wrote Ray, "why would I want to go to all this trouble to record the life of a talentless, grossly exploited freak... whose best filmic efforts had been termed as 'extremely bad taste'..., who could find no acclaim in his lifetime and even less in his death. I think it is important that we remember that there was a lot more to Rondo Hatton... a real man, living the role."

Another artist who would give Hatton his posthumous due was Dave Stevens, whose *Rocketeer* comics stories of the 1980s and early '90s led to a rip-snorting feature film, *The Rocketeer* (1991). Picking up a Hatton-styled character from the funnybooks, the Disney project cast the athlete-turned-stuntman Ronald "Tiny Ron" Taylor in an unnervingly look-alike role. In an interview for *The American Cinematographer* magazine, Taylor told George

Turner about the impersonation: "I learned as much as I could turn up about this Rondo Hatton guy, and the knowledge gave me a sense of tragedy to underpin the menace. I tried to keep one thought foremost in mind: *I* could always take off my makeup at the end of a day's shooting—where Rondo Hatton *was* his makeup. God bless the man."

CREDITS: Producer: Ben Pivar; Director: Jean Yarbrough; Dialogue Director: Raymond Kessler; Screenplay: George Bricker and M. Coates Webster; Story: Dwight V. Babcock; Photographed by: Maury Gertsman; Assistant Director: Ralph Slosser; Art Directors: John B. Goodman and Abraham Grossman; Editor: Philip Cahn; Décor: Russell A. Gausman and Edward R. Robinson; Gowns: Vera West; Sound: Bernard B. Brown; Sound Technician: Joe Lapis; Makeup: Jack P. Pierce; Hair Stylist: Carmen Dirigo; Running Time: 60 Minutes; Released: October 1, 1946

CAST: Tom Neal (Clifford Scott); Jan Wiley (Virginia Rogers Scott); Jane Adams (Helen Day); Donald McBride (Capt. Donnelly); Peter Whitney (Lt. Gates); Fred Coby (Hal Moffat, pre-Transformation); JaNelle Johnson (Joan Bemis); Rondo Hatton (Hal "the Creeper" Moffat); Beatrice Roberts (Nurse); Oscar O'Shea (Haskins); John Gallaudet and Pat McVey (Detectives); Peggy Converse (Mother); Joseph Crehan (Salisbury); John Hamilton (Prof. Cushman); Loren Raker (Parkington); Charles Waggenheim (Pawnbroker); Tristram Coffin (Police Lieutenant); Jack Parker (Jimmy); Jim Nolan (Dispatcher)

BEAUTY AND THE BANDIT
(Monogram Productions, Inc./ Monogram Distributing Corp.)

In the 1907 short story "The Caballero's Way," written by the twist-ending master O. Henry, a murderous roué known as the Cisco Kid pulls an Achilles and dresses as a woman in order to elude the authorities. So maybe it is only right that one of the best—and certainly the weirdest—of the *Cisco Kid* movies features cross-dressing as a prominent part of its own story. But *Beauty and the Bandit* hardly stops there.

The third film featuring the fourth sound-era Cisco, Gilbert Roland, *Beauty and the Bandit* also treats the viewer to a jaw-dropping parade of offbeat elements, including spankings, poisonings (both animal and human), ventriloquism, gender confusion, double entendres and suggestive lines, an Old Dark House finale, and a sea chanty sung by the only actor to play the Frankenstein monster as many times as Boris Karloff!

In a discussion of *Beauty and the Bandit* in the book *Saturday Afternoon at the Bijou* (1972), author David Zinman notes that scripter Charles S. Belden "thought the mistaken-sex ploy would titillate Saturday matinee small fry." The

Ramsay Ames and Gilbert Roland in *Beauty and the Bandit*

romantic content of the Cisco pictures (and of the radio show) sometimes drew negative attention from parents, anyway—the notion of a randy Latin lover as a hero was unique among the kid-oriented B-Western pictures—but this one has such an aura of sexuality about it that, more than a half-century down the pike, it *still* retains the power to titillate.

Much of the appeal lies in Ramsay Ames' portrayal of French rich kid Jeanne DuBois, who disembarks from a ship with a trunkful of silver, intending to buy a bunch of California land and resell it to some moneyed Europeans. Figuring that the California countryside is no place for an aristocratic young Frenchwoman traveling alone, Mlle. DuBois has disguised herself as a boy. It is doubtful that this fooled anyone in those bygone Saturday-matinee audiences, though; the sultry Miss Ames looks like anything but a boy, even an extremely pretty one.

It is doubtful that she fools Roland's Cisco Kid, either. After finding out about the French visitor and all that silver from his sailor friend, Bill (Glenn Strange, who is introduced belting out "Blow the Man Down" in a seaport dive), Cisco boards a stagecoach alongside the new arrival, arching his eyebrows as he pulls a long hair from the shoulder of her jacket.

Much of the gender-switching fun comes after they reach an inn, run by a character named Doc Welles (veteran B-western heavy William Gould). Although the incognito Miss DuBois has been cool to Cisco's overtures of friendship, they head for the bar, where they down shots of tequila. "Puts hair on your chest," notes Cisco. He then tries to hustle the barmaid (Vida Aldana), but she has eyes only for the disguised Mlle. DuBois.

"Hey, the little barmaid—she's making eyes at you," Cisco says, suggesting that the bogus boy make a date and see if the girl has "a little friend." Mlle. DuBois, however, decides to ankle the place, telling the girl to bring the food up to the room.

"¡Si, señor!" replies the barmaid, flashing her teeth and all but licking her chops. Cisco is impressed.

The oddball sexual currents grow turbulent when the girl shows up on Miss DuBois' threshold, visibly disappointed when she spots Cisco, who has become the Guest Who Won't Go. Unfortunately for us lovers of bizarre cinema, this nonsense is over and done with by the next morning, when Mlle. DuBois reveals herself to be a dazzling young woman.

It isn't long before she and Cisco are an item, as he transports her to his camp ("So this is home," she says suggestively. "Why don't you carry me over the threshold?"), where she shows herself to be adept at both shooting and knife-throwing, impressing Cisco's men to no end. She also has fallen hard: After washing Cisco's shirt in a nearby stream, she wraps it around her and emits a moan that would do Mae West proud.

But this is one star-crossed romance. Cisco is a champion of the poor farmers and ranchers, who are being forced by a strange livestock-killing disease to vacate the land Mlle. DuBois is buying. She, on the other hand, has an aristocrat's disdain for the lower classes. It's the Haves vs. the Have-Nots, and the Cisco Kid deals with this moral conflict in an interesting way.

"Did your father ever spank you?" he asks at one juncture. When she replies in the negative, he pulls her down and whacks her generously, with both his palm and a handy board. (Later along, when another argument has arisen, he asks if she wants another spanking. "Yes!" she shouts.)

Finally, of course, Mlle. DuBois sees the populist light, but by that time Cisco has exposed the plot to run the poor people off their land and vanquished the villain in a genuinely creepy sequence involving silhouettes, shadows, maniacal laughter and a death scene that wouldn't be out of place in a David Lynch movie. With everybody happy again but the bad guys, the local *policia* (led by George J. Lewis), and poor Mlle. DuBois (who apparently is going to live the rest of her life in the local mission), Cisco and the boys ride off singing their hearty signature tune, "Ride, Amigos, Ride."

A big-league leading man during the 1930s and early '40s and the former husband of the Hollywood megastar Constance Bennett, Roland was just past 40 when he made *Beauty and the Bandit*, one of his six *Cisco Kid* westerns knocked out over a period of two years by cost-conscious Monogram. But if he was daunted by the career arc that had taken him from the majors to Poverty Row, you'd never know by his performance here, which is packed with a sly sense of fun. He reportedly wrote some of his own dialogue for this one, which may help to account for the upbeat attitude he radiates.

It could not have hurt to have had Ramsay Ames around, either. The darkly sensuous former Universal player is, even now, fondly remembered as the princess whom the undead Kharis (Lon Chaney, Jr.) finally claims as his own in *The Mummy's Ghost* (1944). Miss Ames' glowing presence in this tiny, spirited film suggests that she—like so many others among our genre favorites—never quite got what she deserved from Hollywood.

CREDITS: Producer: Scott R. Dunlap; Director: William Nigh; Assistant Director: Eddie Davis; Technical Director: E.R. Hickson; Story and Screenplay: Charles R. Belden; Based Upon: the Character Created by O. Henry; Photographed by: Harry Neumann; Editor: Fred Maguire; Set Designer: Vin Taylor; Wardrobe: Harry Bourne; Music: Edward J. Kay; Songs: "Viens, Chercher Ton Baiser," by Gordon Clark, and "Ride, Amigos, Ride," by Charles Rosoff and Eddie Cherkose; Sound: Franklin Hansen; Makeup: Harry Ross; Running Time: 69 Minutes; Released: October 28, 1946

CAST: Gilbert Roland (the Cisco Kid); Martin Garralaga (Valegra); Frank Yaconelli (Baby); Ramsay Ames (Jeanne DuBois); Vida Aldana (Rosita); George J. Lewis (Captain); William Gould (Doc Walsh); Dimas Sotello (Farmer); Felipe Turich (Sick Farmer); Antonio Damas (Luis); and Alex Montoya

HOME IN OKLAHOMA
(Republic Pictures Corp.)

A classic-manner *femme fatale* whodunnit plot makes *Home in Oklahoma* one of the best of Republic's many showcases for Western crooner Roy Rogers. The cowboy harmonies are generously deployed as a prerequisite of this peculiar subgenre of the horse operas—and the sentimentality threatens to become a bit thick—but the picture's greater point is Rogers' dogged fight to upset a conspiracy of murder.

Jan Holloway (Carol Hughes) learns that her late uncle, Sam Talbot, had willed the bulk of his ranch to 12-year-old Duke Lowery (Lanny Rees), ward of foreman Gabby Whittaker (George "Gabby" Hayes). Jan's enforcer, Steve McClory (George Meeker), who had anticipated her inheritance of the spread, accuses Gabby of influencing Sam's bequest. Roy Rogers, a newspaper editor in a nearby town, also is an heir: Talbot has willed to him a prayer book, which contains a note asking Roy to investigate the circumstances of Talbot's death.

A visiting big-city journalist, Connie Edwards (Dale Evans), irresponsibly publishes an account of these intrigues, so infuriating McClory that he begins plotting to kill Duke before the will can be probated. A sneak attack on the boy fails, but one of the two shooters eludes Roy. Connie is jailed for refusing to divulge her sources, but Roy bails her out and she joins him in a search for the truth.

Taking Talbot's horse along the same path that Talbot was riding on the day he died, Roy finds the steed leery of approaching a certain creek. The coroner, Jud Judnick (Arthur Space), proves so uncooperative that Roy finds it necessary to rough him up. Roy threatens to exhume Talbot's body.

Duke witnesses a secretive conference among Jan, McClory and Judnick. McClory guns down Judnick, and Jan notices the boy and gives chase. Duke eludes her by diving into a spring. Under siege by Roy, Gabby and their assembled Sons of the Pioneers, Jan and McClory have nothing better to do than start a fight of their own. McClory shoots Jan and rides away. Jan's dying words are a confession to everything from murder to a ranch-grab scam. Roy bests McClory in a fistfight atop a moving freight train.

As ferocious as it is often fatuous, *Home in Oklahoma* is routinely cited as a favorite among favorites among Roy Rogers' most devoted fans—this, despite the lesser role allowed Rogers' famous Palomino, Trigger. The pace is deliberate enough to keep the sappier moments at a minimum. Unusual within this field is the prominence of a pacesetting black actress, Ruby Dandridge (mother of the then up-and-coming Dorothy Dandridge), as a level-headed housekeeper who provides Rogers with vital clues and, later, helps child player Lanny Rees save the life of an ailing calf. The kid is pleasingly headstrong and resourceful. Dale Evans, whose sunnier matronly presence as Rogers' own Queen of the West had yet to take shape, is very good as a near-antagonist who starts off on the wrong foot in her dealings with Rogers. Carol Hughes' show of menace and feigned bereavement is strong throughout: Miss Hughes plays her death scene with a credible mingling of impunity and remorse, making it plain that if she had it to do all over again—she'd probably do it all over again. The musicianship and blended voices of the Sons of the Pioneers are, as usual, delightful.

CREDITS: Associate Producer: Edward J. White; Director: William Witney; Screenplay: Gerald Geraghty; Photographed by: William Bradford; Assistant Director: Lee Lukather; Art Director: Frank Hotaling; Editors: Les Orlebeck and Tony Martinelli; Décor: John McCarthy, Jr., and Earl Wooden; Costumer: Adele Palmer; Music Director: Morton Scott; Musical Score: Joseph Dubin;

Songs: "Home in Oklahoma," "I Wish I Was a Kid Again" and "Breakfast Club Song," by Jack Elliott, "Miguelito," by Jack Elliott & Glenn Spencer, "The Everlasting Hills of Oklahoma" and "Cowboy Ham and Eggs," by Tim Spencer, and "Hereford Heaven," by Roy J. Turner; Sound: Fred Stahl; Makeup: Bob Mark; Running Time: 72 Minutes; Released: November 8, 1946

CAST: Roy Rogers (Himself); Trigger (Himself); George "Gabby" Hayes (Gabby Whittaker); Dale Evans (Connie Edwards); Carol Hughes (Jan Holloway); George Meeker (Steve McClory); Lanny Rees (Duke Lowery); Ruby Dandridge (Devoria Lassiter); George Lloyd (Sheriff Barclay); Arthur Space (Jud Judnick); Frank Reicher (Cragmyle); George Carleton (Marc Kennedy); Johnny Walsh (Jimmy); the Flying "L" Ranch Quartette, Bob Nolan & the Sons of the Pioneers

THE CHASE
(Nero Films, Inc./United Artists Corp.)

Cornell Woolrich, the tormented recluse whose popular tales of bizarre despair made him an American Kafka, a defining figure of the *roman noir* movement in American fiction, reached a pinnacle of erotically charged gloom with *The Black Path of Fear*, a yarn that is stronger on atmosphere and attitude than on narrative thrust. Producer Seymour Nebenzal acquired the 1944 novel as grounds for *The Chase*, sensing in the project a return to the greatness he had known as a filmmaker during the prewar Gilded Age of German cinema.

Nebenzal's Nero Films had launched itself during 1945-46 with *Whistle Stop*, a prestigious starring picture for George Raft and Ava Gardner, and assumed a station some few rungs above Poverty Row with a United Artists distribution pact. *The Chase* took on marquee value with the casting of Robert Cummings, Peter Lorre and, on loan-out from the big-time independent producer

Samuel Goldwyn, Steve Cochran. The spirit of maverick picturemaking prevailed, however, in Nebenzal's devotion to anti-Status Quo subject matter and in his recuitment of Arthur Ripley, the artist behind those bleak mood-poem movies *Prisoner of Japan* and *Voice in the Wind*, to direct.

Cummings stars as Chuck Scott, a hard-luck war veteran at large in Miami, whose survival of a bout with malaria has left him subject to fevered nightmares. Scott chances to find a mislaid wallet and even helps himself to some of the cash therein before his conscience gets the better of him and he returns it to its owner, a crooked businessman named Eddie Roman (Cochran). Roman rewards Scott with paid employment. Lorna Roman (Michele Morgan), Roman's ill-treated wife, prevails upon Scott to help her get away to safety in Havana. Having witnessed Roman's cruelties, Scott agrees.

A nightmare strikes Scott: He dreams of his arrival in Havana with Lorna, whose murder leads to his arrest. Scott finds the killer to be Gino (Lorre), Roman's confidant and one-man goon squad, who in turn kills Scott.

Scott wakes with a fleeting case of amnesia. He finally remembers his promise to Lorna. Roman, learning of the escape plan, rushes with Gino to overtake the fleeing couple. Roman and Gino are killed when their speeding automobile veers out of control. Scott and Lorna reach Havana—where Scott finds that his nightmare appears to have begun replaying itself in real life. Nightmares tend to follow the dreamer into the waking state in Woolrich's bleak view of the Human Condition.

The enactments are pure Woolrich, and so is the evocative photography an ideal visual translation of the author's vivid descriptive powers. Cinematographer Franz Planer was, like Lorre and Nebenzal, an *alumnus* of those glory days of German filmmaking. Steve Cochran captures the brutal eroticism of Woolrich's writing, especially in a scene where Eddie Roman's abuses of his manicurist (Shirley O'Hara) blur the line between harassment and sadomasochism. Lorre is a born-to-interpret-Woolrich actor if ever there were one, and his portrayal of the viciously devoted Gino is prime stuff. The delicate Michele Morgan, a French-born international star who made a small handful of pictures in mid-1940s Hollywood, is poignantly affecting as Cochran's bird in a gilded cage. The film's choicest sequence (barring the climactic breakneck pursuit and the final shrill literalization of Cummings' nightmare) comes in a wine-cellar tour—ostensibly a lighter moment between Cummings and Lorre—that turns abruptly into the purest of horror as Cummings finds himself trapped in close quarters with a vicious dog.

The Black Path of Fear was dramatized twice on CBS' celebrated radio series, *Suspense*—with Hans Conreid and Brian Donlevy in 1945, and with Cary Grant in 1946.

CREDITS: Producer: Seymour Nebenzal; Associate Producer: Eugene [Elsewhere, Eugen] Frenke; Director: Arthur D. Ripley; Screenplay: Philip Yordan; Photographed by: Franz F. Planer; Assistant Director: Jack Voglin; Special Effects: Ray O. Bringer; Art Director: Robert Usher; Editor: Edward Man; Set Dresser: Victor A. Gangelin; Gowns: Peter Tuesday; Wardrobe: Bill Edwards; Musical Director: Heinz Roemheld; Music Supervisor: David Chudnow; Musical Score: Michel Michelet; Sound: Corson Jowett; Makeup: Don Cash; Hair Stylist: Marjorie Lund; Production Manager: Joe Popkin; Running Time: 86 Minutes; Released: November 22, 1946

CAST: Robert Cummings (Chuck Scott); Michele Morgan (Lorna Roman); Steve Cochran (Eddie Roman); Peter Lorre (Gino); Lloyd Corrigan (Johnson); Jack Holt (Cmdr. Davidson); Don Wilson (Fats); Alexis Minotis (Lt. Acosta); Nina Koshetz (Mme. Chin); Yulana Lacca (Midnight); James Westerfield (Job); Shirley O'Hara (Manicurist); and Jimmy Ames

Afterword

This volume hardly draws the curtain on the Price & Turner collaboration, which still has yet a good long way to go in the realms of cartooning and Southwestern regional history. George Turner's *The Ancient Southwest* and *The Palo Duro Story*, newspaper comic strips that have gone largely unseen since their first appearances during the 1950s, are nearing the completion of a thorough restoration and re-editing, following through on the samples of *The Ancient Southwest* that I cleaned up and re-lettered as an appendix to the Midnight Marquee Press edition of *Spawn of Skull Island*. George's and my extensive inventory of Wild West rip-snorters, meanwhile, has yet even to be cataloged—much less re-collected *in toto* from the various newspaper, magazine and monograph appearances dating from the 1960s; a first such volume, known for now as *The Cruel Plains*, is in preparation.

Meanwhile: A fond welcome to John Wooley, who not only has contributed mightily to *FH3* and championed the Price & Turner books over the long stretch—but also has committed his energies for the long term through whatever Arabic numeral will signify a final volume. John and I staged our first research marathon on *FH3* and *FH4* during February of 2001, framing Tables of Contents and unearthing two or three obscurities to every comparatively more familiar motion picture. The fourth *Forgotten Horrors* will edge further into the 1950s, whose onslaught wrought drastic changes in Hollywood's approach to horror-as-entertainment. Any movie buff who has ever witnessed John's celebrated slide-show/stand-up routine, *The Sock, Shock & Schlock Show*, will know pretty well what manner of rambunctious scholarship lies in wait. For all others, that program's title in itself will offer some tantalizing clues.

—M.H.P.

Recommended Video Sources

Film-commentary books used to require more faith than participation on the part of the reader. A Bill Everson or a Carlos Clarens could praise or trash this movie or that with impunity, given the advantage of those scholarly credentials that would get the bearer past the red tape of the great art museums' moving-picture collections and the studios' archives. There was little opportunity for any comparing-of-notes between the reader and the Published Authority.

Video has long since become the Great Equalizer, starting out unevenly with the movies-on-television breakthroughs of the post-W.W. II years and culminating in times more recent with the quick-change pageant of Betamax, CED, VHS and its permutations, plus laserdisc, CD-ROM and DVD and Whatever Comes Next; to say nothing of cable TV's Turner Classic Movies, the Nostalgia Channel, the Western Channel, the Sci-Fi Channel, the Mystery Channel, American Movie Not-So-Classics, *et cetera, ad infinitum.*

The shirtsleeves movie buff is not only better informed as a consequence—but also more fairly equipped to carry on a dialogue with those of us who are fortunate enough to break into print. Conversation and informed dissent are infinitely more fun than tacit assent, and any credentialed critic will tell you that a good argument beats a blank stare or a nod of passive agreement, any time of any day.

To that end, we encourage the reader to dash out and glom onto as many movies as are out there for the glomming. Our Short List of the choicer sources of B-picture obscurities follow herewith. We don't really care to discriminate between pristine, supposedly definitive editions and just plain old watchable dubs. It is too easy, in the struggle for digital perfection-plus-commentary-tracks, to forget the simple pleasure of kicking back and watching some movie upon which one never expected to cast (or strain) one's eyes.

Life Is a Movie—The corporate slogan goes like this: "Life Is a Movie—So Get a Life." The preferred name, Web-wise, is www.lifeisamovie.com. A real godsend in the reference department, with a print of, for example, Spencer Williams, Jr.'s *The Blood of Jesus* (1941), that is noticeably better-looking than the 35mm version reposing in cold storage at the Southwest Film & Video Archive, and the cleanest video transfers we've seen of those W.W. II propaganda gems *Hitler—Beast of Berlin* and *Hitler—Dead or Alive.* The Web-based catalog is also rich with titles from the Mexican movie studios, in the original spoken language. The geographical address is Life Is a Movie, 3639 Midway Drive, B-326, San Diego, California 92110. The telephone numbers are (619) 523-1500 (voice); (619) 523-1599 (fax); and (888) 403-0873 (toll-free).

Hollywood's Attic—A real pioneer in the home-video realm, helpfully allied with Life Is a Movie and known to the rare-movie digger-uppers as a source of scarce titles in clean-if-not-pristine video transfers. Our reference print of that French Revolutionary hair-raiser *The Black Book*, due for a going-over in *Forgotten Horrors 4*, came from one of the earliest catalogs of Hollywood's Attic. On the Web: www.hollywoodsattic.com; on the ground: Hollywood's Attic, P.O. Box 7122, Burbank, California 91510-7122. By telephone: (818) 843-3366 (voice); (818) 843-3821 (fax).

Arthouse, Inc.—This Web-based source boasts an extensive catalog of finely remastered avant-garde rarities, priced so as to target the serious collector (or institutional user) of archival-quality video transfers. At www.arthouseinc.com; 154 Grand Street, Suite No. 208, New York, New York 10013; eFax to: (240) 266-6247.

Sinister Cinema—A continuing source of enlightenment in the retro (both -active and -spective) realms, and an early champion (since the mid-1980s) of the *Forgotten Horrors* project. A high-spirited fan-conversation forum used to be part of the Web site until the Internet barbarians crashed the gate and spoiled the fun for all concerned. Write to Sinister Cinema at Box 4369, Medford, Oregon 97501, or keyword "Sinister Cinema" (quote marks included) on practically any Web search engine. That's invariably more interesting than just keying in www.sinistercinema.com.

Mars Needs Videos—I first encountered Richard Horsey's imaginatively christened company (its cue taken, of course, from Larry Buchanan's film *Mars Needs Women*) while scouring an Internet auction house with the pig-Latinate name of eBay, for relevant titles. We have dealt in person since those first significant discoveries, and Mr. Horsey continues to crop up with the occasional revelation. A catalog can be had from P.O. Box 1116, Woodstock, Georgia 30188-1116. The Web-proficient can call up www.marscollective.com.

Bruce Tinkel—This personable mail-order and fan-convention dealer has turned up a goodly number of helpful reference dubs for the *Forgotten Horrors* books and established himself as a loyal friend of the project. A growing catalog is available from Mr. Tinkel at Box 65, Edison, New Jersey 08818.

Grapevine Video—Continuing growth distinguishes this reliable resurrectionist label, with a particularly strong silent-films collection and a fondness for the Depression-into-wartime B-unit and indie pictures. Address: Box 46161, Phoenix, Arizona 85063. The company's name is its search-engine keyword—beats transcribing all those *http*'s and back-slashes.

Facets Multimedia—The massive catalog is a delight all by itself, with strong concentrations upon independents and imports. Address: 1517 W. Fullerton Ave., Chicago, Illinois 60614.

Video Yesteryear—Long-lived source of early-talkie and silent-screen rarities, including many of the *Forgotten Horrors* selections. Address: Box C, Sandy Hook, Connecticut 06482.

Nor should the enthusiast neglect to browse the video outfits that advertise in such magazines as *Filmfax* and *Psychotronic Video*—to say nothing of the innumerable eBay-and-kindred dealers in the cyberspatial arena. You'd be amazed at what a simple keyword search can turn up. —M.H.P.

About the Authors

Michael H. Price is arts editor and film columnist with the *Fort Worth Business Press* and founding president of the Fort Worth Film Festival. As a radio broadcaster, he delivers a weekly film-review and discussion program to a cool million movie-struck listeners over the Texas State Network.

Price earned accreditation as a working film critic—back in the day when one actually had to *work* at becoming a film critic, rather than just contrive to imitate *Entertainment Weekly*'s pernicious name-dropping snark-isms—as an apprentice to George Turner during the preparation of Turner's seminal film-history book, *The Making of King Kong*, during 1968-75. The numerous Turner & Price ventures began in earnest during 1975-79 with the development of the *Forgotten Horrors* project—a groundbreaking volume whose 20th anniversary the authors marked in 1999 with *Forgotten Horrors: The Definitive Edition* for Midnight Marquee Press.

From the springboard of Turner's rough notes and partial manuscripts, Price has carried on with the present sequels. He and John Wooley are at work on subsequent volumes of the *Forgotten Horrors* series, as well as a monthly feature on later such *Forgotten Horrors*-type pictures for *Fangoria* magazine. Their collaborations elsewhere include *The Big Book of Biker Flicks*, from Hawk Publishing Group. Meanwhile, Price has retooled *The Making of King Kong* as a more expansive genre study called *Spawn of Skull Island*.

John Wooley is a veteran novelist, journalist and scriptwriter whose more recent work includes the movie *Café Purgatory*, co-written and produced with director Leo Evans. Wooley's 1982 novel *Old Fears*, written with Ron Wolfe and characterized as a modern classic by fellow horror writer C. Dean Andersson, was reissued in 1999 to widespread acclaim. Wooley's solo novels include *Dark Within* and *Awash in the Blood*, the latter a sell-out in hardcover. He also is a longtime entertainment writer with the Tulsa *World*.

George E. Turner (1925-1999) was the guiding force behind the original *Forgotten Horrors* collection during the 1970s. He graduated from there to a distinguished career in Hollywood as a cartoon animator, special-effects and scenic-design technician, storyboard artist, and occasional character actor and scenarist—in addition to holding forth as editor of *American Cinematographer* magazine and abiding historical conscience of the American Society of Cinematographers.

Turner's prior career had been no less distinguished but altogether less cosmopolitan, as a newspaper illustrator and writer, magazine publisher and art-gallery proprietor during 1950-78 in West Texas, where his work caromed wildly between the finer arts and thousands of gloriously lowbrow postal-card gag cartoons. His movie-town work is best represented by the rambunctious main-title sequence of Carl Reiner's *Dead Men Don't Wear Plaid*; the storyboarding and on-location supervision of many episodes of network television's *Friends*; and a starring role in the European-made IMAX/Omnimax horror film, *Dangling Death*. Turner had begun work on a contents list and a dozen-or-so chapters for *Forgotten Horrors 2* and *Forgotten Horrors 3* shortly before his unexpected demise.

If you enjoyed this book
check out our other
film-related titles at
www.midmar.com
or call or write for a free catalog
Midnight Marquee Press, Inc.
9721 Britinay Lane
Baltimore, MD 21234
410-665-1198 (8 a.m. until 6 p.m. EST)
or MMarquee@aol.com